Praise for

Man's 4th Best H

T0248940

"Any doctor I know read *House of God* and was transformed by it. It was an honest, raw, and unapologetic journey into the world of a hospital internship. It was like being let in on the secret handshake and all the rituals that accompany it. Best of all, the narrator and author deftly pulled on all our emotions, including humor and anxiety, to spin out a universal human drama that has stuck with me decades later. With *Man's 4th Best Hospital*, Dr. Sam Shem has done it again. This time all of us—doctors and patients alike—are along for the ride into the entire universe of medicine, which is at once both wonderful and ludicrous. The story of doctors, overwhelmed by long noxious hours in front of billing computers called Electronic Health Records, trying to treat patients humanely even as the hospital is more interested in treating the bottom line, feels so timely and relevant. You will get a little pissed off, double over in laughter, and even cry a little. If you read one medical drama, make it this one."

—Sanjay Gupta, MD, associate professor of neurosurgery, the Emory Clinic;
chief medical correspondent, CNN

"In his writing, Samuel Shem has challenged generations of doctors to think deeply about why they chose medicine. His novels illuminate the humanistic core of clinical care, and serve as a bulwark against a system increasingly characterized by avarice and anonymity."

—Jerome Groopman, MD, author of *How Doctors Think*

"Oh my god! This book is brilliant enough to start a revolution. Dedicated nurses, doctors, and all haters of Electronic Medical Records unite! Together we must heed the Fat Man's call 'to put the human back in health care.'"

—Theresa Brown, RN, author of the *New York Times* bestseller *The Shift:
One Nurse, Twelve Hours, Four Patients' Lives*

"Shem's influence through *The House of God* is enormous. Once again he uses his unique writing style, satire, and comedy to allow the most serious examination of the medical profession, both its joys and its seamy underbelly."

—Abraham Verghese, bestselling author of *Cutting for Stone*

"If you want to know why the doctor spends all visit looking at a computer instead of you, and if you want to know how the doctor feels about it, this is the book for you: a mordantly funny tour through modern medicine, with a powerful prescription for how to change."

—Bill McKibben, bestselling author of *Falter: Has the Human Game Begun to Play Itself Out?*

"As he did in *The House of God*, Samuel Shem provides a bitter, caustic, and overdue update on the cold and bureaucratic world that awaits the sick and the dying if they are lucky enough to be able to afford it."

—Arthur Caplan, professor of bioethics at New York University Langone Medical Center

"Sequels rarely outshine the original. . . . But gosh, it comes very close to the brilliance of his 1978 opus."

—*The Irish Times*

"Profound parody."

—*The Wall Street Journal*

Also by Samuel Shem

Novels
The House of God
Fine
Mount Misery
The Spirit of the Place
At the Heart of the Universe
The Buddha's Wife: The Path of Awakening Together
  (with Janet Surrey)

Plays
Bill W. and Dr. Bob (with Janet Surrey)
Napoleon's Dinner
Room for One Woman

Nonfiction
We Have to Talk: Healing Dialogues Between
  Women and Men (with Janet Surrey)
Fiction as Resistance

Man's
4th Best
Hospital

Samuel Shem

BERKLEY
New York

BERKLEY
An imprint of Penguin Random House LLC
penguinrandomhouse.com

Copyright © 2019 by Samuel Shem
Penguin Random House supports copyright. Copyright fuels creativity, encourages diverse voices,
promotes free speech, and creates a vibrant culture. Thank you for buying an authorized edition of
this book and for complying with copyright laws by not reproducing, scanning, or distributing
any part of it in any form without permission. You are supporting writers and allowing
Penguin Random House to continue to publish books for every reader.

BERKLEY and the BERKLEY & B colophon are registered trademarks of
Penguin Random House LLC.

ISBN: 9780593097786

The Library of Congress has catalogued the Berkley hardcover edition of this book as follows:

Names: Shem, Samuel, author.
Title: Man's 4th best hospital / Samuel Shem.
Other titles: Man's fourth best hospital
Description: First Edition. | New York : Berkley, 2019. | Sequel to: The House of God.
Identifiers: LCCN 2019015299 | ISBN 9781984805362 (hardcover) |
ISBN 9781984805379 (ebook)
Subjects: LCSH: Physicians--Fiction. | Medical education--Fiction. | GSAFD: Bildungsromans.
Classification: LCC PS3569.H39374 M36 2019 | DDC 813/.54--dc23
LC record available at https://lccn.loc.gov/2019015299

Berkley hardcover edition / November 2019
Berkley trade paperback edition / November 2020

Printed in the United States of America

Cover art and design by Colleen Reinhart

To Janet and Katie

In memory of John Updike

With thanks to Rosemary Ahern, Tracy Bernstein, Clifton Meador, Christina Robb, Steve Schaffrau, and Mark Vonnegut

"We came here to serve God, and also to get rich."

—Bernal Díaz del Castillo,
*Historia verdadera de la conquista
de la Nueva España, 1632*

Contents

I

Costa Rica

"I'm not rich because I tell the truth."
—Graffiti on dumpster,
New York City, 2018

I

Except for her eyes, Berry is fully clothed. Her eyes show her relief at my close call with death, several hours ago.

Over our decades together, but for the slightest flicker of a butterfly's wing, we wouldn't be here. None of us would—we all ride or fall on that flicker. But for a flicker, I'd now be a divorced alcoholic neurosurgeon on the Best Medical School faculty.

Her relief, yes, and concern—and love. A love that, all those years ago, survived the medical internship that I, Roy Basch, novelized as *The House of God*.

That crucial year, learning to be a doctor, was horrific, but we interns—Chuck, Eat My Dust Eddie, the Runt, Hyper Hooper, and I—lucked out. We had the Fat Man as our teaching resident. Brilliant, funny, earthy, insatiable. Always, amid the illusions of the hospital, being *real*. More than that—being *with us*. If you go through a death-defying experience with a guy like Fats, he's never *not* with you, just past the edges of your sight.

Now, late this June afternoon, Berry and I are on the large back patio of Tierra Tranquila—"Quiet Earth"—our little finca in Guanacaste, Costa Rica, three degrees above the equator. Battered and in some pain, I'm sitting on my lucky red metal folding chair, she beside me. Wishing that our daughter, Spring, could be here. Berry has texted her. No reply yet.

It's the start of the rainy season, a cooling downpour once in the afternoon, once at night, when the drumming of drops on the corrugated tin roof is a comfort. We never sleep past 5:30, awakened by the portent of dawn awakening the birds awakening the day, doves first, cooing. At 6:00 or so, toucans fly in, to feast on the bunch of *plátanos quadratos* I've cut with my cool machete and hung from a close-by mango tree. Other large birds follow: blue birds so big they seem on steroids, and paired-for-life motmots whose two tufted tail feathers are as long as the rest of their bodies, and finally the flocks of small parrots and tanagers. Now the motmots are gone. Last year, high up in the cloud forest near the Arenal Volcano, we saw motmots. Here, it's gotten too hot. The planet is starting to boil. Soon there'll be flamingos in the Arctic, but no Arctic. No refuge anywhere. The sick world is in our rooms. Doctors and patients alike.

We're 2,000 feet up the mountain—no mosquitoes. The patio overlooks fruit trees: bananas, *plantanos*, papayas, grapefruit, oranges, sweet lemons, tons of mangoes—everything you could want. We look past the strangler fig and coconut palm to the stream and little waterfall—we can *drink* the water, imagine?—and then to the rain forest, dark as Conrad's jungle, climbing to the peak. A family of howler monkeys is coming closer. They move from fig tree to fig tree their whole lives, never touching the ground except when they die and fall. Their calls sound like the roars of lions but they're the size of house cats. On the other side of the mountain we see the Pacific, two hours away on pocked dirt roads.

We bought this small finca ten years ago, when America started the Mid-asian War and broke the back of the Middle East. Costa Rica abolished its army in 1948. Uses the money for crazy things like free health care, education, clean energy.

Surrounded by farms, the nearest little town is down a scary 13-hairpin-turn dirt road. No phone, no Internet, no nuthin' except land and sky and whether it will rain today or not. Given our lives in a fractured America, we don't spend enough time here. A peaceful place, this. The national greeting? You ask: *"Cómo está?"*—"How are you?"; and the response is *"Pura vida"*—"Pure life."

I can spend a whole day, on and off, watching a new banana leaf appear, rolled in a tight spiral at dawn, opening to a full leaf by dusk. The sun shining through the slick new leaf is a green to die for.

Which this morning I almost did.

Every time we come here after a long absence, we go with Miguel, the caretaker—who looks 40 but is 73—to walk the property, climbing up the mountain to the highest point, a panorama north across the Bay of Nicoya toward the spine of volcanoes. This morning, because of the rain, mud, and overgrowth, instead of climbing up, we drove the Jeep up the road and began to walk back down. Berry and me, Miguel and Mauricio, a young ranch hand who speaks English.

Going down a steep stretch of the cliff, I stepped on a round rock and my right ankle bent over and I started to fall, and reflexively I put down my left foot on what should have been solid but it too hit a round rock, and I again tried to put down my right but I was moving fast, kind of running fast almost vertically down, and then flying through the air headfirst down, no time to put hands out in front of me, sailed for what seemed an eternity and landed on my face and things went black.

I found myself facedown amidst rocks, hands behind my back. As I raised my head, I saw blurrily a stove-sized boulder a few inches in front of my face. Dimly I heard Berry and the others shouting, climbing down to me. I tried to assess—with a doctor's mind—consciousness, wiggle of toes, eyesight. All, but for my glasses that had flown away, seemed intact. I felt something wet on the left side of my face, viscous and sticky, and wiped it away—bright red, arterial. Blood came across my left eye. I reached to stop it.

But then hands were lifting me to sit up and Berry was staring at my face in horror. I searched with a hand—both my palms scraped bloody—in a pocket for a clean tissue and blotted my face and held it tight on my left eye. They put on my glasses—unbroken!—and I was staring at the stove-sized boulder two inches from me, realizing that if I had gone headfirst into it, I'd be dead.

At that, I started to shake, in shock. I was able to walk with their help up to the Jeep. We sped down the 13 hairpin turns to the village of Carmona and the small clinic.

Then something else happened, a hit of happiness, a kind of *House of God* joy.

I was lying on the examining table in the modern, well-lit room for emergencies, Berry on one side and Mauricio on the other. I'd seen my face in a mirror—a large flap of skin from above my left eye was hanging down.

After the nurse had taken my vitals, in came the doctor. And what a doctor. Standing over me she smiled just about the warmest smile I'd ever seen from a doctor—and she was gorgeous. Black hair pulled back in a ponytail, brown eyes surrounded by makeup, long lashes, eyeliner, a Modigliani face, and, as I said, that smile. She began in Spanish and I, who even after immersion classes spoke like a two-year-old, said, *Non habla español* and Mauricio began translating. It was clear she was a good doc—all the right questions—and, except for my maybe brief loss of consciousness, she got all the "No" answers to rule out bad shit. When she bent over to examine me, I could not help noticing that her purple blouse was—to use a line from *The House*—"unbuttoned down past Thursday," breasts cradled in the lace palms of a pink bra.

All at once, amidst this medical crisis that happened to be my own, where I found myself on what we House of God interns used to call "the opposing team, the patients," I was on familiar ground: sex and death. Especially in the Medical Intensive Care Unit, in the daily horror of lingering disease and death, the healthy sex with the nurses, orgasms crying out *We're still alive and young!* At the threat of disease and death, the sensual, the vital—and, yes, the hope. The thing that kept us going, way back then, and might, just, now.

I luxuriated in it. She did a good job, finding nothing serious in history or physical but the torn face and question of broken ribs. She sutured the eye slowly, expertly, as if she had all the time in the world—though she was the only doc in the clinic—then snapped off her bloodstained gloves, smiled, said I should be okay but to call if things get worse, and passed me on to the nurse to dress the wounds. As she left I noticed she wasn't wearing a wedding ring; hope springs eternal, right? And that she was wearing tight bright pink pants and red high heals—make that heels. The nurse finished up, and that was that.

Standing up, I was shaky. Berry grabbed me, helped me out into the small waiting room filled with people. The pharmacist handed me two pill bottles—pain meds, antibiotics. I went to the window to pay. No charge. Even though I was not Costa Rican. Astonishing. In the US it would have taken hours and cost thousands for tests, X-rays, etc.—because we docs get paid more money the more procedures we do. So we do *more*. And *more* more.

We drove back up the 13 hairpin turns home.

Now, in late afternoon, I'm in pain but clearheaded, Berry beside me.

Suddenly it all hits me, the terror, the chill. Death. Other deaths flood in.

Berry puts her hand on mine. In her eyes is intense care. Touched, my eyes well up. Scared as hell. Grateful she's with me and we're alive.

"What, Roy?"

"Death. All the dead in my life. Fats, others, and . . ." I stop, look down.

She caresses my cheek. "Breathe with me. Look at me. Let's breathe together."

I look into her eyes, and for a moment feel a hit of dread, glance away— but then hear the Fat Man's voice again, saying what he always said. "Y'gotta *be with.* Y'gotta turn *toward,* in this world that as a rule turns *away.*"

So I do turn toward her and, *being with,* tell her without words that I'm still mourning him and so many other dead too—my parents doing better as my parents, dead; and Malik, my resident in Mount Misery; and Potts that year in the House; and some patients, like Dr. Sanders. And all the others floating where the dead *do* float, at best resting. Or resisting.

"But for some reason, of all of them, Fats is close. As if suddenly he's floating nearby—all that weight, *floating?*—just past the level of my sight. I miss him."

"Good."

"Good?"

"Because it's real, his presence."

"Yeah, but it's incredibly confusing."

"I know. And right now he's really with you?" I nod. She pauses. "Maybe the only real resurrection of the dead is in us. We keep learning from them and from their deaths and going on with them till we die too. And then we live on in others." She smiles. Grateful, I smile too. "Tell me, hon."

"Yeah, they're all here—Fats more clearly, right now, than sometimes in person, because he was so . . . so damn *big?*" She smiles. "But yeah, looking back I understand him more and more."

"Understand, and you love; love, and you understand. With sorrow." She smiles. "Love, understanding, and sorrow—they're all words for the same thing."

Suddenly she seems to be *shining.* Her face really *shines.*

"I'm listening." She waits, attentive. Waits some more.

I'm stuck, not wanting to unspool this thread of death any more.

"All right, then," she says, "how 'bout we meditate? Just fifteen minutes, okay?"

She has become a Buddhist teacher. For decades I've been meditating with her. For years, at the end of our silence, she would ask me, "How did it go?"

And I would describe how, in the silence, trying to follow my breath *in . . . out . . . in . . . out . . .* the machinery of my mind roared in, mostly in humiliating flickers of "Breaking News!"—usually bad, my version of the Three Poisons: Craving, Hatred, Delusion. After years of breathing them in, breathing them out, I've learned that they rarely let go of their infernal jabbering, even for a second.

She would ask me, after this torment, "Were you able to stay with the breath?"

"Are you *kidding*?" I'd say, frustrated. "All I get is *busy* mind. Mosquito mind, *flitflitflit . . . slap! . . . flitflitflit!*"

Yet more and more, with practice, the trap would open. A letting go. A lifting up. Hits of gratitude. For the divine in the human. Maybe it would lift me up now?

"Okay."

I close my eyes, focus on my breathing *in . . . out . . . in . . . out. . . .*

But my mind ignites on a letter I'd gotten a couple of days ago—a *letter?* We're so isolated here that in ten years but for two lost girls on foot, Jehovah's Witnesses who'd taken a wrong turn, we've hardly ever seen a person let alone any "mail," but here was a letter delivered by the farmer-cowboy with the Lone Ranger hat who every day rides his horse up from Carmona, past our house to his cattle. And in the upper-left-hand corner of the envelope is the logo of the Best Medical School and beneath it, three royal shields saying *VER-I-TY* and below, an animal, rampant claws outstretched (A lion? The Dean?) and in big red letters THE BEST MEDICAL SCHOOL, THE WORLD IS WAITING. For what? *The world is waiting for the BMS?* To do what? To top off THE $750 MILLION CAPITAL CAMPAIGN AND—

Stop! Stop it! Bring it back to the breath.

In . . . out . . . in . . . out . . .

Despite myself, the 750 million brings back the Fat Man and us in Man's 4th Best Hospital at that grave tipping point when medical care could go one way or another, either toward humane care or toward money and screens— which means money and money, ushering in the decline and fall of all I cared about as a doctor and *damn, it still pisses me off that the money and screens won and this shit—*

"Roy!" I open my eyes. Berry. Touching my good cheek, a worried look in her eyes. "Are you all right, hon?"

"Why?"

"You're really agitated—hardly breathing at all. What's going on?"

"*Busy* mind. Full of shit. Seemed like an *eternity.*"

She looks at her watch. "It was less than a minute." She offers her hand, palm up. "I'm here, right here. It's *okay* now. Let's try again. Hold my hand. I'll be with you the whole time. I won't let go."

"Promise?"

"Promise."

And so feeling her hand tremble a little, I close my eyes, take a deep breath in, and then let it ride out on a sigh, and then do nothing but wait for the miracle of the next breath to spark to life in the brain stem . . . *in* . . . *out* . . . *in* . . . *out* . . . and what floats into the newsreel of this particular mind is a silly question, *Why are 90 percent of all American Buddhist teachers born Jewish and called JewBues?* and the wise answer from one of them, Ram Dass (born Richard Alpert), *Because I'm only Jewish on my parents' side*, bringing an inner chuckle and a giving of thanks for still being alive with my girl, Berry—make that my two girls, with Spring—and then in a surprising refuge from the usual mind hell of memory or expectation, there comes a jolt of just plain joy and a sensation in a body still mostly whole, a sense on the lips of a human being smiling, and the presence of the Fat Man smiling back . . . *in* . . . *out* . . . *in* . . .

II

Man's 4th Best Hospital

"Virtue? A fig! . . .
Drown thyself? Drown cats and blind puppies . . .
Put money in thy purse. Follow thou the wars . . .
fill thy purse with money."

—Iago, *Othello*

2

Man's Best Hospital was the third hospital founded in the United States, through a charter of the legislature by a group of *Mayflower* descendants in the first decade of the 1800s. All funds were donated, including a farm complete with cows and a bull.

Its first patient was a tailor with the pox. He claimed that he did not catch it in the city of Man's Best Hospital, but far away, in Boston. Man's Best mission was summed up in two new-world oaths for its doctors, carved in stone in foot-high letters on the facade of the original Pink Building:

"In pain, everyone is our neighbor."

"Our best charity of spirit is the easing of human suffering."

Everyone our neighbor? Charity of spirit? A best mission, yes, back then.

The lineup of oil portraits in the marble halls was all White Anglo-Saxon Protestants. They had a noble mission: to provide good health care for all, even the poor. Imagine that. If you didn't have the money, you still got the care. In its first year, it became the teaching hospital of the Best Medical School, the BMS.

For the first 100 years, non-WASP docs were non-welcome. There were no places in the city where Jewish med school graduates could go for their internships. This led to a wave of construction across the USA of Jewish hospitals, Houses of God, including a flagship, *the* House of God. This soon filled with red-hot young Jewish doctors—much like some of the ones at MBH, but these guys, like any subordinate group who was denied the best, were *hungry*. By some miracle—a recognition of their red-hotness—the House too eventually became affiliated with the Best Medical School.

The two hospitals were different. The House was run by "God's Chosen People," MBH's by "God's Frozen People." MBH was hard-nosed. The House was *hamisch*, a Yiddish word for a hospital featuring mensches, good-hearted guys.

In the modern era MBH had become a magnificent hospital, in every way.

But several years ago MBH had been bought by BUDDIES, a corporate conglomerate of most of the BMS hospitals. Bought, and being crushed under, the deadweight of BUDDIES—a 73,000-weak bureaucracy—filled, oddly enough, with bureaucrats.

None of them provided any health care.

This 26-billion-dollar cost center, this corporate whale, was inserted into the health-care food chain between hospitals and insurance conglomerates—for no other reason than cash. It had succeeded in its mission: using its purchasing power against insurance, *"To get prices up. To monetize. To cost more."* Never mind that in health care Value = Outcome/Cost. Who cared about "value"? It became the biggest health-care empire in imperial America.

And so a great hospital, its great doctors and other health-care workers, as well as its tens of thousands of patients—all of us became allies, as victims of BUDDIES.

Being bled of cash by BUDDIES, MBH was soon deep in debt. BUDDIES realized that MBH could no longer make any *real* money by honoring its mission of service to the sick poor, and insisted it "reengineer" its mission to make money off the healthy wealthy.

But worse than losing money, Man's Best Hospital was losing prestige.

Many years ago *U.S. News & World Report*, a tabloid magazine that knew nothing about hospitals, for some reason—say, cash—began *rating* hospitals. The ratings, seemingly by whimsy, changed each year. Hospitals were at their mercy, going up and down as if they were passing each other on escalators in Macy's.

MBH was the exception. It was steadily #1. But then in lockstep, as BUDDIES rose, Man's Best fell. Two years ago it had dropped to #2, behind Stanford. And just this year it had dropped another *two* rungs down the ladder to #4, behind New York University—which was kinda, y'know, *okay*—but also behind the House of God. *Not* okay! For some reason the House of God, a BMS hospital, had not joined BUDDIES. Neither Stanford nor NYU had BUDDIES.

Now Man's Best was known as Man's 4th Best.

A few WASPs on Man's 4th Best Board showed hints of a strange feeling: sadness. One even got depressed.

Why did they call in the Fat Man and offer him "whatever he wanted to do"?

Because Fats now embodied, and might just reclaim for them, the two fallen icons of Man's 4th Best, and of America itself: money and fame. Fats had become incredibly rich and famous—first in Hollywood doing "The Bowel Runs of the Stars," then in Silicon Valley founding a biotech start-up, hot on the trail to find a pill to restore memory.

On the morning of July the first, which was to be my first day at Man's 4th Best, Berry and I had a problem and then a fight. Two weeks earlier, with all our savings, we'd bought a house. Two houses, really—a big, crumbly Victorian on a high hill in the dull suburbs, with a huge carriage house in which we three would live and I would write, while I rented out the main house, making just enough money to survive.

Mornings with five-year-olds can be crazy—and this one was. I remembered that Berry, a psychologist, had an early meeting of something or other, so I was tasked with getting Spring out on time to the Whole World summer preschool—her second week there—and walking Cinnamon, our beloved dog.

The fight at the door was our usual one—exacerbated by our hard but exhilarating past two years on Navajo time in Arizona, working in the Indian Health Service, time much less tight and punitive.

"And get Spring there on time—she's all dressed and fed—and—"

"You don't have to tell me—"

"It would be a first." She, as always, had dived into her "I"-phone, texting. "Two minutes don't matter."

"To Margaret, two seconds matter—get her there early, and don't forget that today you've got to get snack." Texting, texting.

I blanked. For a second I couldn't remember if I'd already bought snack.

"You forgot?" she said. "You forgot snack?"

"No, no. In fact I got snack two nights ago. I'm good with snack—in fact, I have a knack with snack." She rolled her eyes. "Gimme a break. I'm a little distracted."

She paused. "You mean, worried? I thought we already talked about—"

"Nah. What's there to worry about?"

"Oh, boy, here we go again."

"No, really, it's not like the House of God—that first day, I was scared stiff, remember?"

"Your fear broke through your denial, yeah. Made you open up. It was good to see." She checked her watch. "Gotta run—can't be late—first meeting." She stopped, stared.

I tried like hell to remember what this first meeting was—and failed.

"You forgot?"

"Not really 'forgot,' but—"

"Unreal. I know you're hassled, but maybe, just maybe, you can tune in to *my* new world a little bit?" She turned toward the door.

"Sorry. Really. I'm psyched that you're back into . . . umm . . ."

"Relational theory."

"And it's great—I mean it." She smiled, sensing I did mean it. She lived in as attuned a relational nature as I'd ever known. I'd watched it grow and blossom, all these years, and envied the depth of her women's friendships.

"Okay," she said, softening. She glanced at her watch. "I'm sorry I can't be the one to take her today, but it's good for you. If we both survive, I'll see you tonight." She turned to go, but turned back. "Okay, okay, what's with you right now?"

"Nothing. What can go wrong? I totally know medicine—and even the Navajo way. Getting back with Fats and the other guys'll be great."

"Oh, boy." She looked into my eyes. "Roy, this is *new*. You're going to be a *teacher* of interns and residents now—which you've never done—in another huge institution like the House and Mount Misery that you never, ever have functioned well in. Plus you've been away from high-pressure BMS doctors for two years . . . and it's gonna be *great*?"

"An outpatient clinic? No night call or weekends, nine to six? What could be bad?"

She shook her head in disbelief. "You have absolutely no anticipatory anxiety."

"So?" Her eyes widened, as if seeing a car crash coming. "Hey, this time is different. Can't be as bad as the House—or, worse, that mind warp Misery. No way."

"It can be. A different bad."

"Like what?"

"How the hell do I know? God!" She sighed. "Don't be late. And get snack."

"I told you I got snack and I'll be on time and it's all gonna be great with Fats—life with him would be great anywhere. And with all my old buddies. It's a chance to create something good in medicine, something human. Fats said they gave him 'total control'—we even profit share. If it works, we make the big fortuna—which, lest we forget, we can really use—I mean, 24 grand for private preschool? So she can learn to do Lunch Bunch?"

Halfway out the door, she paused. "After all this, you are so innocent."

"How am I innocent?"

"See? You're even innocent about being innocent." She shook her head, then stared me down. "On time. Pack snack." And was gone.

Spring was five going on either three or seven, depending on how her day was shaping up. Today, luckily, it was seven. I easily dressed and fed her—and fed and pooped and peed the puppy dog, Cinnamon. We got to the Whole World, where she was learning important things like "water play" and, yes, the dread "snack."

I got there and deposited her—a little early, actually—and proudly handed over a giant bag of "snack" to Margaret, the founder and boss. She was a Quaker, wrinkled and strong and as tall as me and kinda hated me because so far in my two chances I had been six minutes and then eight minutes late. She examined snack. I had bought a variety of Drake's Cakes, including my own childhood favorites, fake-crème-filled, sweet-chocolated Devil Dogs, Yankee Doodles, and the luscious Ring Dings. She glared at me as she laid these out on a table in the Snack Shack, but they passed, barely. The soda didn't.

"Snack is not soda," said Margaret in a voice that could have cut glass. "Snack is juice. Apple juice or grape. You have two hours to get it."

Spring squirmed, looking awful: Dad Was Dumb. Feeling squeezed, I ran out to get juice—and lucked out. Down the street was a convenience store—named Convenience Store. It didn't have any big bottles of juice—but it did have those little boxes. I bought all the apple and grape boxes and went back. Margaret opened the bag and did not smile. "You bought thirty-seven little boxes of juice?" I replied it was all they had. Spring and the other kids stared at a Dad Being Treated like a Dumbo Five-Year-Old. I fled. Only driving like a maniac might I get there on time. Not a good time to have a Prius.

Berry was wrong. I wasn't innocent. I was hepped up, full of earned confidence in my ability to take care of just about anything in medicine. After my year in the House, we'd traveled the world together, me working as a doctor to pay our way, from Australia through Asia to Sweden and a lot of places in between. It had been raw and dangerous and marvelous. After the hell of internship, it took time to rebuild our love. A second rebuilding. We had met when we were in college; a dynamite love carried us through until graduation and what should have been marriage, me going to the Best Medical School, she to Man's Best Psychology. But without working it through with her, I'd applied for a Rhodes scholarship and gotten it—Oxford for three years. We crashed. The love got all twisted; the relationship died.

But we grew up. Back in America, we salvaged it. We both continued our training in psych at Mount Misery, the flagship mental health hospital of the BMS. I went into psychiatry because I thought it would be more human, even humane. As in *Casablanca*, "I was misinformed." There were pedophiles, drunks and drug addicts, borderlines, manics and depressives, passels of psychopaths, and serial sexual abusers—and these were just *the psychiatrists*! Humane? Ha. We lasted there only a year. We wound up at the Indian Health Service. I worked as a general practitioner, Berry as a psychologist. What a time that was! With our baby, Spring, at an isolated clinic near sacred Canyon de Chelly, we were dedicated to trying to doctor the worst poverty, disease, reduced life span, addiction, suicide, violence, and death in America. We witnessed all this, the residue of the postcolonial genocide—but we also saw the Navajo spirit, not only in resistance, but in healing. We both had to become specialists in addiction—alcohol and drug abuse.

I had always wanted to be "the one at the end of the ambulance ride." Now I figured that even if I might have my usual trouble working in big heirarchical systems, I would never doubt my competence in, and caring about, what I at best called "healing." And with Fats again? Driving into Man's 4th Best, I mused on a kind of medical heaven.

I parked in a six-story lot and got lost. I had been here often during med school, but everything had changed. On the crest of a hill, the glorious Art Deco Pink Building and garden and the 1816 neoclassical granite Blue Building were darkened by skyscrapers. I forgot the building name and asked Information for the office of hospital president Jared Krashinsky.

"Oh, that's your Twitter Building." She handed me a map, as complex as linguine.

A whispering rocket ride to floor 40 and out. Staggered by the sheets of morning sunlight backlighting a panorama of sea and threads of bleached clouds and then nothing but magical realism blue. The meeting was in the dimly lit, hushed boardroom, leather and chrome. On a giant bright screen was a slide. As my eyes adjusted, I saw, at a square glass table as big and blocky as my Prius, the Fat Man in a florid and horrific Hawaiian shirt. Beside him was Humbo, a young, compact Hispanic guy in a short white doctor coat. And then what he'd called his "A Team" from the House of God: Eat My Dust Eddie, Chuck, Hyper Hooper, the Runt, and Gath, an Alabama cracker who'd been a surgical resident. A nurse, Angel Jones, the Runt's wife, sat beside him. I hadn't seen most of them for many years. Also, a woman doctor of color, I guessed from India. I slipped into a seat. Panting, wiping off sweat. Way late.

Jared Tristram Krashinsky, of the Lithuanian Krashinskys, Man's 4th Best president and titan of industry, stood at a lit screen in dim light, a power suit reading a PowerPoint:

"—this slide shows Core Concept One: Mobile Self-Management. Notice the two-headed arrow. I *manage up*, and I *manage down*. Man's Best Hospital uses world-class managerial material of the BBS—the Best Business School. I use *both hard and soft* power. I go down *hard*. I come up *soft*, and—"

"*Hraaak-a-hraaak!*" coughed Eat My Dust Eddie, our giant, red-haired, wild-man master of irony, straight from a lucrative Newport Beach cancer practice and wife-lucrative divorce. He kept fake *hraaack*ing and, doubled over, exited.

The Krash stopped. Pissed at Eddie? Nope. He was staring at the screen calmly, with eyes closed, smiling, sucking on something. He was a short, fit-looking guy with a handsome face—plump lips, dimpled cheeks, and, for Lithuania, a reasonable nose. Silky dark hair carefully cut, combed over. Appealing, in a boyish way. He was what my immigrant grandmother, Molly, had called me, in Yiddish, a *zeesa boyala*—a sweet boy.

I looked around. My guys had been sitting there listening to him for a while. They did not look happy, rolling their eyes at one another and me.

Krash shifted the sucking into a pouch of a cheek.

"You may be wondering why I'm waiting, as if I'm doing nothing. I'm not. I'm doing Core Concept Two: Maximum Meditative Mindfulness. Man's Best Wellness Program, directed by Bernard, Lama Llassi. Nickname, Mango. Mango Llassi." No one laughed. *Click.* And there he was, Mango Llassi: shaved head, a diamond in his nose, looking like everybody's uncle Louie.

"What if my religion prohibits meditation?" asked Runt. He'd come into the internship mortally scared of doctoring, and under the thumb of a scary dry poet. Chuck and I had freed him up, into an erotic machine. Eventually he wedded the second-most-erotic nurse, Angel—who had never completed a sentence that whole year, except with a gesture. In Denver Runt had become an orthodox Freudian psychoanalyst. Now he was wearing a lime green bicycle helmet, as if a lid for his id. "What if it prohibits Mango Llassi?"

"Why, then, you, so to speak"—Krash smiled, a boyish smile meant to be friendly—"choose your poison. Or none at all."

"Y'mean, man," Chuck said, "if the sacred ain't sacred to you at all?" He was black, a gentle soul, a magical basketball player and singer, from a poor family of eight in Memphis. At first the higher-ups thought he was just a dumb affirmative action black guy. But he was the best doc of us all—and the kindest. He and I loved to play basketball and drink. Both of us going to work tipsy, if not drunk. Looking back, our internship *floated* in alcohol! I'd come to love Chuck. Now I was startled by the touch of gray in that "cool"-cut hair. Last I heard he'd gone home to Memphis to be a family doc and singer. He was not the kind to stay in touch.

"If it's not sacred," Krash said, "try the 'No-Name Chapel.'"

"But!" cried Hyper Hooper, our high-octane, competitive manic from California, rocking back and forth. His mustache had gone gray, his wavy hair receding. He'd been "into death," winning the prize for most autopsies. But by the end he'd succumbed to MOR—Marriage on the Rocks—separated from his Sausalito wife, and had taken up with an Israeli pathologist in the morgue. He wound up in LA, and through an aqua-nude-couples therapy group, he had repaired the marriage, had kids. A science genius and skeptic about Big Pharma's pills that kill more people than they cure, he'd founded at UCLA the Hyper-Winfrey Nutrition Center, and published a bestseller: *Eat Red, Live Long.*

"But but but!" he went on. "The quote 'No-Name Chapel' *is* a name. Faulty logic."

"Holy shit!" cried Runt. "And Jesus Christ!" Angel put a hand on his shoulder.

Gath, our House surgeon, now a Man's 4th Best orthopedic surgeon, grabbed Runt, surgically whispered in his ear. Runt quieted right down.

"Goodgood," Krash said calmly. *Click.* On he droned on money: "My plan is six ambitious capital tranches . . . derivatives trending to seven aspirational targets at a min 20 per . . ."

I looked around the table. *We're back!* The heart of our team, right here, right now. Back in the foxhole together with the guys you never forget but you rarely stay in touch with after—for fear that they'd changed or that they'd not. With one another, we are *known.* Things had happened. Life had happened.

We had staggered out of our internships and scattered. Each of us with a sense of failure. Down on hope. It would turn out that all of us had done our best to patch up our lives and move on. But we were not doing all that well. And then who should show up? Fats! Was he too still hurting and drifting? I looked at him. He was beaming! Here he was, going full blast into new life. Wanting to do it over again with us, do it good.

"This will be different," he had said, "because I'll have the money and power. Man's 4th Best is at my mercy. Our clinic's gonna be a bullshit-free zone."

All at once I felt hope. Not blind hope, but tattered hope, cautious hope—and yet hope nonetheless. All bound up again with our gargantuan leader.

We're here, hope rising. We'll be free together. A thrill went through me. *Buckle up.*

Later, Fats would tell us about Jared T. Krashinsky—a childhood friend. Raised in Brooklyn on high-test yeshiva. His pop a slumlord in Jersey, mom a force in Hadassah. Pop gave 2 million bucks to the Best College to get Krash in. But Krash quit and enlisted in the Israeli army for two years—trained as a sniper. Married a sabra soldier, had children, Tel Aviv college. Went to med school on the island of Grenada, but quit. Transferred to the BBS—the Best Business School. There, his nickname was *Kopf-Flaum-Radfahrer*: "Head-Down Cyclist"—he walked around head tucked down over phantom handlebars, no eye contact. Classmates never heard him speak in class. Ever. After class, he disappeared.

"He eats *salad*," Fats had said to me.

"So what? A lot of people eat salad."

"For *dinner*? He eats, for dinner, *only* salad! I mean, all he eats is, is a *salad*?"

Now he was taking off his suit jacket, rolling up his sleeves and—surprise!—big biceps? Buff torso? A bodybuilder? Sucking androgens? How had this Jewish nondoctor been picked by a high-WASP board for president of Man's 4th Best Hospital?

Well, boards of directors are selected not only for their big money, but to make sure that nothing ever changes. They run on fear. Their logic? If you're on the board of the "best" anything, anything you do can only screw it up—send it down to "less than best." Their core concept? "Do nothing and make more money." And so when Man's Best began to go broke, and fell to Man's 4th, the board vowed drastic changes. They would do this by making sure that nothing changed. And they found their man: Krash would change nothing but the optics, the branding. He had rich contacts from decades of work in General Electric's tax division. A *lone accountant*, he'd been the boss of *1,000 tax lawyers*. Making sure GE, the world's largest corporation, would pay no taxes. He became a star. Articles were written about him, trumpeting him as "The Man Who Made GE Tax-Free."

Now on the screen was Core Concept Three: Screens Are Clarity.

"Man's Best sees clearly through screens. Man's Best *bills* clearly through screens. Maximally, and trending. You, like us all, will see and *bill* through screens. Computer screens. Our dedicated screen runs on HEAL: H-E-A-L. Our EHR, Electronic Health Record. For billing. All of Man's Best's billing. We *monetize*."

Gath asked, "An' can y'all tell us whut the lettahs stand fo'?"

"Yeah," mused Eat My Dust, twirling what looked like an old-fashioned blackjack or ratchet wrench on a finger, "like, maybe, 'How Eager Admins Live'?"

"Or," Hyper rocked, "'Happy Endings for Aging Ladies'—and great autopsies?"

"I googled it," said the Runt, "but all I got here is a laxative from Mexico."

"Cut the shit!" Krash barked. "I know all about you guys. I know how notorious you all got after that novel came out. I know how you cultivated that notoriety—as if you were famous. Or infamous, like Eddie there, and frankly—"

"Hey, not fair!" cried Eddie. "I'm famous too. I can prove it—"

"Infamous! Infamous in your oncology practice in Newport Beach, for that line of yours—'What could be better than a gomer with cancer?'"

"See? I'm famous for that! And so what?"

"So one morning when you looked out your window and saw your mailbox was on fire and you ran out and found a copy of *The House of God* and a note threatening to kill you? *That's* so what." Krash inhaled. Ex'd. "Let me be clear: we at Man's Best wanted the Fat Man. In his own colorful way he's the best. But bottom-line bottom line? To get him, we *had to take you*. You have a choice. You can do what you're doing right now and cause trouble for yourselves, or you can cut the adolescent shit and fall into line!" A glance at his watch, a smile. "Goodgood. Gotta hop, time to stop. I'll turn this over to Pat—"

"Never happen," said Chuck in a voice that *landed*.

"What?"

"Fall into *line*?" He looked around to each of us. *"Never happen.* Right, guys?"

"Never happen never happen never happen" flew around the table real fast.

A phrase from *Dispatches,* a dynamite book by 'Nam war journalist Michael Herr. When "grunts" were given an order that would put them in grave danger, they refused with "Never happen." This of course wasn't war. But every year, the equivalent of two whole graduating classes of doctors kill themselves. Lots of med students too.

That happens. Because of *this*.

"Before you 'hop,'" I said, "can you tell us what the letters of HEAL do stand for?"

"Why, I don't know."

"Healthy Electronic Assistance Link." A clipped, clear, confident woman's voice.

"Thanks, Pat," said Krash. "HEAL. For billing. Pat, take it from here."

"Wait a sec, Krash," Fats said. "You haven't mentioned the words 'patient' or 'care.' Nothing about 'service.' Is the purpose of HEAL to bill and not good patient care?"

"The answer is yes."

"Yes what?"

"HEAL is primarily for billing *and* primarily to deliver good patient care. So I use—"

"Logical contradiction!" shouted Hooper, twitching. "Mutually exclusive."

"That's old thought," Krash snapped. "Aristotelian logic. Not quantum logic, where you can be in two different places at the same time, like Schrödinger's cat."

We rolled our eyes. *Whoa! Whose cat?*

"Screen logic. You'll each be given an 'I'-tablet containing all the information in medicine. You don't have to remember anything. Just *clickclickclick*. Our interns do eight thousand clicks per twelve-hour shift—best in America. We did a survey of house staff: 'What's the *minimum percent* on their shift they spend in front of screens? Eighty! Eighty percent of their time in my hospital they're in front of screens. Eighty percent minimum." His silhouette trembled with excitement. "Some say *ninety percent*. Minimum."

"And so," Fats said, "if they spend, say, five percent in eating and pooping, how much time is left for face-to-face patient care?"

"Day shift, nine percent max. Night shift, less. Depending."

"That is quite disgusting," said the new woman, with a British-Indian accent. Fats had mentioned there would be at least one woman doctor on our team—and pledged more. Her name was Naidoo and we would come to know her as a brilliant woman of integrity, her life devoted to building "compassionate communities of resistance." "I for one—and I hope we all—resist this, the supremacy of screens—at the expense of spirit—with all our power."

The boardroom went dead. I loved her—looking back, we all loved her.

How would Krash respond to this challenge to everything he had said?

We watched as in silhouette against the glittering dead white screen his chest rose, paused, fell. Maybe, just maybe, he would take Naidoo's challenge as an invitation to some human stuff? I felt sorry for him. Under cannibal pressure at work, what kind of life could he have? As Man's 4th Best president, he had to hide under that ice, all the while projecting "Goodgoods." I found myself rooting for him. *C'mon, Krash, you can do it—be human!*

"2.6 billion?" He stared at us, a game-show host with the bonus question.

He answered it: "The dollars spent to install HEAL throughout all the BUD-DIES hospitals."

Buddies? Who were these buddies? At that point we didn't know, and didn't ask.

He clicked off the screen. Lights up. "My mission as president is to serve. *Service.*"

Again we were startled. Would he finally mention service to patients?

"My *service* to Man's Best . . ." He paused, choked up. Clearing his throat, he went on. "My service is to make Man's Best Hospital *the best bio-pharma ecosystem in the world.*"

I was stunned. Not to serve the patients, the sick? I looked around. *Disbelief.*

He was trending toward the glass door. Fats, with dancing-bear light steps, got there first—he'd always gotten to every "there" first—and blocked his exit, Humbo alongside.

"Hold it, Tristram," Fats said, using his middle name. Krash looked stunned. Fats loomed over him, flag-sized tropical-flower shirt making him seem a powerful Hawaiian king confronting a Dole fruit guy intent on stealing not just pineapples but Hawaii. Fats turned to us. "Okay, team, go on ahead. I'll meet you in our clinic in a half hour." Then, looking Krash up and down as if sizing up a steak, said, "Nah. Meet me there tomorrow at seven sharp."

Pat—a solid, short woman who was pretty pretty and pretty much gender neutral in hair, makeup, build, and pinstripes—showed us out. As we left, we heard the Fat Man shouting in a strange guttural language—Yiddish?—and Krash shouting gutturally back.

Waiting for the elevator, she said, "I'm Pat Riley—Plant and Operations. I work too hard but I do it for love and cash and perks. Two big problems. Number one: parking. With the eternal construction, it's a bitch. Number two: security—cyber and especially personal. Guns."

"I *love* guns!" said Gath. "Guns mean Surgery! Hot damn! Go, 'Bama!"

"Weird. Listen up: this is America. *Think guns first.* Like Emergency, your Outpatient is at the interface with bad and scary armed shit. MBH can expedite your gun licenses. Anyhoo, everything I could tell you is on your smartphone anyways. Use it."

"What if you have a dumb phone?" I asked. I took out my ancient flip phone.

"You . . . a 'Medicaid' phone? Ones we give out free to the poor? That does *nothin'*."

"That's why I have it. If I had an 'I'-phone, I'd never create anything—never write another novel. In fact, I'm losing my wife to her 'I'-phone. She's addicted to it."

"Can that thing text?"

"I get incoming, but it's hard to text back. For each letter, I gotta go through the alphabet. I tell people they've gotta text me a question I can answer with 'OK' or 'NO.'"

"Big problem. Damn elevator—it's express, but you gotta have a special clicker. Which I don't." Finally it came. "We go straight to floor N—what I call Floor Normal."

After Pat left, Chuck, Gath, Hooper, Eddie, the Runt and Angel, Naidoo, and I went looking for the building housing our new clinic, the FMC. We got lost, winding up in a spanking-new corridor—ur-glass, -chrome, -light, and -tech. Large computer screens, with retractable keyboards at eye level, spaced at decorous intervals along one long mauve wall.

A team of interns and residents was making rounds. On one side of the Lysoled, LED-lit hallway were nine figures in short white coats. On the other side, a lone woman in long white. They stood at nine portable rolling tables that are used to swivel trays of food over patients' laps. We got closer. On each tray was an open laptop. They didn't notice us. A sepulchral silence, broken only by the lone woman typing like crazy, *click-clickety-CLICK*. We threaded our way through them, unnoticed, and walked on.

We were too deflated to visit our clinic. In the parking garage we scattered into a free day of sky and optimistic puffy clouds, a classic first of July. The Runt sped off on a severe, glittering racing bike, helmet down over handlebars, a puff of Day-Glo lime green. Why hadn't he taken it off in the meeting? Angel followed slowly on his tail, her silver Mercedes flashing hazard lights.

⊘

"I don't like you anymore, Daddy, and Margaret hates you!"

"Did she say that?"

"Yes."

"Shit."

"A swear! You did a swear!"

"To say you hate someone is a swear too."

"You stupee!" she screamed, and ran up to her room.

"Hey! Hey, Spring, wait! Wait!"

For the first time ever, she slammed her door.

I was floored. And that was only the start. Berry looked up from her texting, stared at me, shaking her head. "Don't say it," I warned her.

She said it. "How could you?"

"Oh, come on. So I got boxes, not bottles—"

"Margaret called me and said it wasn't the boxes and bottles. It was, quote, 'His piss-poor attitude in front of his daughter's peer group. And teachers.'"

"They're five years old—they don't even know the word 'peer' and—"

"They pick up every nuance, especially the way their parents look at their teachers—"

"It's fucking preschool, not West Point. What, did she get expelled or something?" Berry started upstairs. "Wait. Let me do it. That door slam got me in the gut. She's never done that before. I'm sorry—please?" She nodded and gestured me to go upstairs first.

I stood behind Spring's door, eye level with a sticker of Disney's "Mulan, Brave Girl of China." I called to her. No answer. Said I was sorry. Nothing. I tried other enticements but quickly ran out of them. Feeling like crying, I turned the handle of the door.

"No, don't, you kumquat!"

Kumquat? I looked at Berry for an explanation. None came. She gestured us downstairs. We talked. I said I was sorry and, given this strange first day, worried. Spring's door slam was like the starting gun of a race through a new gauntlet. It brought back the slam of Berry's door when we broke up after college, the black hole I got sucked down into and tried to drink myself back out of and failed.

"Maybe this job is a mistake. Coming back for Fats to try to do good in this creepy Man's 4th Best system? A half day and I—"

"'4th Best'?"

I explained. She laughed. "Well, that's progress, anyway."

"Yeah, but a half day, and I'm a mess. Honey, I don't know about this. It was bad."

"How was the Fat Man?"

"I dunno. Last we heard he was screaming at the president, who so far seems like an advertisement for euthanasia. It was great how we all slipped right back into it, the House of God bonding. But this might be even worse." I sighed, shook my head. "Real bad."

"That good, eh?" She smiled. I grimaced. "And thanks for asking how my day was."

"Sorry, babe. How was your day?"

"Don't ask." She shook her head. "I'm in shock. I keep trying to see the Buddha side of it—not the craving side, but the suffering side—to have some compassion for others."

"And?"

"Miserable. Being back here *is* depressing. I mean just walking into my office. Wedged between a Price Slasher, a Burger King, and an Exxon? Compared to Canyon de Chelly and Chinle, it's so ugly! Noisy! All malls. Like our parents' in Florida."

"The mauling of America."

"The culture shock is intense."

"Culture *schlock*." She smiled. *And what a smile she has!* "But why today?"

"Today I put up that poster my mother gave me when I was fourteen, the Camus quote. 'In the midst of winter, I found there was, within me, an invincible summer.'"

"Lovely. I know how much it means to you."

"Used to. I looked at it today, fresh, and I imagined that it was, 'In the midst of winter, I found there was, within me, an invincible winter.'"

"Oh." Our old difference, she toward the downside, I, mostly, up. "That bad, eh?"

"I'm not sure if it's bad or good, but I'm sure it's real. Like our daughter."

"Will she ever forgive me?"

"Yes. But it may take a long, long . . . *long* time."

"How long?"

"Max, maybe an hour." We went back to the kitchen. She started texting again.

I sat on the first step. Waiting. Watching my watch. Time warped to *slow*.

Finally, 47 minutes later, I heard Spring open her door and summon me to come up. I climbed the stairs to her bedroom "office" and listened to her carefully and we both signed a document she had hand drawn on poster board in a strangely bloodred crayon, promising that I would never do that again. A hug sealed the deal.

After two whiskeys, I was in bed. Berry was into her last "I"-phone texts. I read my father the dentist's typed letter. After decades of small-town dentistry in a broken-down town—Columbia, New York—trudging through his half of a bottomed-out marriage, he was still a supreme optimist. Like an old amalgam filling, he was socked into the mastication of the conjunction, his letters always in the grammar of (phrase) conjunction (phrase):

> . . . glad you are through with the Indians and that was a real mistake. Good that you are at Man's Best Hospital with that weird Jewish Fat Guy and I worry about the low pay. I told you not to accept the Rhodes Scholarship and it delayed your physicians earning power for three years. Mom and I played 18 yesterday at Catskill I had my best score a 78 with one Mulligan and she still has that nice compact swing. . . .

3

ook," the Fat Man was saying in a trembling voice we'd rarely heard before. "Beautiful, isn't it? Yummy."

The six of us guys, plus Naidoo, Angel, and Humberto "Humbo" Parza—the short, wiry Hispanic doctor who'd been in the Krash meeting and who would turn out to be the Fat Man's faithful all-purpose man—stood in an alley, looking at what might have been a lot of things, but two things it was not were "yummy" and "beautiful." We were staring at a crumbly red-brick building of four stories, leaning like a gomer for support against a razor-edged Man's 4th Best skyscraper. The bricks were those thin ones that had been healthy at least a century before, and the windows the old kind that light had to wobble through. Above a narrow front door was a wide granite chunk into which was carved: *Pathology*. Under it was a shiny new brass plaque:

THE FUTURE OF MEDICINE CLINIC:
CARE, COMPASSION, AND CANCER

"Yes, yes," said Fats, big head nodding slowly. "The FMC . . ." He paused, stared at us. "C'mon, c'mon—get it?" No one got it. Shaking his head, he raised his hands—I was always amazed at how with those fat fingers, whenever everyone had failed to get in a big IV line or do an LP, with one slick stroke, he would succeed—and now as if lifting each word onto a shelf in the thick summer air, he said: "The . . . Fat . . . Man . . . Clinic."

Shouts, laughter, amazement.

"A dream . . ." Fats stopped, choked up. He snatched a terrible hankie from his pocket, blew that nose, a fat wet sound. He placed the hankie over his heart. "A dream come true."

One afternoon when Berry and I were nearing the end of our two years working at Chinle, Arizona, as we and Spring climbed back up from a hike to the Anasazi "White House Ruin" at Canyon de Chelly, we came around the last switchback in the rock and saw, silhouetted against the low, stark sun and ballooning down from what looked like a pith helmet, a big, fat shape seeming to dominate the exit between the high sandstone walls of the path. I went first. The steep uphill curve had me bending over and sweating and watching my step carefully, unable to look at this figure until I got near the top. There before my eyes were two wide black dress shoes, inexplicably shiny amidst the dust, and then pin-striped pants sailing up over ox-sized thighs and, cinched tightly, a belt buckle rolling over on its own belly like a shiny fish. Above it was a white spinnaker of a shirt over an enormous gut, and then bulging chins. Breathless, gaining the top and looking up into those sharp black eyes, I yelled out:

"Fats?"

"Roy!"

"Roy?" I said lamely.

"Fats!"

I went all teary and embarrassed, and maybe he did too but it was hard to tell because then everything went black as big, strong arms went around me and crunched me to his belly—I'd never been sure if he really had a chest, or if it was all belly—and we hugged the air out of each other. He knew Berry, of course, and hugged her, but he'd never met Spring. She was as usual megashy, hanging back behind Berry so Fats with that dancing-bear agility was all at once down in a deep yogic squat at her level.

"Do you like animals?" he asked. Spring nodded. "Do you like dogs?"

"Dogs are my favorite animal. Our dog is Cinnamon, a cockerpoo."

"Holy moly! Me too, cockerpoo! Wanna see *my* dog?"

Spring looked at Berry and me. We nodded.

The Fat Man gestured to a highly polished black town car reflecting nearby. Humbo, in this case his driver, in plaid shirt, creased jeans, and a farmworker's straw hat, got out and opened the back door, releasing a fat and fluffy white dog, which leash-led him over to us. The dog went right to Spring—animals always did—looked up, rolled on its back, four paws in the air, yearning for a belly rub. Humbo began setting up a full picnic.

"What's her name?" Spring asked, rubbing.

"Chubby Checkers. We call her Chubby. She's just a pup."

"Mom, Dad—Cinnamon will love Chubby. Can we have a playdate?" We nodded.

"Great," said Fats. "Humbo, put it on the list. Let's eat!" *How had Fats known?*

As we ate some suspect Southwest stuff, Fats told us what he'd been doing and why he was there. As with all things Fats, it might have been dead true or live phantasmagoria. He'd left to do gastroenterology in Hollywood. But now, as I asked about his making a "big fortuna," he laughed.

"Back then," he said, "I was flying solo. Now, in Silicon Valley, I founded a biotech start-up. Work with an Oxford neuroscientist who discovered the molecular mechanism of memory storage in the brain. Together we're onto a cure for forgetting, the memory loss that's endemic in the millions of baby boomers like us. The Mother of All Inventions."

"You're de-gomering the gomers?"

"Maybe. But we're going for prevention, for *our* generation, who can't remember where they put their keys or 'I'-phones or kids. It's *functional epigenetics*, not the idiocy of the primacy of genes, the neo-Darwinist *Selfish Gene* bullshit of Dawkins."

Berry and I looked at each other, puzzled.

"The genes are the notes, and life is the music—see Denis Noble, *The Music of Life*. Genes are changed not just by mutation, but by feedback from the environment, from cell to cosmos. Darwin wrote that Lamarck and his giraffe were right. And medical studies show that if you put Type One genetic diabetic mothers on treadmills, their muscles got bigger by phosphorylation and guess what. Their children *do not inherit diabetes*! Gene change!"

He paused to eat more. And went on excitedly, through the mush.

"My scientific partner and I found the biological mechanism of memory.

And we maybe found the treatment for forgetting." He reached into his pocket, brought out a pill bottle, and poured out a few glittering pearl-sized tablets. "Cellular calcium. We discovered that nerve cells have these little railroad tracks with boxcars that load up with calcium at the synapse, carry it to the nuclear membrane, where the boxcar doors open and release . . ."

He saw we didn't know what the hell he was talking about, and laughed.

"Anyway, it's radical, it's hot. Our round B of venture capital financing last year was 34 million dollars, and we're well into phase three clinical trials. I'm CEO. Got an office and labs within eating distance of Google, Facebook, Apple." He sighed. "So many inventures, so little time. Those boxcars are carrying my big fortuna. And doing good in the world."

"What do you call it, the company?"

"Best name so far? 'Boxcars for Boomers'—y'like it?"

"A touch Nazi, no? A bit too Holocaustic?"

"Yeah. My mom, Fritzi, hates it." He deflated, a little, for a second. "How 'bout 'Brainstones for Boomers'?" I nodded. "With the slogan: 'Those who forget their keys are no longer doomed to repeat them'?"

"Keep trying. So, you're still working in Silicon Valley?"

"Yeah, but I can do it all from the East Coast—I'll commute, some. My science partner, Rosie Tsien, a DPhil in neuroscience at Oxford with Noble, runs the show." He sat back, wiped guacamole from his lips, sighed—and spooned up the ice cream melting on Spring's plate. Adopted from China, she preferred salt and soy to sugar and spice.

"Your partner is a woman?" Berry asked nonchalantly. "As in you're married?"

"Phwaa*aakkk*!" Fats choked, coughing and heaving, red in the face.

Was he choking? No. He was blushing. Never, ever had I seen him blush.

"No, no, no," he said. "Nope. No way, no, just a scienterrific colleague of Chinese descent. Good kid and let me tell you why I'm here."

Berry and I looked at each other. *Fats has a woman.*

As if to distract us, he jumped in, speaking fast. "So I'm rich, and with Rosie as chief scientific officer, in biotech slash medicine I'm famous and . . ." He wiped the debris off his face, which had gone from red back to pink. "And so I said to myself, 'Fats, *what next*?' That's why I'm here. Man's 4th Best needs rich and famous. I'm both. I'm it. And all of us on the A Team have got unfinished business. Right?"

"To do what? What's next?"

The dancing dark eyes stopped still.

"To put the human back in health care."

Now we of his team were following him into the FMC. I was surprised to see that the inside had been totally gutted, and was one large space that ran the whole breadth and width of the building, with a circular central desk supporting computers—clearly the nerve center of the place, with admins and nurses hanging around—and a circle of offices up against refurbished wooden walls. The ceiling was high, the lighting not fluorescent but with fixtures designed to look like, well, early twentieth century. All in all an old-time meeting hall, even a union hall—a place that fostered straight talk across differences.

"And we got all four floors," he said as if we got all four hot pastramis in a deli.

We gathered in the conference room, around a well-worn elliptical wooden table with carved graffiti—in the center the inevitable heart with an arrow through it and *JLS Loves SJB*. Placed on the table, in front of the dozen or so old wooden chairs, were sturdy leather-bound three-ring notebooks with *FMC* and our names, and silky silver Waterman pens engraved *FMC*.

Notebooks? Filled with three-hole lined paper? Pens? What was going on?

"Hello!" Fats shouted happily, standing before us. He said it enthusiastically, several times, looking deeply into the eyes of each of us for a moment until each responded with a much-quieter-than–Fat Man "Hello" back. *"Oy gevalt!* Listen up: saying 'Hello' is the second-most important thing you do in life, and in medicine. Y'gotta practice your hello until you do a helluva hello, okay?"

We nodded. He stared. We said, more loudly, "Okay!"

"Great great," said Hooper. "But what's the first-most important thing?"

"Saying 'Good-bye.'" He paused. "All the good-byes, and then . . . the final good-bye, right? Like my Italian landlord always put it, 'Y'know, y'*never* know, y'know.'"

His tone, the sudden solemnity in all that wit, hit us hard. *Wayne Potts. Still dead.*

Fats walked to a big old scarred blackboard—maybe the same age as the building—and picked up a stubby piece of chalk. *Blackboard? Chalk?*

"Next: take out your screens—all your phones." All came out, and out and out. The screens we carried. Who'd have thought there would be so many? "Now," he said, "turn 'em off, and put 'em in the center of the table, on and around that carved heart." No one did this. He got a fierce look in his eyes. "I mean it."

The tension rose. *Let go of our screens?* Talk about radical acts! Put them into a pile, with other screens? How did we know they'd be compatible? In the silence, we began to separate from our screens, placing them as carefully as prostheses in a safe part of the table. The ungainly pile spread from the center. When I threw in my Medicaid flip phone, the others' phones seemed to clatter away from it in disgust. Fats had not yet put his in.

"Good. Now. Those of you who are already big-time addicted to screens, this will be a shock to your systems. You will even find yourself plagued by a new syndrome I've discovered: Google-fingers."

"Which is?" asked Eat My Dust.

"Like when something comes up in a meeting—a piece of data, a reference—or even in your mind as it drifts off toward sex or fear or laundry, and suddenly you notice your fingers twitching in the air to click on Google to find out the 'facts.'"

"But we need to be on call at all times," said Hooper, Google-fingers a-twitch. "We can't be out of touch."

"In these meetings, we gotta be outta touch. In an emergency, they'll find us." He threw his phone in.

The "I"-phone owners looked worried, wondering how their phones were faring in that snake pit. Withdrawal was already starting to be felt. Tension went to eight. Or nine.

"Help! . . . Help! . . . Help!"

What? Who? A plaintive voice from the pile.

"Help, Hyper, help! . . . Help, Hyper, help!"

"This is hell! This is phone hell!"

The phones were calling out? The whole pile panicking? Hyper and others started reaching into the pile, setting off another wave of "Helps!"

"Stop!" Fats shouted. *"Bad phones! Stop!"* The phones stopped.

"Learned that trick in Sili Valley." At the blackboard, he said, "Why am I here? Why are you? One day I looked around and asked myself, 'Self of Fats, what *else* can you do for medicine?' I answered: 'A lot. Medicine has gotten a lean and hungry look, and it's up to you and your guys, Fats, to fatten it up.' Why'd I recruit you?" He wrote in chalk, talking:

TO PUT THE HUMAN BACK IN HEALTH CARE
WE DO IT TOGETHER

"That sums up who *we* are: humane docs. And this?" Chalk-talking again:

MONEY KILLS CARE
SCREENS MAKE MONEY
SCREENS KILL CARE

"That sums up who *they* are: profit-seeking drones of inhuman health care. Why did Man's 4th Best ask Fats to come *here*? 'Cause we got lucky. They're on the way down, in cash and prestige. I'm on the way up in both. But they still get a *lot* of media. So the Krash delegation visits me and makes a sweet offer. And I figure if we can put the human back in here, we can do it anywhere. And if we *do* do it here, because the spotlight'll be on us, everyone will know. So I say to myself, 'Fats, what a chance. Get the guys. And our new gals, Dr. Naidoo and Head Nurse Angel Jones—and Humbo.'" He stood there beaming. "What's *in*human in medicine? It's worse for patients, worse for doctors, and better only for insurance and drug companies—for the health-care *industry*. Why did I choose each of you? 'Cause deep down you each know how bad it's gotten—all over the country, you're dissatisfied playing your part in the industry. Some of you are thinking of quitting medicine— one, who shall remain nameless, is even thinking of becoming a *lawyer*! All of you are pissed to see what's happened to what we love, and have sacrificed a lot for, including marriages: being good docs, in the world."

This hit me hard. Yes, I'd thought a lot about quitting medicine, and yes, because of what he had just described. In Berry's and my travels around the world, we'd seen that some countries have done a helluva lot better getting health care to their people while the docs are a lot happier in their jobs. So it was possible, yes. And we would try to do it here? What was to lose?

"So I chose each of you because you've still got that fire inside! In the House we resisted, brought 'em screaming to the wall of fire that is *truth*—and held their eyes open with red-hot toothpicks making 'em see our agony, the agony of absurdity, right?"

Nods around the table—I felt that fire again, saw fire in those eyes. That hope.

"But, man," said Chuck, "we didn't change nuthin'."

"I know," Fats said, "but from the inhuman, we learned about being human, right? The seeds were there. Remember my slogan to you back then?"

No one remembered his slogan.

"Thanks a lot. Sheesh." He seemed to deflate. And then inflate again. "I kept saying we had to learn to *be with* the patient, remember?" When he mentioned it, most of us nodded. "Make 'em feel that they're still part of life, part of some grand nutty scheme, instead of alone with their diseases. Even young Basch here said once, 'What these patients wanted was what anyone wanted: the hand in their hand, the sense that their doctor could care.'"

"And of course," Naidoo said, "the sense that you knew the science too."

"Yeah. But the science is the easy part. The hard part, the best part, is *being with*—when they let us in, to do our best doctoring and help 'em heal. *Being with*. Empathy."

"Tell it to my ex," said Gath, our surgeon, a stocky, blond-haired ex-Marine from Georgia. "The only way to heal is with cold steel."

"Maybe," Eddie said, "but we didn't change anything—and then we scattered."

"True, because we had no power. When the power came down on us from the top, we got isolated from each other, right? Alone, we started thinking, '*I'm* crazy for thinking *this* is crazy.' But in any power-*over* system—based on race, gender, class, religion, sexual pref, et cetera—the only threat to the dominant group is the *quality of the connections* of the subordinate group. That's us. This time, we got leverage. I've got 'em over a barrel six ways from Sunday—and they only know about three of 'em. Long as we stick together, we got a chance to create something that'll shine. The one thing we gotta do?"

STICK TOGETHER, NO MATTER WHAT

"This is new, different. Here at Man's 4th, we're not trying to survive, but to humanize! Okay, okay—it's grandiose, stupid. It'll never work. Maybe not. But maybe yes." He was all puffed up and beaming, back into his big, fat, capacious joy mode that had inspired us all. He took out a small kosher salami and started peeling it.

I asked, "What makes you think we can really do this?"

"Don't know for sure, but I've seen the best human effort yet." He bit the salami, chomping cheerily.

Naidoo asked, "And where, Fats, did you find this 'best human'?"

"A med school that shall remain nameless. Last year I did a long part-time gig with'em. We'll build on that."

"Okay, man," Chuck said. "So what's with this school?"

"Two things. One, they got the biggest, baddest public hospital in the country—nine hundred beds and noisy and dirty and chaotic and crazy and guess what. Nobody ever gets turned away. So everybody there's focused on—wait for it—service." He stopped cold, nodded his head. Seemed about to cry? The tension went up, say, to nine. Dabbing his eyes with the salami, he wrote on the board:

SERVICE

"Yes, yes. Like my pop serviced customers when he was in Ladies' Lingerie . . ."

I looked at Eddie, who looked at Chuck. *What?!*

He went on. "I asked one veteran doc there, 'How can you stand it—the poor, the tortured, the refugees, sixty-two different interpreters on call?' He says, 'It's hard, but every night when I go home, I try to think of *one good thing* I did to take care of my patients. I can almost always think of one.'"

"How great is that!" said Naidoo.

"Very," Fats said. "So then he said to me, 'But now things have changed. Now every night when I leave, I can't help thinking of one good thing I did to take care of my *computer*! And *that's really draining*! It's criminal. I didn't become a doctor to care for my computer!'" Fats paused. "The docs don't make great money, but they do do good. There, it's 'All for one and one for all.'" He paused, face blank. "Humbo, where was I?"

"La segunda causa," said Humberto.

"Oh yeah." He dropped his salami on the rosewood. It bounced a bit and left a streak of grease. He rubbed his hands together quickly as if they were two sticks starting a campfire for Hebrew Nationals. "It's the tone, the feel of the place—forty thousand employees, and from the docs down to the guy who empties the trash on the night shift in emergency, the feel isn't surly. It's good. How is this possible, this pervasive good attitude? Well, the tone of any institution percolates down from the top. And the top three guys who run it are all refugees from the House of God! Like us, they were abused. So when they got power they were not gonna do it to the guys below. They broke the cycle of abuse."

I tried to get the arms of my mind around this, and failed. I looked at the others; they didn't really believe this either. Another one of the Fat Man's fantasies to help us through?

"So to get me here, they gave me everything. Total artistic control. A no-cut, yearlong contract on the big stage. And we got a secret weapon, the Patient Satisfaction Score. The higher the score, the higher the pay. Man's 4th Best PATSATs are in the toilet. Ours are gonna be in the clouds! 'Course we still gotta relearn the nuts and bolts of *being with* our patients—which ain't gonna be easy and I ain't the world's expert in it either. But we got a chance. So buckle up. *Stick together, no matter what.*" He sighed, then smiled, that big, fat smile. "We're gonna show 'em how to be good docs." He licked his lips. "Lunch!" Snatched up his phone and started toward the door.

"Wait!" said Naidoo. "You forgot to say 'Good-bye.'"

"My bad! Old dog new, right?" He looked slowly around the table at each of us—those dark eyes really looking *into* you—and whispering to each of us in turn as if each were the only one in the room and he were about to die, "Good-bye, good-bye, good-bye . . ."

By the time we had managed to untangle our screens from one another's, I figured he was wolfing down his frightful lunch.

4

That afternoon Fats asked me to go with him to do attending rounds in the hospital. Our titles were "attending physicians." Each of us would be responsible, a month at a time, for rounding and teaching. We were accountable for the care of the patients—and the screwups of the docs—on that particular medical ward. The team we would teach consisted of a resident, an intern, and BMS students doing their rotations in medicine. As interns in the House, we had been near the bottom of the ward team. At Man's 4th Best, we were at the top.

With Fats and Humbo Parza—always at the side of the guy he called "Don Gordo"—I went into a skyscraper, up to floor 11, and out into a con-stricted view of the ocean and the city. Ward 34, our home base. Fats stopped, staring down the long hallway. Observing. He'd taught us that: first, observe—unobserved.

A caravan of white coats, nine rolling keyboards of HEAL, parked at the nursing station and disappeared.

In civilian clothes, we met with the team in the house staff quarters, a two-bedroom on-call suite next to a large room filled to the gills with screens.

We introduced ourselves—"Hello! Hello! *Hola!*"—with an enthusiasm that startled them. The resident in charge, avoiding our eyes, introduced himself. "Dr. Jack Rowk Junior." Short, puffy around the chin and gut, bald-ing, and tight faced. A large purple birthmark started out in the shape of Chile at his blond monk's rim, fading to a pink iceberg calving down his cheek into small pink iceberg-ettes at his chin. Eyes flat blue. Sincere regimental tie, knotted. Tight. And why did he say "Junior" and list it on his name tag?

"Got a *great case* to present! A real puzzler, a toughie, in imminent danger. Going down the tubes!" Was he enthusiastic about this? "Patient of one of the Four Horsemen—"

"Is someone with her?" Fats interrupted.

Dr. Jack Rowk Junior blinked. "I assume so. I mean, a nurse."

"Find out," said Fats. "Now."

"Suresure." He clicked his phone and in an e-moment got the answer. "Yeah, a nurse. The key to the case is that her physican is one of our Four Horsemen of the Apocalypse."

"Meaning?" I asked.

"Agents of death. Book of Revelation. Bad docs. On their last legs. Still use paper charts, not HEAL. We clean up their messes with high-powered care. Mo Ahern here is our star senior med student doing her subinternship with us. It's her case. Mo?"

Mo Ahern was a petite, fit-looking woman in a short white coat. Bright hazel eyed, on alert, sandy hair in a girlish ponytail. Her fear of "presenting" was revealed by her fingering a charm on a string necklace—maybe Mayan. Instead of an "I"-pad, she had handwritten notes on a stack of three-by-five index cards. Like what we'd used in the House? As Fats had said, "There is no patient that cannot be fitted on a three-by-five card." Mo even had the same hand-drawn grid in which to put the crucial labs so they could be seen at a glance. I smiled at her, sent her a silent prayer: *Don't worry, Mo. At least me and Fats won't rip you to shreds and we'll keep you safe from Dr. Rowk.*

As she began, her voice trembled. *How young she sounds. Like 14.*

"Mrs. Burke is a seventy-two-year-old Caucasian married woman who was referred by her local doctor, who had been treating her for decades, with a chief complaint: 'He told me to come in again, for my pacemaker infection.'"

Mrs. Burke had received one of the early types of cardiac pacemakers, where the wire was threaded through the abdomen and hooked on the outside of the heart, the pericardium. This was before pacemakers could be threaded up through a blood vessel, inside the heart. Occasionally the wire would get infected, her doc treating her successfully with an antibiotic, fluconazole, for fungal infection. 14 months ago she was admitted for a fever that the antibiotic was slow to clear up. Diagnosis: "Rule out septicemia." On her second day in the hospital, a mild urinary tract infection was found, another antibiotic added. The fever did clear, but slowly, requiring three additional hospital days, an expense that, to Man's 4th Best's chagrin, was reimbursed at a lower rate than the first two days. The team suggested that her external pacemaker be replaced with an internal one. She refused, fearing surgery.

This admission, the source of infection again was the pacemaker. Fluconazole was continued, but her platelets began to drop precipitously. Bruises surfaced all over her body. Nobody knew why. All the tests for causes of thrombocytopenia had turned up nothing.

"I," Dr. Rowk said, "and all the rest of us including the heme-onc and ID consults have now gone over all data—*all twelve years* of outpatient and inpatient data—in HEAL. The Horseman is not really computer savvy. Nothing's turned up. A great case!"

"How low is it now?" Fats asked.

"Last hour's bloods should be back." He clicked his phone at the big screen in the conference room. HEAL awoke, had its latte, put on its face of 50 horizontal lines in four colors, flickered, and leaped into action—running between the seven or so stationary boxes containing short lines of bouncing data ricocheting off the corners of the screen, like bullets in a video war game. At Jack's quick mouse caresses, layers of colored lines of data scrolled smoothly up and smoothly down. Pausing for breath, a line of HEAL moved from the left (the "Past") to the right (the "Present"). Yes—the number of platelets in her blood.

"It's one," said Jack. "Per mil."

"What?" Fats blurted out. "One little platelet?" We all knew the normal range was between 450,000 per ml and 150,000. This "one" was 149,999 below the lower limit of normal. Platelets are necessary for blood clotting, and life. This lonely "one" meant that she was about to bleed out internally and die. "Shit!" he cried. "She's seventy-two. Young enough to die!"

"Suresure. Gotta be an error. I'll check." He searched the micro-ordered chaos on the big screen, found and clicked a "Question?" box. We waited. My thought? *She's bleee-ding.* We waited more. *Still bleeee-ding.* A second box appeared, labeled: "Gotta be an error?" Jack clicked it. We waited *more* more. *Please, HEAL, don't freeze! Is the box locked?*

Still waiting.

The box unlocked and answered, for some reason in Spanish: *"Uno es correcto."*

"Let's move!" Fats shouted, quickly up on his feet. "Mo?"

Mo led us into the room. Mrs. Burke was a thin, white-haired woman looking younger than 72, restless, fear in her eyes. The nurse was bending over the bed, putting pillows between arms and legs and bed rails. Wherever Mrs. Burke's skin was in view, it was bruised black-and-blue. Her face looked like a loser's in a prizefight.

"Hello," Fats said, smiling, introducing himself, and then sitting on the edge of the bed so he was at black-eye level with her. "How we doin', Mrs. Burke?"

"Not too bad."

"You sure got a lot of bruises all of a sudden, eh?"

"Tell me something I *don't* know," she said quietly, shaking her head, then looking down into her lap. Her attention was focused inward, on her plight, on dying.

"Y'got me there!" he said, smiling. She glanced up at him, managed a grim smile, then, her lip quivering, looked back down. "Scared, huh?" She looked up, her eyes wet—and quickly looked away. And then, strangely, nothing happened—a *lot* of nothing, for what seemed a long time. Finally, Fats put his hand on one of hers, on the edge of a violet bruise shaped like Florida. "I'm sorry you're scared, dear. We'll take care of you." A slight nod. He asked two or three pointed questions. No luck. "Okay, we're gonna figure out why you're all black-and-blue, get you outta here soon as we can. Anything we can get for you?"

"Yeah. Get this damn IV outta my arm!"

Fats paused. "What bothers you about it?"

"You ever had an IV?"

"Sure have. You're right. They're a pain."

"I've always hated 'em. I want to go home."

Fats nodded. Noticing that the small bruise beneath his hand had already spread toward another bruise—say, Cuba—he seemed to stroke it with a finger as if he could push the edge back, push it in, down, away, and then looked up at her. Holding her gaze for moment, he said, "I'm sorry. You still need the IV for now. We'll get it out as soon as possible, and we'll get you home." He smiled at her and led us out, down the hall. "Anybody have any ideas?" No one had any. Someone asked if Fats had any. "I got only one. Slim chance. I need HEAL."

He asked Mo to put up Mrs. Burke's two recent admissions and the Horseman's twice-a-year outpatient records in between. Even these few inquiries were cluttered up, entrapped in an avalanche of data that, I imagined, could have sent Mrs. Burke to Mars and back. For two years in the Indian Health Service, I had used the federal government E-GOV program, used also by Veterans Administration hospitals and clinics all over the USA. It was old and clunky, but friendly to docs and patients. It actually let you open up blank screens to write longer notes. Using HEAL was like deciphering the instrument panel of a 747. I wasn't accustomed to these 50 or so lines of data streaming along, fast, those midget *numerals*. I soon got vertigo, had to look away. No particular number was highlighted—each onstage for a nanosecond, a poor player who struts and frets and then is swept away. No place to elaborate, write a note, highlight what really mattered in all that electronic mush.

Fats seemed solid in these rapids, looking carefully at the admission four years ago, staring at something, and then to the team's amazement writing it down on paper in his *FMC* leather notebook. He then went to the admission from a year and a half ago, at a certain point shouting, "Stop! Freeze-frame, Mo!" Squinting, and then walking even closer until he was big-nose-to-none with the teensy-weensy pixie pixel *numerals*, he wrote something else down. Finally, he did the same with the current admission.

"Y'got a blackboard here?"

"A *white*board, suresure," said Jack, "a dry board. With erasable Magic *Markers!*"

"We gotta move, *pronto*. I'll be brief." On the whiteboard in CAPS, he charted a grid with the values for each of two admissions: platelet count *versus* antibiotic, and the Horseman's outpatient blood values in between—all normal. On the most recent admission, 14 months ago—with the urinary tract infection—by the end of her stay, there had been a small drop in the platelets, with which she had been discharged. She had recovered soon after. There was no note from her resident about that small drop—because, even if it had been noticed, there was no place in HEAL to write a note as to *why*. This time, the same antibiotic had been given, and the huge drop was about to kill her.

"The answer's right there," Fats said. "Anybody else see it?" Nobody did. "Mrs. Burke *told* us what it is." Blank. "What's the difference between her treatment *outside* the hospital and *inside* the hospital?" No one knew. *"Think."* Think we did. Nothing. "Okay. A hint. What'd she say was bothering her?"

"The IV," several of us said.

"Good. So, both outpatient and inpatient she gets the same antibiotic, fluconazole. But outside it's *pills*. Inside it's *IV*. She's suffering a rare side effect of the flucon that's seen *only* in IV administration. Believed allergic. Sensitized via beta-four-y-immunoglobulin. Reversible."

The fingers of the team members flexed Googley to look up the citation. "Stop! Heads up!" Shocked, all stopped. "How 'bout before we google her, we save *her life*? Jack, write the order to stop the IV *stat*—and keep transfusing her platelets."

Jack clicked in the orders. And sat back. "Ja-a-ck," Fats said, "now you go and tell the nurse *in person*." Jack did not move. "Junior? Move!" Startled and astonished, Jack left.

Fats referenced two articles, with the admonition: "Do not look at 'em now. Look at, and listen to, Fats." All did. "So we got bad news and good news. The bad news is that we almost killed her with our 'care'; the good news is that we saved her from our care. It's called *iatrogenica imperfecta*. So, why'd we miss the diagnosis? One: she didn't point any of you toward it when you spoke with her, right?" Nods. "Even though, deep down, she may have had a sense that somethin' bad was coming through the IV. There's no note written that she complained before—'cause HEAL has no box to click for that. Two: I'm all for data, but there's so much data on HEAL that no human, except for the hint we got, and the 'think' we did, could possibly see what was right before our eyes: outside, pills; inside, IV. Nobody noted the big clue from her previous admission, the platelet drop. Again, even if someone *had* noticed and wanted to note it for future interns, Boss HEAL does not want to deter us from its appointed nanosecond rounds. On screens of one med school's electronic record, I created 'blurbs': heart-shaped circles rimmed in hot scarlet that 'pulse' on-screen to get attention, inside of which there's room for docs to write brief thoughts, *understandings*—to tell the *next* doc what to be alert to in this *person*. Here, if there'd been space for just one highlight blurb: 'Unresolved why platelets started down before discharge—find cause.' Bingo! It's top of the problem list upon her *next* admission! If we'd'a had that, she wouldn't'a had this." He sighed. "So with everybody looking carefully at the screen, what didn't happen?"

"Keeping it simple," said Mo.

"Exactly. What *didn't* happen was, simply, a pause. To muse. To think. We gotta think to pause, and we gotta think to think. None of us took that space of time and relief from this million-pixel *mishegas* to think. It was all here. We all technically saw it, but it didn't sink in, so we didn't see it. No time to understand it. You can't click into the same stream twice. And don't forget, the one clue came from what?"

"Suresure," said Jack, back, "listening to the patient. But *everybody* hates IVs."

"Uh-huh, but there was something else in her as she told us—a feeling. Anybody get that?" Mo and another med student nodded. "And why'd she show us that feeling? Because she felt connected, with me, with us." He paused. Others nodded. "I picked up, in my body, a sense. As a doc, sometimes your instrument is your *own* body, your *own* heart—the one thing that you can't screen out." He blinked, smiled. "But hey, let's not blame ourselves. In the face of all that big data, it would take a genius to use common sense, to think to think, and understand. Blame the electrical engineering grads, isolated out in Cheese Country, Wisconsin, who designed HEAL with one primary goal. Which is? Med sudents only."

"Having all the data at your fingertips?"

"Streamlining patient care?"

"Maximizing safety and quality of care?"

"Real-time response to changes?"

"Nope," said Fats. "A hint: clicking boxes. By the way, how many of you *like* having to click on those cute boxes—"

The team began screaming. Two nurses rushed in, were told, and started screaming. Others came, and others, and soon we all together were *screamm-mmming*!

"Ohhh-kay, team!" Fats said. "High fives!"

A lot of high fives.

"Those boxes are a pain in the ass. Why? Because new good studies show they don't improve patient safety, or quality of patient care. With each of us doing eight thousand clicks a shift, mistakes are inevitable—and sometimes deadly! In fact, they don't have much to do with *good* patient care at all." He paused. "And what *do* they have everything to do with?"

"Billing! Money! Cash! Profit! Money laundering!" etc.

"Yes, yes," Fats said sagely. "Finally. The Wisconsin cheesers want money. For us docs to find the key clinical-care data in that cheesy machine is hard! Starling's law: the more data, the less understanding." He rose. "Fun, eh?" Nods. "Basch, Humbo, and I will follow Mrs. B with interest. Come visit the FMC, do a rotation. We love med students."

"Hold on," said Jack. "There's no need, in front of these young physicians and top med students, to be so cynical, to trash high-tech Electronic Health Records and HEAL."

"Cynical? Me? I *feed* on ideals, on ideal care. I'm so idealistic, to you I sound cynical! And I do *not* call 'em Electronic *Health* Records, 'cause they don't help with health, and may well harm it. With a screen between you and your patient, you get distracted, right? A lotta medical mistakes are made— errors in dosages, wrong data entered. Real harm is done to patients. Lots of accidents. *It's like texting while driving.* We docs are *distracted.*"

He paused to let this sink in.

"So, to remind us of the danger, let's call 'em E*M*Rs, the 'M' for 'Medical.'"

"A distinction without a difference," Jack said. "Face it. Without HEAL's recording everything, like the outpatient data, you wouldn't've been able to crack the case, and—"

"The case? You don't mean that sweet Mrs. Burke, do you?"

Jack steamed. "Whatever. You and her woulda been nowhere without HEAL."

"Really? Without it, I woulda paged her doc stat, had a chat, worked it through quick. Or leafed through the written charts—brief, thought-through notes passing along not only the info or knowledge, but *un-der-stan-ding.* What we docs value and are valued for. Y'can forget information and knowl-edge; y'never forget what y'understand. And now? Understanding? Lost some-where out on a cheese farm in Wisconsin."

He checked his watch—pricey, the workings visible amidst a coral reef of gemstones.

"I love great tech. It could be dynamite for docs. I *design* tech for my clinical venture in Silicon. But I can't stand monetized crap tech like HEAL— even if it trumps EPIC."

"Excuse me, sir." Clearly a med student. "What can we do to heal?"

"HEAL the machine, or heal the patients?"

"The patients."

"Any of you ever rotate through the veterans hospital, use those computers?" Nods all around. "What'd you think of 'em? I mean, compared to HEAL."

"Really good," said Mo. "A lot easier to use."

"Yeah," said a student, "they even let you free-write notes on your patients. You can click to get a clear screen to write in. HEAL won't let us do that."

"Jack?" Fats asked.

"Yeah," he said surlily. "More friendly user interface. Everybody knows that."

"And," I said, "the VA and the Indian Health Service are all connected to each other. You can get on every other VA or IHS computer in America, in a flash."

"Which HEAL and the others can't do," said Fats. "So why's the VA much better?"

Silence. Then Mo spoke up. "Because there's no billing, no profit. Like Medicare."

"Exactly. Nobody's makin' money offa it. So we all gotta get together and unhook care from billing. So nobody makes an obscene profit offa the sick."

Jack was turning red, up toward his birthmark. "You want *government* insurance? Where'll you get the money? Eat the rich—" He got redder. "I mean, *tax* the rich?"

"Works for me," I said, "works for the *civilized* world."

Fats mused for a moment, actually *mused*. "No wonder America's left with Velveeta Health." His eyes got hot. "New law: Learn your trade, in the world."

Blank looks from the team.

"What's that mean?" Mo asked.

"The patient is never only the patient—the patient is the world. The family, the friends, the housing, the food, the toxins, where the water comes from, where the garbage goes, the politics, the government, the ailing climate. The world's in the room now. We can't screen it out! The *earth* is in the room. We and our patients are the earth—made of dirt and seventy percent water, with a thin membrane of skin between, right?" Nods. "Dust to dust, ashes to ashes. None of us are here for long. We and the patient are the world." He beamed out Fat Man Gratitude. "You all did good—you listened, about why you couldn't listen to Mrs. B. Don't blame yourselves. We're all at the mercy of the Man and his Machine." He tried to get up from his chair and failed. He grimaced, tried again. Succeeded.

"How can we be sure, sir," said a med student, "that this won't happen to her again?"

"Be creative. And be deft. Find a way to make a note in HEAL that will be noticed by future docs, but not by the HEAL Police. Hey—her next admission, how 'bout going around the hospital and writing it in crayon on all the HEAL screens?" We all laughed. "Seriously. Try to put a noticeable note in HEAL. Mo? Can you find a way to do that?"

"No. I'm only a med student."

"Hey—nobody's ever 'only' anything, okay? And because you're so fresh, you're a gift." She blushed. "Jack? Your thoughts?" Jack sulked. Fats smiled, put his arm around his shoulder. "Jack? Jah-ack! This ain't a contest. We're all in the same boat—it's called learning. We all used to do a lot of it, when we were kids. Remember?"

Jack struggled, then grinned, turning back into Jah-ack. "Yeah. Okay."

"Good. Basch, Humbo—*vamos*."

"Wait," I said. "Someone has to explain to her what happened, tell her she'll be fine."

"Tell her the IV med was an error?" said Jack—going from *Jah-ack* back to Jack.

"You can't not," I said.

Jack looked at Fats, who nodded. "Okay. But d'ya know she's gonna be fine?"

"Telling her she'll be fine—and meaning it—will help her be fine. Read the literature—good news maximizes good results. Bad news, delivered badly, screws people up. Morbidity and mortality rise, confirming the bad news. And when a doc says, 'You have only X months to live'? It crushes people. People die sooner."

"Oh, boy," Jack said with contempt. "The placebo effect, suresure."

"What's wrong with an effect without side effects?" I said. "Better than most meds."

"Great—go ahead and give 'em false hope."

"How can you know it's false?" I asked. "Belief in something beyond yourself isn't false. It's a touch of the spirit smacking up against the medical machine. Hope is sacred. Try it."

"*Sí, sí,*" chimed in Humbo. "The very church miracle is done with the *plachaybos.*"

"Did y'see the new research paper on placebo, Jack?" Fats asked. "They found the enzyme, a COMTgene variant—and guess what turns it on. Good human connection. *Being with.*"

Jack had dived back into his "I"-pad. Clearly these words didn't compute.

"Oooh-kay," Fats said. "So who's gonna tell her she'll be fine?"

"May I do it?" asked Mo. "I really like her. We talk a lot. I'm the only one who has time *to* talk. Because med students aren't allowed to click on the billing boxes."

The Fat Man reached into his shirt pocket and came out with a neon orange plastic fork that had on the other end a spoon, and along one side serrations of a knife. Waving it as a Day-Glo magic wand over Mo, he intoned, "Since you didn't forget to say 'May I?', by the power vested in me by the Attending Woman Doctor in the Sky in the Big White Bathrobe and Beard, I hereby appoint you"—he squinted at her name tag—"'Mocha' . . . ?!"

"I know," she said. "It's weird—they met over coffee at Peet's and—"

"Weird hell. Delicious." He cleared his throat, a royal "Ahem." "I hereby appoint Dr. Mocha Ahern to sincerely tell the truthful and even really good news to that cute Mrs. Burke and bless your heart."

5

*

ater that afternoon, fearing facing Headmistress Margaret alone, I
awaited Berry under the flapping school flag—a charmed circle of children holding hands around a smiley Earth. The words "Whole World
School" arced over the Earth and cradled it from below. Running around the
circle like a smile was "Care Courage Confidence." All slickly done. Given
the fortuna it cost to send Spring there to learn water play, snack, and Lunch
Bunch, I mused on asking Margaret to add another "C" word: "Cash." *Not*.

"How was it?" Berry asked, so startled I was already there that she stopped
texting.

"Fat Man great, med student great, brain-dead ward resident."

"Oh. Well, thanks for being on time—even early." She pocketed her "I"-
phone.

We went in. After six hours of Man's 4th deadly, it was life. Brightly
dressed, real-live lively kids were running around and screaming and laughing
and holding hands (girls) and beating on one another (boys), and never had I
felt so glad to be with human beings. Here we proud parents were, sitting on
tiny chairs, knees up to our chests and eating cookies made freshly by Lunch
Bunch and washing them down with "Bio-Healthy Organic Apple Juice."

"Great snack, Margaret," I said, smiling and nodding.

For once, the big-boned boss lady smiled back. "Thanks. And eco-
friendly too."

"That's why they pay you the big bucks." She scowled. Scary Lady.

The featured event of Parents' Day was the display of each child's "Draw Your Family" picture, about two dozen, thumb-tacked up on one long wall. Spring grabbed our hands and tugged us along excitedly to hers, in bouncing steps. There before us were our three stick figures—five, counting Cinnamon and Olive the bunny: a stick-figure dog with floppy ears, a bunny with a bisected white-and-gray face. The white faces of the stick figures of me and Berry captured my beard and bald head and glasses, and Berry's different-shaped glasses and long hair. Between the two of us was a smaller stick figure of Spring. Her face was dark brown.

What? But her face is hardly a shade darker than ours.

"Y'like it?" Spring asked, hopping with energy. "Isn't Cinny cute!?"

"Wonderful!" Berry said, not missing a beat, not looking at me.

"Really good, Foozle!" I said, on guard, hiding my startle.

"Thanks, guys!" she said. "And I can take it home! Can we frame it, *pleeze*?"

"Sure!" I said. "Right away." Spring rushed off to her friend Eliza's family.

Berry's eyes met mine. Margaret was staring, accusingly.

I whispered, "Is that how she sees herself?"

"And us. A wake-up call. It's a great chance to open it up with her."

"It?"

"Being a family of color."

"Yeah, I know, but she's so light skinned, even being Chinese. Who'd'a guessed such a dark color? I mean, in her mind?"

"A whole new world. It's so sweet, hon! She's inviting us in."

"Man, that Fat Man has changed!" Chuck was saying later that night at a barbecue at our carriage house in the leafy suburbs. He, Eat My Dust Eddie, and I were sitting out in the yard, staring uphill across our lawn at our lit-up Victorian main house, rented out to a Mafia family "in veal." To our right was a stone mansion—a mausoleum, really—of a severely inbred man, Henry Cabot-Lodge the nth. A few years ago he'd bought the historic house, spending millions to "modernize" it. Now, heavy construction vehicles were constantly backing up with *Beepbeepbeep*s, building a driveway close to us, curving away to a granite garage so large the workers called it "the Garage

Mahal." There was an old ditty describing the orginal family, all of whom still lived hundreds of miles away in Boston: "Welcome to dear old Boston, home of the bean and the cod, where the Cabots speak only to the Lodges, and the Lodges speak only to God." Speaking? Fine. Inbreeding? Uh. Not so good.

Now, in neighbor Henry Cabot-Lodge, inbreeding had unhooked the DNA helix linkages of that hyphen, and bad shit had penetrated. He had the aristocratic height and slenderness, and that magical sandy hair that never balds, those impenetrable blue eyes. But the nose was not that hatchet sharp, and the lower lip was wobbly. Also, he had a badly bleeding IQ. Henry was a recession to the mean—the *really* mean. His job was hedge funds.

He was rarely glimpsed in the wild outside the mansion, but when he was, he wore conservative suits, or green sports jackets with a palm tree over the pocket—often containing a puffed hankie—and red trousers. He had one bizarre quirk: always ending our brief conversations with a phrase that had nothing to do with anything except perhaps something secretly dynastic?

"Y'know, I really *love* pizza!"

The stark, mean truth? We doctors chose a job that we loved, and figured we'd make enough money. Henry wanted to make money, and chose a job that was to make money, period. Making nothing else *but* money.

Thus, the decline of the line, and the cause of the fall of the American Empire.

In the still, smooth dark, a blessing of quiet. We were drinking bourbon with beer chasers and smoking Parodi cigars, gnarled, dark twiggy things that had the twin virtues of not staying lit—so they lasted a long time—and a sharp, dark, and dangerous smoke that made you feel like a tough Italian. Spring was in bed. Cinnamon and I were playing fetch the ball. I loved his ears flapping up and down like wings when he ran back, what Spring called "Flying Puppy!" Berry, having had enough male-medical talk, was with Naidoo inside. Over dinner it was clear that Naidoo and she were on the same beam, linked by what Berry had called "our wake-up call on race today at school."

"How's Fats changed?" I asked Chuck now.

"Never heard him say he wanted to 'Put the Human Back in Medicine' before. I mean, gettin' older, man, and bein' *more* idealistic?"

Eddie stared harder at nothing, bushy red eyebrows squinched up. "I wish I was still in Newport Beach. If I hadn't gotten divorced, I'd still be there treating rich gomers with cancer who never die. A gold mine. Pass the bourbon." Chuck and I inquired as to why the divorce. "The dogs," he said, morosely. "Law Number One of my life: Dogs cause divorce. Doin' good in the world? It got so I couldn't even do good in the bed."

"Wait a sec," I said, looking into Cinnamon's "I love you, master" eyes, the pooch hoping against hope for the next ball throw. "How can you say that?"

"Easy. After she saw the mailbox in flames, she said we had to get guard dogs. Next thing I know, two big German shepherds are in our bed—marriage over."

"Yeah," I said, "big dogs are big trouble. Never get a dog you can't pick up."

"That wasn't the issue," he said. "The issue was that they hated me. Wouldn't let me into the bed with them, the three of 'em. I had to sleep in my home office."

"So the dogs caused the divorce?" I asked.

Eat My Dust looked down at his drink, up at us, and, gazing out at more nothing, said, "That and *maybe* when she found out about my affair with her best friend? That might've had something to do with it."

He looked so puzzled, we burst out laughing. Eddie stared at us as if he hadn't laughed since the Great Mailbox Fire, and then he too burst out laughing, and it was that contagious kind of laughter that flips resentment over on its back and tickles it, and we were soon drunkenly laughing at the folly of it all.

When we caught our breath again, he said, "And then, just at the most vicious time with her lawyers—after she'd gone public to all my patients and I'm in court for the execution, guess who's in the front row."

"Fats?" we said, together.

"And Humbo. Somehow he knew that, at that very moment, Dr. Eat My Dust was Señor Chopped Liver. And if the money from his invention comes in, I get solvent again."

"What happened to the girlfriend?"

"*She* got her lawyers after me too. A gun was involved. The twins— they . . . hate me." He coughed a few times. "Mother-daughter bonding. Nice for them, shit for me."

In the summer dusk, sadness.

I had already told them about the Fat Man knowing just the right time— to the minute—to show up at Canyon de Chelly. We turned our attention to Chuck.

"Well, I get married, have a kid—great kid, Alecia. Girls are *great,* right?" Both Eddie and I nodded; Eddie's face turned red.

"With girls," I said, "the love just pours on out, doesn't it?"

"So I go back home to Memphis. Open an office. Try bein' a blues singer but I'm not that good. Get bored. Truth be told, I missed what we had, y'know?"

We nodded.

"So I'm floatin', and call a friend at UCSF—San Francisco—move there, wind up at Kaiser Emergency in Oakland. To pay bills I do too many shifts, don't have quality time for my wife and kid, do some stuff I ain't too proud of, other women. Divorce? Nasty. Not too much custody. Not too proud of myse'f now neither." He sighed. "An' then one day I'm finishin' a round of golf—man, I got to love golf—and I'm comin' off the eighteenth green, startin' to feel all depressed 'cuz I gotta go back to my empty apartment, and I see, sittin' on the deck of the clubhouse, like a beached whale, a fat guy in a dark suit, waving to me with a big hero sandwich. A little Hispanic guy's next to him, sippin' a cool drink with a little umbrella in it. I sit down. Fats hands me a postcard: '*Wanna be a doc in the Fat Man Clinic?*' He tells me what he wants to do. I say, no, thanks. I want to stay close to my daughter, Alecia. So he goes, real serious-like, 'The other good guys are in the same boat as you, not doin' all that well . . . *at heart.*' He says it—I dunno—kinda deep. Y'know what I'm sayin'?"

We nodded.

"An' mentioned you two. So I go, 'What about seein' my kid?' 'No problem. Whenever you want, I'll fly you back out there first-class—or fly Alecia to you. I know she's into animals—y'can take her to Africa on safari, sleepin' in fancy tents with showers. Big chance for father-daughter bonding.'" Chuck smiled sheepishly. "What could I say?"

"Shit," said Eddie. "I shoulda asked for that too. In fact, I'm gonna."

Berry and Naidoo came out, sat down again in their chairs. We greeted them with a boisterous welcome that was 80 proof. Naidoo smiled—what sparkle in those eyes! A startling light green in that walnut face.

Berry stared at me, at us. "What happened out here?"

"What do you mean?" I asked.

"You guys are . . . better." We guys looked at one another, puzzled. "What have you been talking about?"

"Oh, nothing much," Eat My Dust said, "just Nazi dogs in the conjugal bed, the trauma of divorce, the abandonment of children, the hatred of ex-wives—oh, and ex-mistresses too—with guns, outrageous alimony, loss of respect in our profession, suicidal gestures, and two half-assed attempts—but aside from that, Berry, I'm *fine*!" He considered this for a moment. Then shouted: *"We're all just fine!"*

We all laughed, a comfort.

"Well, this must be the Divorcés Anonymous meeting," said Naidoo.

"You too?" Eddie burst out. Naidoo nodded, but was silent.

"Hard to believe, girl," said Chuck. "You're gorgeous, total smart, great doc. Why?"

"Medicine." She paused, lowered her head. "Being on both sides of it."

Oh, God. She was a patient? I assessed her, looking for signs. We all did.

"Breast cancer."

Oh, more God! Divorce and cancer?

"Any kids?" Eddie blurted out.

She smiled wanly, a sad smile. Shook her head no.

"Oh, Christ, I'm sorry," Eddie said.

Chuck and I looked at each other. We had never before heard him use that word.

Dead silence. Divorce. Death. Life with no bullshit or laughs. This was big, sad hurt. The merely humid air turned to stifle. Sorrow spread its wings in each of us.

We all stayed quiet, listening to the lovelorn crickets and the whining of the dog wanting to have the ball thrown again even though in the dark it couldn't be fetched and brought back. Regret eased off, into each of our everyday sufferings, now shared.

Berry said, "It's so sad, your divorces. But it's brought all of us together."

"Fats somehow knew," I said. "Finding us. He always seems to *know*."

"What are you looking for with him, here, now?" Berry asked. She looked at Chuck. "What's the hope, here?"

"Well, gurl, I left home all those years ago for college, and tried to go back there, but can't. And everythin' I tried since then just didn't cut it. I got no home. Fats, for that year, was home for me. For us all, right?" Eddie and I nodded.

"Home?" Berry said. "Now, that—that would be something else, for all of you now."

Chuck smiled. "You know how it is, gurl. You know how it is."

"But we can't do it again," Eddie said.

"The thing that Fats got me on," I said, "was that we might just do it new."

"Yes," said Naidoo. "Sorry. I didn't mean to drag us down, on this fine evening."

"'Down'?" said Eddie. "Sounds like you, me, and Chuck can't *go* down any more. When we make our move, it's gotta be up."

"Thank you, Eat My Dust," she said.

"Call me 'Eat,'" he said. We laughed. "We're kind of related now, right?"

"Yes. I accepted this job for that same reason. It's rare in life, at my age, and single, and . . . and damaged." She choked up, fought back tears, searched for a tissue.

Eddie handed her a folded hankie—we were to learn that for some reason he always carried not one but two hankies.

We waited. "For me, this disease, knowing what's really involved, treating it in my patients . . . It is rare to meet a spirit like Fats." She smiled. "A Fat spirit, like the Hindu god Ganesha, an elephant, with six to twelve arms—and sometimes five heads too."

"Hey hey hey," Eddie said, clearing his throat. "Is that perfect for Fats or what? Nuthin' stops an elephant—y'know what I'm sayin'?"

"Except bees," Naidoo said. "The only thing elephants are afraid of. Imagine?"

We tried to, easing down the softened night into hope.

Berry had put Spring to bed. We went up to see her. Cinny was lying at the foot of her four-poster with its gauzy canopy, Olive the bunny—seemingly two half bunnies sutured together, gray on one side, white on the other—was munching hay in her spacious pen on the floor. Luckily the dog was afraid of the bunny. Spring was fast asleep, clasping Shirty, a piece of an old, soft striped shirt that was her security blanket.

"The best sight in the world," I said. "Best ever."

In bed, exhaustedly drunk, I was crashing.

Berry said, "That Naidoo is wonderful." She had her "I"-phone in hand, but was not yet texting.

"Totally. What'd you talk about?"

"Race . . ." Into her phone. "And gender . . ."

"Great. Tell me more." I yawned, long, and enormously.

"Never mind. Tomorrow." She paused. "Do you really think that Fats has changed?"

"In some ways, but not that elephant essence, no. I mean, I hope not."

"Sounds to me as if he might have changed for the better."

"What could be better than a better Fat Man? G'night."

6

T he Fat Man Clinic was open for business. Kind of. Fats and Humbo were not there. No explanation. I was only partly there, hungover pretty bad.

The waiting area was an open semicircle at one side of the receptionist/ nurse station. It was bordered by a wooden railing like you see in town halls, with a swinging gate at one end—"in"—and another at the other end—"out." A children's corner too. Fats had said we'd be starting off easy. The place was already busy, from babies to elderlies and all ages in between, mostly people of color, a United Nations of sorts. But no gomers? A 4th Best armed guard, to sniff out weapons. With 350 million guns—one for every American man, woman, and child—and 100 gun deaths per day and one mass murder a week and with our own doors wide-open to anyone? Mandatory.

Our individual offices were in a semicircle on the other side of Reception and Nursing—Angel's domain. Gath was the only surgeon. Except for our psychoanalyst, the Runt, each of us was available for any patient. Our specialties spanned a broad range: Naidoo for women's health, Eat My Dust for cancer, Hooper for nutrition/weight, me for general practice and substance abuse, and Chuck for anything. Humbo, a doc with all the alert suspicion of a smuggler, stepped in whenever he wasn't with Fats.

At the main wooden desk carved out of joined old doors lacquered up to shine was the FMC manager—one of those older, salt-of-the-earth and children-out-of-the-house women who'd been doing these things forever in clinics, running each like a complex bowling league, and who was fierce, efficient, and lovable. Ours was named Dulci Cacciatori. She was round in face and torso, and immensely short. Big stylish glasses.

"To set you doctors straight," she said right away, "yes, my name is Eyetalian: first name 'sweet,' second name 'hunter'—like when you order chicken alla cacciatora, it means 'hunter style'—and I don't want to hear another word on this matter, okay?"

A group nod. *Who would dare?*

And billing? We would do it ourselves on our screens. Using HEAL, the EHR or Electronic "Health" Record system that BUDDIES had installed in Man's 4th Best and its other hospitals and clinics, at a cost of 2.6 billion dollars. Incurring a 20-year debt.

Without any data proving that it would be good for safety, or quality, of patient care.

We docs had had an orientation for HEAL. A four-hour-long video and workshop with a rosy-cheeked and smiling, clean young guy dressed casual, named-tagged *Bob*. Bob's first step was to pass out a single sheet of actual paper for our signatures.

"A routine form required for your employment, stating you will not, in public, say or write anything negative about HEAL. Your usual gag order. Like EPIC's, but lots better."

A gag order? Gags? It was clear that Bob was not ordering us to tell jokes.

Bob was waiting. We shrugged, signed, passed the sheets to the front. They would turn out to be just about the only sheets of actual paper we saw having to do with HEAL.

"Folks," Bob said, clicking on the first slide, which printed out his exact words, "we are at war. Against the health insurance companies."

As he went on, it turned out that this war, like all wars, was about money.

"On our side of the screen, we are fighting for the highest payment for our work. On their side of the screen, they are fighting for the lowest payment for our work."

And how did we fight this war?

By gaming HEAL codes of each disease diagnosis and treatment to max out money.

In principle, we could max out cash by clicking on little boxes in two ways. The first was *qualitative*: clicking on the worst disease diagnosis, most severe form, requiring the most treatment; the second was *quantitative*: also clicking on as many *different* worst and severe disease diagnoses, requiring the most elaborate treatments, for as long as possible.

Health insurance, the army on the other side of the screen, tried to minimize our maximums of money. "*Bad* news," said Bob. "And they have *lawyers*. Trained to catch us in anything illegal—like lying, which we do not do. The *good* news? We have *three hundred thirty-four people in the Billing Building*! 'The Billables'—also the name of their a cappella group, by the way—are our allies, our in-house battalion in the war. In real time they track your choices to max out money. We have Man's Best lawyers to fight the insurance company lawyers." The terms Bob used to hide this war of gaming of the system were unintelligible: algorhythmic meaningful-use monetizers, protocolization of chain-link treatment, high-product-gritzel throughput, etc. Bob made clear that the more expensive the Dx and Rx codes clicked, the more 4th Best money was made.

"We nicknamed our elite billing-enforcer team 'Coders 4 Cash.' They work out of a war room at an undisclosed location. We are watching each of you for your choice-of-click codes—from admission to discharge. Fiscally, doing procedures on patients makes the most money. Surgical procedures make the *most* most money. Medical care makes the least." He paused. Then said fiercely, "*Except* for the diagnosis of 'sepsis, severe.' After you click 'sepsis,' the pop-ups ask: 'mild,' 'medium,' or 'hot'—'severe.' Like at a Thai restaurant. But sepsis is *by definition* a life-threatening blood infection—always *severe*. Monetized, compared to mild or medium, severe is a cash cow that wins hands down. We will dog you till the sun goes down: if you click 'sepsis,' you *always* click 'severe.' *The* code for cash."

"But, then, why," I asked, "do you have boxes for mild and medium at all?"

"Camouflage. For this fatal disease, we have no choice Hippocratically *but* to click 'severe.'" He went on. I tuned out, but caught his summary: "It all boils down to earwax."

He spoke passionately about how to squeeze the most money out of earwax. First, in a moving historical tour, he said, "Earwax is an untapped pool. Rampant in our senior citizens, a cause of deafness. How many of you routinely earwax your patients?"

We took this as rhetorical, and did not reply.

"The money in earwax flows by clicking this diagnosis in almost all patients—and removing as much volume as you can." Bob then showed on the big screen a doctor at HEALing. "You have to choose between two codes for earwax removal. 40773 is for just taking a syringe and washing it out, reimbursed at $77.33; but 40774, using the metal scooper thingy to remove it: $182.57. The difference? $105.24. And doing *both*? $259.90. *More* than the sum of the parts. Multiply per person per year? *Millions*. Guess which procedure, for full extraction and max liquidity, is preferable. *Both*. Do the right thing."

The right thing for all of us of the Fat Man Clinic was to walk out. I was with Chuck and Naidoo, walking down the hallway.

"So, Chuck," I said, "what'd you think of that?"

"Man, it all went in one ear, and out the other. Y'know how it is."

"HEAL is hell," said Naidoo, who was an expert in computers from her degree in India. "HEAL is best known for being the worst."

"How's it the worst?" I asked.

"It's the most inhumane."

"Lemme get this straight," I said. "For money, we have to *lie*?"

"Yes," said Naidoo. "One day a few months ago, soon after I joined an ongoing group pediatric practice in the suburbs, I was told that I was always required to click 'yes' on the box for 'cardiac exam normal'—even when I knew that it was irrelevant to that particular child, and I had not done one. The only purpose of that click was to gain a few more dollars. I could not go along with that, and had to leave. We doctors *do not lie*."

"No foolin'," said Chuck. "Or else it's so long, Hippocratic oath, okay?"

"Mind you, I'm no saint about money. I grew up poor in India, and now I value things like food, clean clothes, and safety. In fact, after I graduated from medical school, I worked in a leper colony in Bihar State for a year. I eventually married and came to the West Coast, and I met Fats. One night— over a huge meal, mind you—I told him about my time with the lepers. He wanted to hear every detail. And when I finished he said, 'I wouldn't do that for a million dollars!' And I said, 'Neither would I.'"

She stood there in the antiseptic corridor, quiet, powerful, a beacon.

"Fats and I kept in touch. I phoned him when I could no longer work in the private suburban practice. He invited me to join him, and you all, here. Said we would be a model of integrity. I have hope that we all, standing together in *our* clinic, can do that. Not just to keep our oath, but to keep our common decency."

Each of our offices was roomy, split in half by a sliding curtain. On one side was our "talk" office with desk and chairs. On the other, an examining room. Upon the desk were our desktop screen and keyboard. I took out my leather-bound FMC notebook and silver Waterman pen. Finally I sat at my computer and—*what?*—it clicked itself on and let out a soft, soothing series of chimes as if it sensed my presence and was glad I was with it after a long, lonesome night. On the screen, floating across like a lazy skywriter?

ALL BUDDIES INSTITUTIONS ARE TEAM-BUILDING FAMILY CLIN-ICS TO SUSTAIN GROWTH, COMPETITIVENESS, LIQUIDITY, AND JOY WITH HEAL

Next?

FAT MAN NOTE: I was on Ward 34 all night battling the Nocturnalist and am sleeping late. To make your day go smooth as hummus, as you are seeing patients think: DAMNAP. A special prize for the first to decipher this acronym. We'll start the first day real easy. Do NOT forget to walk patient to checkout and hand them a PATSAT form. Dulci will not let them leave until they fill it out and hand it to her.

I logged in. It took at least five minutes.

Welcome, Dr. Roy G. Basch, MD, to HEAL, at the heart of the BUD-DIES. Have a beautiful day delivering Man's Best quality and reimburse-ment for health care.

I went to the nursing station for my patient. No one had any ideas about what DAMNAP stood for. None of us cared. There was no time to ponder, because here came the patients.

My first patient was Mae Erwin, and as I introduced myself and shook her hand, my doctor scan clicked "on": cataracts; a keloid scar on her forehead; prominent venous pressure; rough, swollen fingers and ankles; and then, from her walk to my office, slight breathlessness. Cardiac. Mild obesity. Question diabetes. She sat on her side of the desk; I reluctantly sat across rather than next to, chained there by the desktop screen. Log in to her name worked: name, age, address, insurance, history. Chief complaint: "I got heart disease, and now when I try to play basketball with my grandson I get out of breath real fast and my neck starts to ache."

Noting her chief complaint, HEAL began flashing a diagnosis box, "Heart Disease," to click on, which I did. Suddenly there were arrays of 20 more boxes flashing with payment codes and dollar amounts—the first bids. I clicked on one box, and another 20 or so opened up—this time with "Other Non-Heart Diagnoses"—from "blood pressure" to, yes, for some reason, "sepsis, severe." Also a flashing header displaying escalating payments for each additional code, to be added to the first total bid. Next, drop-down screens of other boxes for details—open and waiting, coded and priced; I almost expected to see a "daily special." HEAL wanted clicks on the most severe boxes and dollars—as indicated by the throbbing dollar green trim of those particular boxes. Others lay open and waiting, hoping and waiting, the vast majority empty, waiting for that one sweet *click* like the slot machines in Vegas.

The only other data on the screen?

"Care Transferred from Jupiter Satellite Clinic of MBH. No data from Jupiter."

Weird. I said to Mae, "They didn't send the data from Jupiter. I have to call the desk."

Dulci answered. Before I asked she said, "Nope, no patient data from Jupiter. *Their* HEAL didn't connect to *our* HEAL. But ever since they went to HEAL, they stopped writing paper notes. We got nuthin'. Start from scratch. Fun, eh?"

"So I've got no info, and have to fill in this shit screen myself?"

"No need to use that language."

"Sorry."

"I'm shittin' you. Whaddaya think I am, genteel?"

"No, but that'll take me all day."

"Which is why Fats is keeping it light, till you get the hang of it."

"I might hang myself first."

"Do it discreetly. Look. HEAL is hell. The bane of everyone's existence. Drives us crazy. They told us its benefits—population health, patient management, even curin' diabetes. It can't do any of that! Y'think you got it bad? For us to make an appointment on HEAL? Twenty-five clicks—seven minutes. By hand? Two minutes tops! I gotta—"

"Wait. I'm desperate!"

"Oh. OK. Hurry and talk."

I told her how every time I tried to deal with one clicked box, another 20 or so showed up, and I'd never get done if I kept clicking and I'd never used any program like this.

"Listen up. The only way to survive is to use your Work-Arounds."

"What are my Work-Arounds?"

"When your twenty boxes open up, don't click any. Go back and *Work Around it*. Got it?"

"Not really. I mean, won't that distort the data?"

She burst out laughing. "Y'think the data is *un*distorted? Everybody does it to HEAL. The only other thing is, Cut and Paste the patient history. To work around the fifty boxes to click—each visit!—of the patient history, everybody just Cuts and Pastes in the *old* history, and tries to click maybe one key *new* thing. On-screen all histories are out of date, unreliable. It sucks. *Work Around. Cut and Paste.* Got it?" I said maybe. She hung up.

"Okay, Mae, so we have to fill in the blanks." I turned to HEAL. I started to work around in order to enter the clear, simple facts. "Why were you transferred here?"

"Jupiter was closing down. I been goin' over there for years. They tol' me to come here. I used to walk to Jupiter, but to get here it's *two* bus rides. To tell you the truth, I feel worse for all that walking 'n' transfers." I asked why Jupiter had shut down. "Don't know."

HEAL kept green-flashing the hot boxes of cash. I had to click, click, and click. Meticulous work, absorbing, slow. I clicked 39 different screens before I could write a note. *Boring! Even writing it here is boring!* I began to sweat, seethe. Mae fell silent. We stared at each other. I got the sense she was rooting for me. Most patients do, given the chance.

"Did I do somethin' wrong, Dr. Basch?"

"'Course not. Why'd you ask?"

"When you stopped typing, well, not to be, y'know, importune, but you looked right at me but didn't really *look* at me. I mean, not *kindly?*"

I flushed. I had been caught texting while driving. "Sorry."

"Usually the doctors in Jupiter—younger than my grandkids—can type real fast and I wait till they ask another question and then I answer. I get in tune with 'em, like dancin'. You looked blank. I thought I done somethin' wrong."

We were finally eye to eye—cataract to clear. I realized I'd glanced at her only peripherally while I'd boxed HEAL. One thing I'd loved about medicine was the stories, real stories really told, riding on the feeling. And you hear the real story only when you connect. HEAL had no boxes for feeling, or for that sixth sense. It made sure data was fixed—like your car mechanic. Fuck HEAL. I decided to use all my skills as a doc—of doctoring or even *personing*—to find out who Mae was, her history, her suffering, how I could help. But when I glanced back at HEAL, it seemed accusing, as if abandoned? Crazy thought, but . . .

I looked back at her. "Mae, what's really bothering you today?"

"That last time, playing basketball, the pain was scary, and I got little glitters in my eyes. T'day it was worse. I worreh about my heart—what'd happen if it give out. I'm the only one here for the kids, grandkids. Dr. Basch, *I am it.*"

I understood, and nodded. But HEAL was still there, yearning.

"What you said is important. Let me just put it in here?"

She nodded and sat back, accustomed to yet another wait, not for the first bus, for the second.

HEAL had sent me a message: "ROMI"—short for "Rule Out Myocardial Infarction." As fast as I could, intently nose to screen, I started filling boxes from "blood pressure" to "heart" to "scintilla in eyes" and on down through the ROMI fun house. I got a little lost in the stacked-up boxes, bouncing me like a Ping-Pong ball back and forth, but HEAL would find me and smack me back on task, boxing for bucks. When I'd finished the cardiac boxes, HEAL chimed cheerily: "Now click ROMI closed. Click open ROCH—Rule

Out Chronic Hypertension." I clicked and the screen clickly opened another 20 boxes and then flashed:

multinational,qulhuuuu,n.mnnjrip,n,u.

And went dead.

I hit keys at random. Nope. HEAL had just had an MI.

"Something wrong, Dr. Basch?"

"My screen just crashed."

Mae burst out laughing. "Oh, boy! That use-ta happen at Jupiter too. All the time!"

"Excuse me. Let me check at the desk and the screen guru."

I went to the nursing station. The whole team was there—but for Chuck and Runt.

Dulci was on the case, already on her smartphone, texting to the computer gnomes holed up in some padded room. She read the texts to us:

"'Aware of problem. Limited to FMC. All *unsaved* data will be lost.'"

We all groaned and cursed.

"'Will fix.'"

Back in my office, I smiled at Mae and with relief sat down and got out my three-ringed FMC binder and said, "Doesn't matter. This'll work just fine."

At Misery I'd trained my brain to remember—I could write out a 50-minute psych session almost word for word. So I put my Waterman down and *listened*.

But soon HEAL came back, chiming in. I turned away from the person, to the screen, typing away. After doing a physical and telling Mae the treatment plan, I got up and walked with her to the desk and she said, "You know, you're a really good *typer*."

Jesus, and not a good doctor? I looked into her cloudy eyes, and said good-bye.

"Not so fast," said Dulci. "Get a signed PATSAT or I take your car."

⌒

That first day, HEAL was behaving, mostly. But it was tense: the closer I got to filling all the boxes, the faster I *clicked-de-clicked* so that I made more errors and slowed down, sometimes finding a few great Work-Arounds, all the while hitting "saved"—and near the end, HEAL sloshing with filled buckets of cash—*crash*? Screaming, yelling, cursing. Not just from me, but from others outside. Things got even more crazy, then hazy. I realized that HEAL, shredding the connection with patients, made them more vague, less easy to fix in memory. Less vital, more blurry, than if I'd written them down. But a few patients still stand out.

Emma McKenzie, an Australian grad student studying "fairy penguins" off the coast of Sydney, now on a walkabout around the world. She knew she had a UTI—urinary tract infection—and wanted to make sure it was nothing serious. No insurance. Paying out of pocket. She wanted to know what the test would cost.

"I don't know," I said. She was surprised. "Let me try to find out."

I asked HEAL. A speck-sized money box seemed to resist my click and TURFED me to a pea-sized box that lit up with a happy chime and a strobe flashing a green of fresh money and laid out a high-end multidrug treatment—but no dollar amount. I called the HEAL Payment Hotline and immediately—money talks—got a human being, Ferris.

"I'll only know the cost *after* submitting to and getting back from insurance—which she does not have. No insurance, I submit to internal, and won't know till they process."

"You can't even ballpark it, estimate?"

"Honey, Babe Ruth couldn't ballpark it, and Einstein couldn't estimate. Put her on speaker." Ferris skillfully went through all the UTI Dx questions, ruled out anything serious. "Dear, it's just the usual thing we get. Buy some cranberry juice, and it'll go away."

Amid the crush of the sick poor, I saw a legal assistant who sat ten hours a day in front of *her* screen. I thought she had carpal tunnel syndrome, and when I played this bid on HEAL, it came back with $234.98. But, it said, if I gave it a brand-new diagnosis—"carpal-click syndrome"—it rang up $342.76 for the first visit, and since it was, luckily, untreatable, Man's 4th Best physical therapy chimed in with a bargain treatment bid of six visits with a total of $1801.99.

Finally, when HEAL had crashed for good, I had a family doc named Bill Holgerson, with knee pain. He suddenly stared at me and said, as if overwhelmed, "Oh, my God!"

"What?" Was it fear, shame?

"You . . . you're writing notes?"

"You're in luck. Our system crashed." On exam, the issue wasn't his knee, but his hip—hip pain referred to knee. I referred him to Gath for a surgical consult, saying, "He's a bit strange—after surgery, he'll actually do rounds on you, and return your calls. He likes people."

"Wow! That's publishable."

"Here—a prescription for a muscle relaxant." He stared at me, wide-eyed.

"A prescription pad? On EPIC, it's twenty-nine clicks—five minutes—to write one prescription."

Throughout the day the diseases and treatments had been predictable. It's well-known that somewhere around 70 percent of patients going to a GP have *no discoverable evidence* of physical disease—70 percent deemed "psychosomatic," or "the walking worried." In our cracked country, stress is off the charts—people walking around, eyes and ears glued to their "I"-phones, with stress levels of about eight out of ten. Worry makes us sick.

Good doctors treat them in various ways, including placebos and "Tincture of Time." And great doctors treat them much the same as they treat the other 30 percent, who have *discoverable diagnoses*. In their own words, they say, meaning it, four things: 1) "I'm so sorry you are going through this"; 2) "Others have had this and have gotten through it"; 3) "I'm here, and I will be here if you need me"; 4) "We'll get through this together."

And what are the *discoverable* diagnoses? In descending frequency: cardiac, diabetes, gastrointestinal, "lifestyle" diseases (epidemic obesity causing diabetes, hypertension, stroke, renal, and depression, stemming from high-sugar, high-fat, high-junk products in alluring packaging—the special diet of the "poor"), and, down the list, neurology and cancer. Running through all these diseases like toxic streams are two other epidemic ones, though rarely diagnosed, that are the prime causes of the others.

First, alcoholism and other addictions. Considering all the ramifications—death, violence, car crashes, suicide, family breakups, murder and other crimes, loss of work—addiction is the worst disease in the world. Second, isolation and loneliness. Americans are getting more and more lonely—30 percent with no close relationship. Isolation not only feeds the "worried" part of the "walking," but loneliness literally makes us sick—equal to smoking 15 cigarettes a day, increasing the risk of heart disease and stroke by over 30 percent. Socially isolated people have a 30 percent higher risk of dying in the next seven years, an effect largest in middle age. Clearly isolation is lethal. And people try to fend it off with—guess what—addictions, which isolate them even more. Alcohol gives us a sense of connection with others, while it disconnects us from others. The higher up the income scale you go, the more isolated Americans become. Billionaires are the most isolated and have the least empathy for other people.

And the prime addiction of our time? The "I"-phone. Connecting while hiding. Isolation incarnate—without real relationships. Studies show that the greater the sceen time, the greater the misery. Heavy users of social media are 30 percent more likely to be depressed. Suicide is soaring—epidemic in teenage girls. Death by screens. With drugs and guns.

During a break in the action that first day, I sat down with Dulci and said I couldn't get over that the Man's 4th Best HEAL couldn't "talk" to the outside HEALs, and did she have a number to call for the computer geeks to ask about this?

"Call? On a phone? Get real. They only do texts and e-mails. No one calls 'em."

"Which is why they'll pick up when I do." I dialed—actually, I punched. They did. "I'm Dr. Basch at the FMC. Got a question on HEAL." An audible sigh, then silence. "To whom am I talking?"

A pause. "Joe."

"Joe what?"

"Why d'you want that information?"

"Just to be friendly."

A pause. "Hang on." A series of clicks. I hung on.

"What are you doing, looking up my social security number?"

"Passport. Photo. Got it. Okay. My last name is Sole. S-o-l-e. Joe Sole."

I presented our problem: HEAL from MBH did not connect to HEAL anywhere else.

"That's normal. There's no interoperability. HEAL works at MBH only. We haven't rolled out interop between MBH and AE—Anywhere Else. No other health-care nodes."

"You're saying interoperability is inoperable?"

"Affirmative."

"What—are you in the military?"

"I was, yes, in the Midasian War."

"First or second?"

"Actually third."

"Didn't know there *was* a third!"

"Lotta people don't. It's harder than you think," Joe said.

"The military?"

"No, the interop. To get interop between MBH HEAL and the other HEAL sites—even using exactly the same equipment and the same nano-gritzels—is a no-go now."

"'Nano-gritzels'?"

"Technical term. Can't be translated. Used 'em in drones. Third Midasian."

"So you can't send an e-message between Man's 4th and anybody else?"

"The joke is that if you want to get a medical message from here across town to, say, the House of God, the best way is to mail a letter, with a stamp. Even EPIC has no interop between EPICs. It could, but it's the money. They make more if they customize, make sure each site is *non*interop, so each has to buy a brand-new EPIC that can't play with other EPICs. Not totally true: they can connect, but each time it costs us an arm and a leg. EPIC calls them 'i-provements,' but they can make things worse."

"But about HEAL—can't you run a wire or something? I mean a cable or a—"

Hysterical laughter, the blasting kind you hear from someone who doesn't laugh much. I waited. Then went on.

"Why won't it work? Have both ends tunnel in from each side, and meet in the middle, like the golden spike when the trans-American railroad ends met. If they can do it for a railroad across a country, why not across town?"

More hysterical laughter.

"But when will we be interop with the other satellites? Tomorrow?"

Really big hysterical.

"Joe! Breathe!"

Silence. Then heavy breathing.

"This call is protected by doctor-patient, okay?"

"Cool. You asked, 'When?' Answer: NIOL."

"What is 'NIOL'?"

"'Not in Our Lifetime.' This HEAL's a bitch—not as bad as EPIC, but gaining."

"Joe, I don't believe this. I just came back from the Indian Health Service. They were able to connect the whole Navajo Nation across the vast desert at eight thousand feet up—canyons, caves, mountains, lightning storms, flash floods—connect all the clinics to each other—"

"Yeah, Talking Stick's the best we got. The VA's Gun Barrel is a close second. They shoulda used one of 'em here—but I guess it didn't cost enough." He sighed. "Dr. Basch, it helps me to talk with you. No one ever phones us. The human voice? Refreshing. Thanks."

"That's what I'm here for, Joe. Call me anytime." I knew how crucial it was to have a guy like Joe Sole on your side.

"Thank you very much. You look like a real nice guy."

"You can see me?!"

"Oops, that's classified, okay?"

"Our little secret. Safe with me, Joe. And y'know what *you're* here for, Joe?"

"Tech support."

"Nope. You're my Soul. S-o-u—"

"I heard that before. A pun. Truth is, I like being somebody's soul. Roger and out."

At the end of that first afternoon, when most of the patients had been seen, Dulci summoned all of us docs to come out to the nursing station, *stat*.

"I scheduled all of you for an open hour. My girlfriend who used to work at the Jupiter told me that there was a big family who'd been patients there forever, and she said they always liked to come to see their doctors at the same time. They can arrange to do that because they have a family business everybody works in, from the founder to the grandchildren. Very close family. You're going to have to work together. As best I can, I've sorted 'em out to match up with each of your specialties."

We looked around at one another, not sure what to make of this.

"The good news is that they're a nice family—'salt of the earth,' my girl-fiend said. Actually, that's their job—the earth. The grandpa—actually, great-grandpa now—Otto Vance, started it, and everybody works in it: Vance Gardening, Landscaping—and Taxidermy." Turning toward the waiting area, she said, "So now I'll—"

"Hold on hold on," said Hyper Hooper, always into the worst, thinking doom and death. "What's the bad news?"

"Like with your other Jupiter patients, we got no records."

Groans all around.

Again she turned, and called out, "The family Vance?"

We watched as a group of about a dozen stood up and started toward us, led by a wiry, white-haired African American man of at least 70, wearing a neat plaid shirt and neat pressed jeans. With him, limping, was a pale white woman with red hair, of about the same age, wearing a tastefully flowered dress. One by one came the next generation—a set of middle-aged identical twins, stocky but not fat, outdoorsy-tanned, both with their overweight wives, and then at least five children, from a few years old to teenage. One teenager was strange, twitching, affectless—rule out autism spectrum.

"So," Dulci went on, "Nurse Angel and I've sorted them out as to who would take who . . ." Noticing our discomfort with this huge new load with no records, she said, "Don't worry. With all the gardening, snowplowing—and taxidermy—they're all kinda healthy."

I doubted that. In fact, as we all intuitively did our quick Sherlock Holmes checks, it was clear to me that here before us in these three or four generations was a history of the progression of disease in America. The oldest couple thin and—but for her limp—fit and alert, the middle generation with the male twins kind of heavy and maybe a bit dulled down, and the kids of various ages, from chubby to obese, slow to fractious. Lots of spectrums. Probably a family in which diabetes ran, if not raced.

Angel started calling out names, matchmaking. In the House of God, she never finished a sentence with words, only with gestures. Now she was fluent! Gestureless, yes!

The youngest children and their mothers—one with a screaming baby—were assigned to Naidoo and, because of nutrition and "rule out diabetes," to Hooper. Eat My Dust got the twins, Runt the "rule out autism." I got the patriarch, Otto Vance, and Chuck got his wife, Desirée.

As I began leading Otto Vance to my office, we heard a loud exclamation behind us. We turned and saw one of Eddie's middle-aged twins collapse, fall hard against a woman, and then crash headfirst to the floor.

Screams, bedlam.

"Get the crash cart!" I shouted, and went down on the floor, assessing. "Not breathing, no pulse. Call a code."

We lifted him onto the stretcher, and on reflex, all of us started in, coordinating like musicians who all knew the same score, but there was a bloodcurdling scream—the woman whom he'd hit on the way down was clutching her hip, which was sticking out at an ungodly angle.

"I got her!" Eddie said, going to her while Chuck and Hyper and I thumped the guy and put an IV in and bagged him and Naidoo hooked up the EKG and it was flatline, so we got the paddles and jump-started him and luckily got normal sinus, but then I felt something spill onto my shoes and it was vomit from another one of the family Vance.

The woman who'd hit the floor was in terrific pain, and we called Gath *stat* to assess her hip.

The cath lab doc came in, and he and a nurse took the Vance son away.

We explained to the rest of the family that son Lance would be in the cath lab for a while, and they could go and sit there or have their appointments and they'd be notified of any news immediately. Lance's wife and his mother said they'd go, but Otto said he was having some pain in his chest too. He was ashen, breathing hard and sweating, with the classic "fist to the sternum" sign of cardiac pain. I was worried.

"I think you'd better stay," I said. "Come into the office and I'll check you out."

Angel hooked him up to the EKG, ran a quick strip—normal, as was the full EKG.

"Good news, Otto. Your EKG is perfectly normal. Your pain's not a heart attack. Thanks, Angel."

"Here's a wipe, Dr. Basch," she said. "For the vomit on your shoes?" Not pointing—even to my shoes—she left.

I smiled, took a quick swipe, faced Otto, shook his hand. It said a lot about him. Three of the fingers on his right hand were old stumps—probably from work accidents. Rough palm, swollen joints, leathery skin with keloid scars. We talked. Turned out, he had been born and bred in Louisiana; he'd met his future wife, Desirée—he called her "Des"—while caring for her plantation gardens, and both fell hard in love. Across-race love. To both of their families' dismay. They eloped to the North, created a life. "A right good life," Otto said to me. "I went from bein' in sin, headin' toward hell, to living a life of blessings." How was his health? "Well, y'all know, at my age—seventy-four—and a life of hard work, everything's goin'. Hearing, sight, skin cancers gettin' burned off over and over—but the real bad thing is arthritis. Can't work like I usedta for the arthritis. I don't mind not working with my boys in the landscaping, but damn, I miss my taxidermy."

I went through more questions and the exam. Nothing. "Anything else, Otto?"

"Well, no, just arthritis and this pain-in-the-heart thing—I've gotten it before today."

"Your heart is fine. Know what I think?"

"Whut'all do you think?"

"I think it's just worry—it kicks up like when you got scared just now, seeing your boy fall down. I bet you feel things in your gut, that you got worry inside, right in your stomach. Is that right?"

"In my gut? Maybe. Maybe not. I heard that EKGs can miss things. Are you sure?"

"Yeah, but let's do a little test." I got up and got a bottle of Maalox, poured out a big slug. "Take this, and see if it helps?"

He drank it down. In a minute or two, he said, "I dunno. Maybe. Maybe not. I can say I got a twitchy gut though. Y'think it's my nerves?"

"Probably," I said. "Now, you make another appointment to see me, and then go sit with your wife and boy at the cath lab."

As I walked to the bathroom to clean the recalcitrant vomit off my shoes, I was of mixed feelings: pride in how well we had all worked together, dread at just how hard this might be.

Luckily for Otto's son Lance Vance, Man's 4th Best, like all big, modern hospitals, was superb at emergencies and stents and bringings back from the dead, at research, at any high-tech, complex medicine or surgery—like transplanting hands or even, last week, a *face*—and at finding just the right stem cells or immunogenic creations to beat back cancer a helluva lot longer than

years before. And I was, for the first time, impressed with HEAL. It was kind
of a miracle machine for sending me specific information about the patient.
Almost in real time, all the data from the cath lab was available to me, even
videos of the insertion of the stent. Lance Vance would soon be the proud
possessor of a stent in his anterior descending coronary artery—"the widow-
maker"—and TURFED to intensive care, and then, most likely, back home
to landscape, snowplow . . . and taxiderm. He would have been dead, but
now he was saved. A medical miracle: a sure death for all of history until the
last few years, but now a sure save.

My last patient of the day, just before six, was Horace Haskins. I stood at the
"in" gate and called out his name. A light brown African American, he got
up slowly and, helped by an ebony cane with a silver knob, walked to me with
a creaky gait that, with his height—about six five—and trim build, told me
he'd been an athlete, was now plagued with arthritis. I was struck by his
grace, his presence, his cane. His cool. Long, freckled face, a couple of nasty
scars. A hard life, now easier. A remarkable, all-in smile. He wore a dark suit
with a red carnation in the lapel, a blue shirt with a pink cravat. Diagnosis?
Alcoholic/addict, chronic. In recovery. How did I know? By seeing thousands
of addicts. He sat easy in the chair, straightening a crease. Took off his hat—
balding, another long scar from forehead on back, as if from a scythe. No way
I wanted to interrupt this show by inviting HEAL to it.

"What's up, Mr. Haskins?"

"Call me Horace H." It confirmed he was in recovery. "Twenty-eight
years. Word on the street is this new clinic has a guy specializing in
addictions—rare to find."

"How can I help?"

"More like, how can I help you? As you know, one founder of AA was a
doc, the Akron surgeon Dr. Bob Smith, known for saying, 'Our service keeps
us sober.'" I nodded. "I no longer have a paying job. My life's to serve the
suffering alcoholic and addict."

"Good. Do you want to tell me your story?"

"Not now. Y'know—from Park Avenue to a park bench, Sing Sing. Still
here."

"Against all odds."

"The odds now, looking back, are one hundred percent. Same as yours. I can't talk now. Got a call while I was waitin' that there's a guy who needs me. Gotta take him to a meetin'. I want to offer myself to you as a bridge to the twelve-step community. If you see someone in the office and give him a list of that night's meetings and tell him he should go, he ain't gonna. But if you say, 'I know someone who'll pick you up, drive you to a meeting, drive you home'? He might."

"I'd welcome that help. By the way, how'd you find me?"

"I started doing this same liaison thing with a doc you knew, out at Mount Misery. He told me all about you."

I knew before he said it.

"Leonard Malik. Bless his heart."

A jolt went through me.

He nodded. "Like he used to say, 'Spirituality is our connection to reality. We're not the main show. We're just part of the cast. In clear view, for the rest of the world.'" He left.

Malik. My beloved psych resident. A thin, athletic version of the Fat Man, with a mantra of "You can tell everything about a person by the way they play a sport." Back in the office I sat and grieved a little for the loss, all the losses, as one does. As Chuck always put it at times like this, "Man, y'*know how it is.*"

I pulled myself together. Went to the conference room for the Fat Man's checkout.

⌒

"Wowee!" cried Fats, both he and Humbo, for some reason, wearing butcher-length white coats speckled with blood. "Great work with the family Vance. Sorry I missed it—but clearly you don't need me around anymore. Maybe I *will* retire to Kuala Lumpuuuur!"

"Kuala Lumpur?" Hooper asked. "Why?"

"So," Fats said, "how'd the rest of the first day go?"

Each of us said it was good except for HEAL.

"This razor-sharp mind," Hyper said, "got dull. Smart screens make dumb docs."

"The only good thing about that dog," Eat My Dust said, "was when it died. And then it was heaven!"

"I grew up in the dodgy part of India's HITEC City, in Hyderabad," Naidoo said. "Did my first degree there, immersed in computer high tech. I love the aesthetic of elegant IT. HEAL is crap. But thank your lucky stars it isn't a worse machine."

Chuck said, "HEAL was cool. Nuthin' to it." Startled looks. "'Cuz I ignored it."

"Naidoo," Fats said, "I too love elegant info. Sometime I'll show you the programs we built for my calcium boxcars venture—talk about poetry! So I too am pissed we got, here, crap. But moving on. Anybody get the puzzler DAMNAP?" Nobody. "Okay. I'll eat the reward myself. Next, Dulci, let's talk about how our PATSAT was today."

The Patient Satisfaction Score was a numeral, from one to ten, for how satisfied patients were with their doctors—how much they liked us. This one numeral was key to how much money insurance paid to each doc in Man's 4th. It was worth millions. A low score could demolish a career, even a department. On our HEAL dashboards, our FMC running average, to three decimals, flashed continuously, like the Dow Jones.

"I collected all your patient PATSATs, every one—including the Vance family. Today's average rating? One hundred percent."

"That's *all*?" Fats said. "I was hopin' for one hundred ten at least. Everything rides on those numerals. They go down, we go down. Okay, see you all t'morrow—"

"Hey, Fat Guy," said Hooper, "what does DAMNAP mean?"

"'Do as much nothing as possible.'"

We burst out laughing. It was Law Number 13 of the House of God!

"Not fair!" shouted Hooper, twitching. He was the most competitive of all of us. "That is not the complete Law Thirteen. You left out 'TDOMCIT— The delivery of medical care is to.' Trick question. Look." He held up several pages of Excel. "I spent a shitloada time on this, Fat Guy. Not a fair contest. I claim the prize."

Tighter than ever. Must be MOR again—Marriage on the Rocks.

Fats stared at him, then nodded to Humbo. "*Sí, Señor Nervioso.* I get you prize."

"Freud's law?" said the Runt. "'Flies cause disease. Keep yours zipped.'"

Fats sighed, as in "Behold yon lost soul." "Okay. All good. See you tomorrow." We all started to leave. Fats grabbed my arm. "Basch? We need to talk."

"I'm late already."

"It's crucial." The others left. He sat me down, pacing, munching a chalk white health bar with a strange high glitter—calcium? He looked spooked. *Fats scared?*

"Last night, as attending doc on Ward Thirty-four, I went up there to check on things. I tried to find the Nocturnalist on call—their shift is seven p.m. to seven a.m.—no luck. It's rare to catch sight of one in the wild. Me and Humbo were there all night long cleaning up his messes. We gotta do it again tonight so Krash realizes that this necromancy is being witnessed and stops it. I need you with us tonight."

"You want me to stay all night in the hospital?" He nodded. "Nope. You promised no night call, and tonight's Olive's birthday party at home. I'm already late."

"Olive?"

"Spring's bunny. She's two. Turns out, it's a big birthday for a bunny. I promised."

"But y'gotta see this. Especially Mrs. Burke."

"What? I thought she had gone home okay."

"Because of Jack Rowk Junior, she's going down the tubes. We have to save her. Pleeze?"

Fats asking for help? "Shit. Lemme check." I called Berry. Explained.

"I thought he promised no night call?"

I explained it was an emergency. Fats, and patients, needed me. Silence. "I know, I know. I promised Spring. Olive's birthday—"

"Which starts in an hour, at seven. All her new school friends—Razina, Johanna, Katie, Eliza, Kendall—and their parents will be here. Fathers too. Even crazy-driven fathers. Who left their work early. I'm trying to build new friends for her, and us."

"Maybe I can make it for Olive's ice cream and cake at eight?"

"Carrots and cake. And hay."

"Hold on." I explained to Fats and Humbo what was going on.

"Okay," Fats said, "just give me two hours. Till eight?"

"I can be there a little after eight. Maybe you can hold the hay?" She did not laugh. "I'll be there to help put her to bed. Her and Olive."

"Fine."

"What do you mean, it's fine? I *know* it's not fine, and so do you."

Fats and Humbo were pointing at their watches.

"It's the same old story between us," she said, "'I' versus—"

"'You.' I know, I know."

"No. It's 'I' versus '*we.*' The *family* 'we'—which includes me, you, Spring, Cinny, and *Olive.*"

"Got it. Really and absolutely. But I gotta go."

"Not before you tell Spring yourself. Here she is."

"Hi, Daddy."

"Honey, I was planning to come home for Olive's party but I'm a doctor and there're some sick people in the hospital who need me tonight."

Silence. More silence. *Ugh!*

"You won't be at Olive's party? Olive wants you at her party, Daddy."

My heart twisted on its stalk.

"She's a very *opinionated* bunny."

Amazed, I stifled a laugh. "'Opinionated,' is she? How can you tell?"

"Da-ad! She's *my* bunny!"

"Sure, yes, right. I'll be home in two hours. I'll do 'Happy Birthday' then."

"She's dressed up like the White Rabbit in *Alice in Wonderland*, and Cinny's wearing a Mad Hatter's hat. They want you to see 'em."

"I will! I'll just be a little late."

"Me 'n' Olive will be asleep and we need our sleep bye—"

"Wait! I'm sorry, Foozle. Love ya."

A pause. From the time she learned to talk, she would always answer me with an automatic "Love ya too." This time she said, "Here's Mom."

"So when can we count on you being home?"

"Eight thirty. Nine latest."

"Let us know if it's later. Because it usually is."

I felt the jab. She was, of course, right. "Sorry."

"Me too."

Dazed, feeling like crap, I followed the fast-moving Fats and Humbo out the clinic door into the suddenly ugly, pungent summer night and up the grand lit-up driveway toward the soaring 4th Best monolith and Ward 34.

7

*"*ho's my doctor?*"* I would soon come to realize that this was the main question asked by patients in Man's 4th Best Hospital. Most fervently asked between the hours of seven at night and seven in the morning—when all hospitals are scary places. Why didn't they know who their doctors were?

In the House of God, we interns had been on call mostly every third night. We would follow our patients continuously all day, all night, all the next day, and then go home after 36 hours, exhausted. Well over 100 hours a week. But we got to know our patients well—and often it was thrilling. Now this had changed radically, because of the Libby Zion case: a young woman treated by an exhausted intern died, and the court held the exhaustion as cause. Suddenly interns were strictly limited to shifts not lasting more than 14 hours in a row, totaling a maximum of 80 hours a week. This meant they had little continuous contact with patients—never following a patient they'd admitted through a day and a night and a day.

The effect of these lighter hours for medical trainees—and medical students—was profound. At the House we had been dedicated "professionals" who would work on our patients for as long as it took to get them stabilized and handed off to another intern on our team who was on call. All of us *knew* all the patients because we were always at their bedsides, human to human on morning work rounds and end-of-day handoff rounds. If they had private doctors, they rounded on them in hospital, both morning and evening.

During their hospital stay, patients knew their doctors.

Now, rather than "professionals," interns and residents were "shift workers."

When the bell rang at the end of shift, if they weren't outside the legal confines of the hospital, they would be reported and warned. This artificial shift-work mentality fractured ongoing connection and care. Given the 80 percent of their time spent in front of screens and on billing, and the pressure to discharge patients as fast as possible in order to admit other patients just as fast as possible and thus maximize Man's 4th Best's money, the ward team was fractured, hardly a team at all. Hardly any teaching took place. No one had time.

And now there was a brand-new shift-work *sub*specialty: "Hospitalist." (In Obstetrics, there were now even "Laborists" and "Deliveryists.") Patients' regular doctors were barred from caring for them in the hospital. Instead, Hospitalists, who had chosen the ultimate shift work, saw patients *only* in the hospital. Shifts of twelve hours exactly, responsible for all the inpatients on a ward, but rarely on the same ward two nights in a row. Never getting to know their patients. It was the fastest-growing specialty in all of medicine. Strange, since they had no ongoing relationship with patients—the very reason that most of us busted our butts to become docs.

There was a *sub*-subspecialty of Hospitalist: Nocturnalist—nicknamed Somnambulist. These worked only night shifts, prowling the hours of darkness, slipping away quickly at dawn's early light. They rarely *saw* patients, and patients never really saw them. And if a patient did chance to see one, it would be a doctor they had never seen before and would never see again.

We got up to Ward 34 at 7:04, as Jack Rowk Junior was handing off to the night-float intern, a bearded man in a blue Sikh turban. Other docs were rushing off shift to avoid censure.

"Remember, Dr. Montek," Jack said to him, "you just do admissions. Do *not* take care of any other patients. You do not wanna mess with tonight's nocturne. I'm gone."

"Don't you do a face-to-face handoff of your patients to the nocturne?" Fats asked.

"Nope." He yawned. "Whoa, am I tired. Really beat. Finally going home." He raised his arms in triumph. "Home!"

"But there are fifty of your patients in his care."

"Sixty-four, tonight. In her care. She doesn't do handoffs with people—she does screens. Phobic of faces, of humans—some such shit. Have a nice night." He left.

"Hi," said Mo Ahern. "I'm on call with the night float."

"Good," I said. "How did Mrs. Burke do?"

Mo glanced around. The Sikh was in front of his screen. Mo nodded to follow her out into the corridor and then into the utility room, all mops and slop buckets and power floor polishers, all ratchets and rollers.

"She's much worse," Mo said. "I know, I know. All we had to do was 'do nothing' except transfuse her platelets and monitor her. She was all set to be my first patient in the FMC, with Roy supervising." A deep breath. "But as Jack said, she's a 'fascinoma'—a case so unusual that it's publishable—and he said we had to study 'it.' He wouldn't tell us what he was doing or let me or anyone else see her. Ran all kinds of weird immunoassays on her blood. And then—he has hands like a butcher—his bone marrow biopsy hit spinal cord and it got infected and the new antibiotic mixed with the residue fluconazole and . . . she went unconscious, may've had a stroke."

"'Bone marrow biopsy hit spinal cord'?" Fats cried. "The iliac crest is nowhere *near* the spine. Now, *that* . . . that's publishable. Damn—she's young enough to die! Where is she?"

"She's in the TLC—a clinical—"

"The Tender Loving Care?" Fats cried. "In a WASP hospital?"

"The Translational Leverage Consort. A clinical research unit, with all the 'cases' that might lead to 'translation' into patents and drugs, partnered with Big Pharma."

"Uh-oh. I love research—so why do I suddenly feel sick? TLC funded by . . . ?"

"Merck. Merck has first-refusal drug rights to all discoveries."

"Merck, of the billion-dollar drugs Vioxx for arthritic pain—which causes heart attacks—and Fosamax for women's osteoporotic bones—that can lead to broken bones."

"*Sí, sí.* Merck Vioxx kill my *madre!*"

"Mo, listen up. Drug trials usually last only about six months to a year, but patients take most drugs for decades, even lifetimes. Promise me: never prescribe or take a drug that hasn't been used for ten years, okay?" Mo nodded. "And never go to a doctor you see on TV, or prescribe or take a drug you see in a commercial. Swear?"

"Hey, wait a second, Fats," I said. "That's going a little far, don't you think?"

"More than a little. But it's only by going for more than a little that we can get a lot." A shake of that global head. "Where's this ward? Let's go save her."

"You don't have clearance," Mo said. "It's a level-alpha restricted zone."

Fats nearly fell over with laughter. "Lead on."

"What about the night-float mess you needed me for?" I asked as we walked.

"We triage it. First, we got to save Mrs. B."

The TLC was hidden in shadow, down dimly lit corridors and mossy, winding ways, over a bridge between skyscrapers with lovely views. The brass plate on the door:

TLC: MERCK/FOX FOR HEALTH

"Fox?" Fats said. "'All the News Unfit to Print'? Merck and Fox, together at last?"

Mo had the code. "Jack said that working with him would look good on my résumé. I get that creepy feeling that he wants to date me. Yuck."

Inside, we donned stiff, sterile gowns, shower caps, gloves. Passed walls lined with banks of computers and, in one glass-walled room, floor-to-ceiling ones quivering with data.

"DNA sequencers," Fats said. "Industrial-strength, ultrafast. High volume."

There were maybe ten beds and six nurses. They all knew Mo, clearly liked her.

Mrs. Burke lay still, but for her ventilator raising and lowering her rib cage with a precision no normal muscles could. IV line with pink fluid was going in; a catheter with brown fluid was coming out. She looked sunken, but in no obvious distress. Everything had been subdued to measurement. All too quiet. I felt her feet. *As cold as any stone.*

Fats was all business, working on her around the bed like a dancing bear—laying on hands, percussing, palpating, stethoscoping, tapping with his foot-long British reflex hammer—and then barking orders to me to print out her last data from HEAL: the hard-to-find, "clinical" info, sequestered and obscured in the linguine of billings. It was the first time, since the House, that I'd seen the Fat Man's Promethean medico talent in action, and it was so—I don't know—so damn elegant and caring, it took my breath away. By the time I'd printed out the info, he was done with her exam, and with a quick look at her numbers, he perked up: "Ah, yes—I noticed her eyes were a bit pinned. Roy, get me a vial of Narcan from the crash cart. Jack, after he infected her and she was screaming in pain, gave her too much morphine, lighting her up to keep her quiet."

He shot the Narcan into the IV line, and in seconds there she was, a reconstituted Mrs. Burke, groggy but clearly alive. He took out her breathing tube.

"Ohhh. What . . . happened?" she asked.

"Lots of bad stuff, dear, but we'll get restraining orders on Dr. Rowk ever coming near you again." Fats went out to charm the TLC nurses.

"Okay," he said to them, "call me Fats, for obvious reasons, and why don't all of you take the rest of the night off 'cuz I got your backs?" To their stares of *What the hell?* he went on. "I wish. But we got work to do, together, on that sweet Mrs. Burke."

By the time we'd read the whole TLC record, and finished writing new orders, almost an hour had passed, and I was in deep trouble about Olive's birthday.

When I called Berry, she was curt and said she had to get back to the party, which was "going great, and Spring and Olive and friends are having a great time, so I'm not even going to tell her that you called or when to expect you. I gotta go—"

Click. How I'd come to hate those severing *click*s over the years, daggers of guilt that still, *still*, brought up as if it was yesterday our Big Breakup after college as I'd boarded the *Queen Elizabeth 2* for Oxford and left her on a dock in Manhattan, both of us crying our eyes out, I waving good-bye back to her until she was a speck and then nothing human, the ersatz-human Statue of Liberty waving good-bye to me too until she sank into the chill October waves. That jolt? Still fresh? Could it happen again? Destroying all we'd created—she, I, Spring, the dog, and the rabbit. Fucking *click*s.

"Shit," I said to Fats. "It's bad. Gotta go."

"Basch, Basch," he said, eye to eye, "we need you. Very complex what they did to her, lots of ups and downs, ins and outs. Luckily, it'll stand up if she sues for malpractice. But it's gonna be really tough to do as much nothing as possible, with her under the fiscal-pinned eyes of Merck/Fox." He turned to Mo. "Listen up, kid. The treatment now is on two fronts—the *real* treatment of Law Thirteen: Doing as much nothing *as possible*—and the harder *fake* treatment of hiding it, by BUFFING up HEAL."

Mo looked puzzled. "What's 'buffing'?"

"Like buffing a car so it looks good. In the House of God, all of us docs in internal medicine learned to BUFF the problem patient so that we could TURF them to surgery or psychiatry without them BOUNCING back. With Mrs. Burke, we're BUFFING HEAL so it doesn't know what we're really doing—saving her by doing a helluva lotta nothing."

Mo was staring at him, wide-eyed.

"It's hard to understand how it was key to our survival in the House," Fats said. "I mean, y'had to be there. Anyway, Mo, your job is just to go back in there and *be with* her. Got it?"

"Sorta kinda." She looked at us as if we were insane, then nodded and left.

"A real tough case, Basch, especially with this woo-woo, hush-hush TLC shit—high visibility. Gotta be *deft*. I need you with me." He noticed my dismay. "Okay, go. I'll try to handle it. But this is big. This time we're not just up against a hospital—we're up against the whole pharma-entertainment industry. I can't do it alone. Without your help, her odds go *way* down."

We looked into Mrs. Burke's room. Mo was sitting beside her again, holding her hand, talking to her. No response. We could hear Mo's voice cracking, watch her hand falling back down into her lap. The scene, the cracking voice, the falling hand, brought back my own first patients as a real doc, all that sorrow so damn fresh. And that fear.

Fats, I, and Humbo stared at them, and then at one another. I wanted to cry or scream.

How could I just leave? So we started her back to full Mrs. Burkehood. HEAL turned out to be a lot easier to dupe than paper. With so much faked data coding going in already, fake data was easy to hide. And if the fake data could outbill real data, what bean counter would choose reality? It'd be like reporting an error in your favor to your bank.

Thus, the state of the art of the Delivery of Medical Care.

We left her room and turned toward the door but heard, from farther down in the bowels of the TLC, a faint cry:

"Hey Doc wait hey doc wait yeowww!"

And then silence. We looked at one another. Could it be? Harry the Horse from the House of God, here?

"Hey Doc wait yaoww! Hey Doc . . . yeowwwww!"

Harry the gomer, adding a new pain word—"yeowwwww!"—to his House of God signature call? Must be bad!

We hurried toward him.

It was Harry, and it was not pretty. Jack was in a combat stance at the bedside. Harry was connected to so many wires and tubes that the poor old guy looked like a shrunken meatball in a bed of spaghetti. Jack was jabbing randomly at Harry's bruised chest with a large-bore big needle—probably trying to put in a central IV line. Clearly frustrated by repeated stabs with no pay dirt, he was cursing and, enraged, jabbing wildly, way off line.

"Stop!" cried Fats. "You moron! Were you born in a barn?"

Jack kept on stabbing.

"Estop!" echoed Humbo. *"Pene-cabeza!"* And in an *instante*, he had pinned both of Jack's arms behind him and was jerking them up and up. Jack screamed.

Silence. We stared at Harry. Then a whimper. "Hey Doc wait hey . . . hey Doc *you fucker* wait. . . ." But then petering out like a car motor sputtering after the engine had been turned off. For the first time in living memory, Harry the Horse was *silent*.

Fats took his pulse. Paused. Took it longer. "No pulse."

"Thump him!" Jack cried. He tried to break free. Humbo, like jerking up a barbell, cranked Jack's arms higher, into dislocation zones. Jack turned white and went limpish.

"We know you're an idiot, Jack," I said, "but we didn't realize you're crazy too."

"He's . . . he's dying!"

"Agreed. You tried hard to kill him," Fats said. "Luckily you even fucked *that* up."

"He's got no pulse."

"He's just taking his time recovering from your Angel of Death torture routine." Fats looked at his watch. "Fifteen, fourteen . . ." He counted off the seconds. "Ten, nine . . ." When Fats got to "four," Harry's cataracted eyes opened, and at "two" suddenly he said faintly: "Hey . . ." Big gap. "Hey Doc . . ." And bingo, like a car ignition catching: "Hey Doc wait!"

"Jack," Fats asked, "what the fuck were you doing?"

"Looking for genes. Longevity genes. Merck/Fox mission—Nobel Prize protocol. Law Number One from the House of God: Gomers don't die— okay? So logically they must be a subset of humans that has a gene mutation for pretty eternal life. We're gonna find that gene!"

"And how are you going to do that?"

"The standard method—we're gonna knock it out. Once we knock it out of Harry—he's the experimental subject; Jane Doe is the control case—we make a drug to put back into Harry! We CRISPR it, insert it in people when they're young. A blockbuster drug. We're gonna *monetize*! *Monetize the gomers into drugs!* Billions!"

"But, Jack," I said, "if you successfully knock out the gene in Harry's DNA that's keeping him alive 'pretty eternally,' he'll die."

"It's the price y'pay. For success!" He beamed. "And I got animals we're workin' on too. Long-lived turtles. Maybe the gomers and the turtles have the same gene. How cool would that be—"

"Turtles?"

"Yeah. I got two, hundred-plus-year-old Galápagos turtles!"

"What? Galápagos tortoises?" I cried. "They're a protected species!"

"Not from my *dad*, they're not!"

"Killing gomers and those sweet Galápagos tortoises too?

"It's the price y'pay. What kind of life do gomers have, really? Not human, really."

"It's immoral, unethical, and Nazi!" I said.

"Way bigger fish than you—Merck/Fox and the ethics boys—they all say it's fine."

"You moron! You neo-Darwinist!" Fats shouted. "Where's your brain, man, in your scrotum? It ain't the genes. It's their regulation—the feedback from all levels of their environment, from RNA to climate change! Not the notes, you fascist baboon, the music."

"Oh yeah? Well, after my dad hears about this, you're chopped liver. Finished. Nothing good is gonna happen to you here at Man's Best, Fat Man. I swear it."

Fats nodded to Humbo, who dragged Jack away by his sockets, shoved him down the corridor. Jack stumbled, almost fell, vanishing around a severe corner.

Fats told us to wait outside while he spoke to the nurses. We heard, in between Harry's full-throated "Hey Doc waits," what else but a familiar gomere's voice answering: *"Aye . . . eee . . . eye . . . ohhh . . . yuuuuu . . ."* Jane Doe, also of the House of God.

⟋

We went back outside the TLC. Sitting in a small room were an elderly man and a woman of about 40. On their lined faces, and in their restless eyes and tense bodies, was fear. The old man was wringing his hands, big-knuckled, arthritic fingers in fingers, compulsively. When they saw Mo, they got up and rushed to her.

Mrs. Burke's husband and daughter. They had been on a roller coaster of emotion, from the disaster of what had been a routine admission for an infection, to Jack's taking over the case and barring Mo from speaking to them, and then to the sudden transfer to this strange TLC, where visiting hours were severely limited for "security."

"Thank God you're here," said Rick, her husband—and started to cry. He fought back the tears but with no luck, and his daughter, Mary Ellen, offered a tissue. But as she handed it to him and he met her eyes, he was overwhelmed and collapsed into her arms. A wrenching moment—more so for Mo and me because hidden from them was the cause: money, arrogance, more money. "Sorry," Rick said. "How is she?"

"This is Dr. Basch," Mo said. "He and another expert have just been to see her."

I too had gotten choked up, seeing in this scene not only the deaths in my own family, but the savageness of Jack's best distilled medical fascism. I gave a silent "Thanks to the Divinity" that Jack Rowk Junior was a rare case—the exception to the rule that most of us docs do our best, with whatever kindness and care we can summon up at times like this. Like what I managed in the House to show my patient Dr. Sanders, who, in his dying, said: "What sustains us is when we find a way to be compassionate, to love. And the most loving thing we do is to be with a patient, like you are being with me."

"Good to meet you. She's been through a *lot,* but she was awake and alert, resting easy. I'm confident that with Mo and our help, she'll be fine. Later tonight we'll transfer her to a bed on our own ward. We hope she'll be strong enough to leave in a day or two."

"Oh my God, thanks, Doc. Can we see her?"

"Sure. Take them in, Mo. Tell Fats I'm waiting—but that I have to leave now."

They went in. I waited, pissed, staring at the clock. Finally, out came the Fat Man, slumped down into himself, with Humbo, who seemed to be supporting him from some terrible jolt.

"What's wrong?" I asked in alarm. Fats waved his hand weakly. "Dead?"

"The ten o'clock meal!" he wailed.

"The ten o'clock meal?" I asked.

"Dead! I paged Krash!"

"'Dead'?" He nodded. "How can a meal die?"

"They killed it. I said to Mo, 'See ya at the ten o'clock meal,' and she said, 'The what?'" I knew what he meant. In the House of God at ten every night, all the House staff who were on call—every specialty—would come together and eat leftovers from the day's breakfast, lunch, and dinner. "All you could eat . . . for free?" moaned Fats.

"The food was for shit, but the talk was great," I amended.

"Hey, that food was great."

"Fats," I said firmly. "I'm outta here."

"Basch! There's no ten o'clock meal! How do they get through an on-call night?"

"Listen, no one's on call like that anymore. They're all home sleeping. The only ones here at night are whacked-out, antisocial Nocturnalists—they eat alone, if they—"

His phone rang. Fats glanced at the number, snapped to attention. I turned to leave, but his hand was on my wrist, pulling me into a quiet alcove, putting his phone on speaker.

A blastoff in a foreign language.

"Cut it out, Krash," Fats said. "This is an emergency, and Yiddish gives you an advantage!"

Silence from the phone line.

Then not Yiddish, but background music, stirring martial marching music, featuring, of all things, a *glockenspiel*?

Finally, the voice of the Krash. "What's the emergency?"

"Two emergencies. The big one: why isn't there a ten o'clock meal?"

"You paged me at this hour for that bullshit?"

"Food is not bullshit. Food is not even food. Food is gathering around the table, *learning* stuff. Jews invented it. Rip each other to shreds, and then it's 'Let's eat!'"

"Not an emergency. Send me a proposal. What's number two?"

"But what do I eat *tonight*?"

"Don't eat. You eat too much and all the wrong things. Ever since we were kids. How do you think you got to be called Fat Man, Fat Man? Not my problem. Item two?"

I watched as Fats composed himself, taking a leviathan breath in, up on his toes stretching, stretching—then a torrent out. He mouthed me a mantra: Y'gotta be *deft*.

He told Krash without passion the lovely story of Mrs. Burke and how Chief Resident Jack Rowk Junior saw her as a "publishable case" and an MBH patent and a Merck/Fox drug that would make a lot of nice green money with liberty and justice for all.

"What's wrong with money?" Krash asked. "Money is good—"

"Not when it's a clear case of malpractice."

"Clear? She died?"

"Not quite. Iatragenica imperfecta. Malpractice, but the patient's still alive to testify. Picture-perfect loving Irish family—two of the nine kids are lawyers at white-shoe firms."

"You say Rowk Junior did it?"

"None other."

"Badbad. *Oy gevalt.* In fact, *goy gevalt.*"

"That's funny, Tristram. Good for you."

"Don't you condescend to me. But why tell *me* about this mess? *I'm* not responsi—"

"Tell it to the judge."

Silence, but for the glockenspiel. "She's gonna die?"

"Unless I save her. Here's the deal. One, Team Fats takes over her care—in hospital, and then in the FMC. Two: Jack Junior is verboten. Put a restraining order on him, *re* her."

"Done."

"Actually, expand the order to Junior treating any patient on the planet Earth."

"Junior is . . . shall we say . . . through Senior, central to our Merck/Fox health venture?"

"Let me be subtle, Krash. He's an arrogant, incompetent Nazi shithead."

"Ahhh, yes, yes. Given his dad, that lad will go far. Are we done?"

"Not quite. Junior's also trying to kill gomers. And two huge Galápagos tortoises—"

"What the fuck? Those tortoises are protected!"

"So are gomers and gomeres." Fats told him about Harry the Horse and Jane Doe.

"Oh, *that*. Yeah, sure, I know about that. That's the gene work. Immunotherapy. The cutting edge of cancer treatment, yup, for Mrs. Burke and for the gomers. A miracle. Goodgood."

"But neither Mrs. Burke nor any gomers he's trying to kill *have* cancer, and—"

"They say they don't die, gomers, y'know."

"I do know that, yes."

"Well, why don't they? Gotta be a gene for 'not dying,' right? If the knock-out works and one of 'em dies, it's reportable. Except for the kidnapped turtles. But the demographic is exploding. Baby boomers in gomerhood? Like one of your humorous laws: There's gold in them thar gomers. Eternal healthy life." He paused. "Oh, and in terms of humor? Our fifth kid, Moishe, comes home from school today and says, 'The teacher asked us if anyone knew what resurrection was and I raised my hand and said, "It's when your penis stays up for more than three hours and you have to call your doctor."' How could we not laugh? Goodgood. I'll can the turtles and we're done. *Baruch Ha Shem Shalom*." *Click.*

Fats stood there, shaking his head in disbelief. "What you just heard, Roy, is orthodox dingbattery."

"You know him from before?"

"Yeah. We grew up in the same part of Brooklyn, neighbors. He always was in fierce competition with me—the only problem was that I refused to be in competition with him. I just did my thing. And I always won—except sports, which I did not do. It drove him crazy. I was too heavy. He was too, well, heady. Nice, hunh?" I nodded. "We went to the same public schools, rivals for grades. Religion? I was Workman's Circle, secular, inclusive, left-wing, union-joining Jews. He was orthodox, *glot* Zionist kosher. When we were teens, we went on a free, make-an-aliyah trip to Israel, paid for by right-wingers trying to convert American Jewish kids to love Israel and maybe move there. Sacred sites, hot sabras, buff soldiers, *kibitzing* with the *kibbutzim* chicks—big doses of paranoia and pride. Didn't stick with me, but changed him totally. Fluent in Hebrew, Brooklyn Yeshiva, summers in Israel—dropped out of college, moved to Israel, did his two years in the army. In the army he bulked up, got über. Never looked back. Married his lieutenant's daughter, rose like a shooting star. Lotsa kids. Still loves Israel, the hard-body buff stuff, and guns. I'm sure it will come as no surprise that we ain't close."

"But he hired you."

"Exactly. Weird, eh?" I asked why. "He's gotten to the top, but he knows he's in *way* over his head and screwing it up—still in 4th place. Doesn't like me but admires me and knows from all our rivalry that I might just be able to unscrew it, save his ass. But in a distant, itsy-bitsy part of his amygdala he's scared I might somehow be his doom."

Humbo appeared. "That *Señorita* Mo *está* a keeper. She gonna be a real good doc. And she *habla español*—from a year in Venezuela."

"I'm outta here. Olive calls." Fats, puzzled, searched the Roy Basch file for "Olive"—and failed. *That was disturbing. He had always recalled all.* "The bunny? The birthday—"

"Ah, yes. We'll walk you out—Humbo and me'll hit the all-night greasy spoon four blocks down. Bullshit pastrami, but boffo cheese-fried Philly steak. Let's go."

"*Pero la segunda misión, Don Gordo?*" asked Humbo Parza.

"Shit, I forgot! The Nocturnalist! Gotta find her." He looked at his phone. "Name's Edward R. Shapiro—a man's name? No wonder she's weird. Keep your eyes peeled."

⁂

I kept trying to find an exit. We walked corridors as shiny and orthogonal as the place settings at a WASP Christmas, looking for droppings of the Grim Nocturne. Once or twice we thought we glimpsed her shadow flickering away down a corridor and ran to it—but no.

Suddenly Humbo stopped still, hand up in warning. Nothing. But

Humbo's ears were jungle tuned—from time in the Ecuadoran Amazon as the doctor to the Waorani tribe—and he started running, Fats behind, then me. I'd never seen Fats run—all that weight sliding side to side like a rogue piano downhill was scary. Shouts led us to a patient room. There in the harsh pixel light of an "I"-pad held aloft: "You are *not* having pain!" Dr. Edward R. Shapiro shouted, looming over the bed of a cowering LOL in ALOD—a "Little Old Lady" in "A Lot of Distress." Ed Shapiro was a tall, balding woman, granny-glassed, dressed all in black—shirt, slacks, shoes—showing the LOL the screen of her "I"-pad. "See?"

"I *am* having pain! Are you my doctor?"

"You *can't* be!"

"Chest pain! Get me my real doctor!"

"I'm the only doctor here, and—"

"I'm having chest pain, and where's my doc-tooooorrr?"

"Look!" Ed shoved the "I"-pad closer. "These are your real-time cardiac numbers, and they're all *normal*. Your numbers are perfect. You're going home tomorrow, bye-bye—"

"Sorry, Fats," I said. "I'm outta here."

Seeing Fats and Humbo walk in, Ed clapped her "I"-pad closed and in a slick move from Nocturne Night School somehow turned sideways and made herself thin and, bending at the waist, slithered between the two of them. I stepped into the gap like a defensive lineman, but she snapped back up suddenly and whacked her face hard into my ribs—I felt a crunch and sharp pain—and bright red blood spurted from her nose.

"Blood? Real blood? I'm bleeding?!"

"Are you two my doctors?" the LOL asked.

"Lemme outta here!" Ed cried, standing against a wall, free hand dripping blood.

"Shit!" I cried, enraged by the pain. "What's wrong with you? You're no doctor. You're not even a Nocturnalist. You're a fucking *sepulchrist*!"

"No, no," said Humbo, "she is the *sepul-anti-Cristo*!"

"I beg you!" the woman cried. "Are any of you my real doctors?"

"Yes, Mrs., um, Parkman Howe," Fats said. "We're gonna help you. Everybody chill." He grabbed a fresh towel. "Ed? Here y'go." The night nurse arrived. Fats told her in front of Mrs. Howe that he, as attending physician of Ward 34, had caught a mistake—Mrs. Howe would *not* be discharged in the morning. Dr. Humbo would look at her chart and examine her. Could the nurse stay for a few minutes to help? She could. He led Ed and me out to a deserted family waiting area, parking her gently in a purple rubber chair.

"Let's take a look at that, Ed," Fats said. He examined her, gently dabbing away blood, applying pressure. "Not broken." He grabbed an ice pack, pressed it to her face gently. "You don't really want to treat patients like that, Ed, do you?"

This hit her hard. She sagged. Her voice was muffled. We had to lean in to hear.

"No, of course not. I hate myself, how I lost it in there." She looked at him, then at me. "I'm really sorry I hurt you. I'm so ashamed of . . . of this! It's not me!"

Follow Fats. Be kind. Give her something. "Ah, you didn't mean to. An accident."

"I hate this job, this damn night work. Sixty patients? But I'm not that good in . . . in daylight anymore. I try to titrate it—I mean, between . . . doing this, or leaving medicine . . . or killing myself?" Looking puzzled, she went on. "I . . . I loved med school—the BMS was super. All of us there were incredible—every race, nationality, some had already cured cancer or saved Rwanda or something—they were all, you know, good? Full of hope. Even me." She paused. "In med school I was a good person. But then, going into the hospitals, interning here at Man's Best . . . things fell apart. Turned *bad*. Began to not recognize myself . . . tried other specialties—even psychiatry. Psychoanalysis killed off the best in—" She caught herself, started to get up. Then stopped and, looking from one of us to the other with frantic eyes—ashamed? scared?—asked: "What if *this* is the best I can be? And what if it's not enough? I mean, for the real me?" She dropped back down awkwardly like a scolded kid, blew her nose, stared at the red mess in the towel. "I miss patient contact. I really do. The money's good. But this . . . this work sucks. Totally isolated. Burned out. No day life. Look at me!" She raised her head to us, eyes searching. "What can I do?"

"You're doing your best in a tough job, Ed," Fats said. "Like all of us. Aren't you?"

"Not good enough. I oughta quit—can't, with my huge med school debt, but . . ."

"Even the best of us—good people, good docs—do bad in these bad systems."

She was startled. "Y'think?"

"I know. See it all the time, everywhere. The med schools are great, but they're feeding their great students into these big, hungry cash machines. It's brutal. Can turn really good students into shitty doctors. And shitty people." He considered. "And dead ones."

"But this, tonight—is the worst. What can I do?"

"Y'can take a break and join me for a Philly cheesesteak. Humbo will cover."

"Seriously? I mean, *you* want to be with *me?*"

"Don't I look like a serious guy?"

She looked him up and down. With a hint of a hint of a glint of a grin, "Nope."

"Goodgood. All good. Let's go."

"Adios, amigos," I said to them. *"Hasta luego."*

I walked out. Took a deep breath—slicing pain in my chest. *Broken rib? That's all I need! X-ray? Nah. Probably not fractured, and if so, there's no real treatment but doing as much nothing as possible. Tincture of time. Doctors can be dangerous to your health.*

8

Nighttime summer construction, on the narrow road to the deep west, the dulled-down suburbs. A moonless, foggy night. I couldn't see anything, and the traffic jams were intense. Like the night fog in Delhi when our cab almost crashed into a high gray wall that turned out to be the butt of an elephant without its taillight on. I called Berry. No answer. Bad sign. *Very.*

By the time I pulled into my slot at the front of the driveway, I was another hour late—it was close to eleven. The main house was dark and—as befogged Victorians can be—ominous. I got out and, not wanting to be another minute late, decided to take the shortcut to our carriage house in the back, going around under the front pergola of the big house. The mist was thick. The sharp pain limited my breathing. I had to feel my way stealthily up the three granite stairs to the front door of the dark main house and tiptoed carefully across the slippery old tiles and suddenly I felt a strong arm go around my neck from behind and hold me tight and I screamed. I felt a metal stick pressed against my cheek—the barrel of a gun?

"Who're you?"

"Dr. Roy Basch—I own this place."

"Y'mean, youse the landlord?"

The light went on behind the front door. It opened, and there was my tenant, Paulie, an obese shape in a white shirt billowing over his belly like a spinnaker over a trade wind, tied into dark pants, and a guillotined cigar in his mouth.

"What the fuck?" said Paulie "the Veal" Scomparza. "Randolph, let 'im go."

I was released. My neck hurt. "What the hell?"

"Sorry, Doc. Dr. Roy Basch, meet Randolph 'the Clown' Scomparza. My cousin."

"Nice to meetcha, Doc, and sorry for my oversightin' you. Just takin' precautions."

"From what?"

"Never mind what," said Paulie. "Won't happen again. You usually drive all the way up the driveway near the carriage house—y'get me?" I nodded. "A break in protocol. So it was merely a thoughtless error." Shaking my head, unkinking my neck, I started to leave.

"Oh, and I gotta tell ya. I might be going away for a while."

"Oh yeah? On vacation?"

He shook his head as in "You dumb shit," took in a deep breath all through his breadth, and sighed it slimly on out. "Doc. Listen *attentively*. I'm sayin' I might be goin' *away* for a while—y'get me?"

Shit, he was talking about the Big House, the slammer?

Paulie the Veal noticed I'd gotten it—his intuitive skills, fueled by paranoia, were always surprising to me—and nodded. When he had appeared at my door after I'd closed on the property, he had said his only requirement was that he and his wife, kids, and "the girl"—the live-in maid—could move in "right away for tax reasons" and handed me a roll of hundreds. Now he reassured me. "If I go, the wife'll pay the rent. Don't worry. Y'get me?"

"Yeah, but I gotta go—had to stay late in the hospital, missed the birthday party."

"How old is that cute Spring?"

"Not her. Her bunny rabbit, Olive, who's two. Ciao!"

"Touching. One other thing, Doc." With Paulie the Veal, there was always one other thing, and it would turn out to be the main thing. I prayed it wouldn't involve crime. "It's right up your alley, about health—me, you, and our families. It's about the *beepbeepbeep*s."

He was talking about the sounds that the big trucks, backing up, were making every day, from seven a.m. to five p.m., building the driveway to the the Garage Mahal.

"Doc, I think they design the sound parameters of them backup *beeps* to a frequency that pierces like a shiv into the brain—and after weeks of bein' woke up before seven every day after gettin' to bed at about three, well, I think I'm getting a bit demented, and for the veal business, with all them sharp cleavers, I need my cognitive a lot—y'get me?"

"Me too. Can we, y'know, whack him?" I was joking.

A thoughtful look came over Paulie's beefy face. In the shadows he was calm, a philosopher of sorts. "Yeah, but not yet. I been checkin' 'im out first. Last week sold a chunk of bullshit oligarch Moscow Oil bonds to the Princeton endowment. Gotta be illegal. A scared mouse. The usual bloodsucker at the cock of capitalism. Y'want me to *take care of 'im*—y'get me?"

"Can you do that?"

"What? Y'think we're regulated or somethin'? We're more unregulated than Goldman Sachs. Bottom line, Doc? I need my sleep and so do you. I can't hear a *beepbeepbeep* before I leave the house at ten. Is it okay with you if—as soon as I hear the *beep*-fuckin'-*beep* in my brain—" He shot out his wrist and checked his watch—it looked as if it had been hacked from a gold ingot and clearly cost a lot more than my Prius. "But what'm I thinkin'? Element of surprise is best, eh? Me 'n' the Clown'll walk right over there—say, at four a.m.—makin' sure we set off the surveillance cameras trained on us so the alarms go off and he gets a taste of that noise wakin' him up and the doorbell rings and the cops are notified and he peeps his little mousy snout out, scared shitless. And then we have a little *discussione*. And he bends to our will. *Capisce?*"

"Or?"

"Do not go there, Doc. Sorry we shocked your system. Sensitive type, you. Y'need any more veal?" I averred not. "Sweet as honey, right?" I nodded. "Ciao!"

I hurried back down the curling path to the 1875 carriage house, went into the kitchen created out of the horse stalls—all yellow pine walls and brass rails and rings and, in the corners, cast-iron drinking troughs, sweetly rusted. The kitchen area was separated from the dining by a long wooden bar of polished oak, with stools. You could still see the scars of the horse hooves on the walls of the stalls. On the marble dining room table, under the green Murano fixture fluted like a jellyfish, were remains of the cake—carrot cake—with blown-out candles, and a dish of brown glop, once ice cream. A note: "Dad wayk me up Spring."

I looked up at the ceiling to the second floor, once the hayloft. Through the gaps in the old wide boards, I could see that Spring's night-light was on—but our bedroom was dark. There was no way I would wake her up, knowing she had school the next day.

On the bar was a pile of unpaid bills—*more* bills?—and another letter from my father. All at once I felt the blast of my 36 hours up bringing me down. I grabbed the bottle of George Dickel Sippin Whiskey and got a Heineken and gulped the whiskey—ahh, the sharp jolt, calming and bringing out my better, if not best, self—and smoothed it off with beer. Feeling good with one Dickel, I figured I'd feel even better with two and downed another.

Warmed, I clunked up the doubling-back-on-themselves steep stairs and tiptoed into Spring's room. Her Mulan, Brave Girl of China night-light shone a soft amber, making her face burnished gold. Shirty was clutched in her fist against her cheek, a line of drool marking her deep sleep. On a bed table was a slice of birthday cake, the treasured sector, iced with a bunny face. I looked at Olive's hutch, and she twitched her ears and nose at me from her own hayloft, and then went back to being as still and as scared as, well, a rabbit. Spring's breathing was deep—how glad Berry and I had been those first nights with her at four months old in the Xiang Jiang Hotel in Changsha to realize, after five or six visits to the old big-wheeled baby carriage that served as her crib, that she had the magical capacity to keep breathing on her own, through the night. There's nothing as reassuring.

I went to kiss her cheek but feared awakening her and walked out and glanced into our bedroom. Cinnamon looked up from his bed on the floor, got up, and wagged his tail happily and, his nails clicking on the wood, came over to me. Berry, a light sleeper, awoke.

A finger to her lips, she led me back down to the kitchen. Cinnamon followed and came up to me for a pat and a belly rub—my ally now. Dogs are signs of cosmic love.

She stared at the bottle of Dickel.

"I feel terrible," I said. "Sorry."

"How could you?"

"Fats—I had to stay—it's nuts there—"

"You promised—and he promised both of us—no night call—"

"Guilty. It was a crisis, not just with a patient but with—I don't know—

standing up for what we're trying to create, and it ain't easy, so just for now I
have to—"

"With him, it's *always* just for now—always crisis. He's impulsive, no
boundaries in time, place, people. He himself is number one—the 'Great
White Male Leader,' and he expects you to fall in line when he snaps his—"

"Now, wait a sec—he's the most empathic person I know—"

"Thanks a lot—"

"I mean, as a man. You saw it—you said so—in the House of—"

"Yeah, with patients and sometimes, when it serves *him* to be that way,
with you, and even—that one and only night I came into the House—with
me. As long as he's in charge, he's fine. But he doesn't really get to 'mutual.'"

I bristled at the jargon, at her psychologizing. And yet by this time, I had
come to realize that her "take" on things would help us get through these
stupid skirmishes. I took on faith that if I could just stay in it with her, it
would open us up to the best of us. Through gritted teeth, I asked, "How so?"

"Empathy is mutual. If it isn't mutual, it isn't empathy. And even Fats—
with all his savvy, he doesn't get it. So now he's on top, he's got power, and
he's using it to get you to do something he promised he wouldn't."

"Hey—he's the best at relationships of any man I know."

"Does he use the word? The 'relationship,' the 'we'? Does he concretize it?"

I stiffened—"concretize" went too far, set me off again. "Hey, he just does it."

"But can he teach it?"

"He shows it."

"By not caring about *your* 'we'—*us*? Putting us second? He's not married,
no kids. We don't even know if he's ever been in a lasting relationship with a
woman."

"I could have left. He said it was my decision."

"Oh, that's wonderful. Really good."

"Wait. I've never missed *her* birthday—this was just her *bunny's* birthday and—"

"Just? This *was* her birthday. She's so shy. She hates being the center of
attention—you know that—but she did it tonight through Olive. She *was*
Olive. A *great* Olive. You would've been astonished, and proud. It was fantas-
tic, and you missed it, Roy, missed how she really came out! Olive is *her*. Don't
you know that?"

I didn't, but I was smoldering, didn't want to admit it. "Damn it, I can't do everything right all the time and you—"

"Daddy?" Spring was sitting at the turning of the stairs, holding Shirty, staring.

"Yeah, hon?"

"Don't fight, okay, like, especially on Olive's birthday?"

"We weren't really fighting. We were—"

"Liar, liar, pants on fire!"

"Okay, I'm really sorry I missed Olive's birthday. There were sick people, and I—"

"Olive kept looking around for you. She was really like sad you didn't come."

"I feel real bad about it. Do you think she'll ever forgive me?"

"Nope."

A knife in the heart. "Can I make it up to her? Buy her some beautiful timothy grass?"

"Yeah, try that, but listen. You missed her doing it for the first time."

"Doing what?"

"Binkying!"

"What's that?"

"When a rabbit jumps right up into the air and like twists herself around and then lands—it's an amazing! It's called binkying—and Olive did it—she binked!"

"'An amazing'!"

"Yeah!"

"Why do rabbits do that?"

"When they're really happy, and they can't keep it inside and so they just hop hop *hop* and jump up real high and *bink*! I wish you saw it."

"Me too. How do you know it's for happy?"

"Because she *binks,* Daddy. Jeez."

"I wish I'd seen it—"

"And you can. Mom got it on her 'I'-phone." She could hardly contain her excitement.

"You look like you're ready to bink."

"Da-*ad*—it's only for rabbits. Mom, show him."

We looked at each other, and Berry smiled. She took out her phone, and we all—Cinnamon too—sat on the floor. Our heads were close together, a truce of sorts. And then there Olive was, on the living room rug, kids all around, this placid, gorgeous rabbit, face exquisitely gene painted to sector her face exactly down the middle—one side white, one side gray—who had seemed to me not to have much of a repertoire especially in showing humans any joy and she hopped a few times and then launched herself up high into the air and, at the apex, twirled her head one way and her body twirled around opposite a couple of times and then landed. She paused, as if stunned by what she'd done, and then she did it again, and once more. Each time she jumped higher, binked more—to cheers.

"She binks, Daddy, she binks." Spring yawned. "Maybe tomorrow, she'll be so happy to see you, she'll bink for you too."

"I'd be honored."

"Can you carry me and Shirty up to bed?"

I did, with the scent of bathed, warm-child cheek against mine, and tucked her in. Olive was noisily munching.

"Love you," I said, "and love Olive."

"Love you too." And with two snuggles and a yawn, she was out.

Berry and I, relieved, went back into our bedroom, and before I could get undressed, she put her arms around me and tumbled me with her onto the bed, and all at once, she was hugging me hard and kissing me, ripping off— yes, ripping with a *rrrrip!*—my stale doctor shirt and helping me undo my belt and take down my pants and then reached her hand up between my legs so that I stood up at attention and I, really happy at her boldness, slipped her pajamas off and there we were like, yes, bunnies, *binkying!*

And it was, simply, lovely.

As we lay there really close together, familiar body to familar body, Berry surprised me again by saying, in a mock-serious tone:

"Thank you for listening."

"To you?"

"To us. G'night."

9

When all us docs awoke the next morning at a dairy farmer's hour and, with our first cups of coffee, clicked open our home screens, we saw an e- from Humbo, at five a.m.:

"*Caballeros!* Don Fats *es* exhausted to *muerto* from the *noche* of hell with the two Sepul-*anti-Cristos*—the evil one name Rick Hardy who attack us but we beat him bad, save all but two patients dead. Fats schedules 1-hour *URGENTE* meeting today from 12 to 1. He tell me to send this quote, to keep spirits up until 12: 'May I never see in the patient anything but a fellow creature in pain. May I never consider him merely a vessel of disease.' Maimonides 12th century. *El Gordo* say this mean HEAL. *Hasta luego!*"

Fats had found a second, worse nocturne and . . . beaten him up? Crazy.

But even crazier: Fats, *exhausted*? To *death*? Yes, sometimes he had been exhausted in the House. But we had never, that whole year, seen him miss a day. He always showed up. And so all morning long, as we saw our patients, it was with a split attention. One part was doctoring: hypertension to prostate to diabetes to cancer, or to the 80 percent of the "walking wounded" of psychosomata. The other part was trying to fathom a *limit* to Fats. I too was exhausted—my rib throbbed, and my head. Fighting off one of my migraines. And he'd stayed in the hospital for another eight hours?

As we waited in the conference room that noon, we were subdued. Nobody said much.

But his "This mean HEAL" was a balance. He'd have known that by noon most of us would have been half crazy because of the hell of HEALing all morning.

The good news was that HEAL had worked perfectly and hadn't crashed.

The bad news was that HEAL had worked perfectly and hadn't crashed.

By noon all of us—except Chuck, who ignored it, and Naidoo, who embodied the single best quality of a great doc, being able to type while looking at the patient—were fractious and fried. Because it wouldn't crash, we had to use it. Back turned to patients, we clicked boxes. With one patient I got so much into the damn screen, a weird thing happened.

Jimmy Lowry was a 73-year-old retired Irishman TURFED from the emergency room that morning with the chief complaint of "I don't recall anything." Leaving a wake late at night, he'd parked his car in front of the wrong row house. His key not working, he screamed over and over, "Open the fookin' door, Maeve!" Upon arrival the cops noticed that wedged into the front grille of his old Buick Invicta was a mangled tricycle. He had no memory of anything from the moment he'd seen his buddy in the open casket. The cops gave him a break—there was no blood or guts or bone or hair on the tricycle—and there he was before me, looking like shit, sobered up.

His tricycle on car grille brought back the memory of one summer night in England. On my BMW 650 motorcycle, riding home drunk through the forest from Oxford to my rented cottage so damp it was named Noah's Ark, I heard a *thumk* and kept going. Next morning I heard a banging on my door. It was my mailman, asking, "Can I have that pheasant on your motorcycle?" Sure enough, the big bird had been caught by the neck in the right chrome knee protector. I said, "Sure," thinking: "Thank God it wasn't a kid." But that didn't change anything.

I didn't want this "what if" memory, and clicked a box in myself, back to work.

Something weird happened. Despite my key Work-Arounds, as I clicked boxes starting with Dx of "Alcoholism," I got entwined with LOSs, VBNs, CLERs, pop-ups upon prompts, clinical pathways, and, because I'd clicked a "Skin Cancer," a "Secret Question": *Do you believe patient will be dead in six months? Click Yes or No.* By mistake I clicked yes. Up popped "Referral to Palliative Care" and a dollar amount. To squeeze out cash during dying.

But here was the weird part. In all this clicking with my back turned, I had forgotten *who the patient was*. I had to turn, and look, to remember. I TURFED him to Horace H.

As I sat in the conference room awaiting Fats, I realized that, looking back over the week, my patients fell into two distinct groups: the ones who, when HEAL was working, I could not recall clearly; and the ones, when HEAL went down, whom I'd written by hand in my three-ring binder and whom I recalled clear as day. I asked Hooper if he did too.

"Totally! They did studies—teenagers remembered better if they wrote it out. The kinesthetic movement stimulates a link between sensory/motor cortex and hippocampus, the memory nucleus, and that circuit tattoos the memory onto the inside of your skull. If you *type*, no dice. Nobody remembers anything anymore. We're all gomers now."

Suddenly, Fats came in, leaning heavily on Humbo's arm. Behind came an elfish man of large nose, full beard, tinted glasses in two small rectangles. The shuffle of an introvert overwhelmed by the bright lights and people. His face and hands were fish belly white, as if he hadn't been out in a while. Wearing a light brown long-sleeved shirt, he sought a section of light brown longer-sleeved wall, away from the table.

Fats was wearing his usual white dress shirt unbuttoned at the unchecked neck, a delicately flowered tie, loosened, wandering down his chest to rest on the hillock of his gut, and voluminous slacks that were always dark to hide the volume of those thighs. Just below his hairline was a bruise, a scythelike shape. In his hand was a medical instrument: a foot-long chrome metal rod with a point at one end, at the other a rubber disk.

"That thing for lobotomies?" asked Eat My Dust. "If so, I'm in."

"Reflex hammer, from Allen and Hanburys, London. A gift from when I taught at the Royal Society last month—epigenetics, calcium, and memory. Look, I'll show you how it works." He turned to Runt, who was seated next to him in his lime green Day-Glo bike helmet.

"So, how's it goin', Runt?"

"Except for terror and guilt? Okay!" He laughed that wonderful free laugh.

"Good. Cross one leg over the other." Smiling broadly, the Runt did. With the rubber disk, Fats tapped the patellar tendon, which normally makes the foot jerk up. Nothing. He tried again. Nothing. *Weird*. Tried with the other crossed leg—which kicked up just fine. *Asymmetry? Uh-oh. This asymmetry was diagnostic of bad brain shit.*

But Angel, beside Runt, who must have known what it meant, didn't seem upset.

"The point on the end," Fats said, "is for the plantar reflex. Runt? Shoe and sock off?" He took the foot and scratched the point of the instrument slowly down the Runt's sole—the standard test for whether there's any brain stem function. To fail this test would mean that Runt was a gomer. Given the dead patellar response in that same leg, it was a cliff-hanger.

The toes curled down. *Whew. Normal.*

"Whoa! That tickles!" His wide smile seemed more gap-toothed than ever.

"Normal Babinski," Fats said, "but what happened to your patellar reflex?"

"Oh, that!" Runt laughed. "A coupla months ago in Denver, I went over the handlebars of my Cipollini NK1K. Brain damage!" More laughing. "And because the swelling wouldn't go down, they had to leave a hole in my head. I got used to the helmet and kinda like it—cool, eh? Angie says I look like a hot Italian bicycle racer—whaddya think?"

He didn't, but some of us said "Yeah" or "Sure" or "Totally."

"Last week they closed the hole in my head with a plate. Feels less breezy!"

"Hey, Runt," Chuck said, "y'think you got some brain damage?"

"If I do, how would I know? If I don't, I still might. Or, knowing me, I might not anyway. Not to mention the unconscious determinants. But, hey— I'm a Freudian psychoanalyst. I sit behind the patient and try not to say anything *ever.*"

Dead silence.

"Uh, Runt, you're joking, right? Eddie asked.

"And what are your thoughts about my, quote, jok—"

"Runt," said Angel, "we'll"—with a gesture toward her mouth—"talk"—gesture out toward the horizon of time—"later."

Clearly, she was trying to protect Runt from further questions, which might invite further bananas answers—but with Runt she had regressed to her gesture—"word"—defect.

"There's nothing to worry about," Angel said to us, again fluent. "He's almost back to himself. If you want more information, I'll be glad to provide it, in private."

"Good," Fats said. "You keep us posted."

"Deal," she said, smiling. And with head nurse authority, went on. "I'm on it."

"And so *now*," said Fats. "Let's all do a quick check-in—what's up in your life itself, and any problems with patients, staff, or screens. I'll start. I was dead tired, rested now. Rough night trying to keep people vaguely alive. Unlike in the House, where we all shared patients on the wards and covered for each other and knew what each of us was doing, here we don't share patients, so there's not a lotta connection—which is key. So, at morning 'check-in' and afternoon 'checkout,' we'll fill the others in. Two minutes tops. Three guidelines." He went to his beloved blackboard and chalk:

1) YOUR LIFE OUTSIDE MEDICINE.
2) YOUR LIFE INSIDE MEDICINE.
3) DOING YOUR PART IN MEDICINE IN THE WORLD.

We looked at one another. Bringing our outside lives inside? Had he gone soft? But as we went around on number one, it was astonishing. Who knew that Hooper's three-year-old was battling type 1 juvenile diabetes—his specialty; that Chuck was worried about not seeing his daughter and about getting fat; that Eat My Dust was really burned out treating only cancer and "Maybe I should go back to Gomercare, or maybe kill myself"; or that Naidoo was feeling lonely, and "Every day I have the dire thought of a recurrence. A Hindu holy man said that we doctors in the West die of our specialty"?

Each of us envisioned our own Death by Our Specialty. A sense of impending doom.

Humbo crossed himself. "The Holy Spirit in us, making us his beautiful temples of God's presence, in the *oscuridad y* gloom."

"Missing Olive's birthday was a wake-up call about all the crazed work here and"—a look at Fats—"that I can't do night shifts, no matter what."

Fats nodded, slowly, somberly. "For Fats, two things. Life outside of medicine is good, period. I love you guys—and gal. I'm living my dream here. But after last night I was *ferschnickit*! The monster of all doctors, a devilish nocturne named Rick Hardy, sucker-punches me in the gut and then clocks me with his elbow—witness the bruise—and runs off into the, well, *oscuridad*.

He showed the steel point of his reflex hammer. "My nonviolence failed. I feel bad about it, in daylight."

"*El Gordo*, he is like Zorro!" cried Humbo. "*Swish swish!* Blood!"

Fats sighed. "I'm putting this sign at the nursing station." Humbo held it up.

NEVER ALLOW YOUR LOVED ONE TO STAY IN THE HOSPITAL WITHOUT A FAMILY MEMBER OR FRIEND, ESPECIALLY AT NIGHT. IF YOU DON'T HAVE ONE, WE'LL LEND YOU ONE.

"So," he went on, "how'd'ya all feel now? More teamish? Team FMC for all?"

Yes. There was a softening between us, a sobering. Something larger than medicine had come into medicine—a hit of outside life.

Fats checked his watch. "We don't have time today for numbers two and three. Lemme say one thing. In a clinic like ours, all in our own little holes of offices, we get isolated from each other, right? Not a lot of give-and-take. You're all experts in different specialties, which can get boring, so I asked Angel and Dulci to sometimes switch which patients get sent to who so you're out of your safe zone. So maybe go talk to whoever of you's the expert. Talk about a puzzler patient, or a dynamite success. Schmooze. Nosh. Listen. We're not real busy, yet. Use each other. Be with each other. Got it?"

Everybody nodded, even the Runt.

"Okay. Final question. How d'ya like HEAL?"

An explosion of rage, people shouting over one another. Vicious, raw. Then came laughter, starting with chuckles and then a contagion of laughs and belly laughs that you halfway stop and start up again when you see the crazy faces of the others laughing, so hard it brings tears, those breathless tears of laughter that fade with age.

Fats spread his hands palms down like a home plate ump calling *Safe!* "Good!"

"'Good'?" Eat My Dust said angrily. "How the fuck can that be good?"

"'Cuz we're gonna *do* something about it. We didn't become doctors to do data entry. We've started resisting, right?" No one said "right." "BUFFING HEAL?"

"It ain't working!" shouted Hooper, eyes fierce with frustration, tight shadowy face turning pink, arms clasped over his chest, rocking. "Whaddaya gonna do?"

"Yeah," said Eat My Dust. He knelt on the floor. Above the table edge, only his wild surfer hair and crazed eyes could be seen. "Look! I'm *on my knees!*"

"I mean, rilly, Fat Man," Chuck said, hand over his brow, "what'all you gonna do?"

"I'm gonna do Seven Eighty-nine." Fats smiled around the elliptical wooden table and then raised his reflex hammer rubber end up to vertical, slowly pointed it, and lowered it like a priest would a cross, or a magician a wand, into the corner of the elfish man blending into the wall. "Sev, rise up."

Reluctantly, the little bearded guy, still trying to melt into the wall, twitched a bit. *Could it be?* We House of Godders stared. *It was.* We laughed and clapped. The little guy gave a thin smile and acknowledged the applause with the most awkward wave of a hand in history, more like a fin of a dying fish caught in a wave than a wave.

"Not just Seven Eighty-nine," Fats said. "Now *Dr.* Seven Eighty-nine."

More applause. Shyly, he nodded and said, "Call me Doctor Nine."

789 had once been the BMS—Best Medical Student—on the Fat Man's team on the worst ward in the House, 4 North. He was a math genius who had done his senior honors thesis at Princeton on the number 789. Right away we cruelly started calling him 789 or, as we got more friendly, Sev. An isolated math nerd of few social skills, he could have been offended, but he loved it. For the first time in his world of numbers, he was one of the guys. Once, when the Runt had called him "749," he replied, "You misspelled my middle name."

"Sev's on faculty here," Fats said, "in kidneys." Fake oohs and aahs. "He really knows HEAL, and can help with it. Anything y'wanna say, Sev?"

789 opened his mouth and nothing came out. We laughed. He smiled shyly.

"Okay, time's up. Anything else?"

"Yes," said Naidoo. "One more thing." Fats nodded. "It's about the importance of women doctors in health care. I'm the only woman physician, with six men on the team—counting Gath—seven if Fats counts and eight with Humbo. But call it six to one."

"Yes," Fats said, beaming. "I know and it's bad. Y'think Fats likes bein' with all these *guys?* Gimme women! I like 'em better. Go for it." He sat back.

She laughed lightly—a tinkle of Hindu prayer chimes—and blushed. "I find you fellows terrific as well. But we are missing out on something: bringing the qualities that women are valued for into our team and its care. Qualities that even harsh training cannot erase, even in a hard-boiled ob-gyn, sophisticated Bengali lady like me." Her green eyes sparkled. A hit of love, framed by the sorrow of cancer. "Two salient points."

She said that a recent paper—"Benefit Seen from Female Doctors"—showed that elderly patients were less likely to die prematurely or be readmitted to the hospital in 30 days if treated by women rather than men. "If male doctors achieved the same outcomes as female doctors, deaths of Medicare patients alone would drop by thirty-two thousand a year. Equal to the total annual deaths from guns, and also car accidents. And you males would live many years longer." She shook a finger at us—bad boys. "And we women still get paid eighteen percent less."

"Bravo, Naidoo," said Fats. "I'm totally on this—in fact I may have someone for us by end of day." He stood up, shoving his reflex hammer, point down, into a belt loop, a six-shooter into a holster. "Meanwhile, use each other! And I'm here all day—use me! Let's break!"

We broke from the meeting inspired, a real tough team from a locker room—but as I walked into my office, I found my anxiety level, on the one-to-ten scale, rising from two to seven. Seeing HEAL sitting there, I hit eight or nine.

I went back out and got another patient, a 72-year-old woman born in Puerto Rico. Mrs. Jean Perez was a former patient at Man's 4th Best's other clinic, which, when we came, had closed down, and her doctor retired. This meant I had access to her HEAL record. I greeted her and walked her to my office, and then sat down with her, doing the dance of diagnosis.

A smiling, slightly obese woman with a limp. A prominent old scar ran across her forehead toward an eye clouded with cataract. She wheezed a bit asthmatically. Her chief complaint? "I'm having trouble walking, and my old doctor left me."

She was wearing a neat light green dress that buttoned down the front, each button a petaled white flower with a glittery green glass "gem" in the center—a careful person. On her head was a beaked cap in what must have been the colors of the Puerto Rican flag. Wedding ring. Rough palm against my smooth one—manual labor. Her smile was delightful, her grip firm. A firm woman who'd had a rough life, enduring—with a certain prevailing.

She said she'd been admitted to Man's 4th a month or two ago, for a severe asthma attack, and diagnosed with pneumonia, stayed a few days, and got better. Great. I popped into HEAL to find the data for the admission. I typed in her name, opened her chart. Her diagnosis flashed on, with codes for payment. I scanned 21 vertical boxes in the left-hand corner of the screen, and 18 boxes horizontally on the top. I glanced quickly through the 21 and for some reason clicked the 19th box—"transfer admissions billings and medication reconciliation." A drop-down pop-up screen, a grid of boxes with 16 "held orders." I clicked each separately and clicked on "Continue." Not where I wanted to be.

I clicked and clicked, scanned the hundreds of flickering lines of records, and found no admission. Was she sure? Yes. Luckily she had brought all her meds—eight different ones—thyroid, asthma, hypertension, steroids, etc. We went through them meticulously, I with my back to her, avidly clicking boxes, jacking up my anxiety. But for a few Work-Arounds, I did the hundreds of clicks in boxes for the encyclopedic ROS—Review of Systems—each click showing a dollar amount, leading to other boxes, each coded at more money than the previous, until, as always, there was a red-lined box for the biggie, in caps: "SEPSIS, severe." And then: "Yes or No."

Which was the one sure thing Mrs. Perez did *not* have. Triumphant, I mashed "No."

The war was on.

I found myself praying to HEAL as I went. Finally I handed her Man's 4th Best hospital gown and pulled the curtain for her to undress, and tried again to find her alleged admission. Nothing. Physical exam was normal but for slight wheezing and a lump under the skin in her chest—an old pacemaker, she said—slight swelling of both ankles, a sign of a bit of congestive heart failure. But on second look, the "pitting" of the skin was unequal in the two ankles—why would it be worse in one leg than in the other? Partial occlusion of an arteriole? Venous thrombosis? I asked her if this had happened before.

"Yes, ever since my poosy operation."

"Your what?"

"Down here." She gestured to her genitals. "A little cancer. They cut it out."

Aha—the faulty lymphatic drainage on that side, a chronic post-op problem. Not vascular. Nice catch, Basch—saved her a lot of new boxes, tests for nothing. Do as much nothing as possible.

"Okay," I said, "you can get dressed, and we'll talk about what to do. By the way, are you sure that you were admitted to this hospital a few months ago?" She was sure.

I went back to the data, and this time scrolled like a snail even more slowly through it, hundreds of lines—and whaddaya know? There it was, hiding in the quivering 1,000-plus stack of garbage data. While she was getting dressed, I decided to fill up more of her tiny boxes. To my surprise I found I'd gained some skill in checking boxes for checks. I raced through them, and by the time she poked her head around the curtain, I was almost done. Scared to death of losing my work, I pressed "Save/Send to Heal Bank."

Nothing happened.

And then everything happened.

Instead of the usual message from the screen when I had successfully saved/sent my OUTGOING data, there now appeared:

Error. Not saved in bank. Cannot connect to server.

And all the boxes went blank.

I tried not to go crazy in front of Mrs. Perez, got her fixed up with quickly handwritten med refills and advice, gave her a slip for her next visit and her PATSAT form.

When I got to the nursing station, all the others were there. It had happened to all of us. Fats was on speakerphone, talking to our IT guy—my friend Joe Sole. Joe was excited—he had never seen this kind of crash. Fats hung up and faced us.

"Joe says the problem is in the FMC interlink to the HEAL server. No other dis-linkages have been reported in all of Man's 4th. Just us." He shook his head, puzzled. "And here's the spooky part. "INCOMING is fine. We can still receive data coming in. But OUTGOING is gone. We can't send data out. Weird. Joe'll try to fix it." He paused. "The good news is that *all the patient data*—the results of lab tests, procedures, admissions, et cetera—will continue to come in, so we'll have all the clinical data we need." He paused. "But we will *not* be able to click boxes to send out anything we write in

HEAL—no histories, physicals, test orders, or prescriptions. So we'll hand-write all of these things in our three-ring binders and have our lab tests, et cetera, carried out by messengers I'm gonna hire and have running around the hospital. Like in the old days, right?"

As we absorbed this, Fats sat, head down, eyes down.

Strange. Strangely still.

And then all of a sudden, it hit me, and before I could say anything, Eddie shouted, "Hey hey *hey*! *No more OUT boxes to click! We can't bill!*"

Cheers, joy, relief.

Patients stared at us.

We smiled and waved back.

"*Compañeros!*" said Humbo. "Let us give thanks in prayer to *el Señor.*" He lowered his head and—ridiculously and with patients watching—we all did so, with Humbo and Runt and even Eddie kneeling. "*Dios y madres*, make this last—for the rest of our lives. Amen."

That afternoon was a treasure, all of us getting all the data we needed in from HEAL, and not having to click-box any OUT. We went back to tactile: pen and paper, lab slips, X-ray forms, etc. We sailed through our patients with time to spare. When we ran into one another walking back and forth to the nursing station, we smiled and sometimes high-fived, using words like: "heaven!" "bliss," "heavenly bliss!" and "Thank God Almighty—free at last!"

Fats sat in his "office," a high stool at the nursing station, looking out over his creation happily, as if calling it good. Sitting there eating horrific stuff and reading—the *Wall Street Journal, Journal of Functional Epigenetics and Memory.* And a fat volume, *Compendium of American Rail Freight Boxcars.* Often that first day he was on the phone with an excited Joe Sole, who was starstruck by "this isolated meta-gritzel crash. Unique! Publishable!"

Hour after hour, we were safe from click-boxing for cash to HEAL. Fats would wander around and schmooze, sometimes seeing patients, showing us how to *be with* anyone. Total genius at that, a beneficent paterfamilias of care, compassion, and cancer.

After lunch a bunch of kids appeared, junior high age and mostly of color. Fats introduced them as "the FMC Runners." Running from here all over

Man's 4th as messengers for our OUTGOING. They were from a nearby public school, and said they were interested in becoming doctors. The pay was good, and the gold T-shirts and caps reading "FMC Runners" were cool. They also would get help from us on their homework. They were, well, darling! How had Fats rounded them up so fast? Had the caps and T-shirts ready? I mean, he often seemed to see the "What next?" but this was ridiculous.

All afternoon we got only INCOMING. Without the boxes, we had time to follow up what Fats had said: *be with* one another in our work.

It was a revelation, to see how we guys from the House of God had changed.

Back then to survive we had talked a harsh, cynical joking game about old people who wanted to die but never seemed to and the young ones like us who didn't and did. We were crazy with fatigue and frozen with isolation and our souls were crushed by the dumb power coming down on us. Nobody was sticking up for us against the urologist chief of medicine, a man of small urine. And so we, to our shame, had been unkind or, worse, a lot worse.

Now, having time, wandering in to sit with my guys and the new women in their offices as they saw their patients, or they with me, well, I saw real kindness. Kindness that had come from being with suffering. And maybe, just maybe, from being down in the dirt and despair of our own sufferings, compassion.

We had grown up.

I was turning to go back into my office when suddenly there was a commotion at the door into the waiting area. A pale, husky guy in a beaked black cap with insignia and an unzipped blue hoodie was wrestled up to the nursing station by two policemen. The security guard hustled over to them, his hand on his holster. Uh-oh.

A hyperreal, scary moment. Keeping him pinned, the cops spoke to the triage nurse but then saw me and hustled the struggling guy toward me. One of the policemen, limping heavily, was huge, barrel shaped, with red hair growing out of and into most of the slitty features of his fat pink face; the other was a matchstick, decked out, facially, in white of skin and black of hair, with vigilant eyes and an open, large, and worrisome mouth filled with many disparate teeth.

"Gilheeny?" I shouted. "Quick?" The worry vanished. A rush of joy. "You? *Here?*"

Gilheeny smiled. "Would we be policemen if we were not?"

"Or I a doctor?"

"Not if you too were not a licensed *res ipsa*," said Quick.

"Yes yes," said Gilheeny, "and we are now back full-time on the beat, in the city—although we no longer do the sordid, succulent, and violent night shifts." He sighed, as if he missed them. "And the odd SWAT team too. Quick likes the garb."

"But we will postpone the nostalgic catch-up of our lives," Quick said, "until we have successfully employed your Jewish-doctor expertise in the delicate matter of this young Marine veteran Nolan O'Brian, a dear and currently crazed son of my own niece Miles—yes, an aberrant name for a female, Miles, but they're the asterisk-prone side of the Quicks and— *Ugh!*"

Nolan O'Brian had jabbed Quick in the gut and in an eyeblink Gilheeny's nightstick whacked him across the neck, and they hustled him into the office, slammed him roughly down into the patient chair, and stood there beaming, Gilheeny all reddish, Quick pallid.

"Yes yes," said Gilheeny, "the crack of the lead nightstick is a more teleological, sure, and fail-safe blow, much to the consternation of those writing TV cop shows—and remarkably free of guilt. No trace of corporal evidence and no evident blood. And since, as you yourself have told us, the definition of a psychiatrist is, quote, 'a Jewish doctor who can't stand the sight of blood'"—I laughed—"the dull *thwack* rather than the sharp slash, or the bouncing and expanding and exploding soft-nosed cartridge bullet from a gun, is a preferable forme fruste of constabulary in this instancy of these instances."

"Don't worry," I said. "I'm in recovery from psychiatry. I *love* blood now."

"A sanguine adoration," Gilheeny went on, beaming.

"What's up?" I asked. "What's—"

"Up," Quick replied quickly, his sharp-lined, thin face and blue-shaded jaw all squinching up to be clear on this fraught family matter, "is the steely matter of this gun." He took a handgun out of his pocket. "The Glock G30S, a military-issue killing machine, of sweet balance, light weight, and low profile so as to conceal its presence. The Glock catechistic promise is 'Durability, Accuracy, *und Tod*.' Your man Nolan here"—he tapped him smartly on top of his head with the barrel—"we in our surveillance spotted in front of the US Army recruiting doughnut booth in Little Dublin, barrel of said unlocked Glock poking out of his gangbanger hoodie. I'd been following th' lad's isolation from his AA 'home meeting' and relapse—and *here we are*! Before the lad's *final*"—another sharp *whack*—" 'That's all she wrote!' He's sober many months, but no job. He often quotes to Miles and me what the sots say in Ireland: 'Work is the curse o' the drinkin' man.'"

"So why'd you bring him here, rather than to the House of God?"

"Because!" bellowed Gilheeny. "You, Dr. Roy, are here!"

"How did you find that out so fast?"

"From the great orthopedist Gath, who in two magnificent operations redeemed my gait through meticulous repair of the gunshot wound from that bad winter night in the House. And we know that, by the final blowing of taps at the death of Wayne Potts, Officer Quick and I had become dear policemen to you . . . as you are"—he choked up—"so dear to us." Seemingly pinkish tears spurted from his bloodshot eyes. A starched, folded handkerchief was at his nose followed by a loud *ThhhhhronnNK!* He shook his head shyly.

True. When, near the end of the year in the House I was so depressed and acting less like a human than a machine and—worse—was totally denying that this was so, they and Berry and Chuck had physically snatched me up from one of my long-distance runs and forced me into the cop car and saved my life.

Yet as Catholics, they had said while the House was a "warm and friendly place," Man's Best, run by the Protestants, was cold and stiff, "filled with overachievers lacking the human quality of humor."

"But still, you?" I said. "Here?"

"There is one other reason," said Quick. "The House, in this distaff digital era, is more humane, more facile. It was blackballed by the WASPs from BUDDIES—and saves tens of millions, using it in the care of patients and even doctors. Salaries soar past Man's 4th Best. And instead of the fooked-up mess of HEAL, there's the in-House system, homemade by a pimply, red-hot Jewish doc—called TORAH. A user-friendly winner."

"And TORAH stands for . . . ?"

" 'Tough Orthodocs Rock at Healing.' "

Suddenly, Nolan groaned and tried to grab the gun out of Quick's hand, which resulted in Gilheeny's fist suddenly becoming a vise on his nose. As Nolan screamed and blood trickled out between the thick thumb and index finger, Gilheeny suggested we "postpone our reunion until we have gladdened

Nolan's life with your expertise in alcohol treatment, perfected in your two years locum tenens in the Wild West of the *Diné.*"

I was astonished—how the hell'd he know *that,* the Navajo word for their "people"?

"Now," said the quieter, philosophical Quick, "we shall retire to leaning against the walls of this place, with the metallic ease of bicycles leaning similarly, on either side of this smelly malcontent drunk in denial of the tripartite surrender to his disease of alcoholism—vide its physical, psychological, spiritual causes, with treatment in all three arenas, thus the birth of the holistic movement by Bill W. and Dr. Bob in Akron, Ohio, Mother's Day 1935."

"But!" Gilheeny boomed, hand squeezing Nolan's neck hard. "We're ready to provide correction of any fooked-up further foony stuff in his therapeutic alliance with you, Roy!"

The two of them leaned against the wall much as, yes, bicycles might, legs crossed like front tires aslant, arms akimbo like handlebars, elbows to wall. Motionless as metal.

I let all the reverberating "foony stuff" settle, first into a stillness, then softening into a receptive silence, all the while doing a quick Sherlock Holmes read: early 30s, maybe 34, the key age in men when they hit the wall of "self," and if they're lucky crack open and suffer, and let in deeply the love from someone else. Even, rarely, transform. A week's growth of reddish beard (kept things neat, obsessive even in descent to booze); two scars on face, one from a knife, one a burn (combat? domestic?); baseball cap with a US Marines logo, but with some kind of pin attached, covering up the *Semper Fi* (partly proud, partly resentful); a ring on each rough hand with several broken nails, one on the right pinkie, the other on second finger on the left (unmarried, but some symbolic meaning, maybe Marines and high school, maybe a girl or a dead buddy); hoodie (on a hot summer day? Chills from withdrawal or latent infectious disease—question hepatitis, AIDS, TB) with logo and words "Snap-on Tools" (a job? Or trying to keep some kind of identity after losing clarity of who he really was, post-Marines?); his shirt, against a red background a three-photo-by-three-photo grid of identical black Batman faces with a finger pointing out at the world, captioned "Batman's Moods" (all the *same* mood—a sense of irony? Or this squadron of Batmen a cry for help working in resistance, for the good of the world?); dirty jeans worn through to white threads on knees (careless, losing it). And one big clue: in the pocket of the Batman shirt, a pen and a Moleskine notebook (an entry point for helping him?).

In sum? Combat marine in one of the wars in Midasia, menial work until recently (clean shave a week ago), now relapsing, but not far gone yet. No external signs of withdrawal. The pen and Moleskine pad? A journal, and thus hope. The gun? *Bad* sign. All bets are off with a gun. Thank God the cops are here. This is the way that people get killed: a crazed man walks into an office and *bang*. He's full of anger, resentment at not feeling seen, the gun a big fuck-you to the Marines at the recruiting station.

"Nolan?" He didn't look up. I waited. Finally he did. Blue eyes, red sclerae from the booze. Anger. "I'm Roy Basch." Begrudging nod. "What's up?" He shook his head. "A gun at the recruiters?" A shrug. "You must be feeling pretty shitty?" A nod. Getting nowhere, really, and time was moving fast—the Fat Man checkout was in a few minutes. Go for it. "What are you writing?" He was startled. I pointed to his pen and pad.

A deep breath, then, "Yeah, *somebody's* gotta write about this bullshit war."

"Yeah," I said, "I agree."

A blink of surprise, a sheepish nod. "About the bullshit, or the writing it?"

"Yes." He stared at me, then got it, and nodded. "Have you started?" A nod.

Quick, behind him, winked at me. Gilheeny gave a thumbs-up.

He told me about enrolling in a community college on the GI bill a few months ago and for the first time in his life starting to read and write. "The thing that really got me goin' was a play called *Mother Courage*—ever read it?"

"Yeah, and saw it. Not done much anymore. There's not much, quote, 'resistance' anymore, in drama or fiction, given the USA regime, and the screened-out real."

He perked up. "Wish I'd seen it. Fuckin' amazin' story. There they are, a mother and her children—the kids are key—for me, anyways. She has power. They're pawns—what choice d'they have? At the end, *they* pay the price—all three dead—'n' she keeps goin' on. Thirty Years' War, she follows the armies, Protestant and Catholic, sells to both. Doesn't matter a fuck to her, draggin' her cart to one battle, another, back to the first. *Insane.*"

"Totally. Like *Hamlet*—a captain's leading his army to battle. Hamlet asks what the point of it is. The captain says . . ." I closed my eyes to recall. "'We go to gain a little patch of ground / That hath in it no profit but the name. / To pay five ducats, five, I would not farm it.' And Hamlet says, 'The imminent death of twenty thousand men / That, for a fantasy and trick of fame, / Go to their graves like beds.'"

Nolan stared at me. I understood that he understood. Each of us felt seen, and each sensed the other feeling seen. It was that rare, *human* moment we, mortal, live for.

Feeling connected, he told me about how, years ago on his first tour in Afghanistan, the worst place, Helmand Province, "owned by the Taliban," with great difficulty and many dead and wounded buddies, he and his fellow marines had liberated a small town called Nawa.

"Ever hear of it?" I had not. "Well, neither has anyone else. A shithole. Our victory was a total high—we crushed it!" He took a deep breath—and coughed hard, all cigarettes. "But a year later, my *second* gig in Afghanistan? Helmand Province? Totally retaken by the Taliban. Another fucked-up mission in the same town, Nawa, the same more deaths, more wounded, more atrocities, more victory celebrations, medals pinned on, discharge. And guess what. I heard *now*, in Nawa, the Taliban are *more* goddamn dug in than the second time. I mean, *really*? How dumb can the policy pricks get? The Taliban are fightin' for *their land*! *Nobody in history gives up fightin' for their land. Never happen.* And *us*? What're *we* fightin' for? Freedom? Whose? Not *ours*, not *theirs*! They're fighting for freedom *from us*! Fourteen years they fight the Russians—the Russians lose and leave. Like 'Nam—fourteen years of the French, then another twenty of us? For nuthin'! What are *we* fighting for, *really*? The usual. For rich old men with no fuckin' balls. At the end of *Courage*, the soldiers go, 'The war is endless. Money's made by those who stay behind.'"

"'The war is not meant to be won,'" I said, "'it is meant to be continuous.' George Orwell." Nolan was surprised. "America's been at war, continually, my whole life."

He blinked. Took this in. "So back here I start taking a course, writing short stories. And, well, I'm, like, scared to turn anything in, but about a month ago, I had to, to pass. I turn in a story based on what I told you, called 'Nawa Two.' Get it back from the teacher, Miss Heller—a real squinched-up ugly-bugly—yuck. And there's not a mark on it except at the end in little red print, 'See me.' I go see her. She says, 'This story is too terrible to mark. It's below F.'" He looked away—hurt, ashamed. "I ask her what was too terrible.

She goes, 'It's soft, melodramatic, all the gory deaths and wounded. Overblown. Less is more. You need more minimalism. Read Proust, Joyce, Faulkner, Jacqueline Susann.'"

I glanced at the policemen. They were rolling their eyes at all this shit.

"So what'd you do?"

"Shouted, 'Fuck you, bitch!,' went home, and ripped up the story."

"And started drinking again?" He nodded. I glanced at my watch. "Well, Nolan, I like the 'Fuck you, bitch' part, but I feel bad for the guys you ripped up. Every good writer meets up with shits like her. But you can't take it out on the work. Has *she* ever published?"

"Googled her. Nope. She's a PhD. English lit, Iowa. Thesis title?" He grimaced. "'Postmodernism Minimalism: Derrida, Lacan, Nixon, and Disney.'"

The policemen and I blasted out laughing. Even Nolan managed a tenuous grin.

"'Those who *can,* write; those who *can't,* teach.' My hunch is that you can."

I did a super-quick physical, employing "Scruffy's Rhomboid Space"—a diamond-shaped opening obtained by unbuttoning four shirt buttons and inserting the stethoscope bell and squinching it around to allow access to every vital organ. Without the threat of HEAL, in a minute or two I handwrote the salient details, and said I'd take him on as a patient, but only if he had "a meaningful connection to AA: don't drink, go to meetings, get a sponsor, do service. And absolutely no guns." He agreed. Could I suggest a new sponsor? He nodded. I put in a call to Horace, who answered at once, said he was only ten minutes away and could take him to a meeting of Midasian War vets in an hour.

"Good-bye, Dr. Roy G.," blared Gilheeny, standing up unsteadily as if on one flat tire. "We'll stop by on day shifts or on your occasional nights battling the anti-*Cristos,* fill you in on our life journeys in these years since we left our mission teaching our down-in-the-dirt reality to you coddled young medicos at the Hebrew House."

"And to see the new Roy in action," said Quick in his slick, sharp tenor, "listening and responding in mutuality and kindness to my kith, well . . ." And *he* stopped, he the steady rationalist of the two, choked up. Voice wobbling, he went on. "Well, it's a gift horse we and Nolan here will look everywhere but in the mouth. Christ be with you and shal—"

"Hey, wait—one question." The three stopped. "Did you, as you said when we all left the House, enroll at the Freudian Institute downtown and become lay psychoanalysts?"

Gilheeny looked at Quick. Quick looked back at Gilheeny.

"'The horror! The horror!'" cried Gilheeny.

"The horror, yes!" said Quick. "The Freudians tried to destroy us royally, but luckily Gilheeny failed his analysis, and I quit mine. We got out in the quick nick of time."

"The issue was our humor," said Gilheeny. "Humor for Freudians is never humor. Humor is aggression. These bonker shrinkos never just laugh—they analyze. They wear a fookin' filter to the world. Killed us, Quick and me. Let me give you an example."

"Look, I really gotta go—"

"Not to worry. It's the shortest Jewish joke ever, which I told to those anal-stage crackpots at the seminal seminar on Freud's 'Mourning and Melancholia.'" He cleared his throat. "Max and Jacob, two businessmen, meet on the street. Max says to Jacob: 'I hear you had a fire in the warehouse yesterday.' Jacob says: 'Shhh! *Tomorrow!*'"

Even Nolan laughed.

"And how did the shrinks react?"

"Not even a smile—not even a grin on the *roadway* to a smile. Next thing we know, I fail, and the loyal Quick quits."

"And even after a whole cold year of analysis, Dr. Roy," said Quick, "I still had my attraction to bendy-kinky plastic straws. And, warse, I'd still tell the wife when she wouldn't stop naggin' me—'Go bite a fart!'"

"Surely, we are disturbed policemen," said the redhead, red face wrinkling in false concern. "Wouldn't you say?"

"Would you be policemen if you were not?"

Gilheeny turned to Quick. "Yer man Basch here is a you know what."

"A textbook in himself."

Laughing, they wheeled on out, away.

10

Flying high from the company of the policemen, I settled into my seat at the table for the day's checkout. Fats was not yet there. Our phones were all in the pile, but they were not crying out to us for help. Fats calling them "Bad phones!" must have sunk in.

Having had one whole delicious free afternoon of not being able to click boxes for OUTGOING, while still getting the useful data for INCOMING, had us feeling good. A burden had been lifted, our patient load lightened, and our banter was happy—all because we were free. Fats trundled in, bright tie unknotted further, and, sensing the relief in the room, smiled big. Humbo and Mo the medical student followed. We went around the room, quickly checking in. All of us, unboxed, were on a shared high.

"Ohhhh-kay!" Fats said. "Let's pray the OUTGOING stays on the fritz for as long as possible, yes?" Chorus of "Yes!" "Now. About getting more women docs, extending our lives? Well, we lucked out. Two new women docs are joining the FMC, starting tomorrow. So we'll be at three women, six men—not counting me, and I'm kinda both, right?"

"You just think that, Fats," said Naidoo, "because you're a man. But thanks."

"Oh." He considered. "Wow. So we men can't see what we can't see?" She nodded. "But women can see that in us?" Another nod. "And can women see what they can't see?"

Naidoo rolled her eyes. "You don't get it. It's not 'either/or.' It's 'and.'"

"Cool. Betcha there's an invention in that. Get with me later, 'kay? So lemme introduce our first new woman. Almost-a-doctor Mo Ahern. She's now a subintern and a potential great doc, who Roy and I have gotten to know on the wards, and she's as good as it gets." He paused. "And she is a screen genius!"

Amazement. Applause. Mo blushed.

"She's of an age that she has never used paper medical records. And what's your opinion of our medical screens and especially HEAL?"

"All of them stink. But I've tried to be a kind of expert in how to get around them in the interest of patient care."

Oohs and aahs from us.

"Bingo!" said Fats. "She can't sign her own orders quite yet, so we'll all mentor her and cosign. Welcome, Mo!" She nodded. "A few words?"

"Oh. Well, to be honest, I don't—"

We were so revved up and she was so delightful and young, we shouted out, "There's always a first time" and "Don't hurt yourself, Mo" and "Now or never" and *"Alegría!"*

Mo blushed again, her hazel eyes lit up, and her smile got wide in her slender face. She covered her blush with her hands.

"Well, up on the wards, except for the patients, it was demoralizing. We students never got to do much. We could write notes on HEAL but they were secret; the house staff had to *un*click the 'Med Student Opinion Box' to view them! And at the end-of-morning glance-in rounds, when the house staff runs away from patients and jumps into HEAL, we students have nothing to do. We'd wait around, sneak out. Snack out. Waste of time. And fattening."

"And expensive," said Fats. "You med students are *paying* tuition to see patients. The house staff is *getting paid* for clerical work—and also to see patients. The *more* time you spend seeing patients, *the less you pay per hour* to learn medicine. The *less* time they spend seeing patients, *the more they get paid per hour* to do medicine. So for them, spending eighty percent of their time milking that cash cow HEAL, and spending less time with real live patients, pays off big-time."

"When I first saw HEAL," Mo went on, "I go, 'OMG—this has nothing to do with clinical care.' In class they taught us, like, it was a great discovery: 'Patient stay has been cut in half. It's the new era, the era of quote "high throughput."' It's like nobody cares about giving good care anymore." She caught herself. "Oops—not a, um, charitable way to put it. Nobody can give the care we want to. Care like what my mom used to do in her practice?"

"What was her practice?" Fats asked.

"Pediatrics. Just she and a dear friend of hers—a solo, independent practice. At least so far. But they're in crisis mode right now. In fact yesterday she said, 'The vultures are circling.'"

"See, team? Mo's a rough gem. And are we ever gonna polish her up and—"

The door opened.

"Yes!" Fats cried out. "Our third woman doc has arrived!"

In walked Gath, in green surgical scrubs, red hair fluffing up out of his V-neck.

With him was a compact woman in a short white coat bulging over a pregnancy, her brown face aglow. Blue eyes a wake-up call—clarity and power—lids slightly Asian, epicanthic fold of upper eyes, and higher nasal bridge. Dark brown hair, high cheeks. Lips a tight line, as if from holding a rough life together. Her low-heeled shoes were a-dazzle—snakeskin?—her gait striking, each step gliding, as if she was aware of the earth. All in strange sync, but strangely familiar to me. A small pendant around her neck, a silver-and-turquoise animal—a bear?

"Sorry ah'm late, team," said Gath. "We lucked out. It is mah pleasure to introduce Dr. Jude Nanabah. Best orthopedic resident I ever had—and the nicest. Mind you, she's tough too—she coulda just as easily been an Indy Five Hundred winner, changin' her own tires. Jude was s'posed to graduate from Man's 4th Best ortho residency next June, but truth be told, she's had a hard time from the other 4th Best orthopedic residents and the creepy cochiefs, Buck and Barmdun. Jude's filed a gender-discrimation suit. Waitin' for the trial to start. Fats'll find time to explain later?" Fats nodded. "So now they only let her operate with *me*—how lucky can y'get?" She smiled. "A lot of her time'll be here in clinic. She can do anything: family medicine, outpatient surgeries, consult, OB, cancer, nutrition—hell, she can even teach us healing circles, rituals. Build a lodge, get us all naked and sweaty, the works. She'll fit right in, 'cuz she's smart, dextrous, and, like I said, nice. Listen up: this lady has spine, courage. She's a fighter, like us. I'm the only ortho doc who's stickin' up for her in the court case. We gonna win. How 'bout a warm welcome?"

We applauded, whistled. With no OUTGOING that day, we were riding a wave.

"Oh, and how could I forget? She grew up in Arizona, in the Navajo Nation. And the person that got her here to us, a few years ago, is Roy."

I was startled—but then recalled how, in Berry and my first visit to Fort Defiance to look at the Indian Health Service, one of the surgeons told me about a young woman who'd just graduated from the University of Arizona general surgery program and was looking to move east to specialize in orthopedics. I didn't have time to meet her in person. On the phone she sounded great. I sent her to Gath. Never met her in person.

"Yes," Jude said, "that one phone call changed my life. Thank you, Dr. Basch. Dr. Gath has been a wonderful mentor, and he is . . . well . . . still standing with me, in these legal issues. At a risk to his own position." She looked at Gath.

He faked a shrug. "Hey, nuthin' I love bettah, kid, than stickin' it to high-paid lawyers and orthopedic fascists. You watch. We gonna kick ass and win. Go, 'Bama!'"

"Ohhhkay!" said Fats. "The FMC's got your back. Anybody got anything else?"

"Do you mind telling us, Jude," I asked, "what your Navajo name, Nanabah, means?"

"It may be the only cool thing about me. Nanabah means 'went again into war.'"

"You're in the right place!" cried Fats. "The Fat Man Tribe, at war with the White WASP Man. Yes!" He rubbed his fat hands together palm to palm as if starting a fire of glee. "Before we break, let's look around into each other's eyes. Eye contact, okay?"

And so we did. I recalled how one of Berry's great Buddhist teachers, Joanna Macy, always, on parting, made sure to hold your gaze with hers—because you never know if it might be the last time. Now, holding eye contact, awkward at first, ended as a comfort.

Afterward I wanted to talk with Jude, but Naidoo, Mo, and Angel were with her.

Fats asked me to walk out with him and Humbo. We threaded our way toward the parking lot. For once he was silent. I too.

His phone rang—those three ordinary rings like the phones of our youth.

Fats glanced at the number, mouthed "Krash," put a finger to his lips, and put the call on speaker.

"You got no OUTGOING?" Krash shouted.

"I got no OUTGOING!" Fat shouted back.

"So you can't *bill*?"

"I can't bill! And I can't enter any *clinical* data into the rec—"

"Fuck clinical, Fats. You gotta bill!"

"Well, then, fix it, Krash!"

"BUDDIES forced us to spend 2.6 billion, with a 'b,' to buy and install that shit-can HEAL for itself and Man's Best and Women's Best and all other BMS hospitals. Had to take a twenty-year mortgage to pay for it! Could bankrupt us all! So I myself am totally on the line for HEAL actually working—"

"*You're* the one that scrapped BEEMR, your homemade doctor-friendly screen system, for HEAL. *You* hired the numbskulls who can't fix HEAL, so *you're* responsible and I only agreed to come here if it did not crash, *Krash*, so y'better fix it, 'cause *patients* are suffering—"

"Profits are suffering, Fat Boy, and—"

"—but luckily we still got INCOMING data, and so we can still treat patients by—"

"Your response borders on insubordination. We can replace you in a heartbeat."

"Keep talking like that, and Man's 4th loses its stake in the invention, the boxcars."

A pause.

Click.

Krash had hung up.

Fats and Humbo burst out laughing. I asked what was so funny.

"What's funny is that OUTGOING crashing is exactly what we all want, right?"

"Yeah. And what's the 'stake in the invention'?"

"I sold Man's 4th a lotta shares. My 34 million phase two tranche is making him drool."

"So the term 'I have him over a barrel' pertains?"

"Yup." He winked, and said, "He thinks."

"What?! You mean—"

"*Who* said that?" He looked around. "Not me!" He stood there beaming. "Y'gotta be deft, Basch. Deft."

In the garage, at the Fat Man's Tesla, we were waiting for something. Fats took out a Katz's kosher salami, already scarred with nibbles, and peeled back the Star of David wrapper slickly to renibble. But for his prodigal chomp, chomp-de-*chomp*s, it was quiet.

"You said the previous system the 4th had was called Beemer, from BMW?"

"Nope. Acronym. Best Ever Electronic Medical Record. Man's 4th Best figured they had the best computer guys—led by a *doctor* on loan from the House—and designed it themselves. And it *was* the best, for doctors and patients and care. But for billing, the BEEMR was the WEEMR—the worst. They took a 250-million-dollar loss, then bought HEAL for an added 2.6 billion." *Chomp*, de-chomp.

From the shadows a small man walked up, awkwardly, on tiptoe. Sev.

"Oh," he said. Seeing me there, he went on. "Sorry, my bad." He turned away.

"Nah, it's okay. Do that Sev shuffle on over here." He did, actually, shuffle over.

"Roy," Fats said, "I gotta be on the West Coast tomorrow—a crucial moment of the calcium and boxcars and L-amphetamine."

"Amphetamine? The invention is *speed*?"

"Nope. There are two amphetamine mirror isomers: 'L' for levoamphetamine and 'D' for dextroamphetamine. The D is speed. The L has no stimulatory effect. And the L consolidates memory! We mapped it all out, from genes to mouse-memory water mazes. Talk about elegant! Big fortuna. Doing good. Critical moment. Gotta be there in person. Don't know for how long. So I anoint you, Roy, to step up, take charge. Not officially, subtly. Do you *do* subtle?"

"Better than you."

Startled, he choked, turning red, then blue, so I thought, *Heimlich*, and then thought, *Impossible with that girth unless Humbo, Sev, and I link arms around him*—but then he coughed out bits of salami, first big lung chunks through his mouth and then littler specimens out through his nose so he had to dig for a hankie and cough and blow into it for a long time, phlegm-snot-clearing sounds echoing in the clean WASP garage. Finally he spoke. "And part of it is top secret, agreed?"

"What part?"

"No one else in the world but me 'n' Sev knows what I'm going to tell you now. Sev has devoted his genius to electronic medical records—on our side, docs and patients. What a coincidence that *only* OUTGOING crashes?"

"Sev?"

"The best. We four hold the secret. Our only contact now'll be on pristine dumb phones—Medicaid flip phones like yours, Roy. Didja bring 'em, Sev?" He handed us the dumb phones. "These things leave no e-record. Can't be hacked. All these babies do is, well, phone. Got 'em programmed so every number you call or calls you is instantly erased." We pocketed our cute phones, pack rats in our burrows, secure.

"Thanks, Sev," said Fats. "Let's stay in the most intimate touch, all four of us."

Sev squirmed. "Aww . . . shucks." And shuffled off.

"Unreal," I said.

"All too. Man's 4th Best IT will fight back. But there's nobody like Sev. He's been groomed for this moment his whole life, his biggest moment, same as you and me—"

"My biggest moment, this?" I asked, and he looked, for once, sheepish.

"Well, y'got me." He sighed. "I know, I know. You got tsuris from Berry, the bunny birthday, family crisis—but I'm talkin' big picture."

"Nothing is bigger than Berry and Spring—and Cinnamon—y'understand? Nothing."

"Understood. Don't worry. I'm on it, this big enchilada, the FMC dream. It's complex right now—you don't know the half of it. It'll work, Roy, long as we stick together." A yawn. "Really beat. Thank God for private jets. Remember: no e-contact with me; they'll hack it. Dumbo phone only." A hippo yawn. "Whoa! Good-bye and luvya kid and—"

"One question. You gotta rush?"

"Nah. Got lotsa time. The plane waits for me, not me for it."

"How'd you get to be such a great leader?"

His fatigue vanished. He smiled, rubbed his hands together like he was warming himself up, which was strange because it had to be a stifling, humid 90 in the garage. "When I was ten, in Brooklyn, my parents sent me to Hebrew school, to start preparing for my bar mitzvah. One day the woman who was president of the Hadassah took a bunch of us boys into the synagogue to teach us about the traditions that had to be obeyed in the sanctuary. We went up front to the raised, sacred bimah, gathered around—maybe ten of us. She started talking, and we started spacing, fidgeting. It was the most boring moment in my life. I'm standing in the back. My mind wanders, maybe to geometry homework, or to Zetzel Persky, a really cute girl in my class. Suddenly this woman's staring at me, with black holes for eyes, and she raises her arm and points at the doors hiding the Torah, and she has this arm that . . . this arm that . . ." He was overcome with laughter. I waited. "This *Hadassah* arm! Y'know, where the flab hangs down and wobbles when she points?" We let out blasts of laughter. I, in fact, bent over, laughing—I *knew* that flapping flab, yes! "And . . ." He couldn't catch his breath. "And then she says to me, 'Do you have something *better* to do than this?' and up from the soles of my feet to my mouth comes a shout: '*Are you kidding?! And I'm leaving now to do it!*' I turn to go, but then a light bulb goes off in my head and I turn back and I raise *my* arm and wave it toward the door and shout: '*And any a'you who wanna follow me, c'mon!*'" He smiled, breathing himself down. "And all but one of 'em come with me, running down the center aisle of that shabby, moldy synagogue. I stop in front of the exit and look back. Only one kid is standing with her, staring at us."

He paused for dramatic effect. I said: "Jared Tristram Krashinsky."

"A guy that eats *salad* for dinner. We've been rivals ever since." He sighed, satisfied. "Jeez, I can't wait to get back home."

His phone rang again. "Yeah, yeah, sweetie, okay. I'll be there in six hours. Stanford, private terminal, yeah. Bye, honey bunny."

"'Honey bunny'?"

He blushed, stuttered something like "Um, R-Rrr-osie. Discussing the crucial step, boxcars, memory, bye-bye."

Humbo had opened the passenger door and closed it after Fats with the soft *thunk* of a vault and, with a fatigued *"Ve con Dios,"* walked around to the other side, got into the driver's seat—soft *thunk* again—and the world's most expensive electric car whirred like a big cat stalking prey, and drove off, OUTGOING.

11

Several weeks later, after a spell of the climate breaking weird—the wet flush of summer delivering premature cold nights and silvery frosts, and then falling back into a long 90-degree flash of Indian summer—Berry and I were at a potluck supper for the parents of the "Wonderers," Spring's class at Whole World Preschool.

I was always uncomfortable at such gatherings and drank heavily. Berry was a natural. I "wondered" around, seeking out someone to talk with, my plate of kale, buckwheat, and sesame tofu salad untouched and destined for Olive. Next to an empty sweating fireplace were two women chatting. I caught a few words that identified them as doctors—ah, something in common. I sidled up, took an empty chair, and overheard that they were doctors at the House of God. I waited for a pause. They turned to look at me, and I said, "I may not be the most favorite doctor at the House of God."

One of them stared at me and, with venom in her eyes, said, "Well, you can't be as bad as that guy who wrote that *book!*"

And there was this delicious moment. *Do I tell her or not? Do.*

"Well," I said, "I *am* the guy who wrote that book."

She stared at me and then blushed beet red.

And that was the last playdate our daughter would have with her daughter.

"Oh boy," said Berry on the drive home. "Y'got to be careful, Roy."

"All I did in the book was tell the truth, riding on humor and sex."

"You are so naive."

"How else could I write it?"

"Writing's one thing. Admitting it is another. Your problem is you don't run on fear."

"How's that a problem?"

"Because you just jump in and *then* see how deep or cold it is."

"What's wrong with that?"

"What's wrong is when you really hurt someone else—and then the guilt floors you."

"When've I ever done that? And gotten floored?"

She shook her head in disbelief. "Amazing. Get back to me when you re-member a few dozen times—some with me. Times when you've gotten really depressed at what you've done to people or to yourself. Times I've had to mop you up from."

"Ah, yes. Got it. Thanks."

We got out and waved to Randolph the Clown, Paulie's armed guard. Clearly the Veal was still in danger from someone. But somehow he had postponed having to "go away for a while, Doc."

Recently Paulie the Veal had told me that his threat to Henry Cabot-Lodge about the *beep beep beep*s had gone unheeded. Instead, the Veal had recently gotten an e-mail from him.

"It was the savagest, low-class shit I ever got," he'd said to me, "which in my line o' work—where a lot of guys' elevators don't go all the way up—is *sayin'* somethin', y'get me?"

"I get you."

"In Italian he's a *testa di cazzo*."

"Which means?"

"Dickhead."

"What's your next step?"

He had grabbed my arm, turning both of us away from the nearest surveil-lance camera bolted to a 100-year-old pine just over my property line. We watched it swivel in on us. "Doc, *doc*! This is *not* a question you wanna know the answer to, y'get me?"

Now, in the carriage house, I paid his daughter, Pia, for babysitting, and Berry and I went up to Spring's bedroom. She lay on her back, purple-and-white-striped Shirty clasped in her fist to her lips. Olive, backlit by a streetlamp so she was a vigilant, pointy-eared silhouette in the window, was in bunny peace. We tiptoed out.

Berry and I snuggled, so close that my urge to make love eased off. We said our two good nights and turned our separate ways, and with a sigh, Berry said:

"I don't mean to 'can' you, control your daring. It's one of the things I love about you. You dare, for both of us. All in all, your 'no fear' stuff is working."

She considered this, and went on. "So far."

The next morning I walked into the FMC with a lilt in my step—me, a lilt? A kind of *binky*? The Fat Man and Humbo's long absence out on the Left Coast had been okay. They both had shown restraint in contacting us. The Fat Man, intensely focused on the Ca++ Boxcars, trusted us on all our clinical care. But he was available.

To the bean counters of the 4th Best, patients were the rocket fuel of the great sucking engine of HEAL billing. HEAL's dumb machine complexity, interfacing with our human limits—boredom, distractions, rage—assured breakage. In machines and human beings.

"I love numbers and code," 789 had said, "but unless there's a genetic mutation in humans, we doctors can *never* use these machines to help us be human with our patients."

Our other computer guru, Naidoo, in a checkout added, "It's the emphasis on the physical world, the functional, algorhithmic world where my ex-husband lived."

And Berry, having recently gone through yet another one of her aging mother's medical botch ups in Sarasota, Florida: "Good human relationships are the crucial parts of good patient care, and good relationships are exactly what's going down the tubes."

"Yes!" I said. "But ever since OUTGOING crashed, we've had time to be human."

Time with patients, yes. Partly from handwriting prescriptions. By hand, it was about 15 seconds. On HEAL, 20 clicks, 5 minutes (times 3 to 7 drugs for each patient!). Opiates took 47 clicks, 7 to 12 minutes—and the final click-step was to consult our "I"-phones for an app and an 8-digit authorization code, which started a clock hand counting down 30 seconds, in which time we had to feed the code into the prescription code on HEAL. If we did this in *31* seconds, everything crashed. Reboot. Robot. Rage. Start over.

We did non-OUTGOING HEAL visits in half the time of HEAL visits.

Once, as I took the hand of a new patient named Kim Baruch as she entered the office, she stopped, stunned. I asked what was up.

"My last doctor shook my hand with his back almost toward me, while walking away to his computer."

We could face our patients, eye to eye, and be able to pause and consider. We no longer had to text while driving. Errors mostly disappeared. We had time. Being with patients was often *fun*. And we had free time with one another, hanging out at the nursing station, schmoozing. Our differences became a resource. We laughed at work.

The only problem was that the Runners were getting overwhelmed. Too much paper, too few Runners. Fats, from California, quickly fixed it: with the FMC Overachievers.

These were nearby premed college students, hungry for real-life experience in health care. Getting into med school was hard, and this would look great on their applications. And at each college, an especially overachieving Overachiever could serve as administrator for extra credit. Hotly competitive—but young and bright-eyed and more naive than they imagined. We fed off their energy. For once they were facing the real—illness, old age, and death—a rare awareness in a nation advertising health, youth, and everlasting life. They were learning that human suffering is not optional.

Many of the privileged premeds, for extra credit, began to mentor the unprivileged Runners, helping them with homework and how to take tests. Good connections were forged, across race, socioeconomics, culture, gender, language. Rare in America now. The idealism of the young.

Fats had made sure that each of us, in pairs, was on call a month at a time as attending docs on Ward 34. We had final responsibility for about 40 patients' care, for teaching house staff, doing morning and evening rounds, and taking backup night call from home. Fats had told Krash about the cruelty of the Nocturnalists and the high cost of their errors.

Krash surprised Fats by saying, "How 'bout I fire the Noctos and your team takes over? I save money, and you save patients. A win-win."

Fats said yes, but also asked him to offer residents on Ward 34 the option of staying on duty past the regulated shift time. Krash agreed.

Lots of residents stayed! A critical mass of providing continuous patient care for both patients and docs, if only on this one ward, prevailed.

And so all of a sudden the desperate cry of patients at night—"*Who's* my doctor?"—decreased more and more, down to manageable. Their night doctor was a member of the team that they saw on our morning and afternoon bedside rounds. The house staff and students soon realized what a rare good this was, in the era of shift work: continuity of doctor, continuity of patient, continuity of care.

Fats triumphant. All done in a phone call from a calcium boxcar in Sili Valley.

⌀

As the weeks went on with no OUTGOING, the big question was, why?

Tech at Man's 4th Best prided itself on always repairing breakages fast and perfectly. But this breakage had gone on for many weeks. Why?

Joe Sole was on it full-time. At first, checking it out from his undisclosed location, he calmly sent a comment: "No luck." Then he came alone into the FMC and checked it out. "No luck." The third trip, Joe with his higher-ups. "Giga no luck." None of them had ever seen this kind of "selective *and* universal" crash in a major digital sector of HEAL or in anything else.

"This cannot happen," the highest-up said. "In every previous case, either it *all* crashes temporarily, or it *never* crashes—I mean, so far."

Finally Joe's bosses brought in the CEO of HEAL, Akash, and four HEAL nerds. All wore black, mostly turtlenecks with logos. Two wore red looped Hindu threads hanging down their matching, slightly concave chests. Their private jet from the dull underbelly of the Midwest landed at a military airport, and they arrived in a 4th Best medevac helicopter. They expensed a whole day, a cost of five experts times a lot, on the breakage of OUTGOING. From their medevacopter back to the airport, they sent their detailed report entitled: "No luck." The report was one page that might as well have been written in Urdu but probably was in standard computerese—but for the last line: "This is not a digital error in the machine but an analog error in the humans."

To add threat to injury, page two was legal boilerplate: "Disclaimer: HEALInc. by contract has no responsibility for the interface of HEAL with analog interfaces such as humans and their behavior blah blah . . ."

Led by Naidoo, who knew the worst of nerd culture from a summer at Facebook, we wrote back. "We, human beings and doctors taking care of human beings, resent being called analog interfaces. To call us 'analogs' damages our reputations and earnings. We have engaged counsel to file a group claim of libel." As we began to sign our names, Hooper interrupted.

"Wait. I googled 'em. HEAL's ranked *way* down from number one EPIC. How 'bout a PS? 'This machine error would never occur in EPIC—which is eating HEAL for lunch!'"

We added this, cc all.

All of us at FMC loved having no OUTGOING. But over the weeks we sent irate e-mails to Krash: "We, frustrated health-care givers, in the strongest possible terms protest a lack of ability to OUTGO, forced to write on paper, expend money and energy on privately hired messengers. When in the world are we going to get HEAL to go out again?"

Poor Joe. A nice guy on the verge of being canned, going crazy, or both. One morning, I invited him to come to our check-in. The little guy slumped in his chair like a wrung-out rag—as some of us knew, a wrongly wrung-out rag. We offered free psych care.

"Thanks. Medical, maybe. Not psych. Can't open up *that* hornet's nest. Jeepers, I thought healing HEAL was just a matter of rational steps, like with all these critters. But now, nope, no. There's no orelse."

"'Orelse'?" I asked, thinking it was yet another computer term.

"Other side of binary, of either/orelse. A click of zero *or else* one? The orelse?"

"The either/orelse of what?" asked Naidoo kindly. "In the *real* world? *Our* worl—"

"You don't think *I'm in it too*?" he burst out.

We glanced at one another around the table. It was a nerd's worst-case scenario.

"Sorry, Joe. I meant our doctor's world?"

"Oh. Whew!" He took out an ironed hankie, unfolded it, wiped his face, folded the hankie and re-creased it, and considered this. "Either 'no luck' . . . *orelse* the Ukrainians?"

Finally Joe thought outside the box. Since the problem was only in one physical space, the FMC, he called in Physical Plant. We were in the ancient Pathology building, for two centuries drenched in formalin and ripped-up dead bodies, which David Oshinsky, a historian who has written about nineteenth-century medicine, concluded bred "miasmas" causing typhus, TB, flu, and other epidemic diseases. Joe and Physical Plant concluded that the problem had to be the remnants of these "miasmas"—whatever they were—and the only logical solution was to call in Man's 4th Best's de-miasmatist. Frankie Lappe arrived in full antimiasma gear, but her fumigations and miasmacides provoked weeping, sneezing, and hacking in docs and patients alike, and were stopped. Finally, Joe proposed "the logical default algorhythm: blast the shit out of Pathology and its ratty cables, scrape down to bone, and build it back up."

We balked.

It was our home. We and our patients could not tolerate losing the "in" data for even a day, and the noise, dust, and confusion would demolish our delivery of care. Fats drew a line in the sand with Krash—who brought up the matter of billing. Fats told him that billing was taking place on paper, as per the past 200 years, and that everything was working much better—which meant much more nice green money.

A stalemate. The Fat Man had won. It remained a mystery.

No mystery at all, unless the mystery was how one shy little kidney guy with a scraggly beard and a shuffling step could best the best HEAL nerds at their own game.

How had Sev, alone, beaten down an army of high-paid, skilled, thought-to-be world's best techies? And why? I dumb-phoned him.

"That prick Krash screwed me out of a big grant. The average big American hospital spends 30 million a year to fight hacks. I got a big grant to do it, and the prick nixed it." I asked why. "Don't know. My hunch? He's getting a cut of the cash from the hacks."

In this time of having time, Chuck and I even planned a golf day. The day dawned gorgeous. Chuck and I would leave right after morning check-in. We were partnered as attendings that month on Ward 34, and would be back for the handoff to the night intern and resident.

After the FMC check-in, there was a knock on my office door. A tall, thin man with a look of terror in his eyes was pushed in and deposited like a sack of wet sod in the chair.

"A grand good mornin' t'ya, Dr. Roy G.!" bellowed Gilheeny.

"A tee time waits for no man," said Quick, entering.

"How the hell did you know about that?"

"No time for discussion now," blared Gilheeny. "Not just for you, but for us. With the Irish, the teeth are always bolloxed, a great pain, and both Quick and I, finishing our night shift this morning policing the gunplay out there, are soon scheduled to be root-canalled in tandem at a dentist of ill repute."

"Great to see you. What's up?"

"This lad Richard Rowe," said Quick, "a brilliant autodidact, a Renaissance man who's a relation of one a' my relations. He's in grave danger of committing suicide, so we took him to see the Runt, and—

"What? A real crisis, and you took him to—"

"Yes, yes, but we were givin' our dear weird shrinko one more chance to succeed."

"By arranging," Quick added, "that Angel would supervise him. There she was in the room—but suddenly was called out when a novice Man's 4th Best security tried to separate one of her pet patients, Mel—bone cancer—from his only human contact, his dog, Casey."

"And from our own lockup in the Freudian Institute, we knew how much damage even a single fifty-minute session can do. We waited, uptight, outside. Luckily, at the seven-minute mark, Richard came out, screamin'—Runt had been sittin' behind him in mordant silence." He put a thin hand on Richard's shoulder. "Dick? If you do talk now, you'll get Dr. Basch talking right back at you to try to help. *Talk.*"

Richard glanced up at the cops for reassurance, then looked down into his lap. Finally, with a glance at me, and then down again, in a quavering voice, he said, "I'm an engineer on Amtrak, the Acela, the fast train. For six years. I fell in love. Her name is . . . Can't even say it. We were to marry. Her father didn't approve. We were thinking to elope. We had a little . . . what I thought was a little tiff. I got angry. Walked out." He started to tremble.

"I'm listening," I said.

"Yesterday I was at the controls, and I was thinking of her—I'd been thinking of her all along—and I thought I saw something on the tracks and tried to slow down and in an instant . . . it was"—he grimaced—"her. And she was looking straight into my eyes, straight into . . ." He looked up at me, tormented. "No way to stop in time. I felt the . . . *crunch* . . . Stopped way down the tracks. When you hit 'em . . . they just . . . *explode*. Nothin' left. They mop it up. They mopped . . . *her* up."

Time stopped. I looked at the policemen. The sorrow on their faces mirrored mine.

"And you're thinking of killing yourself." He nodded. "Okay, we're going to take care of you. You need to come into the hospital. Right now. Okay?" He nodded. I called the one really good shrink I knew at Man's 4th, Jeffrey Cohen, who'd trained at the House. Having heard about the situation, he arranged a psych nurse to come and escort him to admission.

Richard got up, turned away. I put a hand on his shoulder. He tensed, slumped. Left.

"That does it," I said. "No more patients for Runt. Fats has to find another shrink."

Gilheeny sighed. Quick, nodding, said, "Poor Runt. A sad moment for a good man."

"Luckily, *he's* not sad. And are you screwed-up cops gonna keep bringing me these ugly blood relatives? I mean the clans of Gilheeny and Quick are *sick*."

"Yes," cried Gilheeny, "as are we all. But that's why we get drunk for three solid days of wakes, and after the pebbles dance on the coffin lids, we get drunker."

"Still," Quick mused, a pasty hand at his shadowed thin chin, "I've heard tell, from them that know, that it's allegedly a good way to go. Just stand with yer back to the train, lookin' at the sky, and before you even hear it, you're dead."

"What about the Church's edict that suicide's a sin?" I asked.

"I've heard that, when the decision's made whether y'go up to the climate-controlled pearlies or down to that hot other place, y'can claim it was an accident—say, a catechismic contemplative moment, while walkin' the tracks, on the wonders of a marciful God."

"And in that spirit of hope," said Gilheeny, "can I tell just one last terminal tale of an inspirational story?"

"Be quick!" I said, grabbing my bag. "Chuck and I are attending docs up on thirty-four."

Puzzled, the redhead said, "But I cannot tell it as Quick."

"As quick as Quick?" I asked. "Or *acting* as Quick?"

"What a boyo with the words!" Quick said. "A veritable bard of the bedpan!"

"And so," Gilheeny said, squinching up his face in red rolls of delight, "two alter cocker Jews in Miami—Irl and Siggie—are on their usual gomer morning walk that passes a Catholic church. That day, there's a new sign: 'Come In and Convert. Make 50 Dollars.' Irl stops and says, 'I'm goin' in!' Siggie protests, but Irl goes up the steps and in. Siggie waits and waits. Finally, Irl appears at the top of the steps, and Siggie shouts: 'Hey, did you get the money?' Irl shouts back, 'Ah, that's all you Jews *think* about, is money!'"

I burst out laughing, joining Gilheeny's boomer and Quick's sharp barks.

"Thanks. You cleared the air. It's hard to believe, given what anti-Semites you are, that you do good work. But you're totally wrong about me, talking to me as if I'm Jewish."

Gilheeny looked crushed, Quick close to catatonic. "You, not Jewish?"

"I'm Buddhist. I'm only Jewish on my *parents'* side."

For a moment, they were puzzled. Then they got it.

"Ahh, yes," said Quick, smiling. "Acatalepsy incarnate!"

12

*or the weeks we'd been attendings on 34, Chuck and I had insisted that the handoff at night be done by actually going into rooms to see patients. Mo Ahern was with us.

After the day's golf and bourbon and beers, sunburned and sailing along on a boozy high, we disguised our killer breath with serial Tic Tacs, as in the House of God.

Luckily, Jack Rowk Junior was no longer much involved on any particular ward; he had gotten too big for that—or too scared of us—to show his face. But the Krash had been dead right about Jack. An efficient butcher, he possessed two of the most winning traits in Man's 4th Best firmament: an unawareness of self, and an unawareness of others. He rose like a comet and was now the *chief* chief resident, in charge of all four other chief residents, as well as of the dozen junior residents and the 40 interns and the BMS students. The latest high-gloss *4th Best Bulletin* had a profile—"Rising Star Rowk Junior." Full-color photo with his purple birthmark of Chile airbrushed out. Jack was assistant associate research fellow—or maybe associate assistant research fellow—in the Merck/Fox TLC.

I had asked Fats on our secure phone, "How is this *possible*?"

"Easy. Impossible to *not* be possible. Jack Junior's dad, Jack Senior, made killions in Trireme—a CIA shadow-equity firm, a Laundromat for cash. Witness those two cute Galápagos tortoises."

"How could he buy an endangered species? It's illegal."

"More endangered now—by two. Big bucks, Jack's pop, and—"

"Illegal!"

"Roy, Roy! This is America! Money *makes* it legal!"

That night after a real hands-on-patient handoff, Mo, Chuck, Tic Tacs, and I went out onto the ward. Mostly patients who needed humane care of small things.

A shoe repairman, rail thin but for his bloated abdomen from end-stage liver failure (etiology? Toxic fumes from tanning mordants), who said he would not talk to any doctor until we got a podiatrist to deal with his painful hangnail. ("A lousy foot doctor would be better than the best liver doctor here.")

Also, several congestive-heart-failure patients being diuresed, using House Law Number Seven: Age + BUN = Lasix dose, where BUN = Blood Urea Nitrogen. And even though there was no scientific evidence for this law, it worked every time.

And also lung cases, a palette of "blue bloaters" to "pink puffers."

Many gastroenteric maladies from the simple (long-term use of Prilosec) to scarily complex (total system failures in two immigrants—Mexico and Togo—that remained diagnostic puzzles).

To get home earlier, Chuck and I split the rounds, he with the resident, I with Mo.

Wambui Kamau stood out.

On a gurney parked in the hallway of the ward was a 51-year-old, young-looking woman whom Mo and I soon came to see as an enchanting grandmother. She had been admitted from Emergency with abdominal pain from Kenya—the woman, not the pain. Her pain had started the night before on arrival in the USA. She'd come to visit her son and wife and new grandchild.

Wambui was short and chubby. Her eyes, behind thick black-rimmed glasses, were alert. Despite the worry on her face, when I took her hand—smooth palmed and responsive—she smiled, a striking gap between her front teeth. At her bedside, wearing a fashionable suit, were her son, Harry, a linguist at a local university, and his Caucasian wife, Sarah, in investment banking—and their ultracute baby, whose name I don't recall. In a charming British accent Wambui told us that she'd arrived on the ward after three hours in Emergency and was waiting for a bed to free up in a room. Her diagnosis? Lower-right-quadrant abdominal pain of unknown origin. Slight FUO (Fever of Unknown Origin). Hidden in the Emergency doc's thicket of HEAL billing boxes was his focus on a recent cholecystectomy in Nairobi—gallbladder removal—shown on a CAT scan: "6mm opaque stone retained in the remnant of the cut bile duct."

Harry, with pure worry in his eyes, gave the history. "She'd had a minor heart attack in Kenya—almost died in hospital. I'm not sure she can stand another stay here. But they said she had to be admitted, right away. She—and we—are scared of hospitals."

"That's a healthy start. We'll see if she really needs to be here."

He and Wambui together provided a good history. Mo and I examined her. Mo, bless her heart, like me still used a stethoscope—rather than an ultrasound—our hands touching her chest. I also encouraged Mo, with me, to palpate her belly, testing for rebound pain.

Mo looked at me and, turning us away so Wambui wouldn't hear, asked, "What's 'rebound pain'?"

I was stunned. "You haven't read Cope, *Early Diagnosis of the Acute Abdomen*?"

She shook her head.

Everyone, for generations, had read it, an elegant volume by a modest surgeon, and had learned this key diagnostic test.

"Wambui," I said, "do you mind my showing Mo, a young doctor, a way to check out your belly?"

"I am quite glad to help."

I showed Mo how to indent the skin with a finger, sense the tension, and then suddenly let it go. If, on the rebound, the pain is severe, it means peritoneal inflammation—maybe of an appendix ready to burst. We did it. Negative.

"They didn't teach you that?" I asked.

"They don't teach us much hands-on, say it's all been taken over by CATs, MRIs, and ultrasounds. One attending told me, 'Touching the patient is now unnecessary, error-prone, inefficient. Throw your 'scope in the trash. Learn to read digital scans.'"

"Oh, boy. So much for the healing—and reassuring—power of touch, the laying on of hands. Hard to develop a bedside manner, eh? I bet y'miss a lotta rupturing appendixes?"

"We do! They get sent home, rupture, come back in bad shape. I even saw one die."

Back at the bank of screens, Mo expertly played HEAL for the emergency lab data and comments. All were negative. We looked at the digital CAT scan together—she more skilled than I. The gallbladder was gone, but in the remnant duct was a small stone.

"What do you think?" Mo asked.

"Let's not 'think' yet. Let's pause. And muse. Okay?"

"Summon the diagnostic muse?"

"Something like that. It's called moving outside all those little boxes. Seeing it new."

So she and I together did what would seem to be nothing but was a lot of things, if not all medical things.

I got it. "Okay, Mo, let's wheel her back down to X-ray, where they did the scan."

"I'll text Transport."

"Nope. We do it ourselves."

Mo looked shocked. "Is that legal?"

I laughed. "Y'know, my wife once said to me, 'You're so crazy, you should be *illegal*.' C'mon." I told Harry and Sarah that we were taking Wambui for another test.

All who saw us stared, as if wheeling a patient were like stealing a car. It was a long stealing, through countless cookie-cutter fluorescences, around nonmossy winding ways, and Man's 4th's sharpest and most unforgiving corners. But on the way, on either side of her, we had a chance to talk with her, looking into her eyes, watching her responses, getting to know her.

"I was eldest of eleven children," she said. "Followed in my father's footsteps—he was a farmer, and taught in the local small school. I learned English there—even went for two years to university in Nairobi, before the violence. I married another teacher and had my lovely boy—I could not get to his wedding, and I was so happy yesterday, finally seeing my grandchild." She sighed. "And now this?"

"We'll get you through it, Mrs. Kamau," Mo said.

"After my husband died, I went back to our village, to the family. Things have changed so much! Last month, sitting on our porch, in the distance we saw construction going on—it turned out to be the Chinese building a railroad to the coast. When we went to bed that night, the railroad was about a quarter mile away to our left, and when we woke up, it had passed us and was a quarter mile away to our right. Astonishing, these Chinese."

At the doorway to Emergency, I stopped, pulled Mo aside. "Okay, kid, have you ever before wheeled a patient down to X-ray for another test?" She shook her head. "Or drawn blood or put in simple IVs?"

"No, we're not allowed. Transport and Blood do it all."

"And by not doing it, what are you missing?"

"I don't feel I've really got the skills I need to be able to help. I mean, suppose I were alone in Kenya, and she needed a line for blood or fluids or meds—and it's life or death?"

"And what else?" She was puzzled. "You miss connecting with the patient. This was a pretty long trip, and while we pushed, we talked. Same with blood and needles. When I was in your shoes, in the old City Hospital—back when the BMS still ran it, their only public hospital—we'd spend a lot of time in Transport, wheeling patients through these ancient tunnels that went up and down steeply. We'd learn to run the patient down the slopes so we had the momentum to get up the next one—not to mention take the corners. Sometimes the patients would scream and laugh. It was fun. We bonded on the ride."

She smiled. "But why are we taking her back here again?"

"Gotta talk, face-to-face, with the radiologist who made the call on the X-ray."

This was not easy. The X-ray resident was holed up in a bunker with no identifying signs, behind a steel door with a keypad code. We corralled the Emergency Ward resident who had sent Wambui up to 34. He said—off the record—that admitting her had been a "judgment call" based strictly on the X-ray report. He'd been scared to actually *talk* to the radiologist—it was taboo. All contact with Rays was through digital records sent from screens behind the bunker door to screens in the nerve center of the EW. Looking around stealthily as if robbing a bank, he tapped in the code and ran. We entered a dim, low-ceilinged room.

There she was, alone, lit up by the reflected light of the four screens in this dark and windowless chamber, scented with stale junk food. The walls were peppered with tacked-up announcements and rules, from yellowing and crinkled to bright white virgin, some yellow smiley faces, and a photo of a cat. Seeing us, she did a double take. She seemed hardly old enough to have a driver's license, very thin and pale, as if in her outside life she stayed inside

whenever the sun was out. Her desk was a mess, with empty bags of Korn
Kurls and Kentucky Fried Chicken and styrofoamed Super Salads and gra-
nola, and thick volumes with titles like *MRIs 4 Dummies* and *How to Read a
CAT* and a well-worn slim volume of *Modern Mating*. She wore a mauve
surgical V-neck, jeans, and plastic thong sandals—in purple and also well-
worn, as if she not only wore them here in her, well, "cave" but always. Her
pale face seemed frightened by the undeniable fact that real people were
standing there. But she soon warmed up. Her name was Melody.

We went through her reasoning for thinking this was a serious blockage,
and as she talked—"off the record"—she said that she too had doubts.

"So," she said, *"reluctantly* I consulted Charley. My higher-up backup, the
attending radiologist, Charley Boucher."

"Can we consult with Charley?" I asked.

She hesitated. Charley, clearly, was not to be bothered, just as she was not
to be before we did and she had begun to enjoy human contact in the Dun-
geon of the Digital Rays.

But she got up, walked to the even more dimly lit back of the room, where,
eyes adjusting, we noticed an even *more* massive steel door with prominent
rivets and another keypad. She tapped in a code and opened the door. We
followed her in.

Even *lower* ceilings, even *more* dank and dim. But this cave had bone-bare
walls—and no *more* doors out into the next incarnation. This was the final
hutch in this, well, rabbit warren, Man's 4th Best's X-ray's final *say*. There was
a bed, a desk piled with crap, and a bathroom. At first, it was so dim, I
thought it was empty, but in a corner, in a tattered, tilted-back Eames chair,
was a man doing nothing. Nothing except one delicate medical procedure
requiring total focus: trying to see how wide an arc he could create in the
dank air by extending, between his two hands, a remarkably long stack of
Dunkin' paper cups.

"Charley?" The sound bounced around the concrete walls. "Y'got visitors."

Startled, he collapsed the cups back into a stack and shot to his feet. He
was so tall, he made the room grow smaller, like when Alice in Wonderland,
having eaten a psychedelic mushroom, grew into a giant. His T-shirt featured
a photo of Dylan and a line—"Everything went from bad to worse, money
never changed a thing"—that I knew from one of the *Biograph* albums. His
plaid Bermuda shorts revealed an athlete's bulging calves—a runner?—tapered

into sandals, the high-tech kind that will see you through a hike in the Rockies. His long, thin face, framed by a full brown beard and short-cut graying hair, was set in a scowl, and his black door-stopper eyes shifted from us to Melody and back again. He said nothing for what seemed a long time.

"*Biograph*, eh?" I said, smiling. "My favorite collection."

"Whoa!" Charley cried out as if being saved from a fate worse than human contact. But then, as if to verify I had the password, he asked, "Yeah? What's your favorite cut?"

"'Up to Me.'"

"Cool." He broke into a big smile, delighted that his on-call night would have a spark of human warmth instead of just the challenge offered by those paper cups. And he turned out to be wonderful—too wonderful, because he just wanted to talk and talk—clearly crazily human deprived, especially since I was roughly the same generation and like him caught amidst what he at one point, gesturing to Mo and Melody, called with nostalgia, "These cute infants, these student drivers."

I managed to steer him to the Wambui case. He snapped to, sat us down, clicked onto the largest HEAL screen I'd ever seen. And then Charley said what I'd hoped he'd say, for Mo's indelible learning. We stared at the digital scan.

"Let's get real. These post-op gallbladder stones in the stub of the remaining duct are not uncommon. The literature says a stone has to be at least six millimeters to cause trouble. I measured this all different ways." He demonstrated applying millimeter measuring rules on the screen faster than the eye could see—like a great violinist with impossible arpeggios, legatos, and fortes. "So if I do it one way it's a five. Another way it's a six, another a three. It's a *stone,* not a fuckin'*digit*! Goddamn *digitals*!"

"Agreed, bro," I said, meaning it—and seeing he got that I did, sharing his HEAL hatred. "What's the reality here, Charley?" I asked. "Off the record. For real treatment?"

Again he got wary. Lawyers were in the air, circling, foaming, clawing. "Promise?"

"Promise."

"Nuthin'. It's nuthin'. Where it counts, it's a five, tops."

"And tell young Mo here why you sent the report saying that it was a six."

"You know why."

I nodded at Mo. "Thanks, bro, for this teachable moment. Mo? This is in professional confidence?" She nodded.

"It's a CYA case," said Charley. Mo asked what a CYA was. "Cover Your Ass. Law Number One of Radiology: For diagnosis, always give the worst, the least risky. Everyone knows that. That's why you came down here to talk—only way to get the truth." He went on, sadly. "Nobody much comes down here to do that anymore."

"So no one can sue you, right?"

"Or stand you up in . . ." A gargantuan yawn and another.

We waited.

"Stand you up in Radiology Double Million Rounds, facing a hundred hungry Radiology sharks there to eat you."

"Double Million?" Mo asked.

"M and M, Morbidity and Morality."

"'Morality'?" Mo asked.

"Oops. Mortality. I get so damn tired at night in this cave!"

"Maybe, Charley, you *do* mean 'morality'?"

"Yeah, but up onstage at Man's Best M and Ms, you CYA—everybody does."

"I believe it's currently Man's *4th* Best M and Ms, Charley."

"Dig it. How cool is that?"

"So 'double million' is for 'M and M'?" Mo asked.

"That, and it's the average dollar award when we're sued."

I noticed on the X-ray that Wambui's colon was packed with feces. I pointed it out. "Long flight from Kenya, packed into economy class like sardines, sitting. Maybe a Dx of constipation, painful. Treatment? Laxative. At home with her son and granddaughter, not in here." Charley, Melody, and Mo nodded. "Okay, then. The first laxative starts now."

"I got some in my bag," Charley said. "Want 'em?"

"I wouldn't want to deprive you, bro—"

"Nah, I got lots. Don't get no exercise at this job." As he dug into his battered leather backpack, he waxed philosophic—he actually *waxed*. "Y'know, I was just reading a cool book called *The Digital Doctor*, and the author—Dr. Wachter—interviews one of these AI dicks, Vinod Khosla—Artificial Intelligence?" I nodded. "This Vinod dude says that soon doctors will be irrelevant, and then—poof!—gone altogether. And he says that us *ray guys* are first to go—already going. Quote: 'Our machines already read scans better than humans.'"

Charley located his personal laxatives—high-test prescription bombs called MaxLax that would throw Wambui into electrolytic shock—but I expressed gratitude and said nothing, taking a few.

"Well," he went on, for the first time not mellowly, "can a machine do what we just did, figure this out together? Save this woman from more tests, more machines, more crap? Huh?" He stared at Mo and Melody, who were scared to say anything. Charley cried out, "I mean, I'm askin' for some help on a crucial and uncool matter here, ladies, okay? Can a machine?"

We three all shouted back versions of "Hell no!"

"Exactly," I said. "When those AI guys get their *own* cancers—say, retinal or brain from staring at pixels twenty-three hours a day—and they want a real human being who can listen to 'em, and be with 'em as they die, see if *they* ask for a *machine* t'sit with 'em then, okay?"

"Or if it's *their* wife or kid! Right on, bro! How dumb can these AI dudes get? If they wanna help, work on sane malpractice laws so us docs don't have to lie and fudge and CYA! Like every *civilized* country—the bullshit would just"—he spread his palms along the desk as if smoothing a sheet of it—"melt away."

We turned to go.

"Cool visit, dude. Radical. It's a relief to have a challenge, instead of all the usual horror of 'locate the bullet' shit I get. Like they say, 'The horror, the horror,' okay?"

"Okay," I said. "And since Wambui has not been officially admitted to a room on Ward Thirty-four, can we just discharge from here, from Emergency?"

"Fine with me. I'll clear it with Lebowski, the medical dude in charge. He'll do the discharge summary, prescribe the meds. He's cool. Likes to bowl, though. Go figure." He considered. "Meanwhile, Roy—and med student Mo?" He grinned widely. "Maintain."

"'Maintain'?" Mo asked. She looked at me. "Maintain what?"

"Maintain!" Charley shouted.

"I'm maintaining!" Mo shouted back.

"All good," I said, nodding. We left.

I called the Ward 34 head nurse, told her the admission had been

canceled, and asked her to tell Harry, Wambui's son, to come down to the
EW for her discharge—with her suitcase.

"Another save," said the nurse. "Good TURF to home. No BOUNCE."

Mo told Wambui she would be going home. She smiled at Mo and, shaking her head with gratitude, took Mo's hand. "Are . . . are you my doctor
now?" Mo looked at me—she couldn't yet have her own patients. I nodded.
"Smashing," Wambui said and—on this Night of Cool Things—opened her
arms to Mo, who bent down and hugged her.

"And so, Mo," I said, as we walked slowly back up to the ward, "what'd
you learn?"

"Keep hydrated on long plane trips?"

"And?"

"That you have to talk to—no, talk *with*—people, docs, patients to find
out the truth."

"Not the truth, the real. We can bend the truth. None of us can bend
the real."

"Got it."

"But remember: don't waste time on talk. Spend quality time on your
screen."

"Cute, Dr. Basch. Tonight we saved more time than wasted it—"

"And saved her from the danger of a long workup and hospital stay. Call
me Roy."

She squirmed and blushed.

Ahh, to go back to those days when I blushed!

Mo smiled shyly, and said, "Roy."

Before Chuck and I left to take call from home, all four of us finished rounding on the patients. Mo and the on-call resident introduced themselves by
name, telling the patients that they would be their doctors for the night.
The gratitude—especially of those who so far had been subjected only to
the noncare of the Sepulantichrists—was touching. I called Berry and said
I'd be home early, before bedtime for Spring and Olive. Chuck left.

Mo said she wanted me to go with her to check on one of her favorite
patients, David Smart, who was on another of Man's 4th Best's clinical research wards. She had been volunteering in the Emergency Ward, wanting to

"really be on the front lines, like my mom used to be, before she and Sue opened their pediatric practice. It's amazing what you see there; I mean, you see all the neglected, hidden people. And David is incredible."

As we walked the hospital labyrinth to the 4th Best's Dow/Facebook Clinical Research Unit, she told me David was a 24-year-old gay African American living at a shelter. He'd recently come north from Pensacola. About a week ago, he'd been brought in with a fever of 104. The leading diagnosis was HIV/AIDS, and sure enough, he had tested positive. But he adamantly denied needle use or sexual contact. Treatment was started, but it was so routine that the research house staff lost interest.

"He and I really hit it off," Mo said. "He was totally alone, no friends or visitors, and so we talked a lot. He'd been ostracized for being gay, and thrown out of the house by his parents, and came north as his last chance. I really admired him, his courage. And so after a while, he told me his secret: three days before he came into emergency, in the shelter he'd had unprotected anal sex, and he had been ashamed to tell the other doctors. I asked if I could tell them—saying it would get him better care. He said okay. I told the team leader, Pinky Russell, the world expert in anal-transmission AIDS, and he said this was impossible. There wasn't a single case in the world literature of anal transmission being that quick—three days—and David would be discharged as soon as he was stable. I tried arguing, told them I'd checked with the shelter, and they verified the incident as best they could. Still, the expert was uninterested and said they'd transfer him out ASAP."

"Figures."

"But then," Mo said to me as we approached his room, "for some reason, thinking of you and Fats, I blurted out, 'But suppose it *is* true, okay? It would be the earliest case in world literature!' And Pinky Russell ate it up! He said, 'Yes, yes, he could be a fascinoma. I can see the article already, in *The Annals of Anal Sex*!'"

We laughed.

"I started working on an aftercare plan with David. Told him he could come to the FMC, see the social worker, get on his feet again. I really like him. I think he's going to make it. Here's his room."

It was empty.

We went to the nursing station. He had signed out, AMA—Against Medical Advice—an hour ago. No forwarding address, family, or contact.

"Oh my," Mo said, a hand going to her chin, then her brow. "Oh no. Why?"

I had no answer for her, just shook my head and said, "What a blow. I'm sorry."

She was quiet for a moment.

"I don't know. It's just that . . . after trying so hard, he's going back out there into the world alone? Just to . . . I don't know. You care for them, and they just disappear into that world. It's hopeless. What can we do for him, for anyone like him?"

"We can do what you did, what we all do—we try, try to take on the world, right?" She nodded. "And fail. And try some more. And sometimes, against the odds for people like him, we and they come through. And if enough comes through, we change things. Even, history shows, change the world."

"I'm not having much luck."

"Aw, c'mon." I smiled. "Listen. This is going to seem a little strange, Mo, okay?"

"Okay."

"Keep doing what you're doing—it's working."

As we were walking away from the ward, my phone rang.

"Dr. Basch?"

"Who's this?"

"Dr. Krashinsky. I need a professional favor. My wife's mother's sister, Jean Miller, née Cohen. She's got an unlisted room, top floor of the Jack Rowk Senior Pavilion."

"Technically not our patient."

"*That's* why it's a favor." He paused. Sounds of chomping salad? Swallowing. "She has lots of problems. She had polio as a child, and lately she's had that 'post-polio' syndrome, in the lungs, trouble breathing. She's also been treated for cancer, multiple myeloma—stem cell and all—not going well, kind of end-stage. And because of her compromised lungs, her heart is bad. Our thirteenth best surgeon, Frannie Moore Junior, wanted to open her up and see what was going on, a last-ditch try to save her. He did the operation today and found that nothing more could be done and just closed her up again. She's okay post-op now—back in her suite up in the Rowk, comfy, et cetera, but Frannie couldn't get back to her today to tell her the bad news, because he had to fly out right away to give the Deutsche Bank memorial keynote undress at the American Surgery Hall of Fame Convention in Vegas. Quite an honor. *Someone* has to tell her the bad news."

Did he really say 'undress'? Let it go. "And why not the surgical resident, or her private medical doc, or the heme-onc fellow?"

"None of them are . . . um . . . available this evening."

"That's impossible. *Someone* who knows her should be available, right?"

"Correct." A pause. "Truth is, they don't want to. I want you to do it."

"She doesn't know me. And I know nothing about her."

"She's a nice lady. Suffered all her life. Brilliant psychologist. I checked you out. You're *known* for knowing how to do this darn well. I'd've called Fats, but he's in Silicon."

I said nothing. I wanted to go home.

"She's a really nice lady. Deserves the best." Still I said nothing. "I hear that you're the best—I mean, for your age." Terrific. More silence. "I'll owe you one."

"Promise?"

"You have my word. Whenever you need me."

Why did I say yes? Because of my shame. I had carried it around like a rock on my back for years. Shame for what I had failed to do, on a night like this, in the House of God.

"Mo, c'mon."

As we walked to the elevator and started the *whoosh-up* to the top, I told Mo the story. I didn't tell her that I'd been too ashamed to ever tell anyone—except Berry—before.

"A patient of mine, a forty-some-year-old woman with metastatic breast cancer, had been taken down to surgery to see if they could operate on anything, but they could not and just closed her up. She was back on the ward, alert, but no one had come to tell her the results. The nurse came up to me and asked me to tell her. I said, 'It's her surgeon's job, or her private doctor's, not mine.' She said that neither of them would come in and do it. 'The poor woman's *asking*,' she said. '*Someone's* got to tell her!' And I, well—I couldn't bring myself to do it. I mumbled something like 'It's not my job' and walked away. I never knew who told her."

We got out of the elevator. The atmosphere in the Jack Rowk Senior Pavilion was that sterile one—of the rich.

"But when I was writing *The House of God,* and I came to that point in the story and again felt that shame, I decided I'd write what *should have happened.*

So in fiction, I turned to Fats. I had him overhear the conversation, and say, 'It's okay, Roy. I'll do it.' And then I had him go into the room while I watched from the doorway. He sat on the bed, at eye level. The woman was thin and pale, blending with the sheets. Her spine was riddled with cancer, a honeycomb of bone, so that if she moved too suddenly, she might crack a vertebra, damage the spinal cord, paralyze herself. Her neck brace made her look more stoic than she was. In her waxy face, her eyes seemed immense. I watched her ask Fats her question and then search him for his answer. When he spoke, her eyes pooled with tears. I saw the Fat Man's hand reach out and, motherly, envelop hers. I couldn't watch. Despairing, I went to bed." I paused. "And a bit later, I had Roy look in again, and Fats and she were playing cards. Something surprising happened in the game, a shout bubbled up, and both the players burst out laughing."

Mo's eyes were wide. "Wow. You wrote it to make it right."

"Yes. Now, let's you and me go in there and actually *do* it right. Do it *new*."

We went into Jean Miller's room, together.

She looked nothing like my patient in the House—she was 20 years older and had suffered from her childhood polio and recent recurrent polio syndrome, and complications, all before her cancer. But in the face of all this, clearly she was a fighter and had triumphed in life, no question. In her eyes I was caught up by this sense of strength. Her gray hair and lined face showed decades of illness—but not current pain. Thin, the skin stretched, her drawn face made her eyes seem to bulge.

Seeing us come in, she was startled. In her gaze was fear.

"Mrs. Miller, I'm Dr. Basch, in charge of this ward. This is my medical student Mo Ahern."

"Call me Jean."

"Jean. Can I sit on the bed?" She nodded, her pallid hands limp on either side of her. I took one hand. "I've been asked to tell you what the surgeon found."

Her lips tensed. She nodded.

"I'm sorry to say that there was nothing more he could do."

She stared at me. Her eyes pooled with tears. She wept quietly, shaking her head slowly. In silence, tears eased down her sallow cheeks.

Still she looked at me—*into* me, really, as if in one last search for a way out. I felt the twist of a fist in my gut. She took a slow, deep breath—but coughed it out of her tortured lungs and kept coughing. I gestured Mo to get her the cup of water at the bedside.

She drank, composed herself.

We sat together.

Finally, she asked, "Now what?"

"Now," I said, "Mo and I are here to help you with this."

"Don't you have other patients to see?"

"They can wait. We're here now, Jean, for you. For as long as you want."

At home I felt lifted up.

Berry and Spring and even Olive seemed lifted up with me, and we had a glorious time with Spring, a petulant mom to an impetuous bunny—who, it turned out, had gnawed the hell out of Spring's wooden bed frame. No recent binkys.

After putting Spring to bed, Berry and I talked "your day / my day." I was fascinated by her new passion, the Mahayana sutras.

I told her about my shame and how I felt, teaching Mo, I'd released it, some.

"Wonderful, hon. Maybe that's why you love writing? You go to your edge, and the edges of other people's lives that seem unjust, or just plain unfair, and write them in ways that might just heal?"

"At best, yeah. I remember how, one night in the House of God when a ton of brutalities and abuses piled up, a little voice inside said to me, 'Hey, wait a second. This is so bad, *someone's* gotta write about it. I guess it's up to me.'"

"Your way of living in resistance, babe."

Just before bed, feeling sunburned, tired, and hungover from the golf, and with maybe another crushing migraine brewing—but even with it, strangely relieved—I dared to open a letter from my father:

". . . Glad you are enjoying your new experience of being a physician in Man's Best Hospital and it is an honor to be chosen. Sorry you won't be coming home for the Jewish Holidays and it is the best religion and cooking. Mom broke 100 yesterday with a birdie on the short par 3 and my golf is good too. Money's tight and my Jolly Jews Investment Club is doing badly. Your asking about coming to join us at Thanksgiving in Sarasota is great and of course you won't be able to stay with us because the rules of the condo association at Conquistador Country Club would not allow Spring to stay in our condo and . . ."

13

F ats was back. With food.

After the months he'd been gone, he gave us only four days' notice, on INCOMING:

Coming back. Let's celebrate at Roy's house this Saturday night with
***FOOD** and THE MOTHER OF ALL CHECK-INS/CHECKOUTS.
Starting at 6 for the whole A Team and partners kids and pets. No
"dates" please, cause we gotta reconnect. Fats provides all things: food,
drink, set up before, clean up after. High security. Bring no one you
don't trust. 6 sharp. Theme? THE EXPANSIVE CAN BE EXPENSIVE
AND SO WHAT?

"And he expects," Berry said, "that we all suddenly cancel our commitments, and you and I and Spring get everything ready for the grand Fat Man entrance?"

"He said he'd take care of everything. All we have to do is show up."

"And what's with the paranoia?"

"What paranoia?"

"'High security. Bring no one you don't trust'?"

"Weird, yeah. But he's always two steps ahead, and right."

"Always right? Really?"

I considered my answer carefully and kind of resented having to do so. Why was she messing, again, with my Fat Guy?

"Yes—but this message is unusual. He's *never* done this before—called a 'social' meeting outside the hospital. Must be somethin' goin' on. Needs a safe zone to talk about it. As I said, I can't ever remember him being wrong before."

"In rational ways, maybe. In relational ways, not."

"Y'know," I said, frustrated, "I wish you'd talk to *him* about that. I'm sure he'd welcome it—if you can ever grab him alone. In some ways, he's *too* related, always with other people. I've never been alone with him outside a hospital."

"Maybe it's how he keeps himself unrelated. Protected. As quote 'the great leader.'"

"What would he need protection from?"

The question hung in the air, forlorn. Fats seemed to be one of the least protected people—well, make that "men"—I knew.

"I don't know," she said. "I've only met him twice."

"He *is* a great leader."

"That can be a protection too."

"Why don't you try to get him alone?" I said, irritated. "Lure him away."

"How do I do that?"

"With food. Like you do with other guys—Pup-Peroni treats for Cinnamon, sex for me." She laughed. "But you may not have a chance. I'd guess he'll show up right at six sharp—actually I'd bet he'll come earlier. But when the others come, you're right. He'll probably start with the FMC and expand out to all of medicine, science, health care, and his calcium boxcars to cure memory, especially Alzheimer's, and make a fortuna. The good news is that it will be no work—or cleanup—for us."

Four days later, Team Fats was there to set up precisely at two, knocking on the tall, wide front door of the carriage house. There were maybe a dozen youngsters of equal gender in those all-purpose work uniforms and caps that garage mechanics wear—but the jumpsuits were clean and creased and in lavender, each with a prominent logo:

Ca++ Boxcars

They were smiley and courteous to Berry and me and the excited Spring and the caged Olive and the sensitive pup Cinnamon, who loved only routine and chasing his ball and was as scared of all this as he was of the rabbit. Some of them cleaned up the carriage house, others power-blew leaves off the midautumn lawn and—given the real-time forecast of cloudless, unusually warm autumn weather—called off the tent, spread a lawn cover under the giant sugar maple, and assembled a circular table and chairs that would comfortably seat us all. And in our huge living area, which used to fit two carriages, they set up enough toys, games, and treats to make a child heaven, under direction of an older woman like the dread Margaret of Whole World and two girls with shiny foreheads from We Play Well With, who were so cheery that I wished that I was Spring or, better yet, of an age to date them.

Fats arrived at five. Ringing the bell—an actual bell with a clapper—loudly and happily, with a "Basch, Basch, wake up. The Fat Clan is here. And Mo. And yeah yeah, we're early."

We went out to meet them all: Humbo and that cute black-and-white little cockerpoo Chubby Checkers we'd met on the rim of Canyon de Chelly—and Rosie Tsien! And, by coincidence, Mo, who had arrived at the same time, to help out.

Rosie was a slender, athletic-looking Asian woman as tall as Fats, her oval face California sun sheened and eyes transfixing, intelligent, and alert—a scientist's eyes, zeroing in on the human data to be discovered during hellos, which felt like they rode on a real curiosity and, as we moved along together on our goodwill quest, spread out a blanket of—well, yes—kindness? Her smile felt less culturally reflexive than considered. At least a generation removed from China or even San Francisco's Chinatown. We were to learn that she had been born in Berkeley, her dad and mom refugees from south China—dad, an aeronautical engineer who designed early jet planes, and her mom a professor at her hometown university in Changsha, Mao's birthplace—and Spring's! At MIT she'd coxed the women's eight, was a Rhodes scholar at Balliol—my alma mater—DPhil in neurophysiology with Denis Noble, my supervisor as well. Aha! *That* was how he knew about Denis's brilliant revolution that had demolished Dawkins's silly *Selfish Gene* neo-Darwinists and showed that learned changes can be inherited—in a single generation! What would be the odds that Fats would find her, or she him—and Denis Noble? And now, boxcars. Was there any flaw in this kind, elegant, smart woman?

"I've heard so much about all of you," she said, "but where's Olive?"

"I'll get her!" Spring shouted, and started to run back into the house but stopped and said, "Cinnamon's outside. Can Chubby Checkers play with him?"

"Sure can," said Rosie. "We're early, but I wanted to make sure that Fats and I had some quality time with you. Roy, I can't believe that you and I share Denis Noble."

Berry led us all—except for Humbo, who said he'd supervise the butt-sniffing ritual of the two dogs and monitor the safety of the rabbit—to the oak-slab bar separating the kitchen and the dining room. On stools, and served drinks, warm salted jumbo cashews, and jumbo shrimp, we began to get to know one another. It went well. Fats seemed more open about himself than ever, though he didn't stray far from medicine. The calcium boxcars were mentioned, but soon Rosie, "the brains of the boxcars," called a halt to the thickets of SNIPS and CRISPRs. Berry shot me a look: *Wow, did you arrange this?*

In a lull, I asked, "Why'd you call the meeting, Fats?"

"Great news on our PATSATs, and our future."

"What are they?" Berry asked.

He explained, and then said, "And guess which one of Man's 4th cost centers has the best PATSATs? The FMC." He was beaming, explaining that now Medicare and BUDDIES payments to us would be the highest in the hospital. "Money and fame. That's why they hired me."

"Why is the FMC the highest?" Berry asked.

"Good question. The bean counters, the guys in the green eyeshades and with the short pencils, are trying to figure that out, but can't, 'cause it ain't a bean and can't be counted—it's how we stick together and connect with our patients. And we got lucky—when our OUTGOING crashed, all of a sudden we had more time for it, for *being with* our patients. And they feel it."

"That's wonderful, Fats," Berry said. "Sure is a long way from the House of God. Law Number whatever: The patient is the one with the disease."

"Well, y'found me out! Hey, I was young, trying to help us all survive. Now I'd change it: The patient is not the *only* one with the disease. And I'd call it 'the Doctor's Disease.'"

"Yes!" she said, smiling. "Great. And when you say 'being with' patients, do you mean empathy?"

"Yop!"

"How do you teach it?"

"Hmm. Never thought of how. I just do it. Show it at the bedside, and in our check-ins and -outs—wherever I go, really."

"Yes, I can see how you're a great example of it. Rare these days."

"Goes against just about everything valued in medicine now, for sure."

"Valued almost anywhere," she said.

"No time for it now with screens, and even if we had time, it goes against 'accepted medical practice.'"

"Goes against the dominant culture."

"No foolin'!" He fell silent, brow furrowing. Impatient to try to solve all this, right there, right then.

"When I was at the BMS," Mo said, "we learned empathy in our first year."

We stared at her, startled.

"In the class on interviewing the patient. It was easy. They told us to just repeat the last three words the patient says, and nod your head." She paused. *"Not."*

"A few years ago when my daughter started e-mail," Rosie said, "under her signature she wrote, 'Empathy is when you walk a mile in another person's shoes. That way, you're a mile away, and you have their shoes.'"

She has a daughter?

Fats laughed. "Great kid. Takes after her mom."

"Don't sell yourself short," said Rosie. "You've had a big effect on her."

"Really?" He seemed truly puzzled by this.

"Very really, yes."

Fats blinked a few times, taking this in. Then he looked at Berry and said, "But *formalize* teaching empathy? Nobody can do that."

"We're trying to," Berry said. "Our Women's Institute has been developing ways, for years. The relational model."

Fats blinked. "Tell me!"

"There's not enough time now, but I'd—"

"Bullet points. Please? Pleaseplease*please*?"

"At a party? I don't want to—"

"*Pretty* please?"

Berry, as usual sensing the movement of relationships, looked at Mo and Rosie.

They nodded.

"It's obvious," she said, "but it's the *elusive* obvious. It's a shift to the 'we.' The old model says that the measure of a person's psychological health and growth is in the 'self.' This didn't make sense to most of us women. In the culture, we're valued not for 'self' alone, but for care, concern, nurturing, empathy. *Our* measure of psychological health and growth is in *the quality of our relationships. Of our 'wes.'*"

"Like what quality?" Fats said, two jumbo shrimp on one toothpick dripping bloodred Cajun, suspended on their trip to his mouth.

"For example, mutuality. Good relations are mutual; if they're not mutual, they're not all that good."

Hand still stuck in space with shrimp, he went on. "And empathy?"

"If it's mutual, yes. Mutual empathy."

She looked around. I knew she was concerned about going into this, which was so important to her, now—as party talk. I wondered if she felt she would come off as "psychologizing"—the last thing she would want. For her, this was no theory; it was an affirmation of her life, and of other women's lives. Of blinders lifted. Validated. Unchained.

"But," she said, "I think that's enough for now. Let's get—"

The outside bell clanged. It was a few minutes after six. People were arriving.

We got to our feet.

"One more sec!" Fats cried. "What can we *do*? In the clinic? To improve? To *emp*!?"

Berry laughed. "Later. We do *do* later."

"Gimme a hint."

She smiled warmly at him and took his arm gently. "In every moment, especially difficult moments, take refuge not in yourself but in relationship." She paused and then turned to go out and greet the others.

"Y'*gotta* join us!" he cried, all that weight shivering with hungry, delicious expectation. "We lost the Runt. Roy won't do shrinking. We need a clinical psychologist, and you're it. And we really, really—I mean, *really*—need another woman."

"Sorry. I've already got one hard full-time job in the medical field— teaching, bringing out awareness, Buddhist practice. Exclusive contract. Long-term. High-pressure job. *Very* difficult. Rewarding, but *very*—"

"I'll pay more! What's the job what izzit what izzit?"

"It's Roy."

I recall it as a dynamite reunion—even when the real dynamite came in.

Everybody we invited was there—except the policemen. Even Runt, wheelchair-bound from a third catapult over the handlebars with only a broken clavicle that did not keep him from his new FMC job—greeter. His Freudian training barred him from normal talk with patients and anyone else. But as long as we and Angel made sure that he was not ever caught sitting behind someone, he was all talk, smart talk and happy talk, and he and the waiting patients, the Runners, and the premeds had a natural bond. But at odd moments, if he did chance to find himself sitting behind a person, he clammed up, back in the vacuum of psychoanalysis, silently unmoving for exactly 50 minutes. Angel, glued to Runt as Humbo was to Fats, was a saint. If he happened to sit behind a person, she'd say firmly, "[Runt gesture] . . . No [gesture] . . . *Sit* [gesture] . . . *Behind*." She never gestured now with anyone else, us or patients. We thought she had eyes on his inheritance from Runtsky Rocks LLC, the family construction giant in Boulder—but no. Her goal would turn out to be conception.

Having Fats back provided a marker for how far without our leader we had coalesced as a team, how much we all had come to like and respect one another as people and docs. And the clearest sign that we'd entered a golden age was that this was the first time we'd expanded the work family into the home families. Having kids around, that night, made it all seem so damn normal. Chuck had flown in seven-year-old Alecia from San Francisco for a long weekend. She was one of those dynamite kids who can sing way beyond their years. "I could sing, but that gurl can sing the birds outta the trees!" he said proudly. For the kids, the We Play Well With girls had hooked up a mike and speakers, and with a little prompting, Alecia showed her talent with a rendition of "Let the Mermaids Flirt with Me." This was Wayne Potts's favorite song, by Mississipi John Hurt. Chuck joined in the refrain:

When my earthly trials are over, cast my body down in the sea,
Save all the undertaker's bills, let the mermaids float with me.

I'd never seen Chuck happier. In the aura of marital failure and contentious divorce and few contacts with Alecia, it was an affirmation of the best thing in the world, love for a child and a child's love returned.

Another surprising and yet inevitable love declared itself that night.

As we sat out on the lawn drinking and noshing, we saw at the mouth of the path gently sloping down to the carriage house two tall people dressed all in white—a man in a white suit with a flower and a Panama hat, and a woman in an off-white dress falling sensually to a slanted cut above the knee and a purple scarf at her neck riffling along on the night breeze. A strange and transfixing sight. Who could this be?

The man crooked his elbow, she elegantly took his arm, and they began walking—no, he *escorted* her down the path.

Eat My Dust Eddie and Naidoo.

To a person, a burst of applause, shouts of relief and amazement. I mean, here was the most cynical of us all—the guy in the black leather jacket who'd notoriously said, "What could be better than a gomer with cancer?"—now dressed as Clark Gable in *Gone With the Wind*.

And then, as they both gave a thumbs-up victory sign and joined us, well, if *they* could get together, even for an evening, there was hope for us all. And maybe even for that sideshow called humanity.

When Chuck and I cornered Eddie, I said, "Congratulations."

"What for?"

"Falling in love."

"Is *that* what this is?" His face torqued in puzzlement. "I thought I'd caught a bug from a new patient—Myrna, colon cancer. Sunday morning Myrna calls me at home. I'm not happy. She says, 'You're being *negative* on God's day. With cancer I need to keep *positive* on God's day.' So I go, 'Fine, Myrna—so don't call *me* on God's day. Call God!'"

I smiled, but didn't laugh. Neither did Chuck.

"That," I said, "is the old Eat My Dust, not being able to face anything good. Catch us up, okay?"

"Yeah, I slipped right into him." He slapped his cheek. *"Bad* Eat! *Bad* Dust!"

"Man, you just did him again."

"It hasn't hit me yet, hasn't sunk in. I try to keep it hidden from her. And fail. But I did tell her on our first date, 'I want you to know that I am *not* for beginners.'"

"Eddie, it's . . . it's astonishing. Besides medicine, what d'you two have in common?"

"Nothing. I mean except for the marital fear of big dogs."

"Cut the shit," said Chuck. "Give us a straight answer. I mean, this is weird."

And then he did something I'd never seen him do. He *considered*. And then, when he spoke, it was as if his voice was coming from someone else. "It's not *besides* medicine. It's being *in* medicine. I mean, I love her looks, her smarts, her kindness, all of that. But that would never be enough for . . . well . . . never mind."

"Say it," I said.

"Okayokay . . . love. There'd never be enough for love if we *weren't* both docs. Y'see . . . I mean, well . . ." He choked up. "We're two people who aren't afraid of cancer."

Hooper came in alone, not looking good—a click or two down from Hyper. I asked him where his wife and four girls were.

He scowled. "The girls are hypersocial, out all the time. And, well, because all of you know about me and Kuppy Kushner the Israeli pathologist, Myra felt it would be too embarrassing. She's a California girl. Hates the whole East Coast." He shook his head in exasperation. "Gimme a break! I was crazy—all of us were crazy—but I recommitted. Isn't there a statute of limitations on East Coasts and Israeli pathologists? *Isn't there?*"

"There certainly should be," I said. The guys nodded.

"Why? Why the hell *isn't* there one?"

I had no answer to this except to repeat what he always claimed was his core philosophy: "Stay hyper—it's the best defense."

"Maybe, but it ain't working for shit right now at home."

The only ones who weren't there were the surgeons, Gath and Jude. They were often late, but usually they'd send a text as to why and when they'd be there. No text yet.

Fats led us to the big circular table under the soaring sugar maple. We did a check-in. It was all "Thanks" and "Good to see you" and "Things are going well" and Fats saying "Meet my partner, Rosie Tsien"—all good, but for Hooper, who, without rocking, said, "Whoever said life would be fair?" and refused to elaborate.

And then the food and booze. All of it was pure Fats.

He and Humbo had catered the party/meeting on the theme of, depending on how you saw it, "The Best Food in the World" or "The Worst Food in the World." The best, in his mind, shipped in from Katz's Deli on the Lower East Side. All hot pastrami and corned beef and tongue and other slovenly slavering meats and coleslaws and potato salads and slogging along desserts like triple chocolate knishes with chocolate ice cream and whipped cream—in sum, dead animals with no fresh vegetables. At the initial sight of all this high-fat, high-salt, high-sugar, high-carb food, the revulsion of vegetarians rose, but right away Fats rolled out another banquet of low-fat grilled and raw vegetarian perfection, including a lifelike tofu turkey, from Kale City. And for me a whole bottle of Laphroig single malt whisky.

Fats called the meeting to order. The night started to bed down. The rare last male crickets chirped, leg sawings for departed mates hinting of a certain solitude, say that of Márquez.

Finishing the last forkful of Katz's seven-layer cake with butter pecan ice cream and Reddi-Wip, Fats sighed with satisfaction, took another marzipan cookie, and sighed more.

"I've got three pieces of great news. First, our first-quarter PATSATs are the best of Man's 4th Best!"

Applause, shouts. Slaps on backs and smiles.

"Second, because we're bringing in nice green money, they can't close us down. And third, data analysis shows that *the PATSATs began to take off on the day that OUTGOING crashed.* And that there's no difference between our revenues when we bill on OUTGOING and when we bill on paper."

Sighting a bowl of pistachios on steroids, he threw a palmful into his mouth and chewed, but then, realizing they had to be snapped out of their shells first, spit them back out into his hand and put them on his plate. He looked for his napkin to wipe his hand, saw it on the ground, tried to bend over, but his weight shifted suddenly on the folding chair and almost "went to ground." Humbo grabbed him and with weird strength righted him—flushed and huffing—and gave him another napkin, gently cleaning pistachio bits off his florid shirt.

"Finally," Fats went on, "about that recent cyberattack that totally shut down HEAL?" He trapped a chocolate chip, killing it. "The hospital lost HEAL billing for days—utter panic—lost a cool million." He rubbed his hands with delight, face aglow. "Well, guess what. The only one still billing was *us*. The only secure billing is paper. You can't hack paper. So it all comes down to . . ." He waved his hand like the conductor of a symphony orchestra, and said, "It starts with an 'M' and it's . . ."

"Money!" we shouted.

"Bingo. Under pressure from the board, Krash sent us a note. On paper." He tried to dig into a pants pocket, without success. Humbo had him lean over and dug the paper out.

Dear Fat Man,

Pat P. Flambeau, CEO of BUDDIES, and I congratulate you and the Future of Medicine Clinic, who, during the recent malware infection and crash, continued billing uninterrupted, with your retro-innovative-concept of "paper billing." We are studying use of this method for backup. Please document your model carefully. We need details and solid data to see if this pen-and-paper innovation may be of use to any other cost centers. Even a short publication in the best journal—"The NEJ of Medicine" or, even the more "best," "The Journal of Historic Hacks"—would be a nice contribution to the field.

Shalom, Jared T. Krashinsky, MBH, FRSQ,
President of Man's Best Hospital

"The golden age has begun," Fats said. "Garçon?" Fats called out to the girls. "Champagne. Another round of desserts—go heavy on the whipped crème."

In great spirits, we made toasts, we made jokes, and, following the Fat Man's colossal appetite, even we on tender diets said the hell with it for a night and ate, ate, and ate.

"Fat Man!" cried Hooper. "I can't remain silent anymore!"

During dinner, he hadn't been his usual energetic self. Now his voice was harsh.

Things got real quiet. Fats, caught with an éclair halfway into his mouth and half on a cheek, turned to him, smiling, white stuff between his front teeth.

"Fats, you're fat! Fat fat fat! You're eating yourself to death, and I can't stand watching it anymore. You're eating crap! Your *outside* fat is one thing, but your IAF, *Internal* Abdominal Fat—that spare tire of fat wrapped around inside your belly—is something else! Your body's BIQ—Bioelectric Impedence Quotient? Gotta be off the charts. I'm saying this out of respect, for all you've done for me, for us. But . . ."

He stopped himself.

None of us, ever, had dared to mention fat to the Fat Man before. How would he respond?

Fats closed his mouth, swallowed, took a napkin, and delicately wiped his lips, his cheeks, a stray glob of glop on his cheek. He composed himself, sat back, and said, *"Nu?"*

Hooper let out a long breath. "Look, I'm concerned about you and wanna save you. Like I'm saving all my fat patients—my PATSATs for the last month are the highest of any of you. All of you TURF your patients to me—'nutrition consult' code 37459-N—and almost *none* of 'em BOUNCE back to you. And I almost never TURF anyone back. *Think* about that. 'Cuz what I do *works*. None of you know what I do, what works and why. You never ask me. I tell you I'm in nutrition in primary care, and your eyes glaze over so that when you look at me you see that old-lady nutritionist with a mustache in high school telling you to eat your spinach—well, guess what. She was right."

I, and others, could not help staring at Hooper's mustache.

"How many of you even got back to me on my memo that this month is National Nutrition Month? How many followed the federal guideline 'Bring your fork to work'?"

No one had brought their fork.

"You don't want to deal with nutrition 'cause you don't believe you can do anything about it. Well, guys, I can. I'm into preventing every toxic-food-caused disease we treat—diabetes and obesity, sure, but heart and maybe cancer. The reality? The food industry makes big money by killing us. I hate to say this, Fats, but Big Food's got your number, *bad*."

He bounced a bit, then laser-focused again.

"I'm sayin' this because I love you, Fats. You not only saved my life in the

House but you were key to my winning the Black Crow—which got me my research center at UCLA. So. Death, cause and treatment. Preventive food. Big Money. Five minutes tops?"

Fats looked around the table. Everyone nodded. "Go for it."

Rocking, Hooper launched into something that, well, lit up the night. It was, in a way, obvious, but it was the obviousness of genius.

"The reason we die," he said, "is we eat shit and get fat. Not fat on the outside only. That's just manifest fat. The death fat is that fat tire inside, the IAF. Why? In 1970, a Big Food scientist at a company under the New Jersey Turnpike found the 'bliss point' for humans, the perfect combo of refined sugar, salt, and fat that was optimally addictive to humans—junk food. The reason you die from eating at the bliss point is that the inside fat tire grows and grows and provokes inflammation in the body, and that sounds the alarm for the immune system to rush at it all the time, but it keeps on growing and growing until at a critical moment it outgrows the blood supply and the bloodless fat cells die—really quickly die—and this attracts the macrophages, which migrate to the abdominal fat and eat up the dead cells and kind of circle the wagons."

He paused, assessing.

Fats nodded him on.

"And inflammation goes bananas! The result is *death*, baby, in every part of the body: fatty liver, diabetes, heart, lung, neuro, kidney. Inflammation attacks everything blood can get to, and is a proven factor in breast cancer and maybe colon, pancreas, prostate, kidney. And an outside chance of Alzheimer's—those *fat bodies* in the brain, right? Cancer? Sure, sometimes it's a mutation caused by killer pesticides and all the plastic shit. But we *all* get mutations. Maybe cancer sometimes is a nutritional disease—a lifestyle disease—and not always a chance bolt from the thunder gods! To ignore the toxicity of the shit that we eat is the dummification of the American people, and of us docs too."

He checked his watch.

"Treatment? No time. One stat: a five percent weight loss in a patient— not that hard—prevents fifty-eight percent of new cases of diabetes."

We sat, awed. And all this cancer started by a guy under the New Jersey Turnpike?

"*Immuno*-nutrition?" Fats asked. Hyper nodded. "And it's all the food industry?"

"Big Food, yeah, making big money by loading us—all of us—up to the eyeballs with totally *addictive* carb-based junk food, and we in medicine are stuck trying to clean up the mess of fat? One example, my biggest failure. I focused on red yeast rice—an ancient Chinese medicine—and found the bioactive ingredient. Lowers cholesterol twenty percent, no side effects. Statins, like Pfizer's Lipitor, can eat away muscles so your triceps hang down like wet noodles—irreversibly."

"Yeah!" cried Eddie. "Look." He rolled up his sleeves. His triceps did hang down like noodles, his biceps pulling his arms up like a prizefighter's. "My doc never warned me!"

"Oh, *really*?" said Hooper. "Are you telling me that Pfizer did not *inform* you of this liver damage? Did not alert the nation to this *irreversible* noodling? Imagine that."

Humbo looked at his watch and then at Fats. Fats waved Hooper to proceed.

"For your noodling triceps, I'll give you a thumbnail. I did the study on the active molecule in red rice. Proved that it worked to lower bad lipids. It worked. We began sell—"

"Great!" said Eat My Dust. "Congrats, man! High five! I want some!"

Hooper sighed. "The FDA ruled against it being an approved drug, so it got relegated to the vitamin shelf, lost in the crowd. Merck had gotten to the FDA. They stopped it in order to protect their three statins, the worst noodlers on earth, worth billions and—"

"Merck kill *mía madre*!" A string of obscenities, in Spanish, for a while.

Silence, one of *Even if Hooper isn't crazy, how could he humiliate the Fat Man?*

"Oh, God, I'm sorry, Fats. I feel terrible. You're my hero. It's been a hard month—National Nutrition Month always is because nobody celebrates it. I feel so alone. But . . ." He stopped. Totally still. His face tightened, holding back pain. "But the real big deal right now is, I'm totally depressed about my marriage, looks like it might be MOR. Déjà vu all over again. I can't take my Marriage on the Rocks again." He hung his head.

"All . . . right," Fats said firmly. "I get it. Have you got proven treatments, based on your research, that all of us, in each of our specialties, can really use on our patients?"

Hyper looked up, startled. "Yeah. Tried and true. And use it on ourselves too. At the Hyper-Winfrey Nutrition Center, we train doctors, nurses, PAs, and, yes, *nutritionists*." He paused. "Some with mustaches."

We laughed. He nodded and broke out that wild canyon-to-desert California smile.

"We're eclectic. We work closely with OA—Overeaters Anonymous. The treatment is to snap them out of their secret eating, their craving, loneliness, and shame. Addiction is a disease of isolation."

"And connection heals?" Fats said.

"That's key, yeah. And protein-pomegranate shakes and any red vegetables—tomatoes, red peppers. It's all in my book: *Eat Red, Live Long: Lycopenes, Caratenoids, and—*"

"Okay, okay," Fats said, putting his hands palm down like an umpire calling the runner safe at home. "Thanks, Hooper."

"For . . . for what, big guy?"

"You had the guts to point out the . . . umm"—he smiled—"the *elephant* in the room."

We didn't know whether to laugh or not.

"Laugh!" Fats said. "Laugh—or you *die*."

So we did. Laugh, that is.

"And, Hooper, thanks for giving us the missing ingredient."

"Which ingredient?"

"Money. Big Food. In cahoots with Big Pharma. Big Food's making people sick. So the main causes of death in modern medicine are food, screens, and money." He smiled, relieved. "Hey hey hey! Look at me. *What* internal spare tire, hunh? I'm living longer already. How 'bout a hand for Hyyy-perrr Hoooo-per!"

We cheered.

He rocked, hard.

"Great work, Hooper. We'll follow up at the FMC, under your lead. Any other business?"

No one spoke up. We went back to party mode, high chatter, a kid's pet show and parade—Olive, wearing an all-white vest reading "Olive in Wonderland"; the brave, young, and healthy Cinnamon chasing his ball with astonishing speed and joy, Lady Chubby watching with admiration. There was a sense of having come through something hard together, something that had softened us and *Kaboooom!*—an explosion—followed by *Kabooom!*—another—and a burst of flame from the high spruce alongside the driveway to the Garage Mahal.

We jumped, scared. Something was in flames halfway up the tree—a second fire was in another tree, a century-old sequoia up next to the main house, near the street. Everybody hit the ground. I stood up and shouted:

"It's nothing! Nothing, relax!" I called out. "Relax! Look! *Look!*" I pointed to smoke coming from high up in the two trees. The crisp, edgy scent of cordite floated down.

"There's no danger. It's just my tenant in the main house, Paulie the Veal, blasting away my neighborly hedge funder's surveillance cameras trained on Paulie and me."

Gradually, we settled back down.

Gath and Jude finally showed up, still in their bloodstained operating room gear. A green surgical mask dangled from Jude's neck. They were wired and tired—she very pregnant—having spent a whole day doing patriotic things like extracting bullets from bodies and attaching arms back onto shoulders—real civic-minded stuff. I offered drinks.

"Bourbon?" Gath asked Jude.

"A double," she said, holding her big belly as she sat. "Third trimester, thank God."

"Double that double fo' me." They sat, heavily, at the table. Drank quickly and started in, distractedly, on the food. "We got shit. We're way past critical mass."

"It's about Jude's suspension?" I asked.

"Nope, but they'll make it about that."

Fats put a hand on each of their shoulders. "We got your backs, no matter what. Go."

Jude had been on probation for months on a trumped-up charge—and was restricted to only operating when supervised by Gath. The charge? Not following up with an emergency room patient she'd been called down from the ward to see, for a rare hip injury. She had done everything right: examined, diagnosed correctly—a partial labral tear—and did a non-surgical treatment with a follow-up MRI in the morning, referral to clinic and physical therapy. The trumped-up part was that the MRI had vanished from HEAL, and the patient came back in more distress the next night and was admitted. The chief ortho resident, an ex–football cowboy from Texas who had long been sniping for her—the only woman in the program and a Navajo Indian at that—brought the matter to the two joint chiefs of Ortho-pedics, Buck and Barmdun. They ran the most lucrative practice in America—netting 13 million dollars a year *each*. Walt Buck was called by his residents, with pride, "the worst person on earth." Barmdun was, in comparison, the brains—which was not saying much. His "thing" was mint-condition young women and mint-condition old cars.

A year ago Buck and Barmdun had put Jude on probation, which meant that now, in her sixth and final year of residency, she would not graduate from the program and could not be certified to practice surgery. Jude brought suit in federal court: gender discrimination. She had documented the pattern meticulously. She sued the Big Three: Man's 4th Best Hospital, the BMS, and BUDDIES. The trial was about to begin.

"Last night, when Jude and I were making pre-op rounds," Gath said, "I ran into an old Alabama buddy, Billy Clark. He needed a total hip replace-ment and was told that the best in America was one of the joint chiefs of Ortho, Dr. Buck. I didn't say anything about Buck, but I told him to tell the nurse and the anesthetist that he wanted to be sure that Dr. Buck *himself would do the whole operation*. This morning Jude and I are in the OR suite getting ready for our first case. I look into Billy's OR. A resident was making the first incision, alone. I ask the head nurse where Buck is. She hadn't seen him. I tell her to let me know when he comes in. Jude and I begin our first case. Soon Prudence Kline, the head nurse, comes in, says the resident is still alone and 'He's not all that experienced.' I ask if she'd paged Buck. She had. He hadn't answered. I tell Jude to take over and call him on his cell. I tell him he's got to get back here. He says he's in a cab three miles away headed toward Women's 2nd Best Hospital—which now is Man's 4th Best's fierce steel-cage-death-match rival for BUDDIES affection—to operate on a, quote, 'house-hold name.' I say, 'Y'got ten seconds to turn around or I make a call that'll ream you a new asshole. One thousand one, one thousand two . . . ' He laughed. By eight he turns around and comes back."

"But," said Naidoo, "aren't you afraid of what he could do to your career?"

"Nah. I got a lotta allies here. And y'may not know it, but last year I got the Man's Best Surgeon of the Year Award.' Check it out—it's listed on a brass plaque just inside the Pink Building, where the two 1816 charters are chiseled in stone."

"One more thing you should know— Oops!" Jude's hand went to her belly, and she shifted heavily in her chair. "He's a kicker, for sure." Settling, she went on. "This double booking of operations is routine. Almost *all* the ortho surgeons do it. They book two ORs at once, one slightly later than the other. The resident works in one while they're working in the other—two cases at the same time, twice the money. The patient never knows that the surgeon they signed up with will not be there."

We looked around at one another, shocked, astonished. Who knew?

"And no one tells," she went on. "Not the other doctors, not the nurses, not the anesthetists—its like omertà, the Mafia code of silence. Everybody's scared they'll lose their jobs—as I might. But it never gets out." She paused. "Till now, maybe."

"You think you're gonna get backup now?" Eddie asked.

"Well, my lawyer told me that when my gender-discrimination trial starts, she'll try to find a way to bring it in as evidence. She said that even if we can't, it could be a whistle-blower lawsuit later." She sighed. "It's really sad. They're so into their own money and prestige, they can't put themselves in another person's shoes. I said to them in the OR today, 'You know as well as I do that there's not a person in this room that would allow a family member to be treated this way. And for *money?*'"

"Craving is hell," said Berry. "And craving money's the worst. Money blinds us to suffering. Just what a doctor needs, right?"

"So we're fast approaching Whistle-blower City," said Fats. "And one thing's for sure. We've got each other's backs." He smiled at Berry and nodded. "We're totally *mutual*. Together, we deal with whatever."

"A horror show," Gath added. He yawned. "Gotta go. Early rounds tomorrow."

"Tomorrow's Sunday," I said.

"I round every Sunday morning." He got up to go.

"But why?" Naidoo asked. "Can't your resident on call round for you?"

"Well, one Sunday long ago, when I was just startin' up my practice, I asked the resident on call to make sure to check the EKG on one of my hip patients, Mrs. Daley, a mother of two small kids, before we operated on Monday. Sweet lady, kindergarten teacher, longtime friend of another of my patients. On Monday morning, he told me he'd looked at the EKG and it was fine. In pre-op, Mrs. Daley looked okay, heart sounded normal."

He paused, lowered his head, then raised it again.

"She died on the table." He bit his lip. "Yeah, he'd looked at the EKG all right, but he didn't understand what he saw—and he didn't get a cardiac consult. He didn't know what he didn't know. Imagine my having to tell her husband, the kids? Worst day of my life. So I vowed I'd never again *not* round on my patients every day, *especially* Sundays."

He stood there quietly, reliving it a little.

"But my wife's a devoted Catholic, so it gets me out of havin' t'go to church."

As we were ending, standing in the listless air as the men definitively said good-bye and started walking up the path and then stopped and waited with increasing impatience as the women started connecting with other women about when they'd next see one another and how great it all was—in what Berry said men label "the leaving-the-party *syndrome*"—Berry and I and Fats and Rosie and Humbo and Mo and Chuck and Alecia saw a police car come up the hill and stop.

Out stepped Sergeant Gilheeny and Officer Quick.

14

~

orry to be late," said Gilheeny, "but we were busy on the beat, and when we finally were almost here, we were called by Man's 4th Best TLC norse on an exigent and delicate matter. We must go straight back there, sirens blowing, but we believe that your medico-scienterrific knowledge would help—Fats, Humbo, Roy, and for her genius at genetics, Rosie. Chuck, of course, will stay with his songbird daughter, Alecia."

"Fine, fine," said Chuck, "but what'all's goin' on?"

"We policemen got first call, not five minutes ago."

"Why'all did they call you, man, instead of a doctor?"

"Because the doctor is the problem! This has to be us cops and hush-hush. And hush."

"Sickness, old age, and death," said Quick. "And not just in the patients."

"Sounds bad," said Fats.

"Ominous in its badness, yes," said the sergeant. "The perp being Jack Rowk Junior. Officer Quick? Brief them, with your brevity, which I sorely lack."

"One gomer dead. One tortoise down. To be explained as we drive."

"This Hitler Youth lad is a threat to man and beast!" Gilheeny roared. "I'll never forget looking into the ancient, sad eyes of a Galápagos tortoise. If these two could speak, they'd say, 'What the fook'n' hell has bolloxed up yer so-called *human* race?'"

"To be sure," Quick said, "it's somethin' the cockroaches'll be sayin' soon too."

In the rocking squad car, Quick was at the wheel fighting traffic, lights now flashing, siren yelling.

Gilheeny waxed philosophic, his words landing like glass shards, leaving shiny reflections. "This evening's op, to save the lives of two humans and two tortoises, has a Catholic emolument. Luke Twenty-three, made famous by that red-hot Augustine of the Libyan desert, about the two thieves crucified alongside yer man Jesus: 'Do not despair, one of the thieves was saved; do not presume, one of the thieves was damned.' Our mission tonight, of life and death of these four creatures, proves life is a goddamn crapshoot."

Close to Man's 4th, the siren and lights were turned off in the service of stealth. At a loading dock in back, other black cars and a hefty black truck without a logo sat waiting. Half a dozen figures in SWAT gear, which the policemen donned, so that Quick was puffed up to Gilheeny-size, and Gilheeny to Schwarzenegger.

Up and into the TLC. Quiet but for the machines, and a single female cry:

"*Ayy!—Hey Doc wait . . . Eee!—Hey Doc wait . . . Eye!—Hey Doc wait . . . Ohh!—Hey Doc wait . . . Uuu!—Hey Doc Wait . . . Ayy! . . .*"

Jane Doe! And she'd melded Harry the Horse's cry into her own cry? And Harry?

Fats, Humbo, and I looked at one another with horror.

A stretcher labeled "Forensic" was rolled out of a room by white-clad docs. Upon it was a black plastic body bag. The bag was shaped strangely and straining—we realized that it was in the same posture that Harry the Horse had kept in his wheelchair for years if not decades: legs bent at the knees, head locked almost into chin, viewed from the side as the letter "W"—as if he had been bagged still sitting in his wheelchair.

"So this is murder," said Gilheeny. "I've asked our dear policeman Mac-Cruiskeen to '*hit* Jack Rowk Junior with a few hard interrogations,' if you catch the teleology of my drift?"

Jane Doe was wheeled out, "*Ayy!—Hey Doc wait . . .*" echoing. It was sorrowful and, like all sorrow, strangely inspiring. A call to keep on living and not get dead.

"And where is Jane Doe going," asked Humbo, "and with Harry *el Caballo*'s cry?"

"Back to her favorite nursing home," said Quick. "The Hebrew House of the Incurables, the top floor, the one closest to heaven."

Fats turned to the head nurse, Pegeen. "Where's Jack?"

"With the tortoises."

"At this hour?" I said. "On Saturday night?"

"Tonight when Harry died suddenly," Pegeen said, "I knew it was Jack, and rotten to the core. I called Gilheeny, and he told me to call Jack—and record the call. When I told Jack that Harry was dead and maybe one of the tortoises, he shouted, 'And maybe the turtle too? Yes!' He was here in ten minutes. He's in the operating room."

"What could be better?" said Gilheeny, taking out his walkie-talkie. "Alpha team? It's a GO, but he's armed and dangerous, so treat him with yer maximum you know whats."

We followed the SWAT phalanx to a high, wide door opening onto an operating room. A moldy, earthy scent. The high-pitched shriek of a drill bounced off bare walls and corners.

Two tortoises, one caged in a dim corner, the other on an operating table in light.

The caged one faced us, standing on elephant legs, maybe four feet tall, 100 years old. More than any other living thing I'd encountered, it was *here*.

I had seen them in the Galápagos on a trip with Spring and Berry, but I had forgotten the immensity of them, the constancy and power of them. Now, for a moment, the caged one, slightly sideways to us, was as still as death. Its wrinkled black Atlas shoulders were fitted to follow under the curves of the sculpted, worn, and cracked stone rim of its carapace. Centered, protruding from this mountain, its hawk-beaked head. At the top of its beaked nose were perfectly round pitch-black holes—nostrils—and below, a mouth carved in a perpetual grin. All deathly still—and then a sudden flash of movement? *An eye?* In that immobile oval tiled head, flicked to stare at me—a *face!* Flicked, focused, seized upon, stopped. No wonder even Melville had been transfixed. I stared back at that black pupil—what was it saying to me?

For shame.

And then it looked away. *One was saved. And the other?*

The scream of the drill was horrific. The tortoise was strapped on its belly to a stainless steel operating table. In street clothes and antiseptic bright light,

Jack in goggles was drilling down into the shell, the drill meeting resistance, slipping off the 50 mossy bones welded together by time to prevent anything in nature from getting to the tortoise's vital parts.

He hadn't heard us come in. The SWAT team grabbed both drill and Jack, slammed him facedown on the table, pulled his arms back, and cuffed him.

"What the fuck do y'think y're doing? Do you know who I am?!"

The team leader looked at Gilheeny, who gave a nod that resulted in a whack of a gloved fist into Rowk's kidney, which brought a welcome scream of pain—cut off by duct tape over his mouth and a black bag over his head, and within a minute, he was out the door.

"Where are they taking him?" I asked.

"Forst, in fact, to the House of God, for the rest of the night. Gagged, tied down to a chair placed in the gyroscopic center of"—he licked his lips—"the Rose Room."

Fats and I exploded with laughter.

The Rose Room was a four-bed room on 4 North, the worst ward in the House—the ward that "broke us," driving Eat My Dust psychotic, Hooper to rounding in a wheelchair "to identify with the gomeres," and me to go just plain nuts. It was called the Rose Room because for some strange reason the four beds were always occupied by gomeres named Rose. In fact, one of them, my patient, was named Rose Budz. The worst part was that often each Rose had bowel incontinence, from plain diarrhea to the awful-smelling steatorrheac slime of malabsorption. The stench! The stench! No one could stay in the room any length of time. Jack would be there, bound and gagged, nose open—for hours.

"And now, Dr. Katie Susserman, please examine the tortoises."

A slender, fit-looking, knockout-gorgeous Asian woman of about 30 had come with the cops. She introduced herself as a "large-animal vet" from the Animal Rescue League, and went to the tortoise. With calm expertise and a certain delicacy, she examined this creature looming over her. She concluded that it was still alive, though traumatized.

"Have you ever treated one of these before?" I asked.

"Nope. She's my first of these critters."

"You can tell she's a she?" I asked.

"That part's easy. You look at her rear end. I googled 'em on the way over.

Turns out, they're real sensitive. How would you feel, having someone drill through your shell?"

"Dr. Katie," asked Fats, "is she fit to fly?"

"With me and my tech, Emme, and the equipment on the medevac plane? Yes."

"Magnificent!" shouted Gilheeny. "Quick? Tickets?"

"Here's all the paperwork," Quick said. "Got your passport, Katie?" She nodded.

"Okay," said Fats, delightedly. "Team Tortoise? Go!"

An amazing scene. The SWAT team shifted to tortoise evac—hydraulic rolling lifts, chains, cushions for the cracked mossy carapaces and massive yellow plastrons, and supplies for the long flight, including their favorite food and drink. They worked mostly in silence, with rare grunts and coordinating orders, and soon had packed up both giants in their cages, got them out of the TLC to the waiting black truck, off to the airport, and soon up into thin air. The tortoise-napping was over.

"And they're going home?" I asked. "To the Galápagos?"

"Would they be Galápagos turtles," said Gilheeny, "if they were not?"

"In a private medevac jet," Fats said, "direct to the Baltra airport, a short hop to Santa Cruz Island, and then to their own island, the remote, wild, tourist-free Genovesa."

"I'm worried," Rosie said. "The bosses are sure to find out."

"Ah, yes, darlin', they will, surely," said the sergeant.

"Jack's father's a huge donor," I said. "They could crucify you."

"Ah, but they say it's a good Christian way to go!" boomed the sergeant, "*Vida*, the guarantee of everlasting life, is it not, Quick?"

"Not quick, no—y'suffocate—but I hear that once you get through the nails—oh, and get through the thorst—it's not all that bad. They *do* say that yer thorst is the killer."

"Yes, yes," said Gilheeny, "Jack Senior's LLC is Trireme, its logo a Roman warship. He's a worldwide agent of death. Our department's linked via the Irish into the FBI and Interpol, and both are well aware of the money laundering of Rowk Senior."

"And," said Quick, "in our Darth Vader SWAT outfits, who could identify us?"

"Rescuing tortoises is one thing," I said, "but what about what we did to Junior?"

"Y'referrin' to a young man who could be indicted for the murder of a gomer?" Quick asked. "A veteran gomer who, because of Law Number One, would *never*, otherwise, die?"

"Not to mention Junior's attempted murder of a protected species—kidnapped via the black market by Black Jack Senior? *Very* bad publicity for Man's 4th Best—and fallin'."

"Still," Fats said, "the Krash is tight with Rowk Senior, and—"

"Yes, yes," Gilheeny said, with a satisfied smile, "and yes. But here's the bacon!"

He rubbed his hands together in joy.

"In the Jewish House, our Irishman's power was always tenuous. Between the Old Testament—'eyes for an eye, teeth for a tooth'—and the New—'turn the other cheek, love thy neighbor as thyself'—between these two texts there looms a vast, um . . . Quick?"

"Abysmally yawning *abyss*," Quick shot back, "an unbridgeable teleo-gapness."

"Even at its narrowest, shallowest part, 'tis so. And we—as *Christian* Irish in the *Hebrew* House—we had no potency. But here at the 4th Best, you may have noticed that the Irish patients are as populous as were the Jews at the House. Well, it turns out that when the 4th Best WASPs were desperate for cash, they put a few new-money Irish on the old-money board. And now the chairman of the board is yer man Joey Q. O'Connell, self-made rich as any in the city—loves animals, fanatic about their abuse. How else could this sweet SWAT team be financed? And how silenced will Trireme Jack's filthy gob be after a five-minute chat with Chairman of the Board J. Q. O'Connell?"

"Scheduled," Quick said, "when Senior's money Laundromat opens, to-morra morn."

Silence. Even Fats was awed by the reach of the policemen.

"Summing up," said the sergeant, "does the Irish aphorism 'We got 'im by the short and curlies' ring true in this case?"

We all agreed that it did.

"*Sí, sí,*" said Humbo. "*Tengo mucho gusto* seeing that prick beaten like a *piñata!*"

In bed, when I told Berry about all this, she was astonished and worried.

"This is serious stuff. Are you sure you're gonna be okay?"

"Not sure. But the odds are heavily yes. Fats is always thinking three steps ahead, and the cops are savvy as hell and now connected to real power at the top. I'd never take a risk like this with you and Spring and Cinnamon. The policemen have got all our backs."

"And Olive's?"

I laughed. "Got it. Olive's back is key."

We were quiet for a long moment.

"And you have no doubts about Fats?" she asked.

I was startled. "No. Why in the world would I?"

"Tonight, he seemed, well, different. Vulnerable. When Hooper shocked him."

"Yeah? So?"

"Has anyone ever brought up his obesity before?"

"Not that I can remember. It's just so much a part of him, it *is* him, and how could it matter—I mean, except for his health?"

"That's a big 'except.'"

"No foolin'. And yeah, tonight did send a jolt through me, a flicker of . . . what?" I considered this. "Doubt. Yeah, of doubt. Right from the start, I've had the sense that he'd changed, even that something was eating him—"

"'Eating'? Perfect."

"I mean, something wasn't right in him. Nothing that limits him, but a lot of little things—I mean, in the House, I only saw him vulnerable once, after Potts died—we cried together."

"Yes, I remember you telling me that." She yawned. "Honey, I am . . . *really* tired. . . ."

"Just one more thing?"

She murmured, "'Kay."

"What do you think is different in him?"

"For one thing, he's a food addict. Addicted to carbos mainly. Compulsive overeater."

"Addict? C'mon. It was just the party, the celebration."

"Have you ever seen him in this kind of setting before? Outside the hospital, a purely social setting? I never have. And with a woman?"

I thought about this. "No, except for that day in Canyon de Chelly."

"Right. The day that he was recruiting you, us. He was at his best."

"So?"

"So addicts don't let other people see them in social settings, in their active addiction—*you* know that, Roy. You've treated tons of them. For some reason, tonight he did let us all see it. Maybe it was his cry for help?"

"That's going a little far, don't you think?"

"Could be, sure. But did you notice how he even stared at the dog treats given to Cinny and Chubby?"

"Now that you mention it, yeah."

"When the compulsion gets really bad," she went on, "addicts wind up drinking or drugging alone, right?"

"Yeah. The 'disease of isolation.'"

"Why else didn't you ever see him outside the House that whole intern year?"

"I saw him once, at his Christmas party."

"Hmm." Another yawn. A snuggle up against me. I was losing her.

"If he's an addict, he's the most high-functioning, high-bottom addict in the world."

She yawned, mumbled something like, "He's let himself go. . . ."

"But *why*? Why the change now?"

"Maybe," she said, "maybe he feels that he—and all of you who are counting on him—that he's in over his head, and he's going to, for the first time in his life, in his work, fail?"

"Hard to believe he could—or that he'd really doubt . . . *himself*. But maybe."

"Or . . ." Another yawn. "And this is my *last* guess for the night, okay?"

"Okay."

"Maybe it's love?"

"Love?"

"For him, his first love? . . . In over his head? G'night."

"What?"

No reply. Except a semisnore, kind of charming. I smiled at her.

Sleep tight, dear one.

She was right. I *had* seen doubt in his eyes. *Doubt? In him? My rock? Our rock, our mountain. Shit.* Now, exhausted yet wired, as is often the case in a night of joy and wrenching that pushes you to the edge of your spirit, I opened to sleep and what drifted in was a joyous and dire day in the Galápagos with Spring and Berry. All of us tourists had been dropped off by the Zodiacs from the mother ship on an island with a beach. It was birthing time for seals, and we'd gotten close enough to witness every part from the slipperying out of the babies tied by the umbilical cords and the afterbirths that the gulls prized, and watching the mother seals go out to fish for their older pups and come back.

Walking down the beach alone on the other side of a rocky rise to a more hidden beach, I saw a baby seal lying just above the tide line, alone, still, waiting for the mother and the fish, but the mother had not come back and the little seal lay there, quite still and perhaps dead. Two gulls were close to it, watching. One hopped over and pecked at it and the seal twitched and the gull fluttered away a little farther, watching. I didn't know what to do because it is strictly forbidden for tourists to interfere with any animal on the islands, but this was heart wrenching, and the mother might still appear and save it, and so I went to the seal and sat and watched it, guarded it, really, my doctor's brain noting that while it seemed to be lying completely still, its tiny chest was rising and falling. I glared at the gull, but it wasn't his fault, so I decided to stay as long as I could to shoo it away—against the strict law for tourists on the islands. Hoping the mom would come back. I sat on the sand nearby.

From time to time the gull would sneak in and peck, the seal would twitch, and I would chase it away until a guide was signaling me from the landing area for the last Zodiac of the day. Hustling back to the ship, and sad as hell, I left.

From the Zodiac I saw a few more pecks, twitches. But soon I saw only the small beach and a brown shape and a white speck. And then no more small beach at all but just the big beach, smeared brown with hundreds of seals and no white specks, and I gave up.

But on the big anchored boat as the sun was going down, I found myself at the rail facing the same beach maybe a half mile away and the sun was illuminating it, and my eyes walked from the landing beach and over the rocky rise and then to the curve of the small beach of the baby seal and the gull, but from this distance, I could identify only the larger beach, and the hundreds of seals—mothers, fathers, babies, and youngsters in between—all now little more than specks, and behind me on deck was the after-dinner crowd of tourists hurrying to the stern, where the underwater lights had been turned on to attract sharks. The human chatter was not a comfort.

I felt a flood of sorrow for what had to be the death of that seal, but then I had a gut sense of the millions of years, tens of millions, of that cleaver of death and life over and over again and then billions of years of undersea eruptions giving birth first to raw, hot volcanoes naked of life till vegetation in millions of years conquered them, and then gulls and seals and Darwins, and I felt a . . . yes, a *release. It was all right. It* is *all right.*

A drama of a life and a death that, like our own, and given the billions of years of the volcanoes, was just a speck but because of its speckness crying out to be treated all that much more kindly, with more *humane weight* on the scale of things, just because it and we all *are specktral, and here. Way more. All in the same boat.*

"Hey, Dad, come see the sharks!" Spring called to me. I went to her and Berry.

I put my arms around them, my insanely beloveds, and sensed an immense kindness beyond me yet with me and them and then with the other mere humans and, from a safe distance above, I watched the sharks.

15

Every year, Berry and I spent Thanksgiving with both our families, and Fats had agreed to a week off. Our parents had lived in two Hudson River towns, Albany and Columbia, only an hour away from one another, and played golf together halfway between, at Winding Brook Country Club, which allowed Jews. When they retired, they bought condos in Sarasota, Florida, this time about half an hour apart, at separate golf clubs. After trying hard to be friends, their differences had gotten the better of them, and they rarely saw one another.

Even when Berry and I were hard at work in our doctor training, the one thing we both insisted on, in our scheduling, was having Thanksgiving vacation together off duty. As usual, this year we had only five days, including travel.

We were leaving town in fairly good shape. Berry's practice was almost full. Her training to become a Buddhist teacher was yet another life edge on which she was happy. Jack Rowk Junior had gotten a temporary medical reassignment to a boutique hospital in a wealthy suburb to do a research project on the quality, safety, and profit in boutique hospitals in wealthy suburbs. The policemen, and we of the FMC, had won this round.

"Ready?" Berry asked me as we stood at the front door of her mom and dad's condo on Palme Aire Golf Association.

"No," I answered.

She rang the doorbell. I braced myself. Thanksgiving. You have to understand that I had worked on this moment for weeks. In long talks with Berry, in realms of mind, body, and spirit. She had also led me in several industrial-strength, full-catastrophe guided meditations—walking me through what now was about to happen in reality. I was as prepared as I ever would be. I vowed to try my best.

The subject of all this preventive work? Berry's mother, Roz. I admired her. She was a wonderful woman. Like the other three of our parents, she was a child of immigrants and grew up in New York City. She was well educated, a terrific reader and volunteer at all sorts of good causes. Her paid work for decades had been as the administrator of Albany Region Head Start, a federal program that helped underprivileged preschoolers get a good start in school and life. And she was also a terrific artist, painting huge colorful canvases that echoed Picasso, Klee, and Chagall and that she displayed in local exhibitions; recently she had gotten an agent for her work. She and her husband, Allie, an organic chemist working for Sterling Drug, had for many years taken under their wing foreign students at local colleges to try to help them learn English. Good people, both.

The bad news? Not her. Me.

Always, after being with her for about two minutes, for some reason I would turn into a monster. Two minutes, tops.

Now at the door, Berry offered up a last helpful hint: "Find the right emotional distance from which you can be empathic."

"Sounds good."

The door opened. There she was. Luckily she first reached for Spring.

"My girl Spring!" A hug.

She then greeted Berry with a hug, remarking on her dazzling new 240-dollar haircut from one Antonio, with: "Oh my! I love your hair, dear!"

Berry and Spring were then gone, heading toward Allie, who was beaming with happiness behind Roz.

Next was me.

"*Dr.* Basch," she said warmly, opening her arms to me, waiting, staring expectantly. "Welcome. I've been talking about you to all my doctors—they've *all* read *The House of God* and are dying to meet you. If you like, I could invite a few over for drinks, and you can sign their books."

She was waiting for my response.

I was already frozen.

Sensing my chill, she searched to take my hand, which was frozen to my hip, and so she kissed me on the cheek and I plummeted down into an abyss.

I had turned into a monster.

Stiff, cold, freeze-dried. I knew that there was nothing wrong with *her*. It was all me, Monster Basch.

In preparation for the encounter, Berry had tried hard to offer an explanation. She said that when her mother came toward me, it stirred up Male Relational Dread. This, she said, was "normal" for men. When a woman, yearning to connect, approaches—say, asking, "What are you *feeling*, hon?"— we men often sense a creeping coldness in our guts and then a freezing in our hearts. Our brains lock. Our eyes glaze—women notice this. And what's in our male minds?

Nothing good can come of my going into this. It's just a matter of how bad it will be before it's over. And it will never be over.

Now I was totally in it. I grasped at a straw: *What would the policemen do?*

No transmission came through. I'd failed again.

I knew that Berry was onto something, that most men feel this at some time or other—that it's normal. But whenever in hell had *knowing* helped a person not turn monstrous?

And so, getting only Frozen Neanderthal from me, Roz gave me a warm smile and turned back to Spring.

I shook Allie's hand. I loved the guy, thanked my lucky stars for him. Berry had his looks—sweet face, slender legs and hips—and had both his brilliance and kindness. After all these years, I loved her in him and loved him. He had become a dear drinking buddy.

"How 'bout a Scotch?" he asked. "And a cigar?"

"A double, on ice, with a beer chaser. And a cigar."

All that preparation, and I had lasted, maybe, 30 seconds.

From that moment on, our visit to the tiny-roomed condo alongside the wide green expanse of the eleventh fairway of the "development" was like every other visit. At first we both were glad that Spring would monopolize her grandparents' attention.

Berry and I and Allie, out on the periphery of the Roz-Spring lovefest, started in on the Scotch. I soon retreated to the small guest bedroom and took solace in *Heart of Darkness*, reading it slowly, drinking it in, for the umpteenth time.

⚶

"How bad is it?" Berry asked in bed that night, Spring asleep on the floor. The low ceiling fan, which would whack my head if I wasn't careful, loomed, waiting to attack.

"Worse than ever. I know that your mom is a wonderful person. None of this is her fault. It's all me."

"Just try not to lash out, okay, like the last time?"

"Is freeze-dried okay?"

She rolled her eyes.

"Every fiber of my being will be focused on doing better," I promised. "Golf with Allie will help."

"It's not easy for me either, you know," she said.

"It's horrible for you. I wish I could be human and help. Maybe more booze?"

"Well, being with her isn't as bad as tomorrow will be, with your mom and dad."

"Hey, tomorrow will be easy for me. No problems."

"How's that?"

"I'll kill myself before we go."

⚶

Because my father's letter said that Spring could not stay with the Conquistadores, I had not wanted to do Florida at all, and as an alternative I had suggested we spend Thanksgiving with the Navajo. But Berry had insisted. So we compromised. We'd split our time and do both.

If Thanksgiving Day with Berry's parents was a bit difficult for me, the next day with the family Basch was worse for all three of us. Berry and I were resentful of the Conquistador rules. Rose and Sig were resentful of having only this one dinner with us, to the Moonblooms' two.

The Basch celebratory meal in their tiny fourth-floor condo at Conquistador overlooking a wide expanse of the green-painted parking lot was tense, the food dicey. The main course was what my mother thought was my favorite, brisket. I had told her for decades that I loathed brisket, especially her famous recipe of it: à la burned. It was hard to find any booze in the condo. The horrific Château Mogen David had to do. Nobody else smoked, and I had to go out on the small balcony for a Parodi.

But this time, dinner was punctuated by something new. My father's rage at my mother had finally come to a head. Decades ago she had had an acoustic neuroma whose surgery was botched, leaving her with a facial palsy and deafness in one ear. Periodically when she spoke, my father would mutter: "Stupid bitch!" or "Idiot!" or "Damn moron!"

She didn't hear this, but we did. It was paralyzing, the visciousness. Could it be Tourette's syndrome?

After dinner, I took him aside and asked him about it.

"What?" he said, surprised. "I don't do that and would never."

"Yes, you do."

"I certainly don't and so forth."

I gave up.

When I said good-bye to my mom, she, as usual, started to weep—one of her resentments was "I hate to cry out of just one eye." Now she said, "You never leave enough time for us. We never get to talk."

The sorrow, the rank darkness, floored me. As we walked away, glancing back once at them, two shrunken people standing side by side down the dim hallway, trapped in their shared hatred and, yes, support for each other, I felt my heart wrench this way and that, on its tree of ribs.

On the half-hour ride back on Route 41, Berry asked Spring how she liked seeing them and she said quietly, "Good," and went back to playing with her new digital watch. After she was asleep, Berry and I processed.

"It's so sad," Berry said. "Imagine living in that hell?"

"Hard to. I . . . I feel for both of them. I mean, they started with such hope!"

True. Children of immigrants, they had gotten great public school educations in the city. She was a child prodigy at piano, had graduated from college at 17. He, though rejected by medical schools because of the Jewish quota, became what he always referred to, with great pride, as "a professional man"— a dentist.

"Such hope, and now such hell! I can't remember a single moment of affection between them. But this is the worst. I wish I could help."

"I don't know how you came out of that without going crazy or killing yourself."

"Sports, and you, saved me. You taught me everything I know about being with another person."

"Most men, if they're honest, will say that everything they learned about relationships they learned with a woman."

"Most men are not that honest."

She laughed. "If a man's lucky, he has a good mom and learns from her, from how she does it with others and with him. Without a good mom, if you're lucky, you run into a good woman, someone who loves you and wants to grow with you, and grow you too."

"I remember, early on, you stared at me and said, 'Oh, my God. You are completely *unsocialized*!' I'm so lucky you took on the job."

"It ain't over."

"Thanks, hon. I just wish I could do that for you too."

She smiled. "You do—in your hanging in with me and Spring, and growing us both, and appreciating my trying to live out on my edge too. I never, ever doubt your love."

"Me too. How's it for you so far, this trip?"

"Impossible yet doable. Trying hard for Spring's sake. Finding that empathic distance." She yawned. "I tried to talk to your mom about my work with 'relationship,' and she said to me, 'Hmm. I never knew there *was* something called a relationship.'" She sighed. "It's been a frightful day."

"Full of fright, yeah," I said. "But tomorrow, the Navajo. Talk about irony!"

Among traditional Navajo men, mother-in-law avoidance is a strict cultural rule. If your mother-in-law is in a room, you are not allowed to enter.

The next morning we flew to Arizona, and drove north to the main Indian Health Service hospital serving the Navajo, in Fort Defiance. We had spent two months there in training. The Navajo are the poorest Americans, with the highest rate of just about any disease.

Early on, in an orientation lecture, a Navajo elder who worked at the hospital told a story:

"'We own the land,' the white man said to us. We said, 'The land owns us. We get our stories from the land.' The white man said, 'We own the land.' And we said, 'If you own the land, tell us its stories.' They had no stories." He paused. "An old chief, near death, who had once been free told me this: 'I was poor and thin. Now I am large and fat. Because so many liars have been sent out to me, and I have been filled up with lies.'"

What's there to say to genocide? America *paying* Americans to kill "the savages"?

We just listened.

We, as *bilagáana*—whites—and doctors, had to learn how to read our patients, the *Diné*, the "people." In a meeting with a patient, for the doc to talk first was impolite. Even if it was an emergency, we tried to wait until the patient, or a family member, finally spoke. Direct questions could be assaults. We took care not to look directly at one another. Avoiding eye contact for a while on meeting was a measure of respect. The waiting was a weighted anticipation. Especially when dire physical things brought them into the Chinle clinic. But when it finally came, when the head rose and the burned brown irises met our greens or blues, there was often a jolt, a heated, even hot contact. It said: *now listen, hard.*

Often when I—through an interpreter—asked, "What is the matter?" the patient would say, "I don't know. I'm just feeling somehow." To any specific question—"Is there pain?" "I'm just feeling somehow." It could be nothing or incipient death. Eventually it would come out; blood tests often helped. But we learned that Navajo illness is different—a disease could be an evil spirit called a skinwalker, say, in the guise of a rattlesnake that crossed their path a year ago. This *hózhq*—harmony, or beauty, living in balance—this Native health and healing embraced past events, spirits, and the place of the particular person in a universal history and cosmos. We came to see this as a sophisticated awareness of what we now might label holistic: body, mind, spirit. In cause and treatment.

Being doctors for them in the Indian Health Service meant learning to live and work at the juncture of "traditional" healing and "modern" medicine. We had been taught that medicine was a reductive science of disease. But the Native medicine man—the *hataalii*, or "singer," because the healing was often sung and chanted—taught that medicine was harmony and disharmony: that the bursts of disharmony in our lives were symptoms of endemic, global, spiritual imbalances. All things in the universe are of equal significance—from a little lime green lizard, to a herd of sheep, to a crowd of humans, to a comet. Bodily or mental things are symptoms of spiritual ones beyond any lone person, yet quietly killing that any lone one. As one of the senior white docs at Fort Defiance had said to us back then: "*We* are the alternative medicine here."

Disharmony in the world causing disease? The treatment, harmony?

From Fort Defiance we drove north onto the high mesa and canyon lands, toward the little town of Chinle and the small clinic that had been our home for two years. We had been able to arrange just one full day—and two nights—there.

The drive up, with rare thunderheads and a whiteout snow squall, took longer than we expected. When we finally got there, it was dark and freezing and moonless. Our loyalty had always been to the Thunderbird Lodge, the only Navajo-designed and -owned motel and the closest to the entrance to Canyon de Chelly. When we got out and stretched, the mile-high mesa air tasted like cold quarters and we could see a long way.

We checked in and felt at home—not only because the owners and the staff had been our patients, but also seeing again, in our room, the Navajo coverlet on the bed—lavender with stripes of bright yellow for the sacred corn pollen, blue for sky, white for lightning, and symbols in turquoise and silver of eagles and sacred bears.

Ravenous, we had a celebratory dinner surrounded by friends—word had spread fast. All three of us had been adopted by these remarkably kind people. How had their immense genocidal suffering transformed to kindness?

Visiting Spring's first nursery school—Mesa View, in the center of the small town—watching her lapse into Navajo words, talking about horses and cows and dogs and Olive, and then visiting our clinic—how small it looked!—brought back sparks of spirit from our close hard work together. A real team, in bad and brutal circumstances, trying to do good. It filled us with sharp-edged memories, and joy. But joy soul-shifted, to the nostalgia of sorrow.

We could get out. But we have no tribe. You do. We were part of yours, for a while. We lost something by leaving you.

Out on the street again, Berry said, "This place healed us."

"Yes. The first year eased us down from the insanity of Mount Misery, and the second year lifted us up."

"This is all so . . ." She hesitated, thinking. "So expansive, whole. I'd forgotten so much already. I'm wondering why we left to go back east again."

"Because Richard told us that it was time."

Richard Yázhe was a *Diné* medicine man, a thin, tall guy our age, a dedicated athlete, his square brown face framed in wire-rimmed glasses. We met in his living room on his ranch near Chinle. He listened deeply and did part of the Blessing Way healing ritual with us—an eagle feather and sacred sticks to sweep and tap our bodies for evil spirits; turquoise-and-silver statuettes. He said that, as doctors, we needed to take what we had learned from our two years with the *Diné* and be an example of it back home in our own communities, in our own way. I had said there weren't real communities where we lived; Berry said, "Speak for yourself"—and it was true.

She, as always, had found women friends outside of these "Best" medical institutions, in many different but linked communities: relational psychology, Buddhism, antiracism and other political action.

Richard explained again the core of Navajo healing, Walking in Beauty: not the "beauty" we usually think of, but living in balance and harmony *with* yourself and the world—body, mind, spirit, and the right relationship *with* community, family, the whole natural and animal world, and *with* water, air, earth. If a person honors these relationships, he said, "they walk in Beauty."

He sang parts of the Beauty Way to us in Navajo, and translated the last line: "In Beauty it is finished."

As we left, our steps felt light.

"Yes," I said to her now. "He said we were ready, but . . . but even as difficult as medicine was here, it was more down in the dirt, the trenches, with not much bookkeeper crap. Talking Stick, the IHS computer screen, was *friendly*—no billing for profit, no thousands of clicks, no gaming the system, no lying for big bucks. Like at the VA, no more war across the screen, just writing down what's good for docs and others to know about patients. And it was interop—could send data to all IHS and VA screens in the country. So now, back home, I'm trapped in Big Bucks Medicine at Man's 4th Best?" I shook my head, searching for words. "What I'm caught up in at the 4th is *really hard*. Medicine's tougher than ever. There's no way I can honor the good stuff we learned here. Back east, I've barely even *noticed* sky, land—people living in spirit—not since we left."

"I know, hon. Me too. But let's both keep trying to hold this, the honoring. For better or worse, we belong there, not here."

"I'm not sure I belong anywhere."

"I know that too, and I'm sorry. But finally there's one place you do belong."

"Where's that?"

"In the here and now, with us."

By noon, the sun warming Chinle from 14 to 73, we drive along the south rim of Canyon de Chelly, cut by water from the north, high in the Chuska Mountains, 200 million years ago. The Anasazi first settled there at the time of the woolly mammoth, the giant ground sloth, and camels. In the parking lot, we see a big new sign: "*Warning:* Visitors are Advised About the Increased Criminal Activity of Theft from Vehicle (Car Clouts) at the White House Overlook Parking Area." It lists six things to watch for and do.

As we sit at the entrance to the White House trail, putting on our gear and packing our backpacks, we watch a Navajo woman pass by. She seems to have appeared suddenly out of the high desert along the rim, a lean black-and-white rez dog following after. White-haired, bronze face weathered, she wears a long purple skirt, red velveteen vest, and a Pendleton shirt. Her blouse is the bright red of arterial blood. Gold lightning flashes across it. A turquoise-and-silver bear is around her neck. A golf umbrella, sectored in blue and white and proclaiming *Citibank*, shades her. She walks past without eye contact, slips through what seems solid red stone at the mouth of the trail down into the canyon, her wiry dog following. As suddenly as they have come, they are gone.

"Amazing," I said. "I'd forgotten how they can appear and disappear, like spirits."

After an easy hike down through the Georgia O'Keeffe wind-hollowed and polished red sandstone channels of the path, we come out on the floor of the canyon and, looking up, are hit with that rare sense of awe, that moment when all awareness of "self" is lost to being with, yes, what's in the here and now. Our eyes see it as new. The red iron and stone black streaks of millennia of metal residue fall in diagonal waves down 1,000 feet along the yellow faces of the cliff, as if carefully painted, leading our eyes almost to the bottom to a black gash in the cliff, an eyebrow, inside of which we know is the face of the ancient cliff dwelling called the White House Ruin. On the flat sandbar along the river, we start to walk.

We sit across the river from it. No tourists have come—it's not the season. Unlike in summer, when the river is a trickle, so you can wade across and get closer, now it is a torrent hurrying fast past us, as if herself fleeing winter.

Luckily, we are still in the sun. Out of sight to our right is the soaring Sacrifice Rock, at the entrance to Canyon del Muerto, where the Navajo made their last stand against Kit Carson. Sacrifice Rock is where "Spider Woman" dwells. Mothers tell their children to behave or she'll come down, snatch them up, fly to the top where she lives—and eat them. On the facing sandy bank of the river is a small grove of cottonwoods, now bare of leaves. Berry has always said that their leaves' fluttering in the breeze is really sensual. Boding well for our time tonight in bed at the Thunderbird after Spring falls asleep. In our time here, so immersed were we in the land and the animals and having time with each other, our sex was the best ever—earthy, free, inflamed by the strange present spirits of this ancient world, always all around us. Spirited and spiritual, yes, with the native spirits alive all around us every day. We let go! Sex, love? As close in body as we ever had been.

Now our eyes are drawn to the cave dwellings.

The cave is set in the cliff face like a teardrop set on its side. Our eyes climb the dots of foot- and handholds up, and search the clay structures. The Anasazi, the "Old People," built these dwellings of wood and fired mud. The lower row of dwellings are the red-sand color of the cliffs—some are homes, some are for storing food and water, and two are kivas, sacred meeting chambers with holes in the roofs for fires. Ladders lead up from their flat roofs to the doorways of another house, set back a little, like a hat set back on a head. This topmost dwelling is stark white. It shines in the sun, brighter for the shadows. The current crop of humans named it the White House. After living here for thousands of years, the Anasazi vanished forever. No one knows why.

Before we start back, I lead Berry and Spring off the path along the river, deeper into the canyon. Will I remember it right? We walk. The river curves. I think that I've forgotten, think to turn back—but, finally, yes. At the base of the cliff face, there's a hogan—a traditional dwelling of the Navajo—made of mud and wood, eight sided, positioned on the spirit axes of the *Diné* world, corners pointing to the four sacred mountains. With no electricity or heat, these are ancient homesteads. People raise corn, have orchards, herd sheep, make dyes from the plants, and weave the wool into rugs and clothes that capture, in zigzag patterns, all.

This hogan has a basketball hoop—bent a bit, with no net—and a cleared dirt circle around it. I had gotten to know James Yazzi and his brother, Ben, when James played on the basketball team and I was the team doctor. His grandparents live in this hogan, which is closed down for the winter. The family migrates up to a trailer on the mesa, driving their sheep there. James, a kid with a wide-open heart, once told me: "My best place—like most of my friends—is in my grandmom's hogan."

With the help of a Navajo medicine man, I took care of the whole Yazzi family. After I'd helped one of their women through a rough pregnancy—a risk of preeclampsia—the family asked Berry and me to come to the birth, in this hogan, with a *hataalii* in charge. In the dirt floor they had dug a hole, shallow and covered with a sheepskin. Looped through a hook in the center of the hogan, a white-and-red sash was suspended. The smell of cedar was strong, smudged on the walls, a calming scent. The pregnant girl squatted over the hole, in each hand an end of the sash, to pull and push the baby through. It had a deep simplicity, even an elegance, and all went well.

Finally late that last evening, in the Wildcat Den Field House, which seats about 6,000 in a town of only 4,000, the final basketball games of the season were on, starting with girls' and boys' JV teams, then girls' varsity, and finally boys' varsity. I was friends with the coach, John Nez, who was known to be a genius of Rez Ball and who had once won the league championship for Chinle's archenemy, the Window Rock Fighting Scouts. For the past two years, he'd switched loyalties to the Wildcats and, after a losing season the year before, had made them a power in the conference. The stakes were high: whoever won would win the league, go on to the state championship. For two years I had been the Anglo doctor for the team. Being a basketball player had saved my life, and it was great to be in it again. Here I'd gotten to know the boys, and from Coach John I'd learned every trick and winning strategy of Rez Ball. Since the tallest player was barely six feet, the Wildcats compensated with an energy bordering on insanity, with speed and hustle and heart. Because they lived their whole lives at over 5,000 feet, their high blood hemoglobin carried more oxygen—they could run forever.

So Rez Ball boiled down to run run run, throwing up shots, whirling-dervish cuts and passes and driving hard toward the basket with little idea what to do when they got there, and diving for balls on the hardwood and rebounding with elbows and hard box-outs by hips—to compensate for their stature. John often had trouble trying to get them to play together, to use their spirit and fire not just on an attacking offense but for defense too, and thinking ahead toward plays. They were crackerjack shots, from any part of the court.

John saw himself not only as a coach, but as a mentor. He knew he was teaching them things that might lift them out of the violence, alcoholism, and drugs, the depressed and suicidal culture of teens on the rez—get them coveted scholarships to colleges, to a better life, from which they might come back, to help. But the trap of poverty and all those years of being pissed upon by the dominant white culture made these kids—who seemed so invincible and confident on the court—all the more vincible and doubting off it, doubting they could survive outside. The ripping apart by the long traumas went so deep that even these "star" basketball players, some of whom were also star students, felt a nagging sense of not being worth it. Their bond on the court, their sense that their *team* was worth a lot and this year was winning a lot, made them proud but vulnerable. During the season when I was with them, the team, usually amazing sharpshooters on the court, had two bad games when all of them seemed to be in a shooting slump. They lost games they should have won. One player said that in the last game when he was shooting, he'd sensed a brown blur around the hoop, as if Coyote Trickster were there. A *hataalii* was called in, did a ritual cleansing of the gym and the team—and that night they shot the lights out, their highest percentage of the year. John Nez was a gem, my best friend in Chinle.

I'll never forget one night after a bad loss. John and I at the Wildcat Den Bar spoke about all the hopelessness on the rez, especially the rate of teen suicide, which had exploded. Native Americans already had the highest rates of a lot of the worst things measured in America: poverty, unemployment, high school dropout frequency, twice as much domestic violence and sexual abuse and neglect, PTSD rates higher than those of returning vets, divorce, epidemic alcoholism, drugs, TB, measles, even plague. And the biggest ones, provoked by all this because how could they not be? Depression and suicide. Once Berry asked a group of 15 teenagers she was counseling how many knew a young person who had taken his or her life. The hands of all 15 went up. One told the story of a girl named Little Wind who killed herself and lay in her bed for 90 days before anyone found her—her death followed the suicides of her father and her sister.

"All these things seep real deep into these kids' lives," said John. "The game they're in now, the life game, is dire. But this, this," he said, "this suicide shit is off the charts. Ten times greater than the national average. Mostly girls, but a lot of boys. There's a tamarack tree just out of town on Route Seven, near the Chevron station? A girl hung herself there a few months ago. Young kids are told by their grandmothers not to touch it, not to climb it—it's taboo. In the past six months, we've had eight kids kill themselves. Every kid on this team has known someone who did it." He shook his head sadly; his eyes got moist. He took out an oversized, crisply pressed white handkerchief bearing the Wildcat logo of two wildcat paws in dark blue. He wiped away tears, stuffed the handkerchief back into his slacks.

"Y'know, Roy, the thing I'm most proud of now, after all these years coaching? None of my boys have killed themselves."

We arrived during the boys' varsity warmups. The field house was packed. People drove hundreds of miles to the games. Once I'd gone with the team bus to a game in Tuba City, 280 miles round-trip, all in one day and night. Many of the fans now were dressed in traditional clothing, and had drums and flutes with them. Before the game started, I went to John and the team and was greeted with high fives. I could tell they were ready. John and I arranged to meet after the game at the Wildcat Den Bar.

A hush. The Window Rock Fighting Scouts were introduced and then the Chinle Wildcats—both running on court to wild cheers and insane thunder drumming from fans.

The game was intense. First one team led, then the other, and at the half it was tied. They went back and forth furiously, boys throwing themselves at the basket on drives, and throwing elbows at one another, roughing one another up under the boards. I knew they were longtime rivals—but this was war. For one of them the season would end; one would go on to the state tournament. The refs tried to control the escalating roughness, to little avail. With only 15 seconds left and the score tied, the high scorer and senior captain, Ben Yazzi, going up for a rebound, was elbowed violently by one of the Fighting Scouts, and retaliated with a swing at his head, his fist glancing off his neck. The Fighting Scout went down. A technical foul was called. The Fighting Scout player made two foul shots. With ten seconds left, Ben raced the ball upcourt, faked one way and then crossed over and with time running out had a clear long shot at the buzzer. It looked good all the way and bounced softly once, then a second time more softly, and then, dying, rolled around the rim—and fell out. The Window Rock team celebrated, jumping like crazy into a pile on the two paws of the Wildcats logo at center court. They would go to the Arizona High School Tournament. The Wildcat season was over. For seniors like Ben, organized basketball was over for good.

The Wildcats team trudged to the bench, forced by John to stay. Some watched the celebration; others, like Ben, put towels over their faces. Finally, the coaches formed the two teams in two parallel lines, and with the captains leading, each player shook the opponents' hands. Ben's face was still partly covered. Then both teams walked back through the tunnel to their locker rooms.

After being stuck in traffic and watching the long snake of red taillights winding out of Chinle toward empty mesa, I finally got Berry and Spring back to the Thunderbird Lodge to pack for our early start to the Albuquerque airport. I went back to the gym, knowing that John Nez would take time with the team before meeting me. I sat in the empty gym, in a strange way comforted by my times in similar losses, and wins, which had grown me up.

Finally, he came out. We walked to the bar, got a booth.

I sipped bourbons on ice with beer chasers, John a Diet Coke. He spoke softly, about how the seniors would have to see whether college—or even trade school or junior college—was a real answer for them. It was hard to leave the reservation. Only a few had a dream—like the playmaking guard Willy Grand, who was going to junior college to learn irrigation: "So I can bring it back to livestock and people on the rez."

"What about Ben?" I asked.

"He doesn't know. Grades not that good. Too much basketball, maybe. I'm a little worried about him." I grimaced. "Yeah. I usually feel like I did my best with each of 'em, but tonight, I dunno. I just couldn't get through to them like I always could before. I mean about keeping our cool. I was tough on 'em at halftime, told 'em they were freelancing too much, not playing like a team, like they know how to—at their best. Maybe I was *too* tough on 'em—said they weren't fighting hard enough. Well, I guess they fought, or at least Ben did. He never lost control like that in a game before. Wonder what's goin' on with him at home. No dad, two obese sisters hangin' around, goin' nowhere, mother in a menial job."

All of a sudden I recalled a nightmare I'd had recently about a Navajo boy jumping off Spider Rock. Had I dreamed Ben's face? I couldn't remember. I told John.

"Shit," he said. "Let's go."

We took his pickup, soon leaving the paved road and bouncing along badly, as if the Chevy would rather be in bed. On the moonless expanse of high mesa, there was nothing but black and stars. Finally, in the distance, a light. As we got closer we saw it was shining over a rundown trailer. The trailer was dark. No cars or trucks. Nobody?

I got real scared. I looked over at John. He was scared too.

None of my boys have killed themselves.

We got out and walked toward the trailer but then heard a sound that right then was just about the most comforting sound I'd ever heard, akin to a breech baby's first cry.

Butt . . . butt-butt. Clang.

We rushed around the trailer. Under the streetlamp, a flat hard-dirt patch, a pole with a backboard and rim—without a net—and Ben Yazzi, practicing his jump shot.

John went to Ben, who now, surprised, was holding his ball on his hip like a mom would a baby. He didn't move as his coach walked toward him and then stopped, opening his arms to him. The boy bowed his head into the man's shoulder.

His record is intact. Because of this. Because his players know this. This with. This harmony. This Walk in Beauty.

16

I t was a freezing, windy, icy-roaded Monday morning in mid-December. All of us at the FMC were busy seeing our first patients, the family Vance—a mixed blessing. After the Vances, Fats had cleared out time for a special two-hour check-in. He had not told us why.

All the Vance generations—now into the fourth, thanks to the recent birth of baby Luigi Vance, after a hysterical mother and a normal pregnancy—arrived together for their appointments with us at the same hour. Not all of them, all the time, but it was amazing how religiously they made an unhealthy quorum. Ever since that first day when Lance Vance, one of the twins, had had his cardiac arrest and stent, we had held periodic conferences to compare notes and try to puzzle out the latest Vance twister, in four diagnostic vessels: somatic? Psycho? Psychosomatic? Beyond our cosmologies? It was always amazing and mostly fun—because the Vances maintained, even in dire straits, a certain modest goodwill. Treating them was great bonding for us—to laugh together and at the same time solve tricky problems in the health care of them all.

In them, over several months, we had witnessed the course and progression of the common diseases, especially diabetes and its complications. Too much unregulated sugar in the diet ravages every organ system, from toes, through GI tract and heart, to the tiny vessels in the retina, and it can lead to blindness, mushy dementia—and, per Hooper's research, cancer. Like the pervasive effects of alcohol—which is, after all, a distilled sugar. Carbos kill.

In the family Vance, diabetes didn't just run; it raced.

It was sad to see the acquired type 2 diabetes showing up earlier and earlier, like in a cute nine-year-old who'd been a surprise pregnancy, Chance Vance. And now, for the first time, in a baby, Luigi. He had come into the world with type 1 diabetes, the genetic kind—but with no genetic family history. Were we seeing, in one generation, an acquired trait gone genetic? Unheard of! Except what we'd heard from Denis Noble via Fats.

In our periodic all-team-Vance conferences, we talked about attending to all the psychosocial therapies for diabetes: adequate diet, medical literacy, level of stress, and of course—in those too young to landscape—physical fitness. All fairly futile. The birth of baby Luigi was a warning. Insulin was lifesaving, a necessity for diabetics. It had been off patent for almost a century. Pharma didn't even produce it; *bacteria* produced it. It was brewed up in huge vats like beer, costing almost nothing. But the cost to the Vances and others? 500 dollars a month, 6,000 dollars a year. Not counting pumps and needles. At least the Vances, honest landscapers and taxidermists, could afford to be gouged by Big Pharma.

But they were always kind of kindly, and astute. Lovable.

Naidoo and Hyper Hooper handled the kids, with his Eat Red plan—red and purple veggies and fruits; even watermelon (lycopene) and strawberries (polyphenols) and his dynamite pomegranate shakes—and exercise and attention. The rest of us tried to help the older ones for other, common diseases, but somehow there was often a strange twist, from surgical hypochondria to bizarre and patriotic combinations of red, white, and blue (platelet) blood dyscrasias. Once, narcolepsy: the other middle-aged Vance twin, walking from the waiting area toward Eddie, suddenly sighed and collapsed, asleep. Also, strange infections and rashes, transient paralyses, and virulent sleep disorders. Mostly, we couldn't discover a treatable cause for anything Vance. Despite their real pain and suffering, they were almost always of good cheer, believing in us and our expertise, rooting us on—delightful, in a way. *Patient* patients. And had given us great lawn and garden advice all through the summer and fall. And taxidermy? Well, none of us had animals needing to be taxidermed.

While most of the Vances kept the business going through the winter by plowing and shoveling, my patient Otto was the only taxidermist. For a

75-year-old man he was a model of health: physically fit from a life of hard work, and, as he described it to me, "the joy of bringing animals back to life" kept him sharp mentally. He was a taciturn man, not a talker. It was only in my single meeting with him and his wife, Desirée, that I'd learned how her elopement with this black man had led them to be ostracized from her family—only about ten years ago were they welcome to go to the family reunions, which had been a blessing.

Otto never came in for any health problems of his own, but just to lead the family in. And, I imagine, to talk with me about trees—I'd mentioned how much I loved trees—and gardening. Passing the time with him till the other family members were done.

But today Otto seemed different.

"What's up, Otto?"

In his Delta accent, nubs of fingers worrying his white hair, he said, "I'm a tad jumpeh."

"'Jumpy'?"

"Yeah, tha's it. Jumpeh." A pause. "Never kin recall ever before feelin' jumpeh."

"Where in your body are you feeling the jumpiness?"

A hand went to his midsection. "My guts."

"Anyplace else?"

He considered, those nubs at his chin, his green eyes half closed. "Nope."

"Anything else?"

"Yeah."

"What?"

"Dizzy. Yeah, that's it, jumpeh and dizzy."

"Okay, stand up and close your eyes." He did so. "Are you dizzy?"

"I'm jumpeh. And a mite dizzy."

"Is the *room* going around, or are *you* going around?" A test for ear or brain.

"I ain't that dizzy. I *am* jumpeh, though."

"Any weight loss, trouble with your appetite or bowels?"

"None a' that, no."

The only thing that I knew had changed was the season. His winter of taxidermy. Closed windows, fumes? Neuro or GI? Better do a toxicology check. I tried to get him to elaborate. Nothing. I did a physical, focusing on

the GI tract—nothing—and wrote out some labs for the FMC Runners: a
toxicology and diabetes screen, even at his age.

"So what do I got, Doc?" Otto asked.

"You got jumpy and dizzy."

He considered this carefully. "Yeah, that sounds about right to me."

"Good. It'll go away. I'll have the nurse get some blood, just to make sure.
If it gets worse, you call, y'hear?"

"Thanks, Doc."

"Welcome." I hurried to the Fat Man's check-in.

"I've invited Dr. Mo's mom, Dr. Rosemary 'Ro' Ahern, to come talk with us,"
Fats announced. We were in the conference room. The blackboard was covered with one of Man's 4th Best bedsheets. "All phones off and on the table."

The phones, protesting, formed an unruly pile, then quieted.

"Welcome, Dr. Ro. You go ahead, then my lecture."

I and a few others groaned. A lecture? Too cold. Too early. Too Monday.

Hungover, I was easing out of a migraine from the previous night's Whole
World School "Every Holiday You Can Think Of" party. The kids' opening
song was the most politically correct ever: "At this time of year, in *our* hemi-
sphere, we sing, et cetera." And when Spring's teacher asked me where I
worked and I told her, she said, "Why *Man's* Best Hospital? Why not call it
People's Best Hospital?" The last thing I wanted was a lecture.

Now, around the table, I saw the same roll of eyes in almost all of us—
except the Runt, helmetless, and to my surprise, Angel-less. I prayed her absence was temporary.

Chuck looked bad, slouched in his chair with a slack hand covering his
eyes.

Eat My Dust, looking better but still hellish and sitting with Naidoo, was
staring straight ahead as if at a distant threat.

Serene Naidoo even seemed half attentive—split, I imagined, between the
deepening rapids of Eddie love and Fats attention.

And Hooper was not rocking. The Runt was, well, "Runting."

Gath and Jude were spreading holiday joy in the OR by sawing, hammer-
ing, and nailing bone into metal and metal into bone.

Even faithful Humbo sat sullenly in back, round face a flat disk.

The cops again stood like resting bicycles, leaning against the far wall.

Gilheeny's thick fingers worked his face contemplatively—nose, hairy ears, those horrific Irish teeth.

Quick, but for his eyes flicking here and there like that tortoise's, was stone still.

The dread holiday season had brought hell to our door. The patient load was enormous. There was no replacement yet for the Runt. I refused to see psychiatry patients, but for emergencies. I'd had enough of the walking worried and depressed, now driven more crazy by hearing all the "Ti-eye-dings of Cuh-um-fort and Joy, ComfortandJoy"—and who instead heard "Ti-eye-dings of Sa-ad-ness and Pain, SadnessandPain." They felt badder and then madder and were buying more stuff. Christmas gun sales were up, leading to a holiday spike in gun deaths and holiday massacres from sea to shining sea. And Hawaii.

All this made sick people feel worse. Emergency wards all over the country were swamped. Man's 4th Best Emergency was doing banner business. Gilheeny and Quick were out in the world on the front lines, in hazardous and extended shifts.

And we docs were the *hope*? *We?* Unarmed, and gun naked, at that open door?

Scary. Every commotion snapped us to alert. *Will this be* it?

That morning, stressed-out, we sensed the volcanic rumbling just outside the Future of Medicine Clinic's locked door, ready to break down it and our goodwill toward men, women, and, yes, innocent children. The last thing we wanted was a *lecture*.

"Mo, would you like to introduce your mom to the group?"

"Hi, everybody. This is Dr. Rosemary Ahern, a super pediatrician. She fought to be a doctor—so I didn't have to. When she was at the BMS, ten out of a hundred were women. Now it's sixty percent—all over America. Thanks, Mom!"

"My pleasure." She sat next to Fats, her eyes shining. "I . . . I'm so proud of you, dear one. Well . . ." Gray hair cut short, with the same oval face, cute mouth, dual dimples, and green eyes—but for a glitter of proud-mom tears. She wiped them away, took a deep breath. "I started in the Episcopal Divinity School here, but seeing so much suffering, I decided, late, to become a doctor. Took me years, to go back and take the science courses, and med school was tough. I met my partner, Sue, there. Twenty years ago we opened an office not far from here, a working-class, multiracial practice. I loved my work. Did it for forty years. Six months ago, we were forced out." She bit her lip. "It was like death."

"'Forced'?" Fats asked.

"For years we'd been struggling—the usual financial struggles of an independent practice, doing medicine the way we believed in. Finally, about a year ago, we had BUDDIES assess our practice, to see if we could come in under their umbrella—i.e., have them buy us out? We had a meeting with the acquisition team, including Dr. Krashinsky and a brief appearance by a one-armed African American man, the CEO, named Pat P. Flambeau—of Flambeau Chickens?"

"Flambeau Amalgamated Chickens," I said.

"And Poultry," added Hooper. "Claims he lost his arm in a Cuisinart, but rumor has it that he really lost it in a beheading machine." He considered this. "Or a chicken plucker."

"We began presenting our practice to them, demographics, clinical data—but Krashinsky interrupted: 'Forget patients. If the *dollars* are there, nothing else matters.'"

Catcalls, curses, etc., from all of us.

"Without joining BUDDIES, we were told, none of our patients could go on using their insurance at any of the twenty BMS-affilliated hospitals or outpatient clinics. A classic tactic of a monopoly. But we said okay. It might have worked, but for one thing: we were forced to buy and use HEAL. This meant paying endless fees—installation fees, eighteen-hour workshops to learn it, enhancement fees, user fees *per employee*—so that to survive we had to take our three social workers *off* HEAL. And then the worst: periodic surprise 'upgrade fees.' Next, BUDDIES told all its BMS hospitals, and practices like ours, that patients with 'preexisting' conditions—the sick, poor, black, old ones, the *unhealthy* ones—would no longer be covered or admitted to their hospitals. It canceled its state contract to provide free 'Happy Health Insurance' for low-income patients, which was hemorrhaging cash. As soon as BUDDIES owned us, our patients were told they'd have to find docs *outside* BUDDIES who took that insurance. It was exactly what we had feared if we hadn't joined! Or go to emergency rooms—the new primary care. Our mothers began calling, frantic, or just showing up at our clinic with real sick kids—bad asthma attack, diabetic crisis—because they couldn't afford steroid inhalers or insulin. For a few months, Sue and I saw them for 50 dollars—and if they didn't have that, for free. That kind of worked, until two weeks ago we got an unexpected HEAL bill. We had to come up with 10,000 dollars in a week. And then . . . well . . . one of our kids died. At home. At night. That did it. I mean, it was extortion. A gun to our heads. And for every dollar we made, BUDDIES made nine. We treat. They keep."

She paused, squirmed.

"BUDDIES knew we had many poor, sick patients. We'd been duped; their whole plan was to kill off local hospitals and practices, ones serving *sick* people, mainly of color. Of Man's Best admissions, only two percent are black! Lowest in the whole state. To go with its highest-in-the-state fees. It's happening all over America. Rural towns have no hospitals or emergency rooms within forty miles. Even on Medicare or Medicaid, in emergencies there's nowhere to go. People are dying in their cars."

The room went dead quiet.

"The other piece was how our patients began to blame us. One woman came in angry as hell because she'd gotten the results of an echo test—normal—and she wanted me to call her. I didn't have the time. I mean, she was furious. I apologized, but couldn't really tell her that I spent my time on the phone with some Google child to justify her insurance paying for the test. That I spend two hours with the screen for every one hour I spend with a patient. She said, 'You're just lazy. You don't care!' I mean, patients and docs shouldn't be adversaries—the right relationship is as allies against BUDDIES and Big Medicine."

She shook her head in disgust. Took a deep breath and looked around, her light green eyes asking us if it was okay to keep going. We nodded the signal back: *Yeah. Go for it.*

"Sue and I grew up in the sixties. It's in our blood—if we see an injustice, and stick together, we can change things. Bizarre, right?" She sat up straight. "Well, guess what. We helped put civil rights laws on the books and ended the Vietnam War. We followed your example in the House of God—it's a lot better there now, because of you guys. In fact, it's now known to be the most humane hospital in the city. We read the novel as a primer of nonviolent resistance."

"Can you give us an example?" Naidoo asked.

"How 'bout Chuck?" she said, nodding to him. "When a staff doc would come up to you and say, 'Chuck, wear a tie,' or 'Write my order on this patient,' what did you say?"

"I said, 'Fine, fine.'"

"And what did you do?"

"Nuthin'." We all laughed.

"And at the end, when you say to the chief, 'How can we care for our patients, if nobody cares for us?'"

We all looked at Chuck. He nodded his head slowly. "There it is, girl, there it is."

"Poor Sue. She's a numbers person. Got obsessed with HEAL. Tried to prove mathematically that it could not possibly work for us fiscally. She had a manic psychosis, was in Mount Misery for three weeks. When friends visited her, I told them not to mention the word 'HEAL'—it might set her off again. Luckily, now she's fine. Retired."

"Thank God she's okay," said Fats. "And so now, Dr. Ro, would you say that you understand all the forces in health care involved in your disaster?"

"No. I still don't know what happened to us. Sue and I did everything right."

"Exactly. We all get isolated, so we can't see the big picture. But I've been givin' it a try. Turns out, it's a snake pit of rackets, interlocking extortions, for money. Wanna hear?"

Nods around the table.

"Buckle up!" He was at the blackboard, stubby pieces of chalk in his hand.

Humbo, with the grand gesture of a magician, swept one of Man's 4th Best bedsheets up, up, and away to float down, and folded it carefully, like a flag after a military funeral. Fats stood, assessing—a Michelangelo, of sorts. He sized up his canvas as if it were already a portrait of, say, inflammation, puzzling out clinical signs defined by the first-century Roman scholar Celsus: *dolor, calor, rubor, tumor, et laesa functio.* He underlined:

<u>THE 6 RACKETS OF AMERICAN HEALTH CARE:</u>
<u>FOLLOW THE MONEY</u>
<u>and</u>
<u>*** HOW TO RESIST ***</u>

"Note: Man's 4th Best Hospital is *not* one of the rackets. Like us docs, and patients, it's a *victim* of the rackets." He let this sink in. "So. The goal of the six rackets is simple: to find a way, by not providing health care to unhealthy people—the sick, the poor, and the old—and by providing health care to healthy people—the well, the rich, and the young—to make a lotta nice green money. And each of the six racketeers is holding a gun to the heads of each of the others." He glanced at Humbo. "A Mexican standoff?" Humbo nodded.

It was daring and clear, so it could have been the height either of cynicism and dogmatism, or of pure genius. We were rooting for genius.

"This simple goal," Fats said, "is so complex, so involved, so Byzantine and high-tech and electronic and deceitful, with so many ins and outs, ups and down, with obvious cash that turns out to be hidden and hidden cash that suddenly gushes out all green and scummy like a fiscal oil well. And I think—not sure yet but I think— *finally*, I understand *some* of what's goin' on, and it ain't pretty. There are at least six major billion-dollar moving parts of this moneymaking machine, and that's not counting doctors or patients. It's crazy like a fox. Everybody's trying to game everybody—like Coders for Cash, right?—but none of the six knows what's really going on in the other five. Some try to find big data links to treatment, using algorithms—but don't ask about algorithms now."

"What's an algorithm?" asked the Runt.

"Later," said Fats.

"Okay!" cried the Runt happily.

"But today's news? Doctors now are the highest suicides of any occupation?"

A question floated around the circle: *And that's relevant how?*

"All year long," Fats went on, "we've been asking ourselves two questions: 'What *is* BUDDIES?' and 'What does BUDDIES do?' Well, now I know. First: *there is absolutely no need for BUDDIES.* So it's hard to find what BUDDIES does. The closest I got is this: what BUDDIES does is make MONEY for BUD-DIES."

"Question?" Hooper was once again rocking. "What's it an acromym for?"

"Not sure it *is* one. WASPs don't really *do* acronyms. They paid 100 grand to a 'branding' guru to make it sound like they're your warm and cozy friends—who turn out to be as unreal as friends on Facebook. Anybody got anything on this?"

"Well, we all know what the 'B' stands for," said Hooper, starting to shake.

"How 'bout," Eat My Dust said, "'Best Ultimate Dollar Delivery in Every Sector'?"

"Ooooh-kay!" Fats said, rubbing those big, ardent hands together in anticipation. "*Racket Number 2: BUDDIES*. I'll get to number one, the prime mover in this snake pit, in a sec. In terms of money and care, there used to be, in the old days, just a doctor-patient relationship. A two-party payment system. Next, doctor-patient-insurance. A third-party payment system. And then, suddenly, when no one was looking, somebody slipped in a BUDDIES! It became doctor-patient-BUDDIES-insurance. A *four*-party payment system. One moonless night, some MBAs slithered into the health-care food chain an additional, humongous, *totally unnecessary* 26 billion dollars. A corporate leech sucking out money that serves no purpose *but* sucking. It bought Man's Best, killing the hospital, us docs, and our patients—'cuz that 26 billion cost has to come outta something. Witness Dr. Ro, hundreds of other docs, thousands of patients. Cutting out low-return care."

He frowned.

"BUDDIES is a money-laundering machine, soaking up profits. But BUDDIES is a *non*profit—go figure. Every year they make 150 million bucks in profit—a nonprofit profit paid out to CEO Flambeau, et cetera. BUDDIES reports no income. It pays no taxes."

"*I* pay more taxes than *BUDDIES*?" Hooper shouted. "First, GE. Now BUDDIES?"

"But for years, BUDDIES has had two problems: first, the 2.6 *billion* dollars spent on HEAL, a huge debt; second, the cost of providing health care for unhealthy patients. This year not only do they announce a loss of 120 million dollars, but they are carrying 5-plus billion dollars of debt. HEAL outsleazed 'em. Every year HEAL costs them—as it did Ro—extra millions in fees. So BUDDIES is carrying crushing debt. And WASPs *hate* debt. It'll take forty years to pay it off."

He took out a pack of baby carrots, popped a few into his mouth, chewed unhappily, as if they were pebbles.

"Go for it, Fat Guy!" shouted Hooper, giving a thumbs-up.

Fats rolled his eyes. "So lemme make this complex shit simple. The older I get, the more I realize that the most important thing is history. For the history of this sad, sickening decline of our beloved doctoring, I turn to our memorializers. Gilheeny? Quick?"

"Here!" cried Quick, as if waking up, pushing off the wall to vertical. "Ready for—"

"How much time," Gilheeny asked, "in terms of quickness, do we have?"

"As quick *as possible*."

"*Oy!*" said Gilheeny.

"*Gevalt!*" cried Quick, balanced at perfect vertical. "So. History. How did BUDDIES begin? The borth was when *three* BMS hospitals—the House of God, Man's Then Best, and Women's Then Best (in the separate female ratings)—decided that in order to milk the best money from the cash cow of INSURANCE, they'd band together to negotiate the best reimborsement payments. In the BMS dean's office, terms were agreed upon. The CEO of the House, Abe Schlotzky, celebrated by taking a long-overdue vacation in Italy."

Quick quivered. Gilheeny giggled.

"Imagine Abe's surprise," Quick said, "when, returning, he was met at the airport by a TV reporter who asked, 'And what do you think of this acquisition of Man's Best and Women's Best Hospitals to form and be owned by BUDDIES?'"

"Yer Hebraic man Abe," Gilheeny bellowed, "had been royally fooked by the goyim!"

"And porfectly!" said Quick. "Law Number One of the BMS: *Never* take a vacation. 'Cuz when y'come home, y'don't have yer office, yer job, or, in a few cases, yer wife. Nobody in the know *ever* takes a vacation from the BMS."

"Of course," Gilheeny added, "getting screwed out of a catastrophe like BUDDIES has worked out just fine for the House of God. Witness its rating going up to 3rd Best!"

"Thanks, loyal cops. Now. What do we know so far about this racket, this complex con?" Fats tapped his chalk on BUDDIES. "Formed in deception, it lives on lies, to make money. But now it's burdened by that 5-billion-dollar debt. Much of which is because of the great sucking cost of HEAL. So here are the six interlock—"

He stopped dead still. A hand went to his gut. He looked up and out over us as if from a ship sighting land.

"Holy shit! I see a simplicity, a singularity! There's one key variable hidden in all this cash. The one necessary thing that all national health systems have. What makes health care for all work? *Everyone pays the same price for the same care! There's only one fee scale! No war across the screen!* Once you let these dickheads compete for the highest pay on the, quote, 'free' market, the price goes up, and you screw the sick. You wind up getting health care for some, not all. For the healthy wealthy. Wow." He stared at the board. "Get rid of BUDDIES, we solve a *lot* of problems." He shifted his gaze to us. "Where was I?"

Fats, losing his train of thought? We House vets glanced at one another, puzzled.

"The six interlocking," said Hooper.

"Got it. The six interlocking rackets. *Follow the money.*"

In the center of the blackboard he wrote, in a large circle, HEAL.

Then he wrote, in boxes in a circle around *HEAL*—boxes in descending size to indicate the amount of "Money-Power," from the most to the least: *INSURANCE, PHARMA, BUDDIES, TLC, HEDGE FUNDERS.*

Last in this feeding frenzy for cash, he squeezed, into small tight boxes:

Doctors

Patients

And in the smallest box, hardly bigger than a ladybug:

Health care

And then he accelerated quickly, drawing double-pointed curving arrows between all the boxes from the giant *HEAL* to the ladybug *Health care*, talking, talking—talking.

"*Racket Number 1: HEAL*—a privately held cheesy corporation in Wisconsin—across the state from the worst, EPIC. After the 2.6 billion bucks it charged for installation in Man's 4th and Women's 2nd, HEAL continues to suck humongous money out of BUDDIES for upgrades, daylong trainings, hidden fees every few months. HEAL cost is helping crush BUDDIES under that multibillion-dollar debt. So how can BUDDIES, losing over *100 or 200* million each year, pay the interest on the debt, never mind pay it down?"

"Not by putting *us* out of business," said Ro. "They just do that for fun."

"Yes, yes, the WASPs do love their 'good fun,'" said Fats. "They try to pay down the debt by cutting costs, raising fees, and finding new revenue. Shutting down hundreds of practices like yours *cuts cost*—they're getting rid of low-yield patients, the 'unhealthy' poor, sick, old. But they also have to *make* more money, and are trying everything. For instance, the brand-new Saudi-Kissinger Tower. Flambeau and Krash and their boys are commuting to the Midasian and Eastasian war zones to woo Saudi princes with brain tumors, to Russia for oily-garchs needing new livers, and to China luring billionaires swept up in their epidemic of diabetes.

"*Racket Number 3: INSURANCE.* By the way, before the Renaissance in Italy, there never even *was* a thing called insurance. Before the rise of the Italian mercantile city-states like Florence and Venice, the people, in communities, took care of each other. Crazy idea, eh? The Medicis and Borgias were the first insurers. Turns out that BUDDIES makes deals with INSURANCE to get the highest payments in America. If, say, the House of God gets 2,000 bucks per appendectomy from insurance companies, a BUDDIES hospital gets 3,000. They call this 'enhanced fees.' But *why*? Why does INSURANCE pay premium money to BUDDIES? They *claim* it's because of the 'premium care.' Baloney. It's a scam, a protection racket. They get a kickback—not in cash, but in information. 'If you give us access to all the HEAL data on your patients, we'll pay you more money.' They get *all of HEAL's data on patients! On all of us! In one click!* Why is that valuable? Because then INSURANCE can get the algorithm—don't ask—to find out which patients cost them the most money—i.e., the sick, poor, and old. Who need guess what: lotsa health care. And so INSURANCE *can then strip them off their list*—by raising rates or finding preexisting conditions. And hey—who of us does not have preexisting conditions?"

"Why, none of us don't," said Gilheeny, "none of us at all."

"Like our forst preexisting condition—borth," said Quick darkly. "Which is yer man's main cause of death."

"INSURANCE raises co-pays, deductibles, lifetime limits. They're clever. They disguise this data mining of HEAL as 'population health management' or 'quality improvement' in the guise of 'better health-care outcomes'—and all the other consultant bullshitology—to disguise *what*? That they're getting rid of sick people and insuring ones who are, and will stay, healthy. Like me now eating carrots. We who are resisting Hooper's bliss point."

"Go, Fats!" Hooper cried, rocketing up onto his feet. "Love you, man. You rock!"

"I want salami, okay?"

"As a reward, a little, sure," said Hooper. Giving a thumbs-up, he sat down, smiling.

Fats stopped still, puzzled. "Damn—now all I can think about is salami. Ah, yes, the kickback. INSURANCE cherry-picks patients who are better and healthier and who can be shown to have done better with treatment, so BUDDIES, Man's 4th, and Women's 2nd can now publicly *cite* these high percentages of 'better outcomes' and charge even more money in fees. And what happens to the sick? They come to us, go to emergency—get Medicaid or Medicare, thank God—but basically they live sick and die."

He took a deep breath in, twisted up his face, fat brow in a number of rippling waves.

"A new model. Health care only for the healthy. It's the Fewer-Better-Patient Model."

"Of course most of the 'Better' are white," Naidoo said.

"And," said Eddie, "if you're 'Better,' but then you do get sick, you can get turned into a black man fast! One admission, y'lose your house. Or go bankrupt."

It was astonishing to see Eddie engage in any political thing except Eddie. Clearly love, and Naidoo, was opening his eyes.

"What?" said Chuck, who, like Eddie, would rarely take part in anything like this. "Y'mean that there's racial discrimination in American medicine? Damn!"

"*Sí, sí,* and there is the gomer discrimination too! How many gomers we see here at the 4th? They only admit them if they're rich or *las fascinomas*. Or else, *nada*."

"So the deadly HEAL debt that's burying BUDDIES gets paid off," Hooper said, in pathology mode, "by the fatal trickle-down economics of 'no care,' crashing down on the backs of the poor, sick old people living in the last house on the block. *They* pay for it."

"Exactly. *Racket Number 4: BIG PHARMA* and its subsidiary the *FDA*. As interlocked and invasive as metastatic cancer. Let's call 'em BIGPHAR-MAFDA."

"Sweet Jaysus, whatta novelistic neologism!" said Gilheeny.

"Totally a-teleologic," Quick added. "Doomed!"

"The only barrier between Pharma and FDA is a temporal one, the time it takes for a doctor in BIG PHARMA to quit, take the revolving door into the FDA, oil the tracks for fast approval of his own PHARMA's drugs, then revolve back out to BIG PHARMA, to cash back in. The *usual* kickback racket." He drew another slew of double-pointed arrows. "The link of BIGPHAR-MAFDA to INSURANCE and BUDDIES? They can all charge top dollar for 'the chosen' FDA-approved drugs. Medicare insures millions, and *could* negotiate prices way down—but negotiation with PHARMA is prohibited by law. BIG PHARMA charges whatever they want. Highest cost of drugs in the world. The latest a big-time profit in opiates. Forty-seven thousand dead this year—more dead than in 'Nam. The opiate threat used to come from outside the USA. Now it's from inside. Now we got drug dealers in lab coats."

He sighed, shook his head hard, like a dog coming out of a bath. "Still with me?"

Nods from all of us—except Runt.

"*Racket Number 5: the TLC, Merck/Fox, DARPA.* You all know I'm *totally* into medical research, and in this, the BMS is, well, the best. Their clinical research leads to incredible lifesaving treatments and drugs. But this is different. The 'T' in TLC is for 'Translation'—into money. The TLC, aka the 'Harry the Horse Killing Field,' has a plaque at the entrance: Merck/Fox. A sweetheart wedding of BIG PHARMAFDA and ENTERTAINMENT—each paying millions to Man's 4th and BUDDIES for exclusive rights to all discoveries and drug patents, which are called 'intellectual capital.' Why do they donate millions—tax deductible, mind you—for this? Because just one FDA-approved drug, and all parties *really* party! What else does Fox get? Granted, it's hard to make killing patients entertaining. Maybe Fox gets insider-trading info, and then whispers it into the ears of hedge funders on golf courses. And on the inside door of the TLC is a plaque saying 'DARPA,' paid for by our tax dollars, and don't even ask what it is or does."

"What is DARPA and what does it do?" asked the Runt.

"I could tell you," Fats said, "but I'd have to kill you."

"Oh, okay," said the Runt.

"*Racket Number 6: HEDGE FUNDS FOR HEALTH.* Simple. Insider trading. Easy-sleazy billions—like opiates. Rackets one through five are heavily invested in multiple hedge funds, and vice versa. Betting on both winners and losers. Like the hedge funds buying up private dermatology practices, betting on them. Whether they flourish or fail, the hedgers make big money. The point-oh-one percent that owns ninety percent of the wealth of America. Sixty percent of all yearly income—imagine?"

He paused, again trying to recall something—was it the complexity, a distraction, a memory issue? But no, he had all that calcium on board, right? Still waiting.

"Oh! The last link in 'follow the money' is *between* HEDGE FUNDS and BUDDIES. And here's the real answer to what BUDDIES is and does. Listen up!"

We leaned in.

"Hedgers are dependent on Wall Street. Recently BUDDIES posted a 213-million-dollar loss, a lot of it because of HEAL. Last week the headline in the *Wall Street Journal*? 'BUDDIES Gets Fiscal Health Warning.' The three key securities analysts—Standard and Poor's Global Ratings, Moody's Investors Service, Fitch Ratings—downgraded BUDDIES from 'stable' to 'negative.' One step above junk bonds. Ever since, BUDDIES is on a WASP suicide watch. Given its 213-million-dollar loss and decline in ratings, what does the CEO, Pat P. Flambeau of Flambeau Chickens fame, do? He gets the board to pay him a 2.7-million-dollar bonus. Think what that money would've meant to Dr. Ro's patients and practice."

A spreading hush, of disgust.

"Finally," Fats said, *"finally,* we have the answer to what BUDDIES is and does. First, BUDDIES *makes money* for BUDDIES. Second, given the signature incompetence of its leaders to *make money,* BUDDIES is, really, a program of *affirmative action for administrators.* The worst make the most money." He paused. "Okay. We followed the money. But if there's no money to be made, none of this can happen. The only health-care systems in the world where there's no big money to be made are single-payer, government run— like our Medicare, Medicaid, the VA. With single-payer, there can still be a for-profit system alongside, for the rich—like in Europe, Australia, wherever. If money is no object, let the rich get the worst care, right?"

"Ah, yes," said Quick. "As Count Tolstoy put it, 'Money is the new slavery.'"

Fats sized up the board—all double-pointed arrows, some straight, some curvy and even reversing direction in midflight, making a chalky white web, but also looking remarkably like a plate of linguine, with a meatball called HEAL in the center.

"Oh my!" he said, stunned. "I forgot something. Anybody catch it?"

We stared. No one did. He went on with a sadness in his voice, a slowness.

"The four small circles, clustered together for warmth, at the bottom? *Not* rackets. Victims of?"

We watched his chalk move slowly around each little circle in turn, and as the white dust gradually buried each name within, he called them out with a sorrow that you'd hear in a memorial service for four of the noble dead, these non-rackets of American health care:

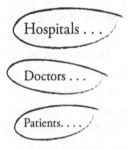

Letting silence build, the final crush of the ladybug:

"And these four are natural allies against the six others." He sat with a heavy *thunk*.

Nobody knew what to say.

Jude and Gath walked in, in rumpled scrubs. "Sorry we're . . . ," Gath began, but glancing at the blackboard, looking around, nodded and sat, Jude beside him.

"Glad you're here. This is Dr. Ro Ahern, Mo's mom, a peds doc whose clinic has just been forced to close by BUDDIES." He checked his watch. "Oops—don't have much time. Anyone want to give our surgeons a thirty-second thumbnail? Thirty, tops?"

"Me, meee!" Hooper said. Fats nodded. Hooper checked his watch, snapped into Hyper focus. "The cost of HEAL crushes BUDDIES under huge debt, so to pay it, BUDDIES makes deals with INSURANCE to pay BUDDIES 'enhanced fees' like for appendixes in return for HEAL's patient database, a protection racket, and INSURANCE trolls the data to cut off insurance for unhealthy poor, black, old, sick gomers and closes practices like

Mo's mom's and does health care for the healthy whites and sheikhs and
Henry Kissinger and BIGPHARMAFDA, which is metastatically inter-
twined with Merck/Fox Entertainment, which buys the TLC intellectual
capital, and all pour insider info into ears at golf so HEDGE FUNDERS for
HEALTH can make huge fortunas—" He checked his watch. "Ergo, BUD-
DIES pushes its huge debt down onto the backs of the family in the last house
on the block—the black, the old, and the sick—and we four allies are *ready*!
Twenty-four seconds."

"Okay! A for-profit health-care system can never work for all. Unless, like
the Swiss and the Dutch, it's heavily regulated. American health care costs
10,000 bucks per person, the most expensive in the world; American quality
of care is 39th, below—I dunno—Togo? Our infant mortality is going up.
Our age at death is going down. Not just health care. In all parts of our
American life, the unregulated profit motive is killing off generosity, shredding the safety net for us all. Health care's the poster child for the shredding
of America."

"The original sin," added Gilheeny, "is the monetizing of whether y'live
or y'die."

"'The *beast* of unregulated capitalism,'" Quick added. "John Maynard
Keynes. Your prescient economist said in the thirties that, if unregulated,
capitalism is doomed."

"Y'know," Gath said, "this all makes me think of what was once Man's
Best's mission? It's carved in the Pink's marble wall I pass every day on my
way to the OR, and it may sound corny, but I've tried to live up to it: 'In pain,
everyone is our neighbor.' And now what would they carve in stone? 'Not *my*
neighbor, no way. I made it. Why can't they? If they stay sick and poor, they're
just not *trying* hard enough. It's their *fault*, not *my* problem.' Well, I grew up
in that last house. Those families were my neighbors. I got lucky and got out.
And every day, I think of them. Y'know, once, when I happened to quote that
original mission to Barmdun, he said, 'In this fiscal climate, that's no longer
valid. Now it's "Our margin is our mission. No margin, no mission."'"

"What's that mean?" Mo asked. "Like excising a safe margin around a tumor?"

"Profit margin. Which depends on how fast we 'churn' patients, round
and round, get 'em in and out, one surgeon doing two—or three—surgeries
at the same time, without the patient knowing. *That's* why I blew the whistle
on 'em. And why I'm in deep shit."

"And why I'm in a lawsuit," Jude said. "Also deep shit."

I noticed that Dr. Ro was sitting quietly, staring down at her hands folded in her lap—suddenly looking older, frail. I asked, "Are you okay, Ro?"

"No." She looked at Mo. "I'm worried, and sad . . . about what we're passing along to you, dear, and your patients. Sweetheart, I'm so sorry." She was shaking her head, and her eyes pooled with tears. "And I'm still so upset about that last child, and family, that I tried so hard to help—*tried so hard*! I cared for her as a baby. Fourteen. A sweetheart. Dead?"

"What happened, Mom?"

"Her diabetes got out of control. She didn't call me. The family didn't have money for insulin and needles—all in all almost *10,000 dollars* a year? Without my knowing, they were *rationing* it, to buy food. What are we *doing*? How can we change it?" She hid her face in her hands and sobbed, crying out all those years of work, doing good, being good—all of it gone.

Mo put her arm around her mother, took her hand. Her mom slumped into her, shoulders shaking, her daughter comforting. "What was her name, Mom?"

"Her name was . . . Mary . . ." She stopped herself, biting her lip, head down. We waited. She raised her head, high, even proudly, and whispered, "Mary Brown."

We all sat there. The only sound was muffled, our patients talking, waiting for us. Sitting and talking to one another. *Our patients, with one another. Despite their suffering, sounding merely human, strangely hopeful. Because of being about to be with us.*

"Dr. Ro?" Fats asked. She turned to him. "How'd you like to join us here?" Taken aback, she said, "Really?"

"Really. We've been looking for a good pediatrician."

She hesitated. Then, taking Mo's hand, she asked, "Would that be okay with you, dear? I wouldn't want to horn in on your—"

"Not just okay, Mom. It would be, like, amazing."

"Deal!" said Fats. "Now, let's go out there and be good docs." He hoisted himself up.

"One thing?" Mo asked. "We didn't get to the 'how to resist' part?"

"I know, and it's *crucial*. Needs time—and we're late. Later, okay?"

No one said okay or moved.

"I'll give you a clue."

He tapped his chalk on *RESIST*, still untouched by the storm of chalk fallen on the snake pit below, and said, "We are the workers. We do the work. . . . Without us . . ." and suddenly, as he kept underlining, the anger turned to such fury that the chalk broke and he snatched up another piece and underlined some more, one line under another, enraged, possessed, shouting, "Without us there's no health care!" And he threw the chalk against the board and went on, enraged, spitting the words out. "If we docs can't stop being so damn self-reliant and isolated from each other and competing with each other for a tighter and tighter drip-drip-drip down of money from numbers one through six, we're dead and our patients are dead—but if and only if we cut the bullshit and stick together and ally with nurses and patients and even hospitals if they're smart—*only then are we gonna change this!*"

He was apoplectic, face beet red. I—all of us, I'm sure—thought "hypertension, fatty deposits in carotid arteries stroke or in coronaries cardiac infarction." We had never, *ever* seen him that mad, that madly determined, losing it, fanatic!—refusing to cover up his rage with Fats the Wise or Fats the Funny or even Fats the Sad, who never lost it like this, ever.

He was panting, but managed to say, "This . . . is . . . lifeordeath. . . ." Gasping. "Firstthings . . . first. Let's . . . go out there . . . and relieve some pain and suffering. We'll do more 'how to resist' another time."

Shaken, we followed him out the door.

I asked myself: *What the hell's going on to drive him to this edge?*

17

*

"D"oc, you were dead wrong about my writing teacher, Miss Heller."

Two weeks later.

We were caught in the icy clutch of January. It was so cold that I saw my hedge fund neighbor with his hands in his *own* pockets!

I was in a rare appointment with Nolan, the Iraqi vet and kin of Officer Quick.

The Fat Man's "six rackets" had stunned us and upset us. While we felt that we had finally come to some clarity on what the hell was going on in the edifice of great American health care, we were even more frustrated with our participation with it. Maybe it was Fats's skipping out on the "what we can do about it," the "how to resist" piece, that had enraged him to sputtering, scary silence.

All of us now were so overwhelmed with the fierce winter rush of patients that we never felt clear or able to take action on anything past the levels of our sight, anything beyond our patients and family. We were hanging on by our fingertips to an icy ledge of our lives. At best we were entrapped by the system; at worst, colluding with it. We were frustrated every day that we were not "resisting" enough, not putting our shoulders against that big wheel of the "rackets" to try to move them even a little. Our ideals were still there, but buried under our daily work. The frigid, windy, slippery weather depressed and inflamed not only our patients but us as well. Ice storms were the norm.

Everyone was slipping and falling. Women fracturing wrists and ankles and hips, men clotting off arteries in heart and brain. Depressions and violence to loved ones were main diagnoses.

It had become a chore even to get up out of bed in the morning and go to work.

Not that we forgot the meta view of our jobs, which showed sharply our being powerless, and "going along with it," lying into our screens. We could not forget all that. But we were too busy and too down to take any real action. I was not alone in feeling all this. We'd get together and talk—in the check-ins and checkouts, and sometimes, in fraught one-on-one moments with one another.

The phrase "doctor's burnout" had started to be tossed around. As if we doctors were "tinder." As if our moral dilemma—being forced to violate our Hippocratic oath in all different ways—was *our* defect? When all along it was that we and our patients and the hospital were being abused by BUDDIES, who, in deepening debt to the other racketeers, was sucking as much money as possible out of Man's 4th and Women's 2nd and, trickling down, out of the rest of us. Labeling us docs "burnouts" was just another insult to our spirit of caring for sick people. And if we were the "tinder," why wasn't anyone fighting the fire? It's not burnout; it's doctor abuse.

In this state of mind, I found myself sitting with Nolan.

It had been months since we'd met. He was in great shape. I was not.

But I was glad to see him looking good. Not only his clean-shaven jutting chin and clear, bright eyes, which seemed infatuated with something, but also his pleated, pressed gray slacks and fresh blue work shirt open at the neck a few buttons down—with that Moleskine notebook in its pocket. A briar pipe in his hand, unlit. Strangely, he wore a red polka-dot bandanna covering his head, tied like an old Jewish woman's *schmatta* or as if he was in a revolutionary polka group. His fingernails now looked manicured. A life cleaned up, yes, but a bit unsettled between the Jewish *schmatta*/revo bandanna, British pleated slacks and pipe, and retro black Converse All Star sneakers.

I sherlocked a little: he was no longer depressed or suicidal, but he was unsure of who he was, and was trying on a lot of different "clothes." Unsure, and not really wanting to find out—witness his not calling for months. But I knew from talking to his sponsor, Horace H., when he would bring in to me one of his AA "pigeons"—new sponsees—that Nolan was staying sober. A miracle. Drinking, all bets were off. Sober, all bets were on.

Nolan had sent a handwritten note for the appointment: "Hey Doc Basch. I'm 'staying sober by helping others'—like I stayed alive helping my buddies stay alive in Iraq. Enclosed, three pages from my first novel, *Nawa Redux*. It's my *House of God*."

I had never seen handwriting so tiny. But even after I'd read the three handwritten pages, I still couldn't decipher its meaning. Something about a desert war, and an obsession with a sport—curling? tennis? pinball? The narrator, never described, was Eye—"a curling/fanatico-world-champ-in-recovery." In order to protect his team from the "stones" that sometimes seemed to be terrorist IEDs, Eye had focused on a "postmodern exegesis of 'Queens Clean Latrines.'" There were no quotes for dialogue, no caps, no indentations for paragraphs.

My carefully considered literary opinion?

It was the most pretentious, unreadable shit I'd ever read. I soon gave up.

"She said these three pages were the best maximal-minimal-postmodern fiction she's ever seen."

"Great. I remember how angry you were at that first 'below F.' You've come a long way, Nolan, from that gun at the US Army recruiting doughnut booth."

He laughed, full barreled—I was glad to see this and, rooting for him, laughed with him.

"Yeah, dude, and that was the last drink I had." He crossed himself. "Through the grace of my higher power, whom I choose to call 'God,' a day at a time. But I took her advice—how I could deconstruct to the combat max what I'd written, shape-shifting out of the real."

Gulping, clenching teeth, hiding my revulsion, I inquired, "And that worked?"

"Sure did. She wrote back, 'F! See me.' Next time? 'D-minus—great work!'" He grinned, ear to ear. "I soon got it up. I mean, to an A!"

"How?"

"Started sleeping with her. I finally figured out her subtext: her 'See me' meant 'See *all* of me, naked.'"

"Minimalist?"

"Hell no. In the sack, max. She's on the editorial board of the best literary journal—they're printing my pages." He threw down a crude oil black volume: *Walt D MM Lit Jrnl*.

"And the 'MM' stands for 'Maximalist Minimalist'—"

"Nope. *Mickey Mouse Lit J*. Clever, eh?" He laughed, sat back, chewed his pipe's stem happily, soon to be a published author. "I stopped smoking. Working out. My agent's giving first refusal of the novel to FSG—the most prestigious publisher in the world. Home of a lotta US Nobels."

My gut churned. How could this shit get published—and by a prestigious press? To hide my contempt, I dropped my gaze, carefully considered my shoes—noticing the white discoloration from the salted ice that substituted, slickly, for real ground.

Silence. I glanced up. On his face was gloat.

"If FSG passes, we'll put it out to auction—floor, 50 thou. Publishers love war novels, as long as they stick tight to the icon of 'American boy as joyful savage warrior.'"

I began to lose it. Tried hard to hide it.

"You know what your problem is, Dr. Basch?" I waited. "You're a psychiatrist. Not a *real* writer. You're a *dilettante*." He left.

⌀

Royally pissed-off, I wobbled through my patients, soon overwhelmed by increased sheer numbers. What Fats had called the golden age was suddenly under threat. Not having OUTGOING, having twice the "humane time" with our patients, had been a gift, yes.

But now word had gotten out about the FMC: your doctor actually looked at you during your appointment. Wrote things down. Didn't rush you in and out. Often smiled! Some even joked around with you—the fat one, the black one, the hyper guy who was into what you ate. And there was no long wait in the waiting room. Sometimes they took you early! A doc, early? Relaxed?

It was like another Horace AA slogan: "Attraction, not promotion."

BUDDIES, losing money, was spending money on big-time promotion. A rash sprouted on billboards in train stations, subways, and airports, proclaiming: "Man's 4th and Women's 2nd. The best Hospitals on the East Coast."

But the public wasn't fooled. Man's 4th was flailing around, failing to attract even well-insured patients.

The FMC—with no ads, and the only part of the vast Man's 4th that was still taking patients on Medicaid and Medicare—was booming.

One day Fats, on speaker, had me listen in on his conversation with Krash.

"You're sending us *more* patients?" Fats asked.

"Affirmative."

"Why are you punishing us?"

"Punishing? No. Rewarding. For your having the highest PATSATs."

"But we're getting overwhelmed—"

"Who isn't? And frankly, there's been friction beween you guys and everyone else at Man's Best. I've heard rumors of talk of possible termination."

"What? You can't do that. By my contract, I have—"

"Of *course* not by contract. Contracts are worth *bupkis*. So far it's moot, because of your high PATSATs. So now you have to increase volume even more—more cash in all our pockets. And with all the new patients we're sending your way—"

"What? What patients are you sending—"

"You'll see. Treat them beautifully, and we'll all make big tax-sheltered bonuses."

"But if we're swamped with patients, the PATSATs will go down."

"With your charisma? Doubtful. But let me offer you a suggestion. The FMC has the best record for seeing patients on time. Shortest waiting time of all Man's Best. Average, thirteen point four minutes. Way below national average, which is thirty-seven point six minutes."

"Thanks."

"Not good."

"What? Patients hate long waits."

"Of course they do. They're patients. But a recent study showed that the shorter the patient waiting time, the more negative the revenue. 'Long Waits for Patients Sign of Good Business' by Drs. Ryu and Lee of Women's 2nd Best. Quote: 'The result of long waits may be chaos, with angry patients waiting an hour or more and dispirited clinicians and staff trying to both appease and care for them . . . ' Blah blah. 'But overbooking makes sense medically, and is good business because sicker patients need more tests and procedures, which translates to more services and more dollars collected.'"

"Keeping them waiting makes more money?"

"Affirmative. Except . . ." He paused. "Except if they're paying cash."

"Cash? Who the hell ever pays cash?"

"Patients in our new venture. You'll hear about it soon. So we're increasing waiting time at every BUDDIES site. But the FMC is making less than your max. Easily fixed."

"How?"

"As I said, see more patients and make them wait longer. Up the volume. *Exceed* temporal-patient-flow capacity. Enhance mean-patient throughput. Which your *zaftig* PATSATs are *doing*, and which we'll help you do even more of, with additional volume, quite soon."

"What the hell are you thinking of doing to us?"

"Nice to be popular, isn't it, Fats?"

"How would *you* know?"

Pause. More pause. "Goodgood. Be well, my friend, and shalom." *Click.*

Fats and I stared at each other.

"What the fuck is wrong with that guy?"

"Lots. Try being an elite sniper in the Israeli army, killing human beings."

"A sniper?"

"A crack sniper. When he joined the Israeli army, he was drawn to sniping. Hiding a long way away, with no risk, blowing heads off unsuspecting people."

"No."

"Very yes. Not a bad way t'go—but still. When I came here last spring to check out the offer, after the official meetings, he suggested a relaxing trip to his shooting range. Turns out, it was on the grounds of Temple Shalom, on whose board he sits."

"A shooting range at Temple Shalom?"

"Which is why he chose Shalom. And sure enough, he leads me down a lovely path edged with pines and lilac, to a peaceful glade with a self-serve bar and things to nosh on, for free. Very convenient, really. You go to a bris and go out and fire a few thousand rounds to celebrate. He had brought two rifles. I declined. I watched him put together his rifle with, well, the meticulousness of a brain surgeon. 'My very own army sniper rifle,' he said, caressing the flashy blue metal barrel. He clicked buttons, and targets started popping up all over, at least a football field away—so that I could barely make out the outlines of humans from the waist up. We both put on fluffy headphones, and he lay down on the ground and rested his gun on a cradle. With a calming sigh to steady his trigger finger, he started shooting them. I saw the heads shiver as they were hit. I think he hit 'em all. Maybe, by his headshake reaction, he missed one head, hitting the torso."

He shook his own head slowly in—what? Admiration? Disgust?

"I'd never seen him so happy."

"Snipering made him that happy?"

"Not just that. You have to understand. We grew up together. He was *insanely jealous* of me—totally obsessed with my success. It got real nasty. And out there on the shooting range, for the first time *ever* in his life, he showed he could outdo me at *something*. He finished, took off his headphones, disassembled his gun affectionately, and bedded it down in its velvet-lined case, and I'd never before seen the look on his face." He paused, searching for the words. "Triumphant. Better than me, even the best. Yeah, he'd 'bested' me. He was in heaven."

"And then?"

"We left the glade. I took the job. He became my boss. You know the rest."

That day with Nolan was a turning point, down. It was the busiest day we'd ever had. The increased patients coming in were of the same class; race, and diseases as before: the poor, the sick, the old, and the sick-poor-old—mostly of color. Many came from the Jupiter and other shuttered clinics, some were TURFED from the 4th Best Emergency. But only the sick-poor-old who had common diseases, i.e., not publishable. The publishables got long, succulent 4th Best stays. Ours—"the wretched refuse of your teeming shore"—got just us.

The main reasons our patients came in were a worsening of common chronic diseases.

Cancer was big—Eat My Dust was going flat out.

Naidoo too, in OB-GYN and Women's Health.

Hyper was in heaven. Ever since his outburst, we all sent patients—"People gotta eat"—and they loved him and the free tofu-and-pomegranate shakes, at a café and health club on the second floor staffed by buff young girl athletes from UCLA Hyper-Winfrey.

Chuck and Mo were family docs. Mo was incredibly curious and avid. Her learning curve with us was spectacular—she soaked up everything. And

her ease with screens was a gift, for any problems we faced even with OUT-
GOING down. Like having a Joe Sole around.

Pediatrics was our grandma figure, Dr. Ro. Under our supervision, she
stepped up big, her learning curve steep.

Humbo was a Mexican Horatio to our fat Hamlet—or, better, a Sancho
to our Don Quixote. Given his kindness and skill, Humbo was a folk hero to
our Hispanics.

Angel was strangely aglow, nursing with expertise, helping out everywhere. She still finished sentences with ease—"I graduated from finishing
school," she joked. Except with the Runt when, and strangely, she still got
jammed up with gestures.

Gath and Jude did surgical care. I was the least busy—lots of TURFS to
Horace's twelve-step network—so I pitched in and did everything else, using
my Navajo-honed all-purpose doctor skills, enjoying it.

Through all this, Fats would perch at the nursing station, feet up on the
counter, chatting up anyone who would listen and doing his reading—no,
"inhaling" books. He was always available—except during his several daily
feedings. We all followed a law of medicine—"Common diseases occur com-
monly," or "If you hear hoofbeats ouside the window, don't assume it's a zebra."
But sometimes a zebra does walk by. And if you miss it, somebody dies.

Late one day, a woman named Trudi Goodman, a thin white 56-year-old
mother of one daughter, dressed carefully in a too-large blouse and plain
pants, came to me, her chief complaint of "difficulty breathing." Sure enough,
she was pale and a little bluish, cyanotic and panting—a haunted look in her
eyes. Not only sick, but scared—a look I'd seen in those sensing they are
about to die. She had been TURFED to the TLC after a workup on one of
Man's 4th Best wards. A fascinoma, she'd had a blitzkrieg workup that showed
only eosinophilia—a rise in the immune system. They'd done all the allergy
tests—nothing. No one could find out why her immune system was aflame.
As an *unsolved* fascinoma, she was *unpublishable*—barred by Jack Rowk Junior from the TLC. She was discharged on heavy steroids.

"Steroids make me crazed, manic," she said. "I'm exhausted but can't
sleep. I'm ravenous, but I don't gain weight, and I'm . . ." Gasping, she stopped,
staring at me. "I don't understand. Why aren't you at your computer? I'm not
important enough?"

"Too important." She looked at me, touched. *So now we're heading into the real, together.* "You must be really scared, Trudi." Our eyes met.

"Yes. I . . . My daughter . . ." She looked away, then back. "I'm scared of dying?"

I nodded. I was scared for her too. "Let's see if we can do something about that."

If you're connected, you can talk about anything; if not, not. I asked her about her life. Between gasps, she said her husband had died suddenly, two years before. Her family and friends had gotten her through. She owned a flower shop. No trouble breathing ever. I asked where she lived. After her husband died, she'd taken in boarders. I asked about them.

"One of them's . . . a real . . . trip," she gasped. "A magician."

I smiled. "He's a trip?"

"Yeah. Part of his act . . . involves trained . . . pigeons. . . ."

"Where does he keep the pigeons?"

"In the . . . basement. . . . The cages . . . are right above . . . my washer-dryer."

My ears perked up. I asked her to go on.

It turned out that whenever she had run the dryer, the pigeon droppings had been aerosolized and she had breathed them in—for the past two years.

"I know what you've got—pigeon breeder's lung disease. You're allergic to pigeon poop."

"Oh my! Is there a cure?"

"Oh yeah! A very very *very* complicated cure." I smiled. "Get rid of the pigeons." We laughed. "We'll taper you off the steroids as we go along. You'll be fine."

Speechless, she got up and faced me. Her face seemed flushed—good to see, a rush of red blood from that hypoxic lung—and hugged me, shaking with sobs.

Fats always said, "The patient is the world." And sometimes hoofbeats outside the window might be a zebra or, if you really listen, the light steps of a common bird. HEAL hadn't picked it up. And none of the ace 4th Best doctors had sat with her, with time enough, and openness enough, to listen.

18

ater that wintry afternoon, Fats appeared, Chuck with him. The afternoon checkout, a sacred time, had been canceled because all of us were still swamped with patients.

"Mo's in trouble on Ward Thirty-four," Fats said. "She paged me stat. Let's move."

At that time, we'd heard rumors that BUDDIES was bleeding out money—with bond ratings still in the toilet—not only from its two main hospitals, Man's 4th Best and Women's 2nd Best, but from the other 18 hospitals and hundreds of clinics it had bought. The main reason was the soaring costs of HEAL—upgrades, breakdowns, trainings, and interest on the 2.6-billion-dollar debt. And so BUDDIES had hired experts—the Best Business School consultants in a brand-new specialty: stanchers of health-care bleed-outs of money. The consultants told BUDDIES—focused on maximum profits—that they could get more cash in by sucking out more cash from Man's 4th and Women's 2nd. How to do this? That day, we would see.

Chuck and I had recently begun another monthlong attending-doc stint on 34. We were responsible for the patients, and for supervising all the house staff, and we rounded on the patients twice a day. We were there also to interface between the house staff and the administrators. When we got there, Mo was pacing up and down, frantic.

"I need help. It's about my patient Wambui Kamau, the grandmother from Kenya that Roy and I wheeled down to the ER to talk to the radiologist. I've been seeing her in clinic—she's done well. Come see."

"You kiddin', girl?" Chuck turned to me. "Roy? You 'n' her *talked* to a radiologist?"

"Long story. Let's go, Mo."

Wambui lay listless in bed. I'd last seen her in Ward 34 when she'd been sent up on the radiologist's cover-your-ass diagnosis of the 6-millimeter stone in the postsurgery stub of her biliary duct. We'd had her discharged directly from Emergency to the care of her son. At that time, she'd never been officially admitted to Ward 34.

Now she didn't look well—lethargic, labored breathing, brown eyes dull. To our questions she slowly gave fuzzy answers, slurring. A scent of ketones was in the air, a flare-up of chronic diabetes, waste products in her blood—ketoacidosis. This caused fogging of sensorium and other systemic problems. Clearly it had knocked her out. Saddened, we went into the hallway.

"As you see," Mo said, "she's not ready for discharge. But I've got big problems with TOSS, and Coders 4 Cash—they're killing me, and may kill her. They'll be here any minute."

Fats, Chuck, and I stared at her. Coders we kind of knew, but what was TOSS?

"They just started it. TOSS is short for 'TURF Out Safely Sub-Seven.' It's to 'churn' patients faster through Man's 4th. Copied from the hotel industry. Y'know how in hotels you check in after three and check out by eleven? A four-hour window?" We did. "Well, Man's 4th met with Man's Best BS's experts—"

We looked at her, puzzled. "Does the 'BS' really stand for 'bullshit'?" I asked.

"'Business School.' Experts in the hotel industry. They found that for a patient check-in after three and checkout by seven—an *eight*-hour window—every day for *one* patient, in three days adds one extra twenty-four-hour room charge—currently at about 1,000 dollars. Per three hundred sixty-five days, 121.67 additional days, or 121,670 dollars. And that's for just *one* patient/room. The added revenue is huge."

"Wait a second," I said. "I don't get it. If it's still check-in at three, why does a larger gap—eight hours versus four hours—get you more billable hours?"

Blank looks all around.

"I know why," said Chuck.

"Yeah?" Fats asked. "Why?"

"Who knows, man? Who knows?"

"The good news," Mo said, "is that published studies show no increased risk or readmissions, and steady PATSATs. But the studies were based on all the other hospitals discharging by twelve noon. A humane hour."

"Sounds good, in a way," I said. "Hospitals are dangerous for sick people."

"Yeah, but Man's 4th Best wanted to be 'the Best' at something—and chose the earli*est* time of discharge. So *we* have to TOSS 'em out by seven a.m., and it is *ugly*. Hell for patients, hell for us. We stay late the night before to BUFF patients and HEAL, and get in an hour early to BUFF some more. Why this insane search for money?"

"'Cause they're losing it hand over fist," Fats said, "and they're neck-deep in debt."

"It's crazy. Starting at admission—diagnosis, treatment plan—they're watching us on our HEAL screens, on their screens, from an undisclosed location. They're the enforcement arm of the three hundred thirty-four people in the Billing Building. They quantify everything. We average eighty percent of our time on our shifts doing HEAL, and they break us down to numbers of clicks for whatever they want. The major thing they track is codes we type in. To make sure we max out codes for cash. They spy on us whenever we're on our screens, especially near discharge, 'cause that's their last chance to code for max payment—and to revise retro, backward in the e-record—to build up, for each diagnosis, the top-paying code. If we resist the top payment, they call us right after we've typed it in—call on the phone so there's no e-mail trace. If we resist, like saying, 'But he never *had* an MI!' next thing we know, the code team's marching down the hall, always three of 'em, to torment us. They're the enforcers for Billing."

"They rilly do *watch* you all the time?" Chuck asked. "I thought they was jokin'."

"All the time. If you balk, they come here in person, so there's no trace of what they say. The fight on codes is hard, but to have to TOSS out at seven? The time pressure's *intense* to click the jackpot box, without insurance catching on so it doesn't BOUNCE back. But then insurance fights back, trying to TURF it back to us without a BOUNCE of our BOUNCE back to them, which would pay the least money. It's a war, a real— Oops!"

Suddenly the ward Muzak get louder. *Mozart? The 40th Symphony?*

She pointed down the hall to a gaggle of three. "Here they come. So if it gets to be the afternoon before discharge and I haven't met their criteria for lying and cheating, they show up. And show up up, all night long, and don't stop at seven but keep pushing through eight or nine. If you haven't met their final bids by nine thirty, they overrule you. To free up the bed, they discharge the patient into the hallway, and give you 'bonus time' to raise the money."

The three were coming closer. Seeming to march, in lockstep, to the Mozart.

"They want to discharge Wambui tomorrow. She won't be ready to go—as you can see. She's still in ketoacidosis, but the indicators of her mild sepsis—after just two days of antibiotics—are gone. She's on Medicaid. If she had private insurance, they'd keep her. They've started TURFING *all* Medicaid patients—if they're not publishable cases. Trying to not admit 'em either. Wambui's got no aftercare, and her son and family are on vacation in Bali. I haven't been able to get in touch with them yet."

Three abreast, they were nearing us.

High noon. To Mozart. In ominous G minor.

"What departments are they from?" Fats asked.

"One from Coder Billing—the Bad Cop. She always has a laptop and a squirrely CIA earphone—listening to the guys stationed in HUC."

We stared at her, puzzled.

"HEAL Undisclosed Central. The second of the trio is Social Work—the Good Cop. The third is an enormous nurse nicknamed 'Thunder.' She's the real boss of TOSS. Überbad Cop."

The Mozart was repeating itself, over and over. "Why the Mozart?" I asked.

"It's the fourth movement. They sometimes set words to it: *'Mozart's in the closet, TOSS 'im out TOSS 'im out TOSS 'im out!'* At six a.m., it gets louder, gets into your brain."

The clash commenced.

The only name tag read "Faith Schenckberg, Social Work."

Bad-cop Coder Billing began, "At admission you coded for diabetic ketoacidosis, which was okay, and *mild* sepsis, S47983—which was not okay. We made the bid of Dx of *severe* sepsis S47985, but you, strangely, demurred. So we raised you to *medium* sepsis S47984, and you *still* demurred, saying you were 'busy treating' ketones and you held at *mild*. Friday morning our chief of Cash Protocolization, Robert Rubin—of Morgan Stanley—called you with *severe* sepsis S47985, and—"

"But by then she wasn't even *in* any significant sepsis, because the antibiotics—"

"—and tonight you're refusing to click her discharge code of *severe* sepsis, life-threatening, maximally coded. Do not refuse. Code it."

"But the antibiotics worked right away, she has not been in *any* sepsis for days, and she needs to stay because she's still in serious diabetic ketoacidosis."

"Ketosis as a code pays peanuts. Discharge her tomorrow with severe."

"How can we discharge a patient who is in severe sepsis?" I asked. "It's malpractice."

"Easy. As you just heard, the severe sepsis has been successfully *treated*—at a high-margin-profit cost. A great reimbursable."

"But if she came in with a Dx of *mild*, and had successful mild treatment, how can you *now* code it for *severe* sepsis at discharge?" I'd be damned if I'd give in to this crap.

"Easy. We code it retroactive to admission. The original diagnosis was human error, Mo's data-entry error click was obviously a slip of her finger into the adjacent box containing *mild*. She was severe all along. Now she's cured. Good work, doctors."

We were stunned.

"Of course, *if* she's *still* in severe," Coder said, "and you don't want the whiff of malpractice, she stays for treatment—with severe, you don't want to discharge too soon, right? Why, it might be malpractice."

"Further treatment for what she never *had*?" I said. "She never *had* severe sep—"

"*Now* she did!" This from the enormous Nurse Thunder, big-boned, big-chinned, big-bosomed, big-hipped, big-calved—but remarkably small feet. "Thanks to Coder."

Nodding, Coder smiled up at her, and then looked back down at us.

"And what about keeping her here for her ketosis?" Mo asked Coder.

"If it's just a diagnosis of ketosis, tomorrow at seven she gets TOSSED. But if she also now has the diagnosis of *severe* sepsis, she can stay for further treatment—and you can piddle around with the ketosis for however long you want. Oh—and cash in on any other diagnosis that pops up, iatrogenic or other. We can help find diagnoses while she's here."

"But won't they notice she had antibiotics briefly, for her mild sepsis?"

"Sepsis. Severe. And who says she *hasn't* gotten the high-dose-antibiotic treatment?"

"Man, y'can retro-treat with antibiotics too?"

"I never said that, and I'm not a man. But yes, it will be a very delicate matter of retrograde clawback." Coder sighed. "And all this trouble because you refused to go *severe*, early and often. We'll retro it, get the money. But it ain't gonna be pretty."

"And so," Chuck said, "stay or go depends on cash money?"

"I never said that—you did. Patient care comes first. Off the record? You bet."

"So she can't stay past seven for ketosis, no matter what?" I asked.

"Unless her severe sepsis gets worse."

"She doesn't *have* severe sepsis!" I shouted.

"Oh-kee-dokey," she said, clapping shut her laptop. "Annnd it seems we have ceased making good progress here. Mo, do the right thing: CODE and TOSS."

"Listen," Mo said, "she's from Kenya, has bad vision, ketones are making her foggy, and her arthritis makes it hard to open bottles of her six meds even if she could read the—"

"Arthritis? Additional code! Why didn't you code for arthritis?"

"—she's a mess. There's no one at home to take care of her and—"

"There's no code for 'a mess,' dear," said Coder. "Enough already."

"What's your name?" Mo asked. "I don't see a name tag?"

A stunned look, as if Mo were asking for her bra size.

Chuck, even though we already knew her name, turned toward the big nurse. "What'all's your name, girl?"

"Thunder."

We waited for her last name, in vain.

"Listen, all of you," Mo said. "Here's what I propose. She's right here, one door down. Come see her with me. You'll understand she's a real person, that this is a reality." Mo, with what I felt was remarkable innocence and courage, held out both her hands, palms up, one to Thunder, one to Coder.

"What?" cried Thunder, shrinking back, hand behind her big back as if slapped.

Coder didn't blink or move.

"It'll make her real to you. A real person." Mo glanced at Fats, who nodded. Mo was coming into her own! "She stays till her brain haze clears, and I will not sign her out with a false fatal Dx code. I, and Man's 4th Best, can be sued and—"

"*4th* Best'?!" cried Nurse Thunder, shocked.

"Dear, believe me, we *hear* you," said Faith Schenckberg, Social Work, nodding—as if trained, like a seal, to nod for a fish, say, a mackerel. "I'll find lovely home care by TOSS tomorrow."

"Time's wasting," said Thunder, looming over us.

"Damn, gurl," cried Chuck, craning his neck. "You are tall! Ever play basketball—"

"I don't play anything." She stared down at each of us in turn, a lighthouse in a thunderstorm—why not? "From the highest levels, we are onto you. Onto your 'empathic care' model of her Dx code. Onto you during her Rx code. Onto you from now until her discharge codes. Don't get yourself into even more deep doo-doo." Thunder handed Mo a sheet of paper. "Discharge note, retrograded from tomorrow. Play it. HEAL it. Or else."

"Or else what?" I asked.

"Bottom line. We've got to game insurance, like they game us. We are at war. Fight fire with fire."

"We have to lie?" I asked.

"I didn't say that—you did. Why would I encourage you to lie?"

"To game insurance, as you said. But lying goes against our Hippocratic—"

"I didn't say 'game' either. Too cute, Basch, too cute by half. I'm onto you, all'a you . . . you House of Godders!" She looked at Mo. "And don't forget to bill that arthritis!"

"And," Coder Billing added, "always remember that *we are watching you*, counting your clicks into the boxes of HEAL, in real time. We total them up. The more clicks, *the more money* for BUDDIES, *the more money* for Man's Best Hospital, *the more money* for the FMC, and *the more money* for each of you as individual stakeholders. *Monetizing*."

"Nurse Thunder?" Fats asked coyly, as if about to ask her for a date or offer her the enema of her choice. "No need to be nasty. Just gimme a minute to iron this out."

He left us staring at one another and, phone to ear, walked to a quiet corner down the hall, his oval body seeming to glide on top of the reflections of Man's

4th Best's polished floor. He said something, then held the phone away from his ear—we heard shouting. A moment or two passed, then silence. He said something else and listened. He hung up. Fats walked down the corridor to us, as if taking a stroll in a park. He looked at the threesome, one by one, saying, "Get the fuck outta here. Any questions, call President Krashinsky."

At end of the day was the PATSATs award ceremony, hosted by none other than Pat P. Flambeau, CEO of the bleeding-out BUDDIES.

Fitting his triumphant great American story from rags to chickens, the event was perfectly protocolized by his protocolers, down to the last feather. Where it would be (in front of the FMC nursing station), who was invited (only staff, no shots of our poor, old, sick-looking, many-hued patients), in what order what would happen—all timed edgily.

Exactly on time, in he came. A tall, broad, fit-looking man—but for the right side of his dark power suit, the empty right sleeve tucked into its pocket—an African American, of much darker skin than in his media appearances. When he walked in, his square face with puffy cheeks and balding dome was set at default levels "high power/medium friendly." His eyes were dark, secreted. Was there any clue in the lips? In his grand entrance, everything was hidden under "hail-fellow-well-met," but I glimpsed quick curl-downs at the lip ends, as if he were a man who'd spent his life with clenched teeth—that lost right arm, and fierce overcompensation of the left—and power and money. Alongside was a buxom woman in a pink silk blouse, with metallic eyes. Later, as the event went on, his face took on a rubbery fluidity that hinted of his inner workings: from smile to clench, from clench to back-slap, or capped rage. For all that steel suit, in that smile, those chicken-flicking eyes? Vigilance. Vulnerability denied, big-time. Craving, bigger.

One of his retinue carried a chicken-sized satchel. We'd heard that this was always with Flambeau. It brought to mind "the football" that contains nuclear launch codes always with the president. Krash was trailing, looking small, Jewish, in over his head—not having achieved the professional slick-ness of chickens.

The story of the lost right arm was not clear. Rumors went from a war injury—though he hadn't been in one—to a reach deep into his invention, the E-Z Decapitator. The real story was the left arm.

Talking about it after the meeting, Gath, who had been in the Army to pay for med school, said, "I was a boxer, pretty good, actually. At Fort Hood, during my surgical rotation, I was in the ring with a one-armed boxer. It was confusing. I felt bad for him, but I shouldn't've. He floored me in round one. Y'think that arm wasn't *strong*?"

As in his left-hand shake—we right-handers at a disadvantage. He crunched us, without mercy. Here was a corporate guy through and through, fair and fowl. Amalgamated breasts and feathers were in the air. It turned out that after a long diet of proudly eating eggs and fried chickens, Pat P. at 42 suffered a bad MI, and a spiritual awakening. This led to an evangelical mission of breeding extremely low-fat chickens, for love and profit. They were so low fat that they shivered in normal sheds, and were raised in high heat. An innovation in fowl that led to his receiving "Business Innovator of the Year" awards. His mansion in Bartlesville was called Cluckingham Palace. Reborn, he'd moved from slaughter to health care.

"Great t'meet you," Fats said. "I love your chickens. Frank Purdue coined that slogan 'It takes a tough man to make a tender chicken,' but *you* took chickens to new heights."

"Off the record?" Pat P. said. "His chickens were tough, and Frank was a pussy."

"Sir!" cried the buxom and severe-eyed woman in the pink blouse.

He nodded and said to us, "They don't want me talking fowl here. Why's that?"

"Why, I don't know, sir," said Fats, rubbing one of his chins sagely. "Why is that?"

"Damned if *I* know. But I like your entrepreneurship, fat boy. You're human, a human being with humaneness. Like me, an innovator. I innovate. Human. I'm known for innovating chicken and amalgamated poultry back from death."

"Back to more humane death?" I asked.

"Less humane. More profitable. By Jesus, I'm gonna do the same damn thing here."

"Less humane?"

"More profitable. Like you boys do right here and how—"

Suddenly no power.

Dark.

It could've been that damn miasma in the wires, but with such a prized target, how could we not flash on "terrorist attack"? Two of Flambeau's men, hands at holsters, shielded him. But almost at once, the emergency lights came on. Clearly this was another breakage in the old power grid to the Pathology Building. While we waited, Pat P. turned talkative, even nostalgic. As if he were visiting a small town.

"Y'know, when Krash told me about you boys, I was skeptical. You think outta the box. But Big Bizniss likes to stay in the box. So you boys are a risk, for me on top of this multibillion edifice placed in my trust. I trusted Krash, but did my own due dil. I like your L-amphetamine and calcium-boxcar venture, son—I'm a sizer-upper, and . . ." He sized Fats up, as if for a role as Thanksgiving turkey. "And you got a lot to size—and what I'm sayin' is this: I trusted Krash and took the risk and guess what. It worked. So far. Like I took the risk early on when I was broke and had to squeeze cash outta chickens? Hit the market, hard—risky stuff—nonlinear derivs? ETFs? Made a few bil. Know what, boy?"

"What, sir?" Fats asked as if interested.

"Biggest problem in 'Murcan health care is where I come from: *rural*. No rural care anymore. Ninety million good folk, neglected. My kin in Bowlegs, Oklahoma, now have to drive 40 miles to Prague to see a doc—and it's never the same doc. It's one foreign visaed Indian or Asian after another. Outta one hundred twenty BMS grads last year, only four went into family medicine— none into rural. Ergo I see your clinic as a model for rural health, an incubator to a whole flock, modeling how we git to Man's Best Rural Hospitals, pronto."

He startled me—not only this Okie down-to-earth stuff that was sensible and crazy both, but with his bone-crackling handshake and by his suddenly saying to Fats:

"Good!"

"Good?" Fats asked.

"Good call!" cried Flambeau, hitting him in the shoulder with that one meaty palm.

"'Call'?" Fats asked, grimacing.

"You 'n' Mo. Deciding not to discharge that poor Kenyan woman in severe sepsis. Saved us from a lotta bad publicity." He turned to me. "And that religious book a' yours, *God's House*? Also good. Funny. Sexy. Great American stuff. And you boys sure know your SATPATs!" None of us corrected him. "Those SATPATs are dynamite, the way Krash here put them on your dashboards to follow in real time, like the Dow Jones of health? Revenue. Brilliant. How'd y'do it? You're twice as SATPATted as the runner-up, Derm—and they cheat. I mean Derm's cushy, right?" He was looking at Eat My Dust.

"You bet," said Eddie. "In Derm, you only need to know three things: 'If it's dry, you wet it; if it's wet, you dry it; and if you don't know, you use steroids.' No emergencies. Millions. Most popular choice of med students now—that and emergency care. These young docs go for the NOPR: 'No Ongoing Patient Relationship.' Just screens and money."

"So how'd you do it, Fats, hit those Dow Jones SATPATs outta the ballpark?"

"The only reason our PATSATs went up, sir," Fats said, "is that HEAL OUTGOING went down for good. So we have twice as much time for patients. And we're not sitting with our backs toward our patients. Not giving them 'the cold shoulder.'"

"I *hate* it when my doc does that! Don't know if I should talk to him or what. Which?"

"Get him to look at you," I said, "and to write notes on paper. We do it here. It takes half the time. And the PATSATs go up."

"Aw, you boys are too modest. Never mind OUTGOING. The real reason is you're damn good. Human. Not like a lot of my boys—like the chicken industry. They're cowards. No risk, no killer instinct. Don't go for the jugular. But you guys, I'm thinkin' of expandin' you. Krash tells me you've got room down here in Pathology to build up, up several more stories." He stared up, down. "We at Man's Best inpatient wards tend to treat the privileged. You, in outpatient, are treating the unprivileged, for less money each. So *we* on inpatient can *cut our volume,* work less, charge more and make more—often for cash, which avoids a shitload of regulation of dealing with *in*surance. And you boys can *raise your volume,* work more, make more. Bottom line? *All* of us make more lucre. You're now the poster boys for our unprivileged care. And soon rural. But y'need more volume."

"We'd need more staff."

"See?" he said to Krash. "How modest can y'get? Yeah, I'll get right on it and—"

"Sir," said his busty pink attaché, "we've got power. The networks are here. Ready?"

He clicked into TV mode. We stood in a row smiling, Flambeau shaking Fats's hand again. He presented the SATPATs award—"To Man's Best Hospital's Future of Medicine Clinic: Care, Compassion, and Cancer, and innovation for *rural* health care"—and left, slightly late.

All of our left hands—men and women crunched in gender equity—hurt like hell and felt like they were going to necrose and fall off. Fats feared a fracture, and rushed to X-ray.

✑

"I call her 'Olive the Destroyer'!" Spring was shouting through her tears.

Late that night.

Chuck and I had gone out drinking at Man's 4th Best's dive, the Diuresis Den.

I had gotten home too mellow for this chaos.

Spring was sitting on the floor, back against her canopied bed, her arms crossed over her chest in righteous anger. Her tone was of an aggrieved mother after a long day, fed up with her child. It was way past Spring's bedtime. I sat on the floor beside her.

Berry, relieved that I was now on duty, was sitting at the foot of the bed, feeding her addiction to her "I"-phone. She thought that she could also pay attention to the non-"I"-phone world at the same time, but she was wrong. I'd say something to her and she'd mumble an answer that she thought was appropriate but really was off target because she was really with a friend or Buddhist colleague two blocks away or in Lake Como or Varanasi or Spirit Rock in California. When I had suggested this, she'd denied it.

Our faithful, aging dog, Cinnamon, who was afraid of Olive, had found a protected far corner of the room and, his back to us and relieved that I was now home, was snoring.

Olive, in a final romp of the day outside her cage, seemed like anything but the Destroyer, prancing around cutely searching for yet another treat—a Whole Foods apple-sweetened dried cranberry. She would stop, stare at one of us, go up on her hind legs, search out a treat, twitch her nose and her ears contrapuntally, then drop down and hop on.

"Don't give her any!" Spring said to me. "Bad Olive!"

"You think she can understand that?" I asked. "Cinny can, but a rabbit—"

"Not a *ordinary* rabbit. She's, like, way smarter than him."

I took that as an insult. A rabbit smarter than my great love? "No way!"

"Way! Y'know that 'plastic food ball,' right?" I nodded. "It took Cinny a week to figure out how to roll the ball to get food out, an' Olive took ten minutes. She's smart, but she's a Destroyer."

"I know she gnaws on things, but—"

"She eats everything 'n' today she got out and ate my bed and spring box—look!"

Sure enough, the wood frame that sat flush to the floor was gnawed through, leaving a hole big enough to let her get in under the bed and start eating the box spring from below.

"Holy shit!"

"A swear!"

"Sorry!"

"Watch out or she'll gnaw *you*! She bit Mom already."

I glanced at Berry. Having TURFED this to me, she was far away in phoneland, texting. "You're kidding."

"Da-ad, she's a rodent. She gnaws and bites."

Great, we're living with a huge, cute rat.

Hand on hip, shaking a finger, Spring shouted, "*Bad* bunny!"

I was coming down fast from a boozy mellow. I asked Berry, "Any suggestions?"

No answer. Still texting away. Recently, her "I"-phone obsession had reached an altitude of empty space, a real pain in the ass for our—to use her thing—our "we."

"Berry?" I said loudly. "Any suggestions?"

"Hmmm?" Two thumbs texting crazily, as if killing crawly insects, say ladybugs.

"Maybe, honey," I said to Spring, "we should take her back to Animal Rescue and—"

"What? Da-aad, I love Olive. She's only *two*. Give her a break!"

"Sorry." I looked again at Berry. Still gonzo. "I'm sorry, hon. Tomorrow, when I drive you to school, we'll figure out what we can do to make her life better and—"

"Rrrwrofff! Owwwrrowow!"

We all jumped, looked.

Cinnamon was twisted around in a way I thought his arthritis would never allow, his nose all the way around to his butt, which already was seeping red blood through his white fur as he sought whatever savage thing had bitten him.

Olive was hopping high and fast toward her cage.

Cinny went after her, but she jumped the three-foot cage wall to safety, Cinny howling and barking like a young dog wanting to kill and eat whatever had tried to kill and eat him butt first.

I knelt to him. Calmed him. Took him downstairs and inspected his wound. A two-pronged fang slash went down his butt toward a leg. I got my doctor bag, irrigated the wound, started to suture.

In Cinny's expressive eyes was a question: *What the hell are you going to do with that fucking rabbit, pal?*

Finally, Spring and Olive were settled for the night.

Cinny was at the foot of our bed. At the head was Berry with her "I"-phone, and me. I was exhausted, my body busily metabolizing alcohol to aldehyde, sending fumes of ammonia up into my brain. Fearing migraine, aspirined up, I hoped the chaos was over. But I wanted to keep up our commitment to talking down any conflict or distance into at least a semblance of connection before falling asleep. Like the adage: Never go to bed angry.

So I hoisted myself up out of my drunk funk and offered what else but an olive branch. "I had a helluva bad day, and I'd like to hear about yours."

"Oh yeah?" She was still texting, the spooky green light on her face making her look, given my mood, like a cartoon martian.

"But I'm so tired, I don't think I can talk."

"Wait a sec." Texting.

Let's try something new, a kind of "I"-phone stress test. "I'm filing for divorce."

"Mmmh, really?"

"My lawyer will deliver the divorce papers to you tomorrow."

"Sounds good, um-hmm."

Text sent.

Pause.

"What?! Did you say 'divorce'?" She was actually looking at me, noting that I was real and really life-sized *there*—not a bunch of pixels in her tiny "I"-phone screen.

I tried to stay calm, but failed. "What the hell's wrong with you and that phone?"

"Don't yell at me!"

"I'm not yelling!" I yelled. "It's the only way to get your attention. You're always in your phone! So much for getting out of the 'self' and getting into 'relationship.'"

"It's not 'either-or.' It's 'and.' My phone *is* relationship. I'm multitasking—women do it all the time and—"

"Not with me right now you're not."

A text rang out, a moment of truth.

She glanced at it. Her thumbs twitched.

"Look, I'm setting up a Buddhist retreat for my women's group. I have to get the program in by tomorrow early. Just gimme a sec—"

"Between your 'sisters' and your 'Buddhists' and your sixteen other Berry groups, you're always on that fucking phone, and it's ruining us!"

"It's just temporary, a crazy week—and you're never around—"

"It's every week! But you don't—"

"—*never* around anymore and you're working—"

"—don't notice it 'cause you're always in your fucking phone!"

"—a ton more hours than Fats promised and you don't even notice it!"

"But when I'm here, I'm *here*—"

"It's getting to be like the House of God and—!"

"—I'm *really* here. When you're here, you're not. You're addicted!"

"And you're drunk!"

I was startled, but still lashed out even though I knew I was lashing out at all the phony shit I'd had to deal with that day and how rarely now I was doing what I loved—taking care of people—but doing screens, and now dealing with *her* screen shit too! Head pounding, I shouted: "Yeah, maybe I am drunk! But tomorrow I'll be sober, and tomorrow you'll still be in your phone!"

19

Maybe a week or two later, in dread February, we three came home from a weekend in New York on a late, moonless Sunday night, chins tucked down into our throats, staggering with our bags, through what seemed solid slats of sleet, down the curving path of iced-up stones to our door. We were exhausted, but glad to be home. Spring had slept in the car. But now she was wide-awake and in bliss to see Cinny and the Destroyer Rabbit—running up the stairs to see if our father-daughter carpentry project in rabbit-proof fencing, designed to protect Spring's bed and box spring from being eaten, had worked. It had. The joy, the joy. I paid the house-and-dog-and-bunny sitter. Happy, we went to bed.

Too early Monday morning, we stepped into the day's "Child Olympics," the first event being "Getting Your Five-year-old to School on Time and Us on Time Too." As we opened the sliding-glass door to the entryway, I saw two envelopes on the tiles, slipped under the big red carriage house door. One was from my tenant, Paulie; the other had no name on the outside. Paulie's handwriting was, strangely, delicate:

> Hey Doc. Like I told you the once before: I'm going away. Henry Cabot-Fuckin-Lodge fingered me to the WASPs runnin' the Feds. The family's gone to Sicily to her family. The girl went back to Georgia. Get the bastard if you can. I'll be on him too. Don't bother sending back security deposit.

You & Berry & that cute Spring will quite soon receive a special gift, a boxed set of 24 perfect veal steaks & best regards Paulie.

"What's wrong?" Berry said, opening the outer door to the wind.
"Da-ad! Margaret!"
"Nothing. Let's go." I stuck the two letters in my pocket.
After I'd dropped off Spring at the Whole World, I opened the other one. Hand-printed in crayons, in childish if not a moron's capital letters:

IN VICTORY, MALICE. IN DEFEAT, REVENGE. SO YOU PRICK NOW IT'S MALICE. LOOK OUT. AND I REALLY LOVE PIZZA! HENRY CABOT-LODGE.

I understood his sense of victory, but why mention pizza? He'd mentioned it in notes to me before—was it a kind of ritual, like a security pizza? A subtle slam of the Mafia motif? A clue to diagnosis? As a shrink, I figured he was a total narcissist—looking at the outside world as a mirror, Projection City. Pizza is him. His love of it is of himself. Insane.

All day at the FMC, I tried to focus on patients—and pretty much failed. Except for one moment when we all were riveted in terror. A nodding addict leaped to his feet and, shouting in Spanish, waved a revolver over the heads of his wife and child, and everyone screamed and hit the floor. A beefed-up 4th Best Security floored him. Luckily it turned out to be the child's toy gun, a lifelike facsimile. But it was a warning. We had been told that we and Emergency were at great risk—even if with knives more than with guns. This was a warning.

Everybody—doctors and patients—was doing a lot worse. That February was the worst in recorded history, all over the world. Worst and the most crazy. One week we'd be freezing, iced in, trees smashing down, electricity snuffed out, huddled around candles, making fires indoors. But the next week, we'd be sweating. The West Coast, in a drought challenging Death Valley, was aflame from Paradise to Malibu. Biblical floods and out-of-season hurricanes hit from Texas to the Carolinas. In the summer in Phoenix, the temperature hit 120— the air too thin for planes to attain lift. No one, anywhere, was safe.

This crazy-climated world seeped into all of us—doctors and patients alike—at the level of mortal dread. Our anxiety was off the charts.

Fats had said to us, more than once: "The world is in the rooms."

And we did try, in the clinic and on the ward, to be aware of the world. We would ask patients questions about their "normal" world, like, "Where does your water come from, and where does your garbage go?" All of us are in this together—we're all *of* the earth—70 percent water, separated from the outside world by a real thin layer of skin—porous to the world. Poison the world, we poison ourselves. If we fail to treat the sick world, how can we treat its effects on sick patients? While there's still time, in our sliver of life, dust to dust.

The patient *is* the world.

But as with all of us busy humans, my main worry was not this. My worry was money. And I knew, from psych patients, how deep that sick human craving for money could be.

Paulie, on the lam, had paid me 6,000 dollars per month cash, 72,000 dollars a year. Other numbers kept buzzing all day. My expenses. Mortgage: 36,000 dollars. Property tax: 28,000 dollars. House insurance: 12,000 dollars. Whole World School: 27,000 dollars. Utilities: 7,000 dollars. Total? 110,000 dollars per year. Plus our "living expenses"—like, oh, *food?*—at least another 50K. Total? 162,000 dollars a year. My salary? 135,000 dollars before taxes. Zero, so far, from profit shares.

I was in a cold sweat. I was now in a money hole. I had to rent the house again fast.

Which, I found out that night, I would not be able to do anytime soon. It was a wreck. Being a "hands-off," trusting landlord, I hadn't been in the house in a long time—maybe six months. Paulie had said that he would take care of everything, all repairs, upgrades. "I'll do whatever it takes to keep this beaut pristine-like, Doc. Y'get me?" I said I did.

Berry and I walked through the house. This gorgeous, grand old Victorian had been beaten up, eaten away from her inside, left in wreckage, stinking. On the quarter-sawed-oak wall in the dining room, a painted dartboard, darts sticking in. The ceiling of the grand living room, with eleven moldings coming out from the edges halfway to the center, where there had been a chandelier, now had a hole, brown water stains from the master bathroom above. Water warping the inlaid oak, mahogany, black walnut rococo floor. The long, stately hallway looked like it had been used for boccie ball. This grand old lady had been raped.

It was unlivable, unrentable. Sad, guilty for not paying attention, I slumped down on the icy stoop, tears in my eyes. Not just for the desecration but also for the fact that to fix it up to rentable would cost, I guessed, 100 grand. The estimate, from structural work in the basement to replacing hand-made Italian roof tiles, would turn out to be two. After the low pay in the IHS, with my salary and Berry's practice, we had no real savings. We could not afford to fix the house up. Just to stay afloat, we needed Paulie's 6K per month.

"I can take on more patients," Berry said that night. "What else can we do?"

"I'll moonlight. I'll put out feelers to emergency rooms."

⌒

"Roy! Eddie!" said Fats. "It's Buck again! Let's move!"

It was a few days later. He'd canceled the scheduled morning check-in abruptly and was now moving fast on those piston legs out the door; we scrambled to keep up.

"Jude's in trouble."

Buck was was the surgeon Gath had threatened when he was in the cab to Women's 2nd Best Hospital to do a second operation at the same time that his first was being botched by a paralyzed new resident. Buck's partner was Barmdun, the other chief of Orthopedics.

The usually quiet, efficient operating suite was in turmoil.

"I shoulda known!" said the head OR nurse, Prudence Kline, a calm, kind, rock-solid 35-year-old. Jude was beside her, in surgical garb and looking very pregnant. "He gave personal instructions to the pre-op nurse not to put his two patients—total hips—next to each other in the pre-op suite, so they can't talk and find out he's booked both at the same time. Right now the resident doing one of the two cases is at his limit, poodling around the hip socket with sharp objects—a lot of bleeding—and he called for Buck, who refused to leave the other patient. I told the resident to stop. The woman's eighty-two, respiratory disease—she shouldn't be under anesthesia for any extra time. She'll come out *ninety*-two. Gath is off duty, so I sent Jude in to Buck to get him back on the other case, but he didn't answer her."

"Oh, he answered me," Jude said, "with four-letter words ending in 'Navajo gal, get the fuck outta my OR.' So I said, 'Buck, you remind me of one of Gath's favorite songs: "From the Gutter to You Ain't Up."'"

Pru looked at Fats, and at Eddie and me. "Can you help?"

"No problem," said Eddie, reaching for his belt. "Just let me reload, okay?"

"Given that it's Buck," said Fats, "we need a higher rank. Is Lena working?"

"Always. Next door. Here, put these on." She handed us gowns, masks, and caps.

"Wait," I said to Pru. "Somebody has to document the time he started in *his* OR, and when his resident started in *his*—and when they both stopped. For the future."

"Got it," said Pru. "Consider it done." She left.

Lena Metz was a rare equal to Fats—they were bosom eating buddies—a tall, hefty, savvy chief anesthetist of the OR. No one messed with Lena. Their mutual admiration was based on poundage and its etiology: high-fat, high-carb, high-salt, low-health deli foods they both loved. And here she was. The two standing side by side were like puffy pylons at a ferry dock. Fats briefed her.

"That fascist *schmucklezager!*" Lena said. "I told him: 'Once more will be your last!' Let's go."

We tied up our scrubs, caps, and masks, and followed her through the maze of ORs, and went in. I love operating rooms, the clean, chill air in slanting bright light, birdlike chirps and beepings and a scent that always reminds me of the essence of hope—ether. If ever a place was "ethereal," this was it.

But not this one. Wagner, "Ride of the Valkyries." Shadow forms cut, as if in lockstep with opera. Buzzing, cauterizing vessels. The scent of burned flesh. We stayed just inside the curtain and watched Lena stand across from Walt Buck, who wore the traditional green gown, but his cap was adorned with daffodils and Cadillacs.

Lena said, "You're needed in the other OR stat. The resident is in trouble. The patient is at risk."

"Get off my case." He kept cauterizing. Scent of burned flesh. Sound of Wagner.

"Dr. Buck. Step away from the table."

"What?"

"Step . . . away . . . from . . . the . . . table."

"You can't order me around. Go away."

"You know I can, and I am."

He kept on sizzling.

"Okay. All of you listen up. Given my authority as OR chief of Anesthesia, I told Dr. Buck to step away from the table. Twice. The rest of you remain, to provide a safe standard of care, until we find someone to continue."

Buck stared at her. Cursing into his surgical mask, he turned and walked past us.

"Hey, Walt," Fats said, "the two families are sitting together out there. Whaddaya gonna tell *them*?"

The fallout came down from Buck's partner, Barmdun. He was famous for the slogan he lived by: "You eat what you kill." "Eat" was money; "kill" was number of patients operated on. And he was famous for double-booking ORs for double pay. Carnage incarnate. A slithery guy trailing two messy divorces. He couldn't go after Fats and me. So with fury he went after Jude, in a letter:

"Your attendance in the theater without supervision under Dr. Gath is a violation of our agreement of your probation from the orthopedic residency. The penalty is suspension from any further operating. Your reporting that two operations were being done by one surgeon at the same time is erroneous and slanderous. The official time logs of each operating room show that Dr. Buck, but for brief openings and closings by two residents, was never in the two places at the same time, but only sequenchully [*sic*] times."

The next morning at check-in, Jude said, "He falsified the time logs. And it was not a case of operating without supervision—Lena had paged me stat for an emergency, to stop the patient from bleeding out until Buck came, a call I could not refuse. He's using it to try to break my probation agreement, to use it at the harassment-discrimination trial. Gath and I have a full day of cases today—and I'm banned? What can I do?"

"What time's your first case?" Fats asked. Halfway to his mouth was a breakfast we'd never seen before, a cruller as big and fat as a shoe, not only glazed but sprinkled with sugar and lunky black chunks of chocolate. Hooper winced, rocked. Clearly carrots had failed.

"I cain't see doin' it without you, Jude," Gath said. "I mean, I could, technically, but that'd be givin' in to these pricks, and any weakness, they'll use it in court."

"The patient comes first," Jude said. "Poor woman—eighty-two, hip revision after a fall? The femur's in three pieces, socket's in bad shape—we'll need wires, plates, screws. I called down. Barmdun's got heavy security there now, to stop me. What can we do?"

"Do nothing," Fats said, "except the operation. I'll handle it. What time's the op?"

"In an hour," Jude said.

Fats balanced his phone on his cruller, putting both to his ear. "Roy? Gilheeny's number?" He punched it in, got up, and, in a corner, whispered into his phone briefly. About 15 minutes later, it rang. He listened, said, "Thanks," turned to Jude. "You two are good to go."

After the morning check-in, as we all trudged toward our offices and Fats, light on his feet, started dancing toward the cafeteria, I grabbed him.

"Gilheeny fixed it?" He nodded. "Here?" Another nod. "An Irishman fixed it at an ur-WASP hospital?"

"Only for my most crucial favors. He never fails. Irish Rule. I'll explain it all later."

"Hey, wait. I know two of the writers in the investigative team at the *Register Star*. They're riding high on that Pulitzer. With Jude's case going to trial, they may go for it?"

"Set it up. Like yesterday."

The next night Fats and I met with the two journalists, sworn to secrecy, at a seedy bar under the Columbia River Bridge. Susan Gray and Mark Vonney, with—yes!—those steno notebooks and pens. If they took a case, and started the investigation, they were like wolves, jaws locked on their prey so that even if you ripped their heads off, they'd die with their teeth still clenched around it. We laid out the whole case. Jude was suing the trio of Man's 4th, BUD-DIES, and the BMS. Gath and Jude had documented every e-mail, phone call, etc. Their case was rock-solid.

"Bad timing," Susan said. "We just ran a discrimation story—they're common."

"But it's heated up again right now," Fats said. "Last year, she went to the chief of Ortho and blew the whistle on a double booking in surgery that almost killed a patient."

"A what?" asked Vonney.

We told them. Their ears perked up, got red. We told them more. They perked up more, even eyebrows, so their eyes looked big, sharp, hungry. Nostrils flaring. Smelling blood.

"The orthopedic surgeons routinely book two different surgeries at once?" Vonney asked.

"Yes," I said. "It's a scientific breakthrough: they're the only two human beings able to be in two different places at the same time."

"And the surgeons are mostly male?" asked Susan.

"All male and very. Jude's the only woman in a residency program of about fifty men. She and her mentor, Gath, are both ortho surgeons at Man's 4th Best Hospital and—"

"*4th* Best?" asked Susan. I told them the story of the rankings. They laughed.

"Gath tried to stop the double bookings, but they told him to shut up, or else. So last week he went to the patient safety officer, Russell Paul, who easily explained it: 'I don't make the orders about what's right or wrong. I just follow them.'"

"Christ!" Vonney cried. "Do we need a Nuremberg refresher course for doctors?"

"What kind of person," Susan asked, "is Jude?"

"The best ever," I said. "Grew up dirt-poor on the Navajo rez, somehow made it here. She's taken the orthopedic residents' abuse for years, and never said a word. By all accounts, she's as good technically as any of them, and has a remarkably humane way with patients. They love her. Now, the final year of her training, they framed her. The chief sent a secret letter around asking the guys for any information they had that could smear her. But there was no bad info on her. So they made some up. She fought back, got nowhere, filed suit. Imagine, after ten years of training, they won't certify her to practice? And in her deposition, know what she said? 'I didn't come here to hurt people.'"

The two journalists looked at each other. Susan said, "Set up a meeting."

A few days later, we all got an e-mail from BUDDIES to announce a ceremony to inaugurate the new Saudi-Kissinger Tower. It would include a traditional sword dance of the prince, Flambeau, and Krashinsky, and Henry Kissinger himself would be there, but not able to dance. Rumor had it that peacock tongues would be served at the luncheon.

Except for urgent patient-care matters, all of us were encouraged to watch on our INCOMING screens. The Kiss-Saudi Tower had come about in a single meeting of the board, because of a grateful Saudi prince who thought his life had been saved by the 4th Best world experts, the chiefs of Surgery, Medicine, and GI. In fact, the experts had almost killed him by their *treatment*—because most chiefs, older docs who'd fought their way up, had for decades taken care of money, not patients. Never go to a chief for care.

Kissinger had suggested that the prince get his open-heart surgery at Man's 4th Best, because he himself had had heart surgery there—by Buck, before he switched to orthopedics. Because Henry was famous, Buck had decided to do the whole heart operation himself from start to finish. Gath happened to be assisting on the operation, and he told me that Buck had never tried the new electric saws, hepped-up versions used for cutting through the center of the sternum to open the chest. Unused to its power, he lost his grip, and with a *vrrrrrooooom*, he veered off course and severed all the ribs on one side. Blood was gushing, flooding the chest cavity. Buck panicked, slapped the bloody saw into Gath's hand, shouted, "Fix this mess and call me after!" He then retired to the surgeons' lounge to eat peanut butter and jellies and watch *Wheel of Fortune*. With baling wire, working for a crucial hour, Gath reattached the ribs. Kissinger, post-op, was in horrific pain—on maximum morphine. He'd lie there, clutching pillows to his chest, screaming. Buck said this pain was normal. Poor Henry never knew the truth. He had touted Buck to the prince, whose gratitude for care led to the gazillion-dollar Saudi-Kiss Tower. It was thought by the board to be the best, last hope to stop BUDDIES and Man's 4th bleeding out.

It was a kind of great pornographic building, straddling the massive granite Blue Building—the signature building of Man's 4th when it really was best. "The Kiss"—on four steel legs crushing the "Children's Cancer Garden"—climbed up, up, and away in space until, leaving a small gap for sky, it started its ladders of floors: numbers 23 to 69. The stainless steel ornament on top looked like either a kind of eternal flame or a Fleet enema. Giant paired flags of Saudi Arabia and Man's 4th Best fluttered around the first floor atop the Blue Building, making that grand old lady look like a carnival ride. The top 25 floors were presidential suites—kitchens, cooks, servants—for Saudis, Russian oligarchs, Chinese capitalists, and other filthy rich who could pay with nice green cash that didn't go through HEAL, who never questioned a bill, and who wouldn't stoop to the dull, chilly, or sweltering Great Plains of the Mayo Clinic.

Below the posh top floors of the Kissy-Saudi were offices of every medical-surgical specialty that the rich might need, from pulmonary to penis, heart to hernia, colon to corns—and gorgeous operating suites, open for business 24/7. The bottom floors would turn out to make our lives in the FMC a living hell, for they housed a new concept: "Man's Ruby Red Rose Carpet Concierge Medicine LLC."

Its logo and branding were, yes, a rose, and red carpets were everywhere, including the bathrooms. It was a private group of GP and Family docs, who for a yearly fee of 50,000 dollars were always at your beck and call. A fleet of chauffeured cars was also at beck, for pickups and drop-offs of children, pets, and visiting relatives and for errands, dog walks, snake feedings—and probably rabbits. Who were the new concierge docs? Almost all were former Man's 4th Best staff, abused not by Man's 4th but by BUDDIES and HEAL. Given the chance for less work at much more pay, they rushed to get in, and left without warning: in the middle of the night before the opening, their offices had been moved to the Saudi-Kissy. It was mostly a payment-in-cash business. Almost no HEALing.

Doctors sat in leather "club chairs," face-to-face with patients, chatting. They never had to touch HEAL! The reason? There were "scribes," who sometimes played HEAL from pools in Bangalore. Hard up Indian doctors hooked into live audio. No video for the stealthy rich. Mostly, these Kissy-Saud doctors were good men and women, fed up and beaten down, exhausted, traumatized. Now they had time, and astro salaries. No more money worry. College costs? Done. Divorce settlements? Man's 4th Best lawyers.

Who could blame them? Before the *1984*-like BUDDIES and the *2001* HAL-like HEAL, they had loved their work, loved the human contact and the sense of doing good in the world. And had cherished the esprit de corps.

As Dick Johannes, a kindly old doc who'd been a leader at MBH when it had still tried to live up to its mission, said at his retirement party, looking straight at Flambeau and Krash: "You money guys don't understand us doctors anymore. We have a secret: *We would do this for free.*"

Good for them, these Ruby Red docs. But bad for us, the FMC, because they TURFED their patients to us. A huge new load.

Seeing Kissinger himself at the ceremony, I thought back to the '60s and what Tom Lehrer, the great protest singer, had said when asked why he'd stopped singing. "When Henry Kissinger got the Nobel Peace Prize, all the fun went out of political satire."

Kissinger was now a loxed-out, quivering, drooling gomer in a wheelchair—in the sick hell of eternally end-stage Parkinson's.

As Reverend Martin Luther King said: "The arc bends toward justice."

⌒

"Molly?"

"Roy!"

I stood there, stunned, staring at her walking toward me as I sat in a chair in the living room with a bourbon and a beer chaser. She had been a nurse at the House that year, in her first real job—as was I—and our passionate-love-in-shared-desperation affair had kept me alive, for a while. Love? Well, a kind of love. The sexual and sensual attraction, heated up by caring for diseased bodies, was astonishing—the eternal pairing, sex and death.

Now, in shock, I looked at her, and she looked pretty much the same, the pitch-black hair now cut more stylishly, framing that round face, and suddenly shining green eyes, a bit-too-large nose, and scarlet lips with glinting lip gloss—and her body! Through memory sharp as first perception, I saw again those remarkably caressable breasts and strangely long nipples, saw her in my rental apartment up in the attic of an old house, I sitting on the edge of the bed and she sitting on me saying, since neither of us could move, "Now what?" and the "what" was my flipping her over on her back, and still in her, moving a *lot*, in tune, until both of us were screaming. She was younger than me and in great shape, with one breast she'd named Toni and the other Sue, and that first night of sex I twirled Toni and sucked Sue and lost it over and over again. Ahh, that first opening up, knowing that it would be *there* whenever I wanted it and when I wasn't seeing Berry—she and I at that time had agreed to our both seeing others.

I stared up into Molly's light green eyes.

"I know where you just went," she said, snapping me out of it. "I went there too."

I nodded. She was one of the most perceptive women I'd ever met. We'd actually met when she was carrying a full bedpan, and I'd said, "Not the most romantic way to meet someone," and she'd said, "No, but it's *real*." I loved the real of her. We were soldiers together down in the trenches, down in the dirt of the real, yeah.

"Oh boy," I said. "It was real."

"Y'think?"

"No question." I looked around for a sec, not knowing where I was, when, or why.

Early March. A party for all of us FMC docs at Eat My Dust and Naidoo's new place, to celebrate their shared house buying, perhaps preengagement(!), the house a sweet three-decker brownstone in a historic district. Everybody had come, but for the Fat Man, who'd been away for a week already, to see Rosie and beloved Chubby and tend to "the crucial results of the phase three trial" of his boxcars of calcium and L-amphetamine, and memory.

Berry and Spring were in Florida for school vacation, trying to make up for the mess I had created with Berry's mom at Thanksgiving. Since then there'd been a growing distance between us. Her addiction to her "I"-phone hadn't eased, and she had also dived headfirst into a new community of Buddhists, for daylong meditations and occasional weekend retreats. She was talking about becoming a teacher of "Insight Dialogue," something new that had you meditating not alone, but facing another person—perfect for her. All of this was mostly with women. I felt the gap between us widen. Add money worry, and it was bad.

With her and Spring away for a few days, my only duties were Cinnamon and Olive.

I'm free all weekend. Is she? No ring on her finger.

"Wonderful to see you, Molly. What are you doing here?"

"I just joined the FMC."

I tried to hide my surprise. A coincidence or something more? "Oh?"

"Yeah. Angel—I've kept in touch with her and Runt—she told me that you guys were hiring, getting really swamped, and the Fat Man wanted gender parity. I've heard only good things—and who wouldn't want to work with Fats?"

"Why, no one wouldn't, darlin'," I said in Quick's accent. "No one wouldn't a'tall."

She laughed. As people age, their laughs never change. I loved that girlish trickle.

"I'm a nurse practioner now. Got my degree at Yale."

"Wonderful! When do you start with us?"

"Monday, and—"

"Hi there, you lovebirds." A familiar voice. "Quite nice to see you together again!"

"Angel?!"

"And my dear, lovable old Runt," Angel said smoothly, with neither pause nor gesture.

The Runt paused and gestured, pointing to his raised finger. "That's"—pointing to his heart—"me!" He was wide-eyed and smiling. Not wearing his bike helmet.

So now she's fluent with both us and Runt? And now he's paralyzed in gesture talk?

"Angel," I said, "you look terrific! And your speech is literally gorgeous. Why?"

"I'm pregnant! Finally!"

"Wow! Congrats!" I looked at Runt, who tried to speak but stopped, gestured an affirmation, much like Angel had always done. They were ecstatic. I felt really happy for them and asked Molly if she'd like a drink and she said, "I don't drink, remember?" and I said, "Still?" I retrieved my own bottle of George Dickel Sippin' Whiskey from the bar and got another two beers for chasers. We chatted about how great it was that Angel's soul sister, Molly, would start Monday.

She had come to the party with Angel and Runt, so I offered to drive her home. It was a great condo in the suburbs and, well, we kissed as we always had and I felt in it that wonderful sense that the woman was melting like her lips were melting soft into mine and as if no time had passed we went into the bedroom—no longer a "little girl" bedroom with fluffy toy bears and bunnies from those years ago but a, well, grown-up-licensed-nurse-practitioner bedroom all order and big-screen desktop that made me realize how far she'd come and how much older we'd gotten and we kissed some more on the bed and I unbuttoned her blouse and unhooked her bra and I was astonished at how Toni and Sue had *maintained* and as I reached up between her legs she caught her breath and said:

"Nope."

"What? Why nope?"

"We have to talk."

"Right now? Can't it wait about fifteen—"

"Nope. Talk."

"About what?"

"About what happened."

"Oh. Okay." I tried to catch my breath and focus, detumesce. "It was simple. You TURFED me. Left me for that idiot Howie Greenstein or whatever his last name was."

"I married him."

"Did you love him?"

"Somewhat."

"He was dull as dirt."

"After you, I needed dull. I loved his not being crazy, and, frankly, at the time I was kind of interested in cystic kidney disease—he was impressive on that. He had promise."

"He was on prescription drugs—did you know that?" She seemed shocked. "On tranqs of all kinds, all year long."

"So? He had promise. And you had . . ." She paused. "You had Berry."

"Wait a sec. She and I were free to see other people."

"Anyway, you were crazy, and I didn't think you'd even live through the year."

"Me too."

"You had a big effect on me, Roy, but you were so bitter. I was getting bitter too. It's one reason I ditched you. But there were two final reasons—in addition to your being crazy and bitter. One time, after one great night of sex, and it was great sex—I give you that."

"Tonight?"

"I asked you, 'If I get pregnant, will you marry me?' You looked as if you'd been shot. And you said, 'You've got an IUD,' and I said, 'Yeah, but it can still happen,' and you without even thinking about it said no." She was staring at me as if I'd committed a crime.

"Sorry. I guess I was really shocked by the idea of marriage, not to whom."

"Maybe, but I heard it being about me."

"What was the second reason?"

"Again, after great sex, I asked you a few questions about the other woman you were seeing. You were evasive. Finally, I asked, 'What's her name?' Remember that?"

"Hmm . . . Yeah, I do, yeah. There was something about that—"

"You said, 'Berry.' And in the *way* you said it, I knew that you really loved her." She nodded. "I was in a crucial place in my therapy, and my therapist said I was replaying my Electra complex."

Shit. My love life crunched by a jerk psychoanalyst. "You didn't go to Runt, did you?"

"Nope." We stared at each other, grown-ups now. "I did fall in love with you, Roy, but you were too angry for me. And when the book came out, I got really angry at you."

"For including you?"

"For not using my real name! You used Angel's real name. She told everybody, 'How can he *do* that to me?!' but was proud of it. Why didn't you use mine?"

"Out of respect, not wanting to hurt your feelings."

"Oh, so you felt guilty, and were mollifying me?!"

"Molly-fying Molly! Tell you what. In the new novel I will." She smiled. Touching her inner thigh, the most incredibly smooth skin anywhere, I said, "I'm not angry anymore."

"But you're married. It's over. I'm incredibly into you—really, um, wet— oops, I shouldn't've *told* you that—but you're with her now, and—"

"I was with her at the end of the House year, but it didn't matter then, remember?" She shook her head. "That night, both of us on call at Four North, you getting off shift. I said, 'Come sleep with me in Kirstein,' and you said, 'It's illegal' and I said, 'It's illicit,' and—hey—it was amazing! When you sat on me in the bottom bunk and grabbed the box spring of the top bunk, you said, 'This is like making love on a night train across Europe!'"

"Oh my God, I forgot all about that. Oh, God, that was so good."

I bent toward her and, caressing her nipples, kissed her, and she responded. I slipped my palm farther up the smoothness of her thigh, and she pushed it away and said, "Nope."

"Yes!"

"Nope."

Feeling like an abuser might feel, I sobered up enough to stop, soften, talk for a while, go. Feet feeling way far away from body and sounding loud on the chill brick street as I searched endlessly for where the hell my car had gone, I stumbled to one knee, ripping a hole in my pants. Kneeling there, I took a few breaths and, as if in prayer to the God of Big Things, looked up and whispered, "Thanks."

20

oney.

Like sharks scenting blood, the bills started to circle and bite.

Fear of going broke for me is a bad fear, like fear of getting sick or dead or worse—stroked out. Every month I had to come up with an extra 6,000 dollars just to stay even. In April, I was going to get killed with quarterly bills and taxes, almost 30,000 dollars.

Now, with a family and a big mortgage, I was scared shitless.

All of us at the FMC were close to hitting an upper limit of patients. Why? Our reputation of being human had gotten around; the cash crisis in BUDDIES and the revved-up turnover because of TOSS; and all the new patients abandoned by their docs who'd joined Ruby Red Rose Carpet Concierge at the Kissy-Saud. It was a huge stress that had us all racing around, cutting things short, seeing patients outside our comfort zones, missing lunches, getting irritated with one another.

Fearful, frantic for cash, I found work on night shifts in Emergency wards all up and down the coast, deep into the dire suburbs, and even all the way into Massachusetts.

My shifts were seven at night to seven in the morning. The pay was great—1,200 dollars a shift. I took as much work as I could. Luckily in my training at the Chinle clinic, I'd handled bad disease, drunken brawls, gunshots, knifings, car crashes, and obstetrics emergencies. I could handle just about anything that came through the EW doors. Exept car crashes and multiple gunplay—stuff that, if I got advance call from the ambulance barreling toward me, I could page the on-call surgeon about, stabilize the blood and the guts and the heart and the brain as best I could—shoving things here and there, tying off bleeders, in some sense of redeemed bodily order. I loved more than anything the arrival of a surgeon. I would assist when he or she came in.

On my first moonlighting night, a one-year-old who'd fallen and had a laceration beneath the eyebrow was brought in by his mom. I had a hard time at first—maybe because, in that baby, I could see Spring.

I strapped him down to a "papoose" board to keep him from squirming and, taking the smallest suture needle, started toward the eye. The baby was screaming louder than any other baby in human history, face red, and with superbaby strength he wrenched his head away. The mother screamed, the nurse shouted at her to "please go away," and as the nurse held the head, I made a second approach. The sharp tip of the needle wavered above that eye and I said to myself, *Whatever you do, Basch, do* not *stick this needle in that eye*, and my years in the House and Chinle clicked in so my hand was robot steady, and three quick sutures later, it was done.

I checked the baby out with a helpful acronym to assess facial health I had learned at the BMS: TEON. Two Eyes One Nose.

It was a strange world. I was totally in charge, the only doctor in the EW, and often the only doc in the hospital.

A few of these hospitals were enclaves of the rich, with espresso machines and nice clean sheets on the on-call bed, and not all that busy—valid emergencies of articulate people accompanied by worried family members.

But most others were in severely neglected cities of the poor with, at best, wounded, dented vending machines dispensing sugar-soaked soda and pancreas-testing Ring Dings and Korn Kurls. Often there was no on-call room to sleep in. Once I slept in an operating room on a hard upholstered gynecology table, feet up in the stirrups. That night, I never slept more than ten minutes at a time, because the EW had the city's only night doctor for poor people, with really *badass* chronic diseases of multiple organ systems in fierce acute decay: alcohol, drugs, and the resultant guns, knives, cleavers, and even, once, a ritual Nepalese ice ax. As opposed to the surburbans, the poor often came in alone, or with police. I was their only care. Often after a shift, I was ashamed that I hadn't been all that nice.

Most wrenching are gunshots known as "talk and dies." Especially the young. One moment they'll be talking to you clearly as you assess the bullet's damage, and then they die.

After one particularly gruesome gun death, I asked the on-call trauma surgeon who had tried and failed to save the kid, "How do you keep on doing this?" And she said, "The day you don't cry is the day you should quit."

And yet I was startled to find, in the midst of the carnage and suffering, moments of goodness, if not grace. At one of the worst inner-city emergency wards that was the only chance for the poor to get care, but so understaffed that nonemergency patients had to wait at least two hours to see a doctor, many patients when they finally saw me were really angry. It was understandable. I can't say I handled these interactions well. But I noticed that the head night nurse never lost her cool or even showed a sharp edge. Terry Malick was about 40, thin, and fit, with strawberry red hair and blue eyes that were vigilant but not hardened. She had worked there for decades. I was amazed at how, in the chaos, she was calm, steady, even kind. When I left, totally frazzled, I asked her how she kept working in a place like this, often on night shift, with such, well, what Berry called "equipoise."

"I wouldn't work anywhere else," Terry said. "Yeah, it's a bitch, mostly. But we're a real team—lifers, many of us girls. Sometimes a person, when they're finally seen, starts off by giving you the finger and a 'Fuck you!' But then, if you take care of them, when they leave, they give you a hug."

I hated the exhaustion. Caffeine, nicotine, and alcohol couldn't cut it. If the day before I'd been at the FMC, then up late on Ward 34 or with Spring and Berry or at a party (though I soon cut out all social life), and then worked the next full day, then drove an hour to an EW and didn't sleep on that shift? I'd be totally wiped out on my dawn drive to the morning check-in. After one of these long, sleepless stretches, driving back from the boondocks, trying to keep my eyes open as they repeatedly closed, the radio on full blast, the window open to freezing, I suddenly heard not rock and roll but scratching, grinding sounds and opened my eyes to see I was moving fast toward a row of bushes and then trees and whirled the steering wheel left and fishtailed back onto the shoulder of the road and stopped.

Drenched with sweat. Trying to breathe.

On adrenaline, I drove to my ten-hour shift at the FMC and, that night, Ward 34.

One evening during my crazed do-or-die, take-care-of-your-family money-making, I was at home in a wired-up, exhausted-down state—with an assiduous titration of caffeine and bourbon. I sat at dinner with Berry and Spring and, under the table, Cinny, he hoping against hope, *Just this one time, God of Dogs, make an exception and slip me some table scraps!*—and Olive the Destroyer, gnawing her steel cage. It was a birthday celebration with old friends, the Robbs. Christine I'd known at Oxford, a Pulitzer Prize–winning journalist at the city paper who'd introduced us to the *Register Star* investigative team.

Since none of us adults had time to cook, we'd gone crazy with a serious load of takeout from Tienja Dong Garden—specializing in heavy, greasy, salty Chinese. As we sat talking, all of a sudden I felt a sense of dread—something was badly wrong in my body, in the region of the heart. I put my finger on my radial pulse. It was fast, wildly irregular. The dread turned to impending doom. The clammy sweat of terror.

My father's heart attack. I'm gonna die. Wait. Be a doc. Assess.

Abnormal pulses can be regular or irregular. If irregular, a lot of them can be regularly irregular. There is really only one that is irregularly irregular, and this was it. Atrial fibrillation. Diaphoresis—the clammy sweat of terror. Leading to an MI?

"Um," I said, "Berry?"

"What's wrong?"

Not wanting Spring to hear, I said, "C'mon. Let's talk."

In the hallway, I said, "I'm in atrial fibrillation. We'd better go to Emergency."

"Oh my God, is it serious?"

"Dunno. That's why we're going. Don't tell Spring why or where. Ask Bill and Chris if they can stay with her for a while."

Nothing like this had happened to me before, and Berry was as scared as I. On the way in to the Robert Grossman Hospital, named after the only creative dean ever at the BMS, I called my local doc and pal from the House year, Bob Press. He said he'd get a cardiologist to come in.

Luckily, the EW wasn't busy. But after my vitals were taken, I sat with Berry, waiting. And waiting. Thinking clot, and then stroke, and then gomerhood.

But I had learned that if I—or any of my family—go to a doctor, it's help-ful to say I'm a doctor, and when they ask what kind, I tell them and then ask, "Have you heard of the novel *The House of God*?" Almost always they perk up and say, "Oh yeah, it's my favorite book!" "Well, I wrote it." Their responses range from "Really?" to, with a suspicious look, "No, you didn't." I did. "No, you didn't—you can't have—that was written by Shem, and you're Basch." I say it's a pen name, and offer a card with both names. And then the word spreads throughout the EW, and we all get a lot of attention. Docs and nurses crowd the room, want to chat, almost always telling me where they were when they'd read my novel.

I play this card shamelessly. It got us of the family Basch good care. And it worked that night.

The EKG and the monitor showed atrial fibrillation. Bob Press arrived, with the cardiologist, a kind-looking, bearded, shy guy named Steve Abramson. They stayed, supervising the attempts with meds to convert me to NSR—Normal Sinus Rhythm. I watched as if from a distance, focused on the sound from the heart monitor. Wild jazz riffs of the randomly random:

Beep . . . beepbeepbeep . . . beepeebeep. . . . . . . beep . . . bbbbeeeeeeep! . . . b . . . eee . . . BEEEEP!

I tried to calm down, and performed all the ways to stimulate the vagus nerve. Nothing worked. I feared death or having to go through cardioversion—the docs putting me under and shocking the heart, stopping it. And then waiting—hoping!—it will decide to start up again on its own, and reset into NSR. Press chatted for a while and left.

After three hours, nothing. My heart was drunkenly rumbling along at 150 like a ganja-high steel band. Was I imagining a tightness in my throat? Angina, the sign of coronary insufficiency, maybe heading toward an MI? Being a patient, I suddenly felt the whole package of dealing with doctors, waiting, hoping, fearing, left alone on a gurney. Being a doctor, I felt bad that mostly, lately, with patients I had not been terribly nice.

At eleven, change of shift, Dr. Abramson said, "Your signs are stable. I don't want to cardiovert you—how 'bout how we TURF you upstairs, under the care of the resident on call for the night?"

The thought of being at the mercy of the resident upstairs shocked me, and I felt something go *BANG!*

Normal Sinus Rhythm. Beep . . . Beep . . . Beep . . . etc.

The cardiologist and I looked at the screen. It lasted.

"Thanks, Steve, but I'm out of here."

"Wait. You need some meds. The one thing you do *not* want is a clot and a stroke and winding up locked into paralysis and silence. And you should do a twenty-four-hour heart monitor, echocardiogram, and—"

"Okay, okay. Write me a 'scrip' for propranolol, and if I have another one of these, I'll follow up with you later."

Berry and I left. Relieved, sobered.

Spring was up, waiting. Chris had told her I was having a "heart flutter-wutter" and would be fine. She ran up the hall to me and I squatted down and she jumped into my arms, and her arms around my neck felt as strong as the woven-leather lanyards on one of those Navajo necklaces she'd made last year and she said:

"Olive had a bad heart flutter-wutter too. It was scary but she's okay now."

After that, both Berry and my FMCers were adamant: I had to stop working so hard for money and take care of myself. Fats was gone again—he'd had to go back to the Left Coast: "Presenting great news to investors about the calcium boxcars and L-amphetamine proving how memory works." When he heard about the A-fib, he called at once.

"Probly just once-in-a-lifetime, Chinese-food-induced," Fats said. "Surviving A-fib without chest pain for all those hours is a stress test of your heart and you passed and don't worry about it."

Berry reminded me that I'd never done anything just for money, except summers as a toll collector on the midnight-to-eight shift at the Rip Van Winkle Bridge—money to take her out that summer when we first met, when she had been wowed by me in my Bridge Authority uniform and the gun in the booth, not fired since it had been put there in 1939.

"We'll get through it," she said. "I've got a waiting list. I'll take more patients."

"And you'll wind up in the Grossman EW alongside me, getting cardioverted."

"Don't think so. When I get stressed, I get *more* involved with all my people, get more support. When you do, you withdraw, try to do it alone, draw a line in the sand, double down—"

"I'm just trying to make enough money to keep us all going."

"Spring and I—and Cinny—want you alive."

"Not the rabbit?"

"No. She knows you don't like her."

I upped the propanolol but kept going, startled to see how much I'd in-herited the "male provider role." Luckily, our FMC insurance was great. Made me think of all the poor and middle-class patients I'd seen who were only one illness away, in our nation's piss-poor health-care system, from bankruptcy.

Got cancer? That's the good news. The bad news? Y'lose your house too! But hey, you're in good company. A million households a year.

I soldiered on, sometimes with that jolt of the heroic. Or that sweet hit of masochism.

"I'm *really* worried, and I wish you'd stop it!" Berry said after a while.

"I haven't had any A-fib since that night. It had a clear etiology—the egg foo yong."

I understood her concern, but lately I was on edge with her, more and more—maybe because of my close call with Molly.

After a month of moonlights, I paid old bills. Without Chinese food, I hadn't had any further atrial fib. But my big challenge would be April 15. Not only taxes, but several other big payments, including the 7,000-dollar quarterly payment to the Whole World—the cruelest cut, because my 24,000-dollar city taxes would have paid for excellent public school. But we'd tried it with Spring—it didn't work. She was terribly shy, and with the Navajo, she had learned to be even more reserved. I needed money. I dived deep into a lot more seven-to-seven emergency shifts.

All of us were stretched by the new, huge FMC load—and attending on Ward 34. With Fats gone, we no longer took time for check-in and checkout. We just came in and opened the gates, and in they came.

At four one afternoon, I went up to 34 with Mo, into a nightmare. Jack Rowk Junior, promoted to best chief resident of all less-best chief residents, in Fats's absence had claimed more authority to suck humanity out of care. That afternoon as he "taught" residents with Mo and me, someone asked a question about a guy dying in a room. Jack had never seen him, but he rushed into the room, parting the gathered sad family, and said:

"I know you're dying, but I've gotta look into your *mouth*!"

He did so, searching for something publishable in there—maybe a fungus or a lost tongue depressor—and, finding neither, rushed back out. I blasted him in front of the team, told him to "Get the hell off our ward!" and got ready for the blast back from the Krash.

I was getting ready to drive to my night shift at a horrific EW two hours away when I got a *stat* page to the FMC. When I got there, everyone was gathered at the nursing station, in shock, as if someone had died.

"What's up?" I asked.

"Man, the worst," said Chuck.

"Worse than that!" said Eddie. "We're gonna be *on our knees*, forever."

"What?!"

"OUTGOING," said Naidoo. "It's back!"

"It's the worst," said Hooper almost in a whisper, his lips trending down. For the first time ever, he was still, hands and arms dangling down by his sides lifelessly, as if dead.

"Can't we fix it?" I asked.

"Fix it? What the hell are you—"

"I mean, keep it broken. Sorry. I'm really, *really* tired. What's the Fat Man say?"

"He ain't answerin'," Chuck said.

"What? He always answers—"

"Ain't!" he shouted. Him shouting at me? "We tried everythin' stat—nuthin'."

Silence.

This could be the death of the clinic.

"What are we gonna do?" I asked.

More silence.

Glancing at my watch: "Sorry—gotta run—got an EW gig tonight up in Lawton."

I drove fast to the tough, understaffed, and ill-equipped hospital—I don't remember the name, but I know it was whoever is the Saint of Lost Causes. I would serve as primary-care doc, general surgeon, and every specialty in between for poor, sick people barely making it through in a Catholic mill town that still had a bare, ruined cathedral but had not had a mill or another job maker since 1916. From the car, I called 789 on his secret flip phone. "The number you have dialed is not in service. Please check the number and—"

"Fuck you!" I screamed. "And fuck you too, Fat Man. Where the hell are you?!"

The hospital was the catchment area for the worst health neglect I'd ever seen, fueled by drugs and violence. A phantasmagoria the whole long way through my twelve-hour shift. For a while my mantra was Edgar's eloquent one in *King Lear*: "The worst is not / So long as we can say 'This is the worst.'" But near the end of my shift, something happened that was pure down-in-the-shit Beckett: "I can't go on, I'll go on."

It might have been about four a.m. I'd gotten almost no sleep. Once in a chair, once standing up, nodding off—and then, like a cop was snatching me up by my collar, snapping to, taking a few seconds to figure out where I was. I was so exhausted, and the patient load was so big, that I had a hard time remembering what I was doing with whom.

Hazel Thompkins was her name, an African American, accompanied by her pastor, Reverend Carter. A short, roundish woman with a wrinkled chipmunk face and white hair making her look older than her 62 years. She'd worked for most of her life with a large and kind family as maid, babysitter, and cook, but they'd recently moved to Florida. Her children, unable to make it in America, had moved far away: a daughter to Chile, a son to Africa—maybe Togo? She'd been in pretty good health—well, I mean, with diabetes, asthma, high blood pressure, and arthritis—but had awakened at two in the morning with a scary fever, rigorous chills, and drenching sweats. She felt she was dying and had no one else to call but Reverend Carter, an aged, frail-seeming man who looked, from his tremors, fearful eyes, and breathlessness, as if he needed my care too.

"Are you okay?" I asked him.

"N-no," he said with a stutter, "b-but not so b-bad as to need you, Doctor, yet."

"Well, tell me if you do," I said, a little loopy. "We're featuring a special tonight—bring a friend, no extra charge."

They smiled. And that kind of got me, her smile. It was just, well—maybe in the way she shook her head in resignation, in a "What a life!" way—it was just so real, clear, enduring. And no one else for eight hours had smiled at me that night, nor I at them.

It got me. Calling me to cinch up my belt and to be real and clear and enduring as well.

She had no doctor, no health records, no insurance. I took a history, examined her. Even without the labs, from her vitals and her history, I was worried she was brewing up a sepsis. I put her on a saline IV, drew the bloods, sent them off, and went to work on the rest of the packed waiting room. Finally, the labs came back. Everything pointed to sepsis—but mild. I had to jump on it right away, or it could kill her.

I of course had treated a lot of sepsis on the wards of Man's 4th—mostly nosocomial, acquired while in the hospital. Not long ago, Fats had given us a talk on a brand-new nationwide study and a new protocol, a three-drug bolus treatment. I'd been totally wiped out from being up two days in a row. He'd started to talk about "algorithms," mathematical formulas that turn Big Health data into treatments. Now I recalled him saying, "This research was done using a complex algorithm that analyzes data based on a simple binary rule: if *this*, then *that*. If *this* is the sepsis data, then *that* is how you treat it. But there's a core problem in any computer algorithm, and it's called GIGO: if you put Garbage Into the computer, you get Garbage Out of the computer. Algorithms are useful *only if* the data are valid. If not? You all know that the 'I'-phones have an app designed to calculate when and how much insulin a diabetic needs to take? Well, guess what. Studies show that seventy percent of the time, the dosages are wrong. The more complex the algorithm, the more difficult it is to maintain. . . ."

At that point I'd fallen asleep, waking up at the end with "national sepsis health-care protocol."

So I asked the nurse at the desk if she had seen this new national sepsis protocol. Yes, they were using it. She handed me a copy. The usual directions in terms of hydration and blood pressure maintenance to save renal function, etc., but a new three-drug combo was listed for treatment. We had always used the first two, with success. The third was a brand-new Big Pharma drug called Xylolaxenda, which, in my blitzed-out fatigue, sounded like a combination of a laxative and a sugar substitute. I looked at the protocol's small print instructing me in what kind of sepsis—mild, medium, hot-severe—the three-drug treatment was indicated: in *all* sepsis. Then, with my nose to the page to decipher the even smaller print, I checked out the side effects. They ranged from minor to disastrous, ending with "sudden death." But hey, almost all new drugs had side effects from minor to disastrous, ending with "sudden death."

Fats had always said, "Never give a drug that hasn't been on the market for ten years."

Clearly he'd been exaggerating—what would he say about his boxcars?—but I agreed with him; irreversible side effects can appear years later, like with the antipsychotics that turned coping schizophrenics into crippled tardive dyskinesiacs for the rest of their lives. I was ultraconservative in trying new drugs to treat old diseases.

So I hesitated.

But now it was a nationwide directive for treatment, for all cases of sepsis. Did I really want to risk this with that nice Hazel Thompkins, with only mild sepsis?

I stood there at the nursing station, wobbly on my feet, trying to think.

The nurse came up and said that a family shooting was on its way in, and had I signed the med orders for "the sepsis case"? I heard the siren, signed the order, and asked the nurse to please, *please*, check on Hazel Thompkins every 15 minutes—all the usual vital signs.

Before I went to the wounded spouse and child, I pushed the bolus of Xylolaxenda into the IV port, into Hazel's system. I wanted to be there in case she had an allergic reaction to this new drug and suddenly went into anaphylactic shock. I watched, epinephrine in my hand, for two minutes, the nurse trying to drag me away. No sign of reaction. I left to stabilize the mother and child awaiting the surgeons.

Soon I was in overwhelm, maybe for an hour or so.

Suddenly, the nurse grabbed me, ran me to Hazel's cubicle. She had crashed and was unconscious. Temperature way up, blood pressure way down, heart racing horribly to try to keep pushing blood through her vital organs. A disaster.

I snapped to attention. Asked the nurse to look up Xylolaxenda on Google *stat* to see if there was any antidote to it. Nope.

With adrenaline clarity, I used everything I knew to save Hazel.

The morning shift came in, and I signed out, but said I'd like to stay on with Hazel Thompkins.

When I'd done all I could do, I invited Reverend Carter to come in and sit with me and her. He was praying, hands sometimes in his lap, sometimes lifted, palms up, to God. At one point he took my hand in his. I too prayed—to any divinity who might be out there beyond me. At times like that, we all do "God" in some form, even us docs. Y'*got* to.

Finally, she seemed to stabilize. She woke up, dazed but alive. Whatever the drug had done had passed. As long as no one did her any more harm, she'd make it.

With relief I let go and let myself feel like shit.

How could you do that? Go against yourself? What the hell were you thinking?

Before I left, I wrote notes on what had happened—there actually was space for notes on the old, clunky surplus Veterans Administration machine.

And then I stopped, still, and groaned. It came back to me what Fats had said, as part of his algorithm talk. In my night's fog of exhaustion, I hadn't dredged up the most important fact—it went something like this:

The Big Health data on sepsis was collected from virtually every hospital in America. And virtually every hospital in America used HEAL or EPIC or some other electronic medical record system that torqued data big-time to "sepsis, severe" for maximum money. Rarely could we get away with "mild" or even "medium." So the *real* nationwide data, a combination of mild, medium, and severe sepsis cases, was not the same data that the algorithm analyzed. It was falsified badly toward "severe." And so the protocol recommended, for *any* sepsis, using the three-drug treatment for *severe* sepsis. And it almost killed Hazel Thompkins.

What was it that Fats had said? Ah, yes: "It's caca! *It's Money In, Caca Out!*"

In my note before I left, I described all this fully, ending with:

DO NOT USE XYLOLAXENDA OR THE NEW SEPSIS PROTOCOL ON MILD OR MEDIUM SEPSIS.

Leaving the hospital, still shaky, I flashed on all the "Work-Arounds" and "Cut and Pastes"—which was the phony data we doctors clicked on just to survive the screens, distorting the data and any protocols derived from it! *And what other diseases are being maltreated because of how money distorts Big Health data, how money destroys the real?*

I drove not to the FMC but to the federal courthouse. We were going in shifts to support Jude in the first days of her harassment-discrimation trial. There had been a couple of days of nice, vicious sparring, the usual parody and injudicious shows of justice. The first objection was filed by Jude's lawyers, to demand that the judge, Dinny Crisper, recuse herself on grounds that her brother had trained as an orthopedic resident at Man's 4th under the accused

Buck and Barmdun. It was trial by judge, not jury, and Judge Dinny dismissed this with a sneer that said, *Just try to appeal that one, you bozos.*

Because Buck and Barmdun were members of Man's 4th, BUDDIES, and the BMS, all three were being sued by Jude. Each institution had its own hassle of lawyers. On their side of the aisle were 16 lawyers all dressed in black pin-striped shark suits. 15 white men and a woman of color. On Jude's side were two women lawyers in similar black suits, and Jude in an off-white pregnancy outfit. Seated behind her was her husband, in uniform with one of those hard-won green berets.

I was woozy. Lawyer jokes ricocheted around the inner surfaces of my skull: What do you call 300 lawyers at the bottom of the ocean? A good start.

As the morning proceeded, it seemed the kind of event that satire can't satire. For almost every statement that Jude's lawyers made, one of the 15 defense lawyers—say, from Man's 4th—would shoot to his feet and yell, "Objection," which the judge would either affirm or overrule. And then, like Whac-A-Mole, as each sat down and Jude's lawyer continued—"Objection!"—up popped another lawyer, for BUDDIES or BMS. Comical.

Many witnesses for the defense were suffering from a contagious disease: acute loss of memory. "I don't recall." Worst was Delise Blieberman, an elderly woman in charge of the BMS Office for Discrimination and Harassment. When confronted with hard evidence, a letter she had written that would have helped Jude's case, with a terrified look, she said, "I don't recall," several times, but as she was pressed by Jude's lawyer to tell the truth, she got more and more flustered and, trapped, said: "To my best recollection, I have no recollection of recalling that." She did recover and recall, photographically, evidence to hurt Jude's case.

Another affliction had hit and run through witnesses for the defense: a penchant for perjury. This was most beautifully suffered by a former chief resident in Orthopedics, Pavorad Pene de Capo, a certified dolt central to the case. He had flown his plane up from West Palm for the day, where he had hit gold drilling for gomere hips. Pene had started this whole mess. In the crucial event—Jude's volunteering in Emergency, after her shift was over, to treat an indigent patient's hip injury because no one else would—Jude had proof of perfect treatment and follow-up in her detailed notes, with her supervisor's co-signature. Pavorad Pene said that as chief resident, he'd tried to help Jude, giving her factual—in fact, "kind"—advice: "Your problem is, is that you're a woman who acts too much like a man, in a man's world."

Evidence substantiating Jude's story was her contemporaneous documentation of each of many discriminatory encounters that clearly showed a pattern of harassment, with gender and racial insults, escalating in frequency and vehemence. The guys in the ties popped up burning and popped down coolly. Upon cross-examination, Pene did admit that after that first Jude "incident," he'd gone to Chief Barmdun, who then wrote and sent out a "sealed top secret memo" to all orthopedic residents *except Jude*, and to all senior staff, with "Warning: To Be Destroyed" at the top, urging all to: "Secretly document examples of her bad practice and/or insubordination."

But there was hope. Admitted as evidence on Jude's side was a telling episode.

Chief Barmdun was a corn-fed former Kansas State defensive lineman, all fattened up and with his footballer's helmet head shaved bald. He seemed rich and happy. With slits for eyes and slits for lips—in a best suit that made him look dashingly feminine. Taking the stand, given the many stands he'd taken for lying and cheating and billing work he did not do and winning all of these cases, well, he was smooth. The scent of his Chanel reached back to the row I was in. It was unclear if it was Chanel Homme or Femme.

His lawyer's first, introductory question: "Chief Barmdun, would you state that you are the best orthopedic surgeon in the world?"

"Well, yes. I mean, I *am* under oath."

Jude testified that Barmdun, in his office, had confronted her, saying that she had not shown proper respect for her superiors, Chief Resident Pavo Pene de Capo and others. After putting her on probation, basically ending her career, he said to her: "I am surprised that you are not crying. Now I *know* that you're guilty, because I've never disciplined a woman who did not cry. Every single woman I have disciplined cried. You are abnormal, with no insight or feelings, no ability to take ownership of your mistakes in surgery, and really bad judgment."

Sick at heart, I left early for that night's emergency gig.

A two-hour drive to the ocean. The rush hour traffic out of the city was insane, the hospital worse than insane. A fishing city where the catch had declined because of overfishing and greed. Now the drug trade had prospered. Highest rate of opiate addiction in the state and the most gun deaths. The city was a poster child for the new CDC study revealing that America had an epidemic of "Diseases of Despair," drugs and suicide, which had lowered the life expectancy of Americans for the first time in decades.

Soon I was flat-out.

The only bright spot was a call I got at about ten. A three-car smashup was on its way in—a trauma surgeon was too—but I got a call that I had to take.

"Daddy, it's me."

"What's up, hon?"

"Olive is sick. She didn't eat, and her ears are twitching."

"Don't they always twitch?"

"No. I think she works too hard at her job and is scared."

"She has a job?"

"Da-ad—her job is being a rabbit!"

"Oh yeah, binkying and hopping and stuff. Sorry."

Stretchers were coming in, lots of medics swerving into the two trauma rooms.

"I'm at my night job too, hon, saving lives. Humans."

"Will you save Olive? 'Cuz she's scared to die."

"Yes."

"Promise?"

"Yes. Love you."

"Love you too."

It was the worst twelve hours I'd ever spent as a doc, and I was sustained only by mission (money), caffeine (bad coffee), nicotine (cigars), aspirin, propranolol.

At three in the morning, I failed to save a "murdercycle" crash of a young woman high on coke, a "Wailers" tattoo on her biceps. I'd gone all the way—cracking open her chest and squeezing her heart, all slick and tough, in my hand. After looking at that bloodless white young face, I shook my head, feeling, only, dulled to feeling. From the hallway, I stared back at the operating room. Blood in red puddles and smears, red footprints of our shoes. Stained green gowns thrown all over as if by a pissed-off wind. Machines dead.

Maybe four a.m. Rag of a person. Stench. Found leaning against a dumpster. Seems dead. Not dead. My patient. Stench. Filthy clothes in tatters.

Double-glove-and-gown technique. Filthy. Cut off boots. Find stench. Maggots. Brown rot. Cellulitis or worse. With maggots. Identify putrid stench. *Clostridium perfringens.* Gangrene. Revulsion. Effort not to vomit. Wet gauze with alcohol to nose. Start IV. Try using Berry's loving-kindess mantra, "May all beings be free from suffering." Doesn't work. Call surgeon. Needs AKA—Above the Knee Amputation. TURF to surgery. Whew. But stink stays.

Suddenly I had a migraine prodrome scotoma of jagged rings of flickering lights—kind of clear and clean and lovely, really and thank you, retina—and I did all the usual things to try to catch it early, but two more aspirin and four Advils and two Valium didn't touch it. Pounding headache, photophobia so bad that I had to dim the operating lights as I sewed up the knifings, falls, domestic "accidents." Luckily only one gun death—of the 100 to come in America that day—and two gun wounds, one a six-year-old girl. Mass murders were now averaging one a week, but it was almost Sunday and *there'd yet to be one*! I thanked the Gun God for not sending one in to me.

As I left after my shift, I had a coherent thought: *In all of that horror, none of the patients cried.*

I was afraid to total the number of hours' sleep I had gotten in the past 72 hours, three days on call every night and day, and carefully and slowly drove the two hours down to our house, having the day off, wanting to just crash. On the kitchen table was a note in careful printing:

> Welcom hom dad. Olive is tired and sick. She's twitching ears no binks. (Honey, this is me, Mom, we're in a rush to school. We are worried about Olive and can you—before noon—get some lettuce, cilantro, parsley, kale, and apple-infused dried cranberries? There's only a half day of school today and I'm helping with Lunch Bunch and we'll be back by 12:30 and really want to take care of you. Right, Spring?) YES! Love u too! Me and Mom.

I washed my blank face, took some more Advil, dragged myself out to a Price Slasher near the health club, figuring that after I shopped I'd hop into the whirlpool to see if that would help reconstitute me to face all the ones I loved more than life itself.

I found myself with my shopping cart at the vegetable section, searching for Olive's salad, and I felt something funny. I mean, I was staring at the rows of lettuce and they were moving by themselves kind of back and forth back and forth really strange and—

Next thing I know, I come to in an ambulance, looking up at the roof, hearing the siren.

I'm dying try to move nothing moves try to speak nothing comes out shirt covered with blood Dx atrial fib threw a clot into my brain and stroked out bye-bye.

III

The Sick Empire

"To create is to resist; to resist is to create."
—Stéphane Hessel, *Time for Outrage!*, 2010

21

Eyes opening. Floating. Everything hazy, misty. Clouds.

Through the clouds, Christ on the Cross.

I'm dead and in heaven but it's the wrong heaven! I'm on the opposing team!

Below Christ on the Cross, a "BIBLE."

Below that, a sign: "READ THE BIBLE."

I will I promise I will if I'm alive I swear I will!

The clouds part. Doctors come in.

So I know I am not in heaven. They say I'm in St. John's Hospital.

Two thoughts: Brain tumor? Stroke—from another atrial fib throwing a clot from my heart up into my brain? Try to move legs—Yes! Try to speak—"What the hell?" *Yes!*

"Did someone call my wife?" I heard my voice, as if it were separate, at a distance.

One nods. "You were brought by ambulance from a Price Slasher, in status epilepticus. A grand mal seizure. No injuries except a gash in your forehead, probably from bashing something on your way to the floor—the rail of the vegetable section?—six stitches' worth."

Aha! Those dancing lettuces were the prodrome of my seizure. They looked like they were dancing across a stage because my eyes were moving horizontally back and forth.

"What caused it?" I asked.

"We did a CAT scan of your brain. There's no lesion, no vessel occlusion or bleed." He "presented the case," reading from his "I"-pad, and summed up: "There's nothing in your brain."

"People have been telling me that my whole life. When do I get outta here?"

No one laughed except a tall, bulky, older doc wearing a white shirt and regimental tie, a long white "attending doctor's coat," and, in a lapel, a red rose. He had a round face with wrinkles, gray hair, a laugh twinkle in his blue eyes—and a sweet smile. His voice seemed high as a choirboy's, and gorgeous.

"Th'name's James 'Jimmy' Barnacle O'Toole."

He settled his bulk carefully to sit on the edge of the bed, on my level, looked into my eyes, offered his hand—his felt meaty. We started to talk about my life and the seizure. I told him about my money issues, my moonlighting crazily.

"I confess, Dr. Basch, I luved the comico-tragedy of *The House*—the real, the sorrow. A contortion of words and a seminal woark!"

Is he really talking like the policemen, or am I out of my mind?

"So how're ya feelin'?"

"Good! Euphoric!"

"Ah, yes, your seizure is like having electric convulsive shock therapy. The 'high' will wear off, lad, and you'll come to deeper terms. Enjoy it while you can." We chatted back and forth. I felt he'd "gotten" me—and that I'd gotten his caring. "Anything else we need to know?"

Take care. If you wanna get outta here in one piece, do not reveal anything like your killer migraines and atrial fib or they'll have a field day and keep you here for tests that could make you dead.

"Nothin'. I've just been workin' too hard. You know how it is."

"For your safety," said a third doctor, an infant, "we have to find a cause." He reeled off maybe 15 causes, beautifully and fluently. He fell silent.

"And trichinosis!" A boyish voice from between the cute, pillowy cheeks of a medical student.

This, an uncommon infection by trichinae from eating rare pork, was a quest to get an A in his "medicine" rotation.

"And so," said the red-hot chief resident, ignoring him, "the further tests we need—"

"Discharge me *stat*."

The resident protested. Jimmy stopped him. "Back in Ireland, my dear late mother's philosophy was: 'Maybe everyone's entitled to *one* epileptic seizure in thur life,' and so—"

"Dr. Roy, here? At a devout Catholic institution?" A familiar resonant voice.

"And on the opposing team, the patients?"

"And top o' the mornin' to you," Gilheeny went on, "Dr. James Barnacle O'Toole of our childhoods, with all our knoockles now gone arthritic from the raps on 'em from the mustachioed Mother Agnes of the Ruler." Jimmy smiled, nodded.

"How'd you know where I was? You got a chip planted subcute in me, like a dog?"

They glanced at each other for an instant. Pause.

"Oh my God!"

But then they shook their heads no.

"We'll discharge you at once," said Jimmy. "I'll see you two cops at *not* church."

The team followed him out in rank order, the med student looking at me, nodding at me, and mouthing, with a thumbs-up, *Trichinosis.*

I was sore all over—I'd been in status epilepticus, a total-body clench-down of the neuromuscular system that sometimes cracked bones.

But I felt strangely good. Everything—from the shiny badges of the cops catching slants of sunlight, through the way Gilheeny was probing a molar with a pinkie, to a sad smile on pietà-faced Quick—all seemed hyperreal, freshened by a narrow escape.

The cops, exquisitely sensitive to sorrow and relief, picked this up, and Quick, with a wave and a wan smile, said, "We'll wait and take you home in the cruiser."

Quiet. I propped myself to sitting against starchy pillows. I felt strangely peaceful. Like that moment as a six-year-old lying on my back in a field when I watched clouds slide across the sky and heard the words *Something else, I'm part of something else!* Or like in England when I, in depths of despair from losing Berry, sat on top of a centuries-old Cotswold stone wall and found myself speaking out loud into the crisp, clean night air, solidified in transient mist: *At least I am.*

I hadn't understood these words at the time. But I sensed that they were a first step out of despair. Later, hearing this, Berry said, "A moment beyond your self, a moment of the spirit." It didn't last, but it never left. It was a beginning. I felt it now. *At least I am.*

"Roy?" Berry, in the doorway.

She rushed to me and hugged me, and we both were sobbing, yes, sobbing for our lives.

Bizarre sounds from the doorway. The policemen, blowing their noses—Gilheeny florid, Quick meticulous. Both waved, shyly, and left.

She sat on the bed. Our eyes drinking in each other. "What's happened to you?"

"Had a grand mal seizure."

Berry stared at me—into me, really. "But, I mean, you're different."

"How?"

"You're just—I don't know—open! In your eyes, you're like I've almost never seen you before—totally opened up, totally right here now *with* me, open *to* me. It's amazing." She was looking curiously into my eyes.

I had often felt her sustained look as awkward, and would look away. Now I stayed with it. I sensed she was waiting for words to describe it. "I got no words for this. Sorry."

"Honey, it's wonderful."

"Let's hope it lasts. Get me outta here before they kill me."

"Daddy, you look like a piggy bank." Spring had Olive in her arms.

I had bent down to pick her up as she ran across the living room toward me—but she stopped, pointing to the sutured-up laceration arcing across my forehead.

"How am I like a piggy bank?"

"You've got a slot in your head like my piggy bank."

"So I'm a piggy?"

"Daa-ad! You're my daddy!" We hugged. She pulled away, raised a finger. "Look at Olive." To me she looked as she always looked—who knows from rabbits? "Olive's mad at you! Two times going to the hospital. Olive told me to tell you this. We wrote it down." She took out a piece of lavender construction paper, pointed out each word as she read: "'*Bad* Dad. No More Sicks!!!!'"

I sat at the kitchen table, listening to her and throwing aging Cinny his ball—away from the scary rabbit. He too, perfect-pitched pooch, was upset. I was still full of euphoria, but already it was grounding—back into the concerns of the world. But I was open to everything. Staring at Berry's treasured jade statue of Kwan Yin the Bodhisattva, which we'd bought in China the day before we were handed Spring. Seeing Kwan Yin as if for the first time—her crystalline gaze, her 50 hands encircling her head, each hand lifted up and, in each palm, a sitting baby Buddha. Lines from Wallace Stevens floated in, settled in, as if in a palm tree: "Tired of the old descriptions of the world, / the latest freed man rose . . ." I forgot the next lines, then recalled: "To be without a description of to be . . . / to be changed / From a doctor into an ox . . . / It was how he was free."

"I feel like an ox!" I cried out to Berry, Spring, and Cinnamon. Wide-eyed stares.

Was I finally free? Would it last?

To my surprise and delight, that night I did stay that way with Berry and Spring—I seemed to see, as if solid, our daughter's five-year-old spiritual energy, wound up all tight and ready to unspool for the rest of her life through first love and lost love and finding at last a lasting love and giving birth to her first child and then, like me and Berry and Cinnamon before her, losing her energy but not her spirit as she aged, with dignity, walking to her death smiling. No gomerhood. And I saw Berry still walking along with all I loved in her until death do us part, yeah. And I would be with them. You bet.

Spring put Olive to bed; we put Spring to bed. Neither of us was tired. We and Cinny went downstairs and talked on, totally into each other, wide-awake.

Cinnamon started barking. A voice outside yelled: "Hey, Basch, open up!" I looked at my watch. 2:15? Opened the door.

The Fat Man, Rosie Tsien, Chubby—and Chuck?

"Figured you'd be wired," Fats said, "so we came right from the airport."

"Hey, man, how's it goin'?"

"What are you doin' up?"

"Well, without night call wearin' me out, I can't sleep—y'know how it is."

He was *worried* about me? Our eyes met, for a moment. He looked away.

"I'm so glad, Berry," said Rosie, "that you're still up. I warned him to wait." She glanced at him and shook her head. "He doesn't *do* 'wait.'"

"How do you deal with that?"

"Badly. Sometimes I restrict access."

In they came with, I could see clearly, joyful relief on their faces and frisky-smelling joy in both dogs.

"Here," said Fats. He handed Berry a food basket made of designer twigs. "Hungry?"

"Famished."

Rosie removed the purple cellophane. We dug in.

"So what'all was the cause, man?"

"Nobody knows. I mean, except exhaustion."

"*We* all know," said Fats. "Two related etiologies: one chronic, one new."

"Which are?"

"You tell us, man. I mean, tell us what you didn't tell the Saint John docs."

"What're you talking about?" They stared. "I really have no idea."

"What's a main cause of seizures?" Fats asked. "Alcohol and alcohol withdrawal."

"That's crazy—I haven't had a drink in, maybe, the last three days."

"But what was your daily intake before then?"

"I don't drink *that* much."

Silence.

"Aw, c'mon, Roy," said Chuck. "Face it."

"You should talk."

"I can now. How many times you seen me loaded lately?"

I tried to think, and couldn't find any.

"There it is, Roy. There it is. Like my old man said, 'There's no education in the second kick of a mule.' Clean and serene. And even more cool."

"I didn't have any symptoms of withdrawal."

"Seems to me you did. Could be daid. 'Doctors die of their specialty,' okay?"

I turned to Fats. "You think I'm an alcoholic?"

"Dunno. But your stopping suddenly was the proximal cause. The chronic cause is that, over the past month or so, you pulled away, got isolated from us, working all the time."

"I had to. We needed money, bad. We're going under!"

"Why didn't you *tell* me you needed money?" Fats said. "I woulda given you money, as much as you needed."

"You were gone. You bailed on us. Even when we could get you on the phone, you weren't really there. We're blitzed, no check-ins and checkouts, no time to schmooze. Where's that talk you were gonna do on how to resist? What's going on with you, Fats? What's wrong?"

He took a deep breath, a belly-to-chins inhale, a hold, and a flop down. He glanced at Rosie, who gestured him to go on.

"I dunno. Yeah, it's the boxcars, sure. But I kinda got beaten down a bit, trying so hard to make this thing work—trust me, there are a lotta problems every damn day that I handle by myself, protect you all from: dealing with Krash and BUDDIES, all this screen shit and money shit. They're takin' all the *fun* out of dys-*fun*-ction. Y'see, I always felt I was putting one over on 'em—Flambeau, Krash—by getting the FMC. Lately, I've been thinking that they *knew* I was trying to put one over on them by getting it, so they put one over on me by giving it to me. Heavy admin crap."

"Well, it ain't okay with us or the clinic—*our* reality, which used to be yours. We love you, Fats, but what we've noticed in you lately is, well, a flabbiness of purpose."

Stunned, he blinked, his mouth in a little "o."

"And that," I went on, "is the good news."

"Good? Since when is flabbiness good?"

"Because now, *kid*—" It was his word. He smiled. "It'll get you and us going again, to resist. We're in the shit. Time's precious. We gotta act. Are you ready, or—"

"Ready!" He seemed to reinflate, pump up his bulk. "I gotta do it."

"Hold it," Berry said. "Not 'I,' *we*. *We* gotta do it, together."

Fats paused, sighed, settled. "I'm listening."

Berry went to him, sat next to him. We gathered around.

"When we talked here before," she said, "you told me you could show people how to connect, but you couldn't really teach it, in any deep way, right? Those Hadassah arms? 'Follow me!' That's the old model. It can only take you, and the clinic, so far."

Fats nodded.

"It's because you know how to lead by being at the top of the ladder—isolated, as in 'It's lonely at the top'—but do you know how to lead by being *one among*? How, in a power-over system, to get to *mutual*? How the ones 'down the ladder' can also *grow you*? That's the secret of leading. *Power with, not power over. With* is healthy; *over* is deadly. For every 'the Best,' there's a '*More* Best.' If you buy into self, comparison, you suffer. The shift is to 'identify, not compare.' You talk about *being with*, which is great. But do you know how to *not* be just the boss? Can you learn?"

He paused. His eyes screwed up in a fierce, famished attention.

Berry looked around at us. Chuck and Rosie and I nodded. She put her hand on Fats's hand lightly.

"It's a big weight, Fats, to carry all by yourself—and not just at work. I'd guess that outside of work, but for Rosie and Chubby, you don't have a lot of good friends?"

Fats glanced at Rosie, then at Chubby. He choked up, cleared his throat. "None."

Silence. What could we possibly say? Real thin ice, this.

"But." We all looked at Berry. "Maybe you can learn how to lead *with*."

"Can you teach me?"

"No."

He blinked. His fat face fell.

"I could teach not a 'me' but a 'we.' A new vision of 'us.'"

"*Our* vision, yeah," Fats said, eyes wide. "Let's start right now."

Berry frowned, piqued that at a time like this he'd try to press her.

"Sorrysorry!" He smiled. "Berry, join us. We're so busy. We need help—in psychology. And we're only one woman doctor shy of parity—you could be her. Join us?"

"I'd like to. But my priority is Spring and Roy—which right now is a lot, and this sudden money thing is—"

"Here's the deal. Work as much or as little as you want. See patients, teach your 'we' model, guide us, whatever. It's a chance to try the model in a new clinic, right?" She nodded. "And make money. I'll pay you and Roy whatever you want. Or hell, I'll just make a big gift to the family Basch. I'm rolling in dough now. Means nothing if you got it. A good family like you shouldn't have to worry about moronic shit like money."

Berry considered. "Spring and Roy come first. Work second. Part-time work, on my schedule." He nodded. "And you, Fats, have to be here, at least for now, all the time."

Fats looked at Rosie. "I agree," she said. "I'll take care of the boxcars."

"Good. But . . ." He stood up, reached into his pocket, and came out with a few pigs in a blanket, hot dogs in dough. Going down on one knee with an

"Ooof!" he held out a pig in a blanket to his dog on a blanket and whispered, "Chubby?"

Eyes in that fat dog face opened, and like a shot, Chubby was on the food and scarfing it down and looking for one more pig in a blanket. Which Fats gave. And then ate two at once himself.

"How the hell am I going to live without Chubby?"

"Is *that* why you've been spending so much time out there?" I asked.

Sheepish again—a giant sheep—he nodded.

"Don't worry," Rosie said, going down on her knees beside Fats and Chubby as he gave her a third hot dog. "I'll take care of her, and I'll fly out with her on weekends."

Fats, after yet another dog was inhaled by the dog, looked up at Berry. *"Nu?"*

"Okay. Let's try."

"What's this thing called?"

"The relational model. Putting relationship at the center. Let's all get some sleep."

"No, no—tellmetellme! Just gimme a taste and we'll go?"

"Fats. I told you before. Obviously, it didn't sink in." She made him look at her. "The measure of a person's psychological health and growth is not in the self, but in *the quality of her or his relationships.*"

"Holy moly! It's obvious."

She smiled. "As I said before, the *elusive* obvious, yes." Berry took his arm firmly and, turning him like a tugboat would turn a liner, moved him out, away, toward the opening dawn sea. "Good night."

22

cruel March had given way to an April Fools'. Berry and I dropped off Spring at the Whole World early and beat the traffic into town and the Fat Man Clinic.

"This is crazy!" Berry said, stunned as we waded through the swarm of waiting patients to the morning check-in.

Crazy busy, yes, a torrent. Woozy during my moonlighting, I knew things were getting worse but didn't know how much. There were not enough chairs for the patients. The sturdy stood; others sat or lay on the floor, some playing with children. The entryway was way over-entered, a jam of diversity. Two burly 4th Best Security guards were trying real hard to be nice. In addition to our sick poor, now we were getting middle-class city and suburban whites, many of the 4th Best house staff, and private patients who couldn't afford to follow their doctors onto the Ruby Red Carpet of the Kissy-Saud.

Many new patients came because they'd heard a rumor that we did not turn our backs to them and dive into our screens. But with OUTGOING now working, humming along like a dental drill, we did turn our backs. You could feel their hope fade. With no real human contact, things took twice as long. Back to doctor as adversary. Our "work" was the computer.

On our screens was a scary note from Hyper Hooper.

"Attended an advanced HEAL training at a hotel: 'Billing-4-Diets.' During a break, I saw down the hall a 'HEAL-4-Lawyers' training: how insurance company lawyers can catch and sue doctors gaming the codes for more cash. Focused on 'workarounds' and 'cut and pastees [*sic*]'." And then, in response, a note from Eddie: "No problem. *We* have to do our own training: how our 4th Best lawyers can catch and sue the lawyers' insurance companies for gaming *us* for cash—and hey, we sue them for slander too. Man's 4th can't survive without us—so Bring It on Baby and ***Eat My Dust!***"

I felt a jolt—that cold fear triggered by the word "lawyers" and their bills.

But our Work-Arounds and Cuts and Pastes were a matter of life and death. Hyper's words soon vanished, a faint etching on a glass wall.

Our hope now lay in the return of Don Gordo—and his faithful Humbo Parza. That first day we watched as, up on his toes among our huddled masses yearning to be seen, he cut a swath, triaging, stopping a family to guide them to one of us, giving a quick diagnosis and even "It's nothing. Take two aspirin. Call me in the morning" and "treating" them, playing with a kid or a dog—lapsing from English to Spanish to what sounded like Chinese. Carrying on high a giant pink Slurpee from 7-Eleven, a torch for the masses in the chaos.

Morning check-in. Putting our phones on the table. Berry, startled, stared at me.

"You too," I said. Caressing her "I," she balked. "Think of it as your 'I' joining a 'we.'"

Carefully, she slipped her "I" to the edge of the pile—it seemed to jerk, back away a bit. She grabbed it as if to protect it from the riffraff, including my dumb phone. We all burst out laughing. She smiled tightly. Nudged her phone gently, like pushing a child forward on the first day of school, up against a rival Samsung—which let out a *Squeeep!* like a fart.

Fats welcomed her, citing her credentials in psychology and "Head keeper of Basch. She's a pioneer in the 'relational model,' which is just what we need, to resist the tough stuff we got now." He paused. "I'm making amends to you for being unavailable. My bad. After talking with Berry and our postictal Roy, I'm gonna stay on this coast till we get a handle on our success. And—wait for it—bringing in Berry gets us to gender parity! Let's hear it!"

Lots of noise, from all. We all turned to Berry.

"Glad to be here." She smiled around the ellipse at each of us. "We had a real scare with Roy, but he's okay. That crowd out there—it's overwhelming. How can we survive?"

"By killing ourselves?" said Eat My Dust.

"Edward, please do not go there," said Naidoo.

Chuck and I glanced at each other, worried.

But Eddie surprised us: "Sorry. I'm just a passionate dude, can't help it sometimes."

"We'll survive by not see'n' 'em one by one," said Hyper. "TURF 'em to my Eat Red food groups. Eat healthy. Bye-bye, death." He sang: *"Bye-bye, death. Bye-bye, loneliness. I think I'm gon—"*

"Hyper," said Angel, aglow, pregnant and fluent, full of words and confidence, "please control yourself so we can problem solve."

The Runt said, "I think that"—gesture—"I"—gesture. Laughing, he stopped.

"Yes," said Molly, "the crowd out there has got us all anxious, even dysphoric. This is a bottleneck of logic, as in a Goldman Steven Mnuchin beta caregiver fiscal flowchart."

What? Molly talking consultantese? Where the hell did she learn that?

I don't remember the other comments—my memory for this period is really bad, because my brain had blown fuses from sensory to hippocamp to frontal. My check-in was simple. I said, "Glad to be alive. But who's gonna put a bullet into OUTGOING?"

"Be cool, Roy. Do nuthin'," Chuck said. "An' if anybody asks, just say, 'Fine, fine.'"

"Works for you," Eddie said, "'cause you are cool, black, and proud, and they defer. Try being me, with all the charisma of an Episcopalian."

"Fats," said Dr. Ro, "you promised this would be fun, but now this is *not* fun."

"Okay, okay. Our problem is we did good—too good. And I neglected. I *promise* to kill OUTGOING, either by this afternoon or, latest, plan B, tomorrow by seven a.m. Y'see, when I was away, Krash kicked out the Runners. So we're probably stuck with OUTGOING for today. The good news is that, last month, when we had OUTGOING, our PATSATs went back down into the toilet. We lost money—that's all Krash cares about. So we got leverage. To get through today, go heavy on House Law Thirteen: Do as much nothing *as possible*."

"But even when it was broken," Mo said, looking at her mom, who nodded and smiled with mom pride, "with the increasing numbers of patients, it was hard. Listen."

A constant, growling roar. We, gladiators with stethoscopes, facing lions.

"It's scary," said Fats. "But I'm on it. We need more docs. Luckily I'm getting a *ton* of calls, lotta interest from health-care workers—fed up with the industry. We got two empty floors to fill. Flambeau said we should expand, and we will."

"And forgive me," Naidoo said, "but do you have the funds to pay them?"

"Yop. Without OUTGOING, the PATSATs'll come back. If we need more, I got ways. And we're attracting new blood, as volunteers—med students, house staff, old docs who are retiring rather than learning HEAL. They're ripe."

This was met with eye rolls and shakes of heads.

"Hey!" he shouted. "Hey hey hey! The bad news is we're overwhelmed. The good news is that being overwhelmed in our good cause is gonna bring out our best"—he glanced at Berry—"by sticking together." He was on fire. "Let's break!"

⌀

Like a starting gun at a race, we—and our patients—broke.

Soon we were all backed up, overwhelmed.

But I was in a strange, sharp, free focus. The "high" was wearing off, but wearing on was a heightening, a synthesis of all my senses.

Everything seemed more acute and to be explored. After all, I was alive, having been kind of dead. Each of my five senses was acutely attuned and echoing down into a sixth—a well of intuition. It was as if I tasted what I heard, touched what I smelled, saw clearly with the other senses, as if I were clairvoyant. One patient's rough skin would let me see her incipient immunological challenge; another's scent of sweet, musty dimethyl sulfide said "liver disease." Our doctors' credo—"to relieve pain and suffering"—was easier. I sensed others' pain as never before. My openness opened up patients. It was weird. Through the responses of my patients to me, I could sense what was going on.

My old patients would say, "What happened to you?" or "You're different, Dr. Basch." This sharpened sense was mostly good. But my openness was blasted by one thing in the FMC that I'd never really noticed before: the six big TV screens in the waiting area.

I had always screened them out. Now I was drawn into them, with deathbed clarity. As if I were a visitor from another planet or a child encountering them for the first cogent time. Shifting from my usual view in the hospital as a doctor to a new view, as a patient.

I was riveted and appalled.

The screens were big and beautiful and loud, and the news channels had sincere cookie cutters of handsome men and pretty women looking like windup dolls talking and joking, and shouting "Breaking news!" and horizontally trending banners with not-so-breaking news and atrocities and movie star betrayals and the human-interest stories like a dog named Moby who swam across the Hudson River and made it, and in the corners of the screens the stock exchanges and the weather and a lot of other numbers as if on scorecards.

*

I was sucked into two usuals: shootings and drug commercials.

One gorgeous news anchor listed, in breathless, almost joyous tones, the mass shootings of the past month—the restaurant in Tennesee, the multiplex in Iowa, the middle school in Maine, and the baby store in Montana. One handsome anchor excitedly drew me into the more *usual* shootings around the USA, from intentional murders to heartbreaking ones like a four-year-old in a shopping cart grabbing a gun from his mother's open pocketbook and shooting her dead. The running totals of our great American pandemic?

Every day, including suicides, 315 gun deaths. One every 15 minutes.

Once a week, one mass shooting.

The patients and we, watching this horror and carnage, and mourning the latest high school massacre, would stop and stare—a hush would fall. We'd each look around and wonder if it could happen at *my* kid's school—was it happening there *now*? We'd all stare around at our shared vulnerable "here," with the old wooden Pathology doors and a cachectic 4th Best Security guard—and then we'd all just go right on.

How could it be that in an instant, when all was going okay— *Bang!* Dead. Dead?

The usual.

The waiting in the waiting room kept waiting; we docs kept doctoring— enraged.

I asked Chuck, "Why can't they just lock up these shooters?"

"Because, man, they'd have to lock up half the country."

For relief, I found myself ignoring the slaughter and being drawn to the commercials—gorgeous dramas, especially for drugs, which comprised maybe 25 percent of all peak-time TV ads. The purpose was to snare the worried. They were stoking the fires of suggestion and, in our patients, of deep and nagging fear about their own diseases. Riveting. Clearly, drug commercials had become the classic American success story, in three acts.

Act one: Pain. A beautiful, spotlessly clean fake patient—usually a woman—clutches her stomach with a grimace. This *causes* the viewing customer to identify with her, for who has *not* had stomach pain? No one at all! And so she feels hints of the same pain in herself.

Act two: Solution. A handsome young doctor in whites or a rumpled good ol' family doc hands her a pill bottle of stomach de-painer.

Act three: Happiness. The woman is smiling or hugging a child or playing a hole of golf or winning a triathlon.

Amazingly, the TV drug *cures* all the things that the TV ads *caused*. And, of course, induces people who *do* have an ailment to request the latest drug, which the doctor might go along with, even if it's worse and more costly than the old one.

Finally, the warnings about *taking* the drug, starting slowly with slight indigestion and faster and faster into cancer, ruptured spleen and—old Mr. Reliable—"risk of sudden death and if so call your doctor."

It was sickening.

But our real patients, despite the shit on TV, held true to the hard reality of their lives—at least many of them. Soldiering on, limping or wheeled into my office, some angry and bitter, but many rooting for their doctor to just plain help them out.

That day my heart opened to them. My brief suffering and afterburn were now a bridge to their chronic.

We are all more human than otherwise. Living human-sized lives. What our patients want is what anyone wants, the hand in their hand, the sense that their doctor can care.

I asked Chuck, "Has anyone in a commercial ever cried?"

He considered, stroked his chin soberly. "Never happen, Roy, never. Their ain't no money in cryin'. Us black-skinned people have done a lot of cryin', and the jury's still out."

One patient that morning stands out. I finished a follow-up with my pigeons-on-dryer woman, still in recovery from the magician, and was coming out of my office when I heard someone yelling in a high-pitched voice as he backed out of Chuck's office, stumbling.

"—so donchu dis' me!" said a rail thin, tight-faced thirty-something man with blazing eyes and a goatee, limping backward, leaning heavily on a cane with one hand and jabbing a finger at Chuck, standing in the doorway of his office. "You Uncle Tom!"

Quickly, a security guard was moving toward him, and something in me said, *Do not let the guard get there before you do*, and I hustled over to him. Chuck approached warily. I scanned the worn leather coat and baggy jeans for bulges of "dangerous"—a gun, a knife—worried that the cane hid a stiletto. Nothing in sight. But that meant nothing.

"I'm Dr. Basch. How can I help?" My using "how" implied that I *could* help; it was only a question of finding a way. The man's eyes were accusing—the pupils not pinned, no opiates—but wide with rage. His knuckles on the cane were deformed, swollen, and angry. I held out my hand.

He stared at it. "How the hell *you* gonna help *me*?"

"What's your name?"

He hesitated. "Pen. How?"

"First, Pen, by keeping security off of you." I waved the guard away. "Okay?" He nodded. "Chuck, what's up?"

"Chronic sickle cell, in crisis now. Talking about dealing with the pain."

"And he won't give me relief! Thinks I'm an addict. Pain, man. Sickle cell pain!"

"Oh! Well, then, you're in luck. Pain is my specialty. We're busy, but how 'bout you and Chuck come into my office, we try to figure out *how*?"

He didn't move, looked around at the hushed crowd. "What you people starin' at?"

"Pen, do you have anybody with you we need to include?" He gestured for his wife and child to come. Horace was in the clinic. "Do you know Horace Haskins?" He shook his head no. "He's a recovering addict, our link to twelve-step programs—y'ever been in one?"

"Like I said, I ain't no addict! I need somethin' strong, like OxyContin."

We sat together in my office. Chuck had offered nonopiate pain meds, but Pen said they weren't enough. He was staring at me. I met his gaze. *What is there?*

"So," I said, "you felt that Dr. Chuck didn't believe how bad your pain is?"

"Yeah, man, he's dissin' me. I wouldn't ask if I didn't need it. Donchu know African Americans have a higher pain tolerance than any other ethnicity cohort?"

"I do know that, Pen. With all that pain, it's amazing you're functioning at all. And on top of that, you come here asking for help and you feel your doc disrepects you?"

"Big-time. This sickle cell—my joints, head, gut—it's worse than withdrawal!"

Saying "withdrawal" meant that he had been an addict at one time—but was he telling the truth now? We stared at each other. I felt a hit of a new clarity. He was an active addict. I said nothing.

He caught his slip and my catching it. "Shit! Let's go!" He stood up and left, wife and child following.

We stood there and watched him limp out.

Fats was bending down to a kid, handing him a lollipop. Just as Pen, moving fast and mumbling, got to him, Fats straightened up and they collided—hard!—the Fat Man's mass knocked Pen off his feet to the floor. The Fat Man reached down to him, but Pen scrambled up and with his cane popped him hard in the chest, rocking Fats back. Fats struggled to stay on his feet, and Pen got into his face, yelling, and to my surprise, Fats lost it, and they were shouting practically nose to nose, and we watched Pen reach back under his leather coat to the back. *No, don't let there be a gun in that belt.*

But no, Pen saw the guard coming, took his hand away, and, cursing and shaking a finger in the Fat Man's face, shouted, "I'm gonna get you!" and hustled out.

Chuck and I stared at each other, wide-eyed, stunned not by the addict but by Fats losing it so badly. We joined the crowd. He was okay. I was in a cold sweat. We went back to work.

*

At lunchtime Fats collared me to follow him out. He had picked up a large bag of food from Demos, which consistently won awards from us as "Worst

Greek Restaurant in the World." Munching a piece of soggy pita, he kept on
trundling along through the thin and chilly spring sunlight, down a maze of
old streets. All at once, he stopped, shifted the Greek mess into his other
hand, and grabbed me with a greasy arm, pulling me into a stairway that led
down three flights of a nasty parking garage into a dim, urine-scented corner.
A finger to his lips indicated "silence." We sat on the hood of an old Capri, he
noshing, me watching.

Shuffling feet—and a misstep and recovery—coming closer. A small
bearded man.

"Seven Eighty-nine?" I cried. He raised a flipper and nodded.

"Where the hell've you been?!" Fats cried. "Why haven't you been answering?"

"Too dangerous. Physically. Man's 4th is Man's Best, at threats. We gotta
hurry."

"Why did OUTGOING come back?"

"Seven *Ninety*-nine. Nicknamed 'Niners.' He's the House of God screen
maven. We're rivals. But he's better. Makes me look like chopped liver. No
social skills, but boy oh boy. He's as good as those 400-pound bedridden
Ukrainian hackers."

"Is Seven Ninety-nine," I asked, "the guy who invented TORAH?"

"Yup. Best for-profit system in the USA. If Niners or the House had any
sechel, they'd put EPIC out of business and make a fortune."

"But can you hack and break OUTGOING again?" Fats asked.

"Nope. Niners will heal HEAL as soon as I rebreak it—he'll easily unhack
my hack. And it's not 'healthy' for me to be in touch with you. Me, my wife,
Emma, and our little Pinkle are moving to Miami, Ponce de León Dialysis
LLC. Founded by Molly's ex-husband, who's settled in Jerusalem." Sev peered
into the dank gloom, scanning. "Gotta go. Man's 4th Best Intelligence is
onto me."

"Throckster," said Fats, chewing hard on something tough, say, burned
baklava—I had no idea what he was saying. We waited for a swallow, then
another, figuring he'd talk, but, unable to, he waved and nodded and for some
reason gave the sign of the cross.

"Sev," I said, "one last question. Do you think that screens will ever be
better for the care of patients and the care of us doctors?"

"If billing is involved? Nope. If not, yup."

"You sound pretty sure." He nodded. "Why so sure?"

"Seven *Ninety*-nine said so." He started to shuffle his feet as if doing a dry run for walking.

"But why did he say that?" I was suddenly on edge, seeing clearly, wanting—even, then, almost yearning—to have this basic question in medicine answered with clarity.

"Niners was real cryptic, dismissive, as if any idiot including me should know why. He said, 'They, the screen machines, are *iterative*. We, the doctors, are *integrative*.'"

"Can you explain that?"

"I can, but I gotta go."

"Sev," Fats said, "we need to hear this. Give us the thumbnail."

The little urologist was sensitive, and sighed. "Okay. The screen. 'Iterative' means that it demands we fill in its *own* box-filled protocol—click a box, a new screen drops down, click a box on its list, drop down, et cetera. We have to *teach it over and over again each time, click by click*. It's just plain dumb. Twenty-six clicks for a prescription? Waste of time and money—it'd be cheaper to teach docs penmanship." He looked at his watch. "Us docs? 'Integrative.' It's what we've always done. Gather the data from the patient's paper record, talk to and examine the patient, then let it all riffle through our experience and creativity, and, without us doing anything, *it gets clear*. We think, feel, and *intuit*. We write a prescription in five seconds. It's HAL verses human."

He started to shuffle, but stopped himself.

"One more thing. I know a lot of the hot-shit artificial intelligence idiots. I used to be one of 'em, but I chose med school. They don't care about patients, so they just don't get it. Never will." Another shuffle and stop. "One really last thought? As a doc, not a nerd? It's not that billing machines are too *complex* for docs and other humans—they're too *simple*. We humans get bored, make coding errors, like in that *Lancet* article 'Why do British men get pregnant so often?'"

"Just to make money!" Fats spat out with a morsel of gop. "All because of the Jared Krashinskys of the world, seething greed!" He was panting, scowling. "Screens are terminally boring! And boredom leads to rage!"

I was startled by this explosion and tried to cool him down. "Easy, Fats, easy, okay?" He didn't say okay.

"Gotta go," said Sev.

"Thanks for trying, Sev," I said, feeling sad that I might never see him again.

"Welcome." He turned away and shuffled off.

Fats finished eating. Calming.

"Y'know, Basch, I hate to say it—and don't tell the team—but I feel I'm starting to lose some of my power. I mean, we are up against a fucking monster."

"Lose power? Really?"

"It's a toughie." He gathered himself, puffed up. "Plan B, at six a.m. tomorrow."

⌀

"'The Five Good Things of Relationship.'"

Berry. Standing at the blackboard for the day's checkout, chalking as she spoke.

Everybody was there, even Gath and Jude, Gilheeny and Quick. Fats had given an effusive introduction. I was worried about how she would come through to the others. All of us were really worn down by our day on the front lines.

"Thanks," Berry said. "Now. Take a few seconds, eyes closed, to picture a *good connection* you've had with someone recently, say, a lunch or a coffee or a walk. Anything, really."

We did.

"Okay. If it's a good meeting, both of you leave with Five Good Things." She wrote and said, "One: you each have an increased sense of Energy, or Zest. Two: you each feel an increased sense of your own Self-Worth and the Worth of the Other person. Three: an increased sense of Self-Knowledge and Knowledge of the Other. Four—and this is crucial for being a doctor in these huge hierarchies of the House and the 4th: Power. You each leave with an increased sense of Power, and that of the other person. Five: you both leave with a Desire for More Connection—you each say, 'Hey, let's do this again,' right?" Nods. "That's a good connection. A bad connection is the five opposites: Decreased energy, decreased self-worth, self-knowledge, power—and no desire to do it again. What's that describe—?"

"Depression!" shouted Eat My Dust. "Berry, that's me! That's my life!"

"Thanks a lot, Edward," said Naidoo.

"Until I met you. All the guys who knew me then know it's true."

"Right," Berry said. "It's a *relational* definition of depression—and of health. What do I mean? Take number four: power. When you went to the lunch, you may have, say, come from a really bad morning here—you may even have felt that you just couldn't make it through another afternoon. But if it's a good connection, you leave with a sense of power to take action—*doing* things in medicine that afternoon that you had been putting off or didn't have the stomach for. These huge systems *dis*empower us. But at that lunch, in our connec*ting*, power *arises in both people.* Good connection makes you a better doctor. Good connection is good medicine." She looked around the circle.

I sensed an electricity in the room, as if each of us had been, well, powered up.

"The usual, 'normal' model in the dominant culture—power over—says that power resides in this"—she gestured to her body—"in a person. Like saying Henry Kissinger is a powerful person and—"

"Hey," said Hooper, "he got his name on the Kissy-Saudi Tower, didn't he?"

"We can't *all* be that *un*lucky," Berry said, to laughter. "In a tower, the power flows down, top to bottom. The lower down we are, the more down-and-out we are made to feel. More isolated, 'outsidered,' retreating into 'self,' alone and lonely, without support. Bereft. To get to mutuality in a power-over system is a real challenge! I'm talking about a different model of power, the"—she chalked it up—"*relational* model. Power *arising in relationship, mutually.* Not power *over.* Power *with.*"

"What do you mean by 'mutually'?" Molly asked.

"If the connection at lunch is good, the five good things are felt mutually, by both people." Her eyes showed her excitement. "Each person *sees* the other, each *feels seen by* the other, and each *senses the other feeling seen.* There's that *click*! Not just empathy, mutual empathy. All good connections are mutual; if it ain't mutual, it ain't that good. We've all felt it sometime, right?"

Many nods.

"Let's be radical. Let's call it 'love.'"

She let this settle and looked around at each of us as we considered "love."

"Our job here," she went on, "is to deal with suffering. Mutuality brings compassion to suffering."

I found myself opening up to her, relieved that she was here now with us all. The room fell still.

"But how's that going to help us here?" said Fats. "Can you give us some takeout? Oops. I mean take-home?"

"Next time. But let me frame this even more grandly." She wrote on the board:

SELF MODEL: "SELF" AS CENTER OF
UNIVERSE—EXCLUSIVE
RELATIONAL MODEL: "RELATIONSHIP"
AS CENTER—INCLUSIVE

"The basic shift? The measure of a person's psychological health and growth is not in the *self*, but in the *quality of their relationships*. Their *connections*. Their *'wes.'*"

"Oh my God!" said Molly. "That is amazing."

"It's true," said Angel, "and real."

"Finally," said Naidoo, "someone has understood and put this into words."

"There's not a *male* surgeon on earth who understands that," said Jude.

"Agreed!" said Gath.

Mo and Dr. Ro smiled at each other. The men, mostly, seemed puzzled.

"Sounds good," said Eddie, "but if I go deeper into the relationship with Naidoo, won't I be less myself?"

"But haven't we found," Berry said, "that when we're in a good connection, we feel *more* ourselves, not less? Like right now?"

We men considered this. Then light bulbs went on and out came "Yeahs" and "Damns" and two "Holy shits!" and a *"Mia Madre!"* The women laughed.

I was really happy for Berry—for not just talking it, but showing it, just really being there with all of us. I sensed in the room relief, even euphoria—that crinkly, fresh texture when actually, often when you least expect it, you hear something that might just change your life. To us, beaten down that day, she offered some just plain hope.

"If only I'd larned this," Gilheeny said, glancing at Quick, "before I met the wife."

Quick glanced back. "My own spousal torment often devolves to harsh words. But this shifty paradigm offers a way out for suffering humanity—and hu*woman*ity?"

"But are you saying," Hooper said, "that these things are genetic?"

"There are genetic gender differences, sure. But here's the good news. The science with newborns proves that we all come into the world with *a primary desire for connection*. It gets crushed in boys—a whole other story. But it's always still here in us. It can always be tapped through good connection."

"Bravo, bravo!" cried Fats, beaming, a happy pop seeing wisdom for the first time in his child or in his Chubby. He looked at his watch. "How 'bout a few helpful hints for our work"—he winked—"in relation here? Or even at home?"

"'Or'? 'Even'?" she said, teasing. "How 'bout 'and'? 'Both'?" Fats squirmed. "Maybe we can do a gender workshop—learn to connect across our gender differences?"

"Workshops, yay!" cried Hooper. "An aqua-nude workshop saved my marriage."

Berry took the chalk. "How 'bout three more laws, to add to the laws of the House of God?"

"LawBerries! I love it." Fats beamed and took out what looked like a stick of foul reindeer jerky or something and began wrestling, trying to peel its airtight wrapper.

"Law Number Fourteen: Connection comes first. Fats has already said this, in different words: 'be with' the patient or 'stick together, no matter what.' Think of a patient, or your wife, husband, child. If you're in good connection, you can talk about *anything*. If you're *not* in good connecton, you *can't* talk about anything! Taking a new patient's history? If you connect, they'll tell you all the important stuff. If not, not. Right?"

"Can you give us a 'how to connect'?" asked Angel. "Nuts and bolts?"

"Sure. Even *before* you see the patient, *pause. Breathe.* When you meet, look into their eyes, say, 'Hello. I'm Dr. So and So.' And—these last two are really hard—give a little smile and offer your hand. Don't wait till the physical to touch your patient."

"We don't touch patients much anymore," said Mo. "We're too busy."

"Really?" Berry said. Mo nodded. "Oh. Oooo-kay." She picked up the chalk.

"Law Number Fifteen: Shift to the 'we.' All of us here have been trained to live our lives in the either-or, the I-you—the adversarial stance, which is normal in the hell realms, the realms of lawyers. Try using the 'we,' which includes, and amplifies, both the 'I' and the 'you.' A good example is from surgery."

She nodded to Gath and Jude. "The old-time patriarchal surgeons would say to their patients, 'I've done the tests. I'm going to operate on you'—that's the I-you. More recently, surgeons might say, 'I've done the tests. I think I should operate on you, but you can get a second opinion'—again, still in the I-you. But what if a surgeon said, 'We've done the tests. Let's talk about what we're going to do'? That's the shift to the 'we'—three times, counting the 'let's'—in one sentence, right? And what will the patient say back to the surgeon? 'I think *we* should do . . .' That's the magic. The doctor, using the word 'we,' puts it out there between them, almost as a 'thing.' The word 'we' concretizes the fact that there is a relationship here. We're in it *together*. This is the shift from 'self' to 'relationship,' from isolation of both doctor and patient to connection. And what do studies prove is the major reason that surgeons get sued by their patients?"

"Yeah," said Gath. "It's if patients feel they had no relationship with us. And guess who's never been sued." He raised his hand. As did Naidoo.

"It's so simple. The 'we.' Try it. Use it. Use the 'we.' With your loved ones too.

"Finally," she went on, "Law Number Sixteen: It's not just what you say or do—it's what you say or do *next*. Nobody gets relationship right all the time—we're always screwing it up. There are always disconnects. When you're in a disconnect, if you keep the 'we' in mind and hang in through the disconnect, you'll move to a better connection. Even saying 'We're in a disconnect' is a connecting statement."

She groped in her pocket to take out her "I"-phone to check the time.

"It's in the pile," I said. "You've got two more minutes."

"Okay. Forgive me if I end by going to a 'meta' level—not just what we're doing here now, but what all of us are dealing with in this fractured country. Okay?" We nodded. "Teaching connection and compassion, teaching kindness in a power-over machine that runs on craving and greed—i.e., on 'self'—is necessary. But it's also dangerous, because it provokes the rage in the machine, in the whole world. It can kill us."

We were stunned. Who ever talked, in places like this, about "meta"—meaning "larger, opening our focus *into the whole world*"?

She and I knew she also meant *metta*, the Pali word for "loving-kindness," the path of the Bodhisattvas in the world. Seeing my smile and nod, she returned them. Sensing each other being seen.

"Damn," said Chuck. "Girl, you nailed it."

"In some ways," Berry said, "it's just all about being present with each other, being a presence." She turned to Fats. "Like you are, Fats, to everyone in this room."

All eyes turned to him, the slick hair, the dark eyes, those cheeks, the greasy, thick fingers on that stick of venison jerky—all of it. The Fat Man blushed. He really blushed. Pomegranic.

"I'm, um, oh, jeez . . . but I'm not sure my mere presence helps that much."

"Presence," I found myself saying, "is never mere."

Berry smiled. "And it can be better than words. The simplicity of shared presence."

The room fell silent.

"This is the first time," Dr. Ro said, "in my training—and life—that I feel someone in medicine is sharing my experience. Berry, you're speaking my truth." She looked at the other women. "Our truth?" Nods. "How great is *that*?"

"I'm so moved by all of you," Berry said. "It just goes to show: truth is relational. We find it together. All of us working here in this giant . . . *thing*, with pressure coming down on us from the top and the clinic being overwhelmed, we *know* how to take refuge in our selves. But we don't know how to take refuge in our relationships, in our 'we.' But we can learn it. The practical essence, the takeaway law? Use the word 'we.'" She paused, looked around the circle at each of us. "And don't we all feel the five good things, especially more power, right now?"

Nods and yeses and, from Eddie, "Let's rock 'n' roll!"

Time was up. She smiled. "Now I've *gotta* rescue my phone!" With lightning dexterity, she extricated her "I." Fats, Humbo, Chuck, Mo, and I left, late for attending rounds on 34.

23

Up on Ward 34—after a whole day of chaos in the FMC that made me keep asking myself, *How will I survive?*—suddenly, I was dead tired. Whatever ictal jolt had been keeping me up had pretty much stopped working and was shoving me back down. As if I was trying to sit down and rest, only to have some joker pull the chair out from under me so I had to catch myself and stay on my feet. Blurry, I stumbled. Fats, as always, insisted on doing rounds in person.

George, a retired black postman in liver failure, was being evaluated for a transplant to save his life, but he had tested positive for cocaine—which would deny him a transplant and doom him to death. The liver team was ready to cancel. George, a devout Baptist, asked his wife to bring in the family Bible and, witnessed by the liver team, swore on it that he hadn't had a drink in decades, since joining in AA. He also swore that a night ago, celebrating a birthday with his old postal pals, he'd snorted one hit of cocaine—just the one—and that he had not touched it for years.

"My wife said she'd never cook me another peach cobbler if I ever did."

The house staff and liver team had examined him, but no one had sat down to listen to him. With fierce competition for transplants, the drug test was enough to reject him.

"Talk with him, Roy," Fats said. "I'll tell the liver docs to hang on till you're done. It's your call."

I sat eye level with him on his bed, did the *pause, breathe, hello, eye contact, smile, handshake*—his hand was worn, calloused, evidence of a life of hard labor before passing the postal exam. Orange abdomen puffed up with ascites, jaundiced yellow sclera, skin flaking from the urea burden, panting lungs exhaling the sweet scent of ketones. Everything goes through the liver, the great filter of our waste. Scared but calm. On his face were the long creases of his history, going on his appointed rounds. A good first connect. He opened up about his parents, his children and grandchildren, and how it had been a mistake to take that one snort. I sensed a stability, a continuance, a peach-cobbler romanticism. In our fractious, perilous, collapsing country, where jobs now were transient routes to survival, not callings, here was a postman's creed, a clear good.

I asked about his faith. He described his baptism in the river vividly, six decades of remembering. His said that his faith was still rock-solid.

I felt for him. As our eyes met and held, I sensed him sensing my feeling that.

Back out in the hallway with the transplant team, I said, "He's telling the truth. The cocaine was a slip, a onetime thing."

"How do you know that?" asked the liver fellow, glancing at her liver chief.

"I've been an addiction doc for decades. I can tell."

"Yeah, yeah, but what's the evidence?"

"You're looking at it." She was startled. I added, "I'd bet my job on it."

"We're talking a 200,000-dollar investment," said the chief. "We need more than hearsay. No evidence, no liver."

"I'm certain. I—"

Suddenly, Mozart.

The chief glanced at his watch and started to curse.

It was exactly seven o'clock, and Amadeus was announcing that we now were only twelve hours away from "TOSS 'em out, TOSS 'em out, TOSS 'em out!"

Down the hallway came three night shift CODE-'n'-TOSS commandos. They zeroed in on the interns and residents who were now hunched over, eyeballs glued, deep into their roiling screens.

The chief and I, now abandoned and bonded in our disgust, chatted. He brought up *The House* and how he had loved the tragic farce of the Yellow Man's liver.

He gave George's transplant the go-ahead.

After a few more consults, we heard, coming down the hall from Memory Lane toward us an insistent call: *"Fix the lump fix the lump fix the lump!"*

Max? Could it be?

"Fix the lump fix the lump fix the lump!"

Max! A *third* House of God gomer, here? Being pushed along the corridor past us by two burly Teamsters from Transport. 300 pounds of flesh, naked but for dirty underpants, with huge herniations of his abdominal wall, a great medicine ball of a head with little slots for eyes, nose, and mouth, and a bald skull covered with purplish crisscrossing neurosurgical scars so he looked like a box of Purina Dog Chow. And all of it convulsing. An unhooked frontal lobe. Parkinson's for 63 years. Bowels blocked so you could see the lumps— intestines pushing out through the scars in his belly. All feces. Each House admission had been to disimpact him manually. In the House he'd been an Eat My Dust patient, and finally Eddie had paid a Japanese BMS violin prodigy with fingers like wires to do the job, promising her the internship of her choice.

Law One: Gomers don't die. But why was this loyal House gomer TURFED to Man's 4th? Why here?

Answer: because following him was Jack Rowk Junior. Somehow his research—to knock out the "eternity gene"—that had led to the cold-blooded murder of Harry the Horse had not been stopped.

They disappeared toward the Merck/Fox Translational to "monetize" Max. The liver chief and I looked at each other, seeing, in each other's eyes, a revulsion. *Sick. All of it, sick.*

⟋

My last ward visit was to Otto Vance.

Chuck, who'd been taking care of Otto's wife, Desirée, came with me.

After he first told me he was having gut pain and feeling "jumpeh and dizzy," I had put him through the usual outpatient workup. Everything was normal. I'd suggested that maybe he'd been working too hard and was getting tired of the extreme, harsh winter—and not getting his ususal "lift" out of taxidermy. He declined to take antianxiety or antidepressant drugs, and he dismissed all my relaxation suggestions, such as mindfulness meditation.

He also dismissed religion with a rare eloquence: "God ain't for me."

Finally, I convinced him to take a break, a vacation back in Louisiana with his wife. They would stay at her sister's plantation near Oak Alley, on the Great River Road south of New Orleans. They had done so.

But now, a few weeks after the trip, he was clearly worse. Thinner, even more "jumpeh and dizzy." He wasn't eating, was losing weight fast. He had super insurance, and I admitted him to Ward 34.

As a potentially publishable fascinoma, he brought out the best in Man's 4th—it was dazzling. From whole-body scans with red, white, and blue contrast, to genetics and molecules—all the way down to single atomic elements; the World's 4th Best gastroenterologist had found that number 42 on the periodic table, molyb*denum*, had the same last two syllables as duo*denum*, and he guessed that treatment with pure molybdenum might somehow crack the case. No luck.

They exhausted all diagnostics, which exhausted Otto. There was still no identifiable cause for his weight loss, except that he wasn't eating enough.

No paper could be published. By seven the next morning, Otto Vance would be unceremoniously TOSSED.

He was lying in bed, a rail-thin, muscle-wasted guy looking years older than when I'd met him, that first Vance family visit. All of us liked them, looked forward to seeing them. All except Otto were doing well—especially the diabetics, with Hyper Hooper coordinating, manically: from exercise to genetic manipulation using his Eat Red diet.

Now Otto's face was more than worried. It showed dread. The face of a dying man.

Desirée was sitting at the bedside, dressed and made up meticulously in shades of purple, her red hair in a neat bun. Her face was tight, stern, her eyes in squints of fear.

Otto's slack hand was in hers, like a tired child's.

"Just dropped in to say hi," Chuck said to her. "Come see me anytime." He left.

"How are you, Otto?" I asked.

"Not bad," he said as usual. "Gut pain same. Not jumpeh, though. My insides cain't jump no more. So that's good."

"All the tests were negative. So I'm going to discharge you tomorrow morning. We'll keep on trying to find out what's wrong."

"'Preciate that, Doc," he said morosely. "But don't you waste yo' time on me."

"You have *got* to start eating again. Maybe the trip south upset your gut somehow, and being in the hospital made it worse. Maybe home cooking'll do the trick?"

He shrugged.

I turned to his wife, clearly at her limit. "Anything you want to put in, Desirée?"

Tears in her eyes, she shook her head no.

"Listen to me." She looked up. "If you ever want to come in with Otto, or even come along by yourself just to talk, call me. Here's my cell phone number. I'm available twenty-four seven."

"Thank you kindly," she said. "Maybe it's in God's hands now?"

"The hell it is!" Otto said in a rare angry tone—a snarl. "The *hell*, y'understand?"

I was a startled—it was so unlike him. I left and from the hallway looked back.

Otto's eyes were closed, his hand still in hers.

Fats and Humbo were at the nursing station finishing up their losing arguments with CODE 'n' TOSS.

Mo, our high-tech genius, was busy on-screen and, at the same time, talking on the phone, eating kale chips, and drinking pomegranate juice—another Hooper convert. She was being ultracareful in arranging the admission the next morning of Mrs. Burke, her very first patient, coming in again for an infection of her pacemaker wire.

"I have to make sure they don't start her on IV fluconazole again."

As Fats, Humbo, Chuck, and I started walking down the hall, I glanced back and saw, as if miniaturized for efficiency, the eight or so cubicles with these smart, good, young docs and med students who had fought fiercely for ten years to get in here, now forced to be—with their backs turned toward their patients and even toward the other docs on their team—totally out of the life of the ward, in the banks of the screens.

Treating the screens, not the patients. Our work is screens.

Before we parted, Fats got a phone call. Seeing the number, he signaled all of us to be quiet, led us into an empty family waiting area, put his phone on speaker, and picked up.

It was the Krash, frantic, breathing erratically, sounding as if he were in tears. "I need help, Fats. You're the only one I can call—you're my only friend!"

Fats rolled his eyes. "Glad to help. What's up?"

"Terrible stuff . . . I . . ." Long pause, panting, trying to get himself under control.

I wished he would. I was tired of this hospital, this constant fight, this Krash.

"Two things. First, I blacked out, maybe for about ten minues—maybe it was a seizure. I don't know. When I came to, I still had an erection."

"Excuse me?"

"Did I mention my Viagra?" Fats averred no. "I took a big dose of Viagra—with all the stress, y'know, of the job—and another big one just popped up and—"

"Another erection?"

"No, a stress! I'll tell you about that next. Y'see, Bronia keeps on wanting it—needing it, really. I mean, with the five kids. And I keep it up for Israel—y'know, the *numbers*—but it's hard, so I use Viagra, and when I took it this time and was about to penetrate, all of a sudden everything went black, and when I woke up, she still wanted me to, you know—but I was scared I had brain cancer and called you, my only friend. Whaddaya think's going on?"

Rolling his eyes at us, Fats asked all the right questions, including "Did you poop or pee the bed?"—a common effect of seizure—and got all the healthy answers and finally convinced Krash that it was clearly *not* a seizure but just a blackout and probably due to exhaustion from his job, and too much Viagra for his putz.

"Will you tell that to the wife?"

"Sure."

"And tell her that, as a doctor, you say we can't have sex for a while?"

"Yeah. Tell her to call me tomorrow at the—"

"Shalom, Fats. It's Bronia."

"*Shalom aleichem*, Bronia."

She sounded more mad than scared. The conversation was not pretty. She ended with a dictum: "Please tell my husband that I and my family need his sexual-slash-reproductive health, and commitment, to make more Krashinskys."

"I can assure you that Jared is totally committed, but a little overworked and stressed-out. Don't worry. He'll be fine. Put him back on."

"Thanks," Jared said with a sigh. "You did a mitzvah. It's a lot of stress, sitting on top of this big pyramid!"

"Yeah, sitting right on *that point*? Yeow!"

A pause. "You have no idea."

"And so," Fats went on, "what was the second thing that popped up as a stress?"

"I got a real tough decision to make, and I've got to make it before morning. A new admission today, Beef Kripke, of Kripke's Rent-a-Philospher dotcom? Orthodox. Based in Long Island but wants Man's Best because of me. Admitted today for, quote, 'ballistic flatulence and diarrhea.' CAT scan with contrast of bowel. So he's lying in his bed and in comes his doctor and it's an Arab, a Muslim. Beef goes bananas, refuses to be examined by him, and says, 'There must be a hundred Jew boy docs here and I ain't gonna be under a—cussword—Arab.'"

"And?"

"Man's Best's policy is to not discriminate, okay?"

I was again late for dinner and said, "Gotta go!" Fats held up a finger—wait!

"So that's that," Fats said. "Nice talkin' to you and—"

"Wait! If I say he has to deal with the Arab, he'll raise the roof. Very influential, and not only on Long Island. This is a big—no, a *very* big—deal. And I have to decide before tomorrow at seven for the TOSS."

"And if you accede to his wish?"

"I betray our mission. The one carved in stone, about how even an Arab is our neighbor. It's an old *goyishe* mission, but a mission is a mission, right?"

"Unless it goes misshing."

A pause. "Humorous joke, yes. Humor is *good*. Defuses. I feel calmer."

"Maybe you can ask for help—run the decision past your higher-up, Flambeau?"

"No no! He said when I came on board he expects me to make decisions myself."

"Goodgood. So decide."

"But I need *help* deciding. That's why I called you. You're my only friend!" Fats held the phone at arm's length, scowled at it. "Flambeau's *exact* words? 'Don't be a chicken. Be a decider, like me. I only want to hear about the really big deals.'"

"I thought you said this *is* a really big deal?"

"No, I said it's a *very*, but I'm not sure it's a *really*. Is it?"

"How the hell do I know? If I were you, I'd risk it."

"Y'mean risk ruling for the Jew or the Arab? Or risk telling Flambeau?"

"The latter, which will get him on board with the former."

We heard his tortured, even stertorous, breathing. Once again I shook my head in a "Gotta go."

"Sorry, Krash," Fats said. "Gotta run—"

"*Nooo!*"

"Okay, you heard what Flambeau said. You have to be the decider."

"That's right. He did say that. Except for the *reallys*."

I found myself thinking, *Nothing's more explosive than Arab-Jew shit and it could easily turn into a really,* so I said, "Roy here. I was just walking by—"

"Hi, Roy. Thanks for your help, my good friend."

"I think you better tell him. Because if things go south, he can blast you to bits."

"'South'? You mean, so to speak, south into the administrative desert, the Negev?"

Rolling his eyes toward us, Fats said, "Good metaphor, Krash. You better call him up right now and tell him, but now Roy and I have to go see an urgent patient—"

"Wait! He *implied* only the reallys not the verys and—"

"Yeah, but what if in this case the verys really are the reallys, so you can't be the only decider and we're done?"

A pause on the other end. A hiss, like a train makes releasing its brakes. "But maybe not. Which means he definitely does *not* want to hear this one. Wants me to be *the decider*. If I involve him wrongly, he'll wring my neck. I'm thinkin' chickens here."

"So don't tell him," Fats said. "Decision made. Like an adult."

"But maybe if I *don't* involve him, he'll wring my neck."

"You're a decider. Go with your gut. If there was no Flambeau, what would you do?"

"Hmm. Good reframe. The choices are clear: I tell the Jew he accedes to an Arab doctor or else I discharge him, or I tell the Arab doctor he's off the case and get the Jew a Jewish doctor. And I can't threaten to split the baby, like Solomon."

"Right, it's not a pediatric case," Fats said. Silence on the line. "Bottom line bottom line: what's your *gut* telling you to do? Quick, Krash, don't think. Go gut level."

"My gut is telling me I can't decide."

"Look, y'remember that day in the synagogue, with that Hadassah arm?"

"Who could forget it? You walked away. I stayed. I always worried that you did what was right and I should have gone with you."

"And I thought you were right too. We each did what was right for us. Not on a thought level, on a gut level. What is your gut telling you to do right now?"

"Do . . . it . . . for . . . Israel."

"There you go. You are the decider. We're done."

"But maybe not and—"

Click.

"Man, somebody better distract that guy with a shiny object," said Chuck.

"*Está mucho* discombobulay. *Mía madre* say, 'Think of words of Jesus—Blessed are the merciful, for they will be shown mercy'—but me, I kick him in the *cojones*."

Fats stayed behind to work with Mo on Mrs. Burke.

Lucky he did, because his emergency note in HEAL warning against ever giving Mrs. B. a fluconazole IV had been deleted—and HEAL, on its own volition, had on admission ordered an IV to lower her platelets and kill her dead. Fats would cancel it.

She would be saved.

⌒

Berry and Spring and Olive and Cinny were still up, happy to see me.

Cinny had a new toy, a pink flamingo with long, stringy legs and a squeaker.

For the first time in a while since she'd become the Destroyer, gnawing things to sawdust, Olive was outside her cage on a round rug, centered near the table on the gleaming, wide-planked yellow pine floor.

"Hey. We can't have Olive pooping all over and eating the floor."

"Da-ad, I'm on it. I learned rabbits are scared of floors 'cuz it's slippy, so she can't run away from hawks. She'll stay on the rug. You watch."

"Watch what, her pooping?"

As we ate, Spring was talking and talking about how nice I was being since my piggy bank flash and how at the Whole World there was a boy she liked, John, who liked her and they did water play but Margaret screamed at them to be neat.

"Margaret screams?" Berry and I said together.

"Real loud. And lots. Mostly in Lunch Bunch when we make messes."

Quaker Margaret? The Whole World? 24 grand a year?

"Olive's mad and lonely. Both of you were away all day and me too in after-school, and Olive got mad at me."

"How can you tell?"

"She got out of her cage and ate the windowsill."

"That's it!" I cried out. "She's history!"

"She's lonely and needs rabbit friends. She's an *only* rabbit!"

"No more rabbits!" I cried.

"Mom said you would say that."

"Maybe she should get out more, let her run wild in the yard and find other rabbits, make more friends, have playdates, join a soccer team—"

"Jesus Christ!" Berry and I stared at each other.

"Where'd you hear that, honey?"

"From John."

"It's a swear," Berry said, "and you—"

"You guys swear sometime at each other. I hear you through the wall."

"We're old enough to swear," I said. "There will be a time when you can too."

"Next week?"

"Not that soon," Berry said, "but someday."

"Promise?" Berry nodded. "Will you tell me when? 'Cuz it's quite cool."

"Anything to help you with your relationship with John," I said.

"It's not like that! He's just fun. And *he* can swear."

"About Olive," I said. "Maybe we should send her away to have some time with other rabbits so she gets to be more friendly."

"She's friendly, but she's an only and doesn't like it."

"Honey," Berry said, "does this have anything to do with *your* being an only child?"

"Ma-ahm! I am not a rabbit!"

"Rabbits," I said, "live together, right? So they learn not to gnaw the windowsills in their hutches and houses, right?" Spring did not reply. "How 'bout we coop her up with another rabbit—at the pet store or Animal Rescue—so she learns how to get along?"

"Yeah, sure," said Spring. "Why not tie her up to another rabbit and throw 'em in the clothes dryer till they both die?"

We soon moved off the rabbit to the food, and to Spring yawning, and to bed.

I realized that for the first time in decades, I'd had nothing to drink. I was still drunk on being alive, being with— Hey, call it good connection, why not?

"I'm really worried, Roy," Berry said after turning off her "I"-phone and putting on her sleep mask and turning out the light. The only two things she ever turned off.

"Mmmm?"

"I can't see how we can take care of all those patients. No way without help."

"I know. Scary. But I'm glad we're in it together—and that you're with us all. You were great today."

"So were you all. It's rare to get to a little bit of 'mutual.' But how in the world are we, and it, going to survive?" Silence. "And you heard Spring loud and clear, right? Olive being 'mad and lonely'?"

"Got it."

"If it gets too much for her, hon, I stop."

"And I do too."

"Promise?"

"Promise."

24

❦

elp came.

It started at six the next morning with the FMC Runners for Health protest outside Man's 4th Best's Pink Building, the main entrance, with the two missions carved into the facade. The early hour was chosen because it would catch the type A docs and staff hurrying into the hospital at six to get a jump on the lazybones who came in at change of shift at seven, including Pat P. Flambeau, described by Gilheeny as "a titan of early birds who always gets the proverbial worm."

"Whose first two names," Quick said, "were given by his mom after she saw them on a new invention in chicken husbandry, an automated disembowler: 'Pat. Pending.'"

The Runners were all there at 5:30, organizing. Astonishing, that high schoolers would be up at that hour. The Runners had grown a grassroots movement, mentored by us who hated OUTGOING more than gum surgery. It looked like a United Nations Youth Delegate Program—every color, shape, religion, and ethnicity.

Dark April air was crisp and astute. Security spotlights were on. Carrying posters, we sent chants clattering up metallic sheets of sound, echoes sliding back down the Pink.

NO RUN NO FUN—RUNNERS FOR HEALTH!

TIME FOR RUNNERS, DOUBLE TIME FOR PATIENTS!

RUNNERS LOOK GREAT ON MED SCHOOL APPS!

FOR GREAT PATSATS BRING US BACK BRING US BACK!

RUN DON'T GUN—RUNNERSFORPEACE, RUNNERSFORPEACE!

Pat P. Flambeau was known to arrive at six sharp, though he was often away milking cash cows. Sure enough, a limo the size of a whale calf rode an invisible wave in, gently parting the crowd. As if startled by the gathering of urchins, it just floated there, seeming to bob. A chauffeur held open a door. Dead quiet. Authority fluttered.

Pat P. Flambeau de-whaled, stood up straight. With smooth rotations of his head, he took things in, saw Fats. "Hey hey hey! Fat Man Clinic, I love it!"

He waved as if he were responsible for their joy. Then he expertly put his one hand palm down, to stop their yelling, and turned to Fats again. We gathered around.

In a deep voice amplified as if by a microphone by the scalloped facade of the Pink, he said, "And who are these fine youngsters and what's a 'Runner'?" Fats explained. Pat P. listened and asked, "Fired? Why were they fired and who fired them?"

"President Krashinsky. He did it when I was away."

At the word 'president,' Pat P. started to mutter, "Fuck. And when did this happen?"

"Maybe a month ago exactly."

"That explains it—the SATPATs. After leading the league in SATPAT, you toileted. And the reason you led the league was because HEAL OUTGOING broke?"

"Yessir," said Fats. "It was the best thing that ever happened to us. We had twice the time to see patients, and we didn't turn our backs on them anymore—so they loved it. But we needed an OUTGOING, so Roy, here, and I started Runners for Health. Some are in college, some premeds. Most come from a local public school."

"Inner-city public?"

"As inner as it gets. The premeds are mentored by us, learning what real medicine is like, and they help the inner-city kids with homework. It's inspiring. A lifting up."

"Lifting up is good. Truth t'tell, boys, 'Climb up, lift up' is my motto. Y'know, that HEAL's a som'abitch! I hate it! I don't use it. Rowland, my admin, is fluid in it, so he does it for me."

"So," said Fats, "after all these great months of no OUTGOING and with Runners for Health, when I was away OUTGOING suddenly was back! Despite my protests, Krash fired the Runners. So now we're overwhelmed with patients because with OUTGOING we have to see twice the number in half the time. And the Runners are really bummed—just look at them!" Pat P. did. They were. "What can we do?"

"Why, it's easy. We'll turn off OUTGOING again, hire the Runners again, and let the SATPAT toilet be filled with—I dunno—Path and Psych and prostate guys."

"Amazing, sir. You solved our problem."

"Don't patronize me, Fats," he snapped. "I didn't lose my arm for nothin'."

He turned to the Runners and the crowd. A hush.

"Runners and others! I hereby this morning am crashing OUTGOING, and hiring all of you back! By noon!"

Cheers, hip-hips! He waved left-handed to the crowd, and gestured me and Fats to follow him through the Pink lobby to the BUDDIES LLC skyscraper, and straight up to the top.

"That group o' kids brought back a lot of memories," he said as we elevated. "I grew up in Bartlesville, Oklahoma. We had nothing, except chickens. Wasn't easy bein' black with nothin' but those birds, a drunk dad, and a great but clinically depressed mom. I took paper routes, manual labor, worked my way out—first in rabbits, then in chickens. A great man named Buster took me under his wing. And then this arm?"

We were now stopped at the top of things, and got out. Stunned by the 360 of sunrise, ocean, city. An aerie, a nest for birds of prey, Masters of the Universe.

In his office, he kept talking, as if lonely. "Losin' the arm brought a lotta suffering, but it made me what I am today. I was always a little guy. I'm a big guy now. Buster's voice is always with me: 'Pat, help the helpless. Be big to the little. Strong for the weak. Cocky for the chickenhearted.'" He sighed. "Suffering made me grateful and generous."

I was struck by this. It was almost Berryan: suffering attracts compassion. *Whoa.* I glanced at Fats. He had a look I'd never seen on his face before, of puzzled awe.

"That Krash, deciding to fire those Runners? I keep tellin' him, 'Let me help you with decisions. You don't have to be the decider. Work with me.'" He shook his head. "But the money now, the disparity, how rich the rich are and mostly shittin' on the nonrich? I never had money growin' up, so I look at money like it's lead: if it gets into your body early, it gets into your brain and you're crazy for it forever. We forget—in health care, we really are our brothers' keepers. If we don't care, who the hell are we and—?"

Rowland, his admin, came in. A sleek and slender boy-faced man of maybe 40, with slick black hair combed back, wearing a tailored pinstripe suit and thin pink tie, nodded.

"Boys," Flambeau said to us, glad-handing us with the one left, the left, "you're the best. Haven't paid as much attention to you as I shoulda but that's a-gonna change."

Astonished, as we walked to the elevator, we were silent. It was the only 30 seconds of silence I could recall ever having with Fats. I floated through my patients, and went home happy.

The next day, local TV had the Runners and us of the FMC and Flambeau himself, his lone big arm raised and meaty hand waving happily, like a kid's flag. Interviewed, he had great quotes: "Good health care isn't a luxury. It's a right—and these fine boys and girls are the right generation to assure that right for us all. Right?" The six a.m. TV reporter, a woman who looked 14, was flummoxed but managed a "Right," and everybody laughed. Flambeau smiled. "Runners! Guys and gals, show us some runnin'!" The video caught them running back and forth, screaming and laughing.

We walked into the morning check-in to applause. Berry, in charge, asked, "So, how'd it go, using the 'we'?"

Around the table, in turn, everyone had something good to say—each in their own way. While the women said it had been easy and natural, giving them a word for what they already did, the guys were using the "we" differently.

"Dynamite," said Hooper, hard-rocking in his chair. "I used it sixty-seven times yesterday, on all the nineteen referrals from you of all those diabetics and cardiacs, and in my four Eat Red food groups. I use 'we' emphatically—eye to eye as if I were delivering bad weight news: 'We! We!' Result? Out of the sixty-seven times, fifty-nine said it right back to me—ninety percent! It works. Anybody beat sixty-seven?" We rolled our eyes. "I win. What's the prize?"

"I too love it," said Eddie. "Y'gotta be very delicate with cancer patients, and the 'we' works like a charm." He seemed sincere. Naidoo looked worried. "I see the 'we' with a capital 'W,' the royal 'We.' My cancer patients can't argue with King Eddie—"

"This is the very opposite of what Berry means!" Naidoo burst out. "It is not royal. It is communal. Royal will lead to disaster with them—and with us, damn it!"

Everyone in the room must have had the same thought: this "we" will not last.

Berry broke the tension. "My bad. Sometimes men, especially, see the 'we' that way. There are different kinds of 'we.' The *exclusive* 'we' is 'we' against 'them'—like an army or a team or a bad king, yes. But here we're talking about the *inclusive* 'we.' One that expands to include anyone who wants in. An open circle. Get it, Eddie?"

"Yeah, I do. I'm eatin' my own dust." Red in the face, he glanced at Naidoo.

"So in this disconnect with her, Eddie, anything you want to say or do next?"

Eddie squirmed, hung his head, grimaced. "I'm really sorry, Nai. You're the best thing that's happened to me since . . ." He clenched his teeth. I knew he was fighting like hell against his demonic sarcasm, which all us guys—except the Runt—knew was like a vise around his heart, squeezing out venom. "Since *ever*. I'm totally in awe of you, Nai, totally in love. Because of you, I'm, secretly, behind my office door, *kind* to my cancers. I tell 'em that they're facing *hurdles*, not death—and I'll help 'em over our next hurdle. You're so, well, in the 'we' all the time. Uhm, I sound cynical 'cuz deep down I want perfection and no one except you ever gets near. You're the one. With cancer, even. Sorry."

They stared at each other. Naidoo burst out in tears. She tried to talk, but could not. Eddie put his hand out to her, palm up. She took it. They hugged, both shaking. All of us, a minute ago, had been on edge. Now this? Their softening softened us. We saw ourselves in this; we'd all been there in our loves—and some of our loves hadn't made it.

Looking back, that check-in was a healing in our FMC "we." As I walked out to the mass of patients, I seemed to float.

⌒

That day, among the onslaught were a lot of new patients. The poor, people mostly of color. But among them now were other health-care workers, nurses, techs, a few doctors who'd retired rather than deal with HEAL, and one woman who was suicidal from EPIC. She had been a Nocturnalist who'd developed, in daylight, an impenetrable insomnia and a rash of cruelty at home. The doctors were amazed we'd killed off OUTGOING. Often, not knowing *how* we FMCers were different, they sensed we were more *with* them. Not realizing our using "we" to them, they used "we" back to us.

Later, at checkout, the team talked about this. Every one of us had had one or two health-care workers who'd asked about joining us, either for pay or to volunteer. One of them even said to Naidoo, as she left, "I really admire your cause." We all looked around at one another. *Cause? Yes, we once did have one—to put the human back in medicine. Maybe we still do. And is it as simple as being in connection? Getting to mutual, the we?*

⌒

Midafternoon in any job is tough. Diurnal cortisol is at its lowest, and any more coffee will make you crawl right out of your skin. *One short nap—God, just give me one short nap! God said nope.* A well-worn, inch-thick paper chart (!) of a new patient: Pam Sheen, a long-practicing doctor, now wheelchair bound. She had been treated well at a small hospital, but BUDDIES had bought it and shredded it. Her GP, rather than learn HEAL, retired to Italy. Pam had a terrible history: 64, myasthenia gravis diagnosed ten years ago with all the exacerbations—once being on a ventilator, heart disease, renal, liver, etc., and now on a chronic downhill course. The domino effect, each organ toppling topples others. The chart had lots of numbers. Not much about her as a person.

Her written chief complaint: "First, I need a new doctor, and I heard good things of the FMC. Second, a surgeon botched a drain of my infected index finger two months ago. He tried to repair it and couldn't. It hurts like crazy, and I can't use it."

I did not look forward to taking all this on—a multisystem-chronic-organ failure of an untreatable disease. I managed a smile, took her hand, introduced myself.

"Call me Dr. Pam," she said, having wheeled herself into my office. An obese, panting woman, wearing a brown, almost liturgical smock, with a crucifix. Her face was puffy, breath strained, but her eyes were remarkable: in all that congestive bloat, light blue and lively. A woman whose body had been giving out for a long time.

"What shall we talk about, Dr. Pam?"

As if reading my mind, she said, "Yes, this body is giving out—but this body isn't *me*. It just happens to be my body, not me, and—"

A loud knock on the door. Another, louder. I opened it.

It was Mo. "Sorry to interrupt. It's a code red in the OR."

I jumped up. "Sorry, Dr. Pam. Make an appointment with Dr. Gath for that finger today, and another one with me as soon as possible—like tomorrow. I look forward to seeing you."

We raced to surgery—too late. Lena Metz, the anesthesia chief, was coming out of an OR, shaking her head. Through the open door, angry shouts. We went in.

A scene of carnage. Blood all over the operating table and sheets covering the body—the patient clearly dead. No one was moving to clean anything up. The OR team was gathered around Gath and a young resident, who were shouting at each other. I'd never seen Gath so enraged—red-faced, shaking the resident by the shoulders, spitting out words. I shouted at him to stop and pushed my way between them, Mo following.

The resident looked at us, terror in his eyes. He was a giant, six five at least, smooth cheeks now flushed, crew-cut blond hair, regal nose. Holding a banana?

"I . . . I'm sorry," said the resident, name-tagged "Prince Whiteside III."

Gath shook his head, took a breath. Asked everyone but Prince and us to leave.

"What a mess," I said.

"You don't know the half of it," Gath said. "This is the limit. My limit."

"Why'd you call Mo and me?"

"Bad news. It's your patient. Both of yours."

A chill. Mo's eyes and mouth fell open. We stared at the covered body.

"Her name is Wambui Kanau—"

"No!" shouted Mo. "It can't be. What? Noooo!" She moved toward the body.

Shocked, I went with her, put my arm around her. She looked at me, and I nodded. She pulled off the sheet and gasped in horror. I felt sick to my stomach.

What we had come to know as her lively black face was not peaceful in death. Contorted and lighter, like a man's dark shirt washed too many times. Eyes wide as if seeing horror, mouth open, blood drenched—splashed all around her. Mo delicately pulled the sheet down but got only to her upper chest—between the circular burns of the electric paddles was her roughly sliced-open chest, the heart a dead blue fruit on a tree of ribs.

I pulled Mo away. Put my arms around her.

"Tell 'em what happened," Gath said, "Prince fucking Whiteside the Third."

Prince sat, looking exhausted and scared.

It turned out that Wambui Kamau had come to Emergency for acute and severe upper-right-quadrant pain. The previous CAT scan was the one we had seen in the EW, showing her gallbladder gone but with a stump remaining in which was that small stone, at 6 millimeters the borderline of dangerous. Mo and I had sent her home because, in private, Charley, the X-ray guru in Emergency, had said that 6 millimeters is a standard for taking it out, but he needed to cover his ass for legal. With laxatives, and Mo at the FMC, she had been fine for months now—except for the recent admission for uncontrolled diabetes.

"But she's *my* patient!" Mo said. "I know her story! Why didn't you call me?"

"Or me," I said. "I cosign all of Mo's notes."

"Must've slipped through the cracks," said Prince. "And when we saw that the EW CAT scan said a six-millimeter stone—that was was the red flag for us to pull the trigger."

"That was just to cover the radiologist's ass!" Mo shouted. "She was constipated!"

The word bounced around the tiled walls and died.

Gath shook his head and said, "Keep going."

The story got worse. Wambui's son was married to a prestigious invest-ment banker downtown. She had recently bought a Platinum-Plus Aetna Health Insurance package for the family, including Wambui. The Platinum paid the highest reimbursements in all of America. Like blood does sharks, it attracted a cruising Chief Barmdun. Never mind that a gallbladder isn't a bone—he took the case, inviting Prince to scrub in with him.

"I was honored," Prince said to Gath. "I scrubbed in. But . . . but *he* didn't. He told me, 'You start. Open her up, expose down to deep tissue, then call me. I've got another case I have to start. I'll come down when you need me.' I tried to tell him that I hadn't ever done a gallbladder, but he said, 'Hey, anyone— even a resident—can do the exposure down to the deep tissue,' and left. So I started, and, well . . . I got confused and asked myself, 'But that's the *bowel*, isn't it?' and she bled a little and I cauterized it—I thought I'd gotten all the bleeders—but I called him and he didn't pick up and . . . shit . . . I waited . . . called again and finally he answered and said he was up in the Kissy-Saudi doing a complex hangnail on a sheikh and he'd be there in a few minutes, and when I came back in here, well . . . it was all going to hell. . . ." Prince's face clenched up and his jaw clenched up and he was all set to cry but just sat there, clenched up, fighting.

"Okay," said Gath, straining for control. "Listen. Here is what you will do. Her son is totally dedicated to her, and his wife's a real player downtown. They and their lovely little girl, her grandchild, are sitting out there, waiting. Someone has to tell them—"

"I can't!" Prince was terrified.

"Did you talk to them before surgery? Would they recognize you?"

"No, Barmdun talked to them. After that, he happened to see me—I was coming off a really bad night shift: two days straight, totally wiped out, seeing double, heading home—and he grabbed me, told me to do this. He's the chief. How could I say no?"

"Lucky for you they never met you. We'll take care of them right now. And then you can bet we will be taking care of Barmdun. Mo and Roy will tell the family. You and I will wait till they're told, and then we will walk by, *slowly*, and you will *look*."

"'Look'?"

"Yeah. Because then you might just never forget it and become a *real* doc." Gath paused. "Listen up, Prince." He waited until Prince looked him in the eyes. "There's a 'Golden Rule of Surgery': 'Do operations unto others that you would want done unto you'—or your mother, father, wife, child, your family. One more thing. If you or me or any of us were a patient, do you think we'd *ever* agree to this, to overlapping surgeries?"

"No, sir."

"So why the fuck would we do it on someone *else*? For the money? Shit!"

"Mo," I said, "do you want to tell the family, or do you want me to?"

"I can't lie to them," she said.

"Let Roy start," Gath said, "and then just be there with them for a while, with all your own pain, and with your strength. Tell them exactly what happened—and write it all down. Because, believe me, with our help, they *will* sue. And your notes—cosigned by Roy—will be crucial contemporaneous evidence." He turned to his phone, hit some keys. "I just sent you all the Barmdun contacts—even in the Caymans. Before you leave them, forward these to 'em now. Tell 'em to call him."

We walked to the OR suite doors and out to the waiting room. The son, his wife—holding their little girl—rose up as they saw Mo and me come toward them, their eyes asking.

We all sat down together. I told them the bad news. At first, they couldn't take it in. I nodded. Told them again.

They all collapsed down on the couch into one another, cried out and cried and cried, all three in a little clump on this stupid, dead purple plastic couch. We sat with them. The saddest end of a journey I had ever seen.

I saw Gath walk Prince Whiteside III up to us, pause a long moment, for a long look, and walk him on.

⌒

At that day's checkout, Gath asked if Mo or I wanted to speak about what had happened.

Mo was too broken up to talk.

"We've all seen tragedy in medicine," I said, "but nothing as bad as this, death by greed. She came to America with high hopes, living her dream of joining her family, and she's going back to Kenya in a box. Gath?"

"I've had it," Gath said. "I mean, I really have *had* it!" He shook himself out of his rage, from his head on down, a wet-dog shake. "Now we're gonna make our move. Gonna go all out to the *Register Star* team on double booking. Lena is key. As chief of OR anesthesia, for years she's documented Buck and Barmdun—and three others who routinely double book. She's got exact in and out times each surgeon was actually in each OR. She's got their clearly falsified time charts with their signatures. She and I have collected data on the bad outcomes of double booking. Wambui Kamau is the clincher."

"Won't it interfere with your trial?" Hooper asked Jude.

"The trial will be long gone by the time the *Star* exposé comes out."

"But," said Naidoo to Gath, "you put yourself at great risk. Won't they fire you?"

"I'm squeaky-clean. Got my Man's Best Surgeon award in bronze—when it still was, in fact, Best. Got my name chiseled in a wall along a corridor in the Pink, on the way to the OR?" He paused, closed his eyes, and sighed. Eyes open, a glisten in them, he went on. "Always reminds me, before I operate, of our original mission: 'Charity of spirit is the easing of human suffering.'"

We fell silent.

"*Fire* me? Fire *me*? Fat chance." He smiled. "And when they *do* fire me, hey, I'm a surgeon. I can take my tools anywhere in the world—if the wife agrees."

"Gath, you're the best," said Fats softly. "Resistance incarnate. Kiss me."

"*Never* happen."

We laughed. Laughed harder for the pain.

Then we fell silent.

No one knew what to say.

"None of us can stand up to this giant alone," Berry said, fiercely. "*We do it together.* Yes?"

We went "Yes" all around the ellipse, a sober "Yes," the voice of a solid "we."

25

Over the next few days, some of the health-care refugees who had come to us for care did join us, as volunteers. And first- and second-year BMS students—having been immersed for a couple of years already in "the Best bio-pharma ecosystem in the world"—were hungry for something merely human, not only real-live patient contact, but for a lifting up to a higher good, a sense of service to those being crushed down, the poor.

We matched them with docs who were hungry for real-live student contact.

One morning, I watched another old doc who was volunteering trudge off into an office with a med student, to mentor. His brow was set in layers of frown. He seemed crunched down by the blows of screens-and-money medicine, maybe facing a lonely future of golf and a big, empty house for just him and his wife. Later, I chanced to see him come out with the student. He'd gone from crunched, hunched, and slouched to standing up straight. Trudge had morphed to light step. Frown reset to grin. At their good-bye, the student said something, and they both burst out laughing. Each walked away lighter.

As Berry put it, "Any good connection is mutual. The mentor gets as much out of it as the mentee. If it works, it's that *click!*"

Even some 4th Best residents—TURFED to us as patients, sitting with us as we looked at, talked with, listened to, touched, and didn't OUTGO—

had their eyes opened. Seeing us connect with the poor and sick, watching the world-famous Fat Man—all this in the shadow of Wambui's death and our fresh sense of resistance—the residents were *inspired*. Some would hang around after their appointments and, given the crush, help out with patients, writing with pen on paper, which was handed to the cute, spirited Runners. A few asked shyly if they could do something with us, more formally. We said, "Yes."

Take away the screen, the human rushes back in. Rushes curious, and lively.

The other wonder was how much patients loved being interviewed on their medical histories and having physicals done by the preclinical medical students—supervised by the old docs, or us. The med students were so nervous that the patients often felt they had to help them out. Real bonds of curiosity, both ways, were formed. Chronic patients had never had such acute doctors. Patients love novice docs. It was alive, crackling.

A 52-year-old woman, a longtime Man's 4th internist, seeing what we were doing and the crush of really sick patients, said, "I've been in the BMS system for decades. I'm a 'star' here at Man's Best, and I'm the most burned-out alum you'll ever meet. I can't *stand* it anymore. HEAL, elitism, killing myself, divorced, joint custody. Can't stand making money for *them*, killing *me*. Don't know why I went into medicine in the first place. But this, here, is different. Patients scraping bottom, risky, on the edge—unsolvable problems scraping bottom in the culture—and you really help. What keeps you going?"

"Good question. I guess . . . I guess it's all heartfelt. I don't mean to be—"

"No no, heartfelt is good. I need heartfelt. Go on."

"Buckle up." We laughed. "I came to see that our job as docs is to use our experience with others who suffer, and our vision born of that experience, to bring someone who's out on the edge of the so-called sick into the current of the human. To take what seems foreign in a person, and see it as native. Being with people at crucial times in their lives, walking them through suffering, taking care. That's healing, right?" She nodded. "That's what we signed up for years ago, remember? This is what good doctors do. We are *with* people at crucial moments of their lives, healing."

"Oh my," she said, blinking back tears. "It's so true. So true it might be— I don't know—*litigious*?" We laughed. She blew her nose. Blushed. "Haven't heard anything like that in decades."

"We're looking for more docs. Maybe you'd want to join us?"

She hesitated, then calculated. Metrics piled up. "Oh, God, I don't know."

Others said yes. The Future of Medicine Clinic—Care, Compassion, and Cancer—was attracting some good souls. We might just be gathering mass, making momentum.

Through attraction. Getting traction.

⌒

"Billin' is killin'!" said an Irish voice from the doorway of my office. It seemed vaguely familiar—as if from a recent sharp dream.

"Dr. . . . O'Toole?"

"James Barnacle O'Toole, lately of St. John's Hospital!"

Suddenly worried, I asked, "Are Gilheeny and Quick okay?"

"Would they be policemen if they were not?"

"Thank God! What are you doing here?"

"I've come here, in my quite queer Ulyssical quest, to look into joinin' you."

"Dynamite! You showed up at just the right time—our team checkout is now."

"Strange, is it not, that I happened here at this prescient particular moment?"

"You seem to have the same gift as Gilheeny and Quick."

"Which is?"

"Seeing around corners I can't even imagine."

And so all three of the Dubliners, and Gath, Jude, and a ballooned-up Angel, joined us that day. Fats was finally getting around to part two of his lecture:

*** RESISTANCE ***

"This," he said proudly, tapping his chalk on the word, "is now crucial." He winked at Berry, then looked around the table. "How're *we* doing, being with the 'we'?"

All of us except the Runt indicated that we were doing well, having fun with it.

"Dynamite!" he cried, rubbing his hands together happily like they were two old friends meeting. He was so excited that he wriggled. With all that bulk wriggling, he charged ahead, weaponizing the chalk.

"The six rackets of health care wind up being 'the World's Best' only in having the highest cost per patient of any country—over 10,000 dollars for each man, woman, and child. And America's 'the World's *37th* Best' for quality and safety of care—wedged between Slovenia and Croatia—*not* the place to be. The USA can't afford treatment for ninety percent of our addicts, or reduce lead for half a million of our kids? And the costs? We spend eighteen percent of our 21-trillion GDP on health care."

He sighed, shook his head, then brightened up.

"*But!* Finally, the data about screens has come out. Recently a few super-good studies on doctor, quote, 'burnout'—defined by the Maslach Burnout Inventory—have proven that the introduction of screens to medicine has *not* increased either patient safety or quality of care." He smiled, as if hitting a food jackpot. "And here's the *brisket!* There are three attributes of physician 'burnout'—one, lack of sense of accomplishment; two, lack of enthusiasm; and three, cynicism-depersonalization. The studies show that *all three are correlated with one and only one variable: the date that the Electronic Medical Record machines came in, and began to take over medicine.*"

This was astonishing—and made perfect sense. Here, at last, was proof.

"Wait a sec," I said. "You mean, we docs don't get up in the morning with a real zeal to have a meaningful relationship with HEAL?"

"Hard to believe, yeah. So the six rackets are worse for doctors and nurses, patients, and hospitals, and *only better for the six rackets.* The rackets run on money and screens, 'death by a thousand clicks.' The only screens worth anything are the ones that *do not launder money*—the VA, Indian Health, Medicare, and Medicaid. The big question? How to resist the screens that *do launder money?* It's simple."

He searched in an old wooden box of chalk, found a piece fat as a sausage, and wrote in the boldest, chunkiest letters we'd ever seen from him, talking as he wrote:

WE GOTTA SQUEEZE THE MONEY OUT
OF THE MACHINES

"If we stop clicking screens for cash from private insurance, and click just for care, the main problems of doctors, patients, and maybe hospitals are mostly gone. Like in the thirty-six countries ranked above us in care, we'll have two parallel systems. One, national *nonprofit* health care for all. The key? Each data code—say, 'appendectomy'—pays the same, all over the USA. No dicking around with insurance. That data is our first click—and done! The second system will be supplemental *for-profit* insurance, and our second click will be to send that data to them. And they handle billing and supplemental payment, not us. On *their* screens, baby, *not on ours*. We can keep all the Kissy-Sauds, for those who pay cash."

He sketched on the board a child's drawing of the Saudi-Kiss, which looked like an elongated wasp, stinger on top.

"Squeeze out the money, and the three hundred thirty-four people in the Billing Building and the Coders 4 Cash? *Gone!* No more war across the screen. And what a savings! What's the biggest cost in American health care? Administrative cost—which is thirty-three percent, 3 *trillion* bucks a year. Think what that money could do for real-live care. *No billing* on our doctors' screens? What a relief!" He paused, mused. "And the care itself has to change. What's most important for patients? Quality. Quality is paramount, maybe even more than access—'cause access without quality sucks. So we have to pay docs more, for more quality care. The other big thing is to pay not for procedures and process, but for outcomes. For improved care. How to get there?"

He stopped, looked around the table.

"Maybe one thing to try? Have outpatient clinics like ours be run by nurses, nurse practitioners, and PAs? You can do most anything we docs can, and you're better at getting to the 'we,' right? To treat the sixty percent of the walking worried?"

Nods all around. Made sense.

"And then the screens, no longer going crazy with billing, will be at *their* robotic best, sharing data with the clinics, answering questions—even assisting in minor AI surgery. I mean, it's happening already, right?"

It was true. All yeses.

"Finally, we gotta deal with social problems: violence, guns, diabetes, and—"

"Diabetes!" Hooper shouted, shooting to his feet. "The epidemic is here! Right now, *half* the population of California is prediabetic! The Midwest and the South are total fat and sugar! We gotta get 'em *before* they get sick. When they come to us sick, it's too late."

"Exactly," said Fats. "And what's our goal? National health care, for all."

"And are you saying," Molly asked, "that your goal is Medicare for all?"

Fats hesitated. "Well, kind of . . . I mean, yes, but . . ."

He stopped still. Two or three of his brows rolled up.

"Well, yes, but no," he went on unsurely. "Mind you, it ain't gonna be easy to redesign Medicare and Medicaid to jibe with a national system. Real complex. Lotta ins and outs, ups and downs. Complex. Real *tight* . . . In terms of infotech and servers, retro-engineering and retooling? *Way* high start-up costs. Complex bureaucratic shuffling, firing, hiring . . . lotta time, money . . ." He shook his head. "I hate to say it, but so far, I got no answer for that."

Silence. Just beginning, and Fats was stymied?

"I do."

We turned our heads. Mo, our in-house computer wizard. She had been able to help solve any glitch in INCOMING—and snafus in our cell phones.

"You do?" Fats said. She nodded. "Okay. Go."

"Okay!" She stood up next to Fats and took his chunky chalk. The two of them looked like a dangerously obese dad and a trim, sparkly daughter. She wriggled with excitement. "Once we get approval for Medicare for all, it's a snap to roll out. I pick up the phone." She held the chalk to her ear. "Hello, is this Medicare? . . . Good . . . Can you get me the techie who's in charge? Thanks . . ." She waited. Drumming her fingers—who knew she had such stage presence? "Oh, hi—what's your name? Merlin? I'm Dr. Ahern. Are you sitting at your computer that handles Medicare? . . . Good. Now, go to the box for 'age setting,' okay . . . Got it? . . . Good, Merlin. Just to confirm, what does it say? . . . Sixty-five? That's correct. Now, Merlin, I want you to click 'delete' on the 'sixty-five,' okay? . . . Yeah, sure I'll wait. . . . It's deleted? Good. Now click on 'zero.' That's right, the *number* zero? . . ." More finger drumming, staring up at the ceiling. "You did it? Great. Now click 'save'. . . . You clicked 'save,' great. Now, just to double-check that it's changed, close it and then open it ag— You already did that? . . . No, I *don't* think you're a dope, Merlin. I think you're a real smarty. . . . You're welcome, my friend. . . . What's that? . . . No, we'll do the nano-gritzels later. Hey, thanks for giving us Medicare from zero to death for all!"

We laughed, hard.

"It sounds ridiculous," Mo said, "but it's—"

"It's true!" Fats said. "We got a whole great national computer system already in place, so it's *just one click*! Wow-wee! A star is born! Let's hear it for Dr. Mocha!"

We applauded. She blushed. The first blush I'd seen in the FMC all year.

"I can vouch for Medicare," said Dr. Ro, "both as a doctor and as a patient. It almost never makes a mistake; everybody likes it. And a few years ago they *did* lower the age two years. Without a glitch. Y'know something? If you chart the health of Americans over our life spans? It peaks at about twenty, and then goes down, down, down until sixty-five—when it shoots up in a hockey-stick curve of better health. Why? Because Medicare kicks in. We gomeres love Medicare! With cheap supplemental insurance, we never see a bill—"

"And what happens," Fats went on, "once we have national insurance? What happens to private for-profit health insurance? Still there, still available as *a parallel system* for those who want additional coverage. *Heavily regulated.* Like Holland, Germany, Australia, and most other sensible countries. BUDDIES? Blackmailing INSURANCE and sucking money out of HOSPITALS and outpatient clinics? *Gone.* BIGPHARMAFDA drug prices? Not totally gone, but—wait for it—prices negotiated wayyyy *down.*"

He chalked an arrow, going down off the board from *BIGPHARMAFDA* and, bending clumsily, continuing on the floor until he hit the Runt's shoe. Fatly, he straightened up.

"HEDGERS FOR HEALTH? Unable to place bets on the stocks of health INSURANCE or even derm practices? *Gone.*" He beamed. "And since *every procedure costs the same nationwide,* no more war-gaming the codes, no Coders 4 Cash! *Gone.*" He shook his head in amazement. "And the final miracle, done with that *one click?* No more HEAL, no more EPIC! Picture it! The billionaire cheese farmer in Dogpatch-as-Disney, Wisconsin, dumping machines into the trash? *Gonzo gone!*"

"But," said Runt. "How"—gesture—"to"—gesture—"pay for it?"

A solid fiscal question? Go, Runt!

"*Good* question," said Fats. "Back when Man's Best *was* best, a pediatrician named T. Berry Brazelton went before Congress to solicit funding for a national preschool health-care program for kids that would save a ton of money for care in their futures. He presented the whole thing in detail, and a congressman sneered, 'How are you going to pay for this?' T. Berry replied, 'All it costs is *one missile* per year.' They shot him down. No program." He shook his head. "You want depressing? Now fifty percent of our tax dollars go to the military. Ten days of Defense is about a whole *year* of the National Institute of Health." He let this sink in. "So we gotta change our priorities. I bet if we stop just *two* of our wars—say, the Midasian and the Eastasian—we can start great health care. Like the more *civilized* nations of the world that're not screwed up by sick dreams of being 'the Best Country.' That—and a teensy-weensy one percent tax on the point-zero-one-percent rich, who own everything—gets you all the money you need, forever, to provide health, instead of making money off disease."

"I doubt that will ever happen," said Jude. "We on the rez have been lobbying for those two things for, oh, only about a hundred years."

"Probably not," said Fats. "But here's what will. First, admin costs. When we get rid of the for-profit system, we automatically cut out the thirty-three percent *administrative costs* and free up each year 1.2 trillion dollars. As opposed to the *three percent* Medicare admin cost. So we save thirty percent. Second cost cut? A huge decrease in drug costs from our leverage in buying drugs in bulk from the monopoly of BIGPHARMAFDA. And then lots of other cost cuts kick in. Like freeing employers from having to pay for their workers' health care—and collecting what they had been paying, as a tax."

"Well, Fats," said Hooper, rocking hard, "this is totally great. But how do we actually get rid of insurance?"

"Y'mean get to that one little 'click'?" We all nodded. "Not easy. But listen up. Has anyone, in a crowded theater when somebody falls down onstage, heard the cry go out: 'Is there an *insurance executive* in the house?'"

Laughter from all.

"Exactly. *We are the workers. We do the work. Without us, there is no health care.* But guess what. We doctors don't even have a union. Nurses have a union, a great union—Angel, Molly?"

"The best," said Molly. "I've been on strike three times now."

"And how many of those times did you win—get what you wanted?"

"Three. The Women's 2nd Best caved before we even *had* to strike. Nationally, we've never, ever lost. They need us to function at all."

"Bingo! Nurses have a union, teachers too—but docs? Ally with nurses? 'Oh, no, *I can do it myself*!'" He looked at Berry. "Women! They actually *like* getting together—and look what they've gotten. They've never lost."

"So how do we get to national health?" asked Eat My Dust. "Write our congressmen? The guys with spines of linguine? Paid for by the world's biggest lobby, insurance? Fat chance." He looked at Fats. "Ooops. I mean, uh, thin chance."

"Forget our representatives. They only act when they're paid off or trapped." He wrote:

WE DO THE WORK
WE GOTTA DO WHAT WORKERS DO

"Es-strike!" shouted Humbo. *"Indignación! Juntos!"*

"We'd get killed for striking," said Naidoo. "For putting our patients at risk."

"But the way our nurses' strikes worked," said Molly, "is *we got the patients to join us.* Almost *all* of them have horror stories of treatment. Health care's the number one issue for Americans."

"Totally," said Fats. "The key is getting patients, doctors, and nurses—and even hospitals—to *join together as allies.* All three groups hate BUDDIES, and *really* hate INSURANCE, right?"

Shouts of "Right!" "Yeah!" and *"Caramba!"*

"Patients are taking their own action now," Dr. Ro said, "against the same things as us—yesterday there was a huge protest downtown of mothers against Sanofi Pharma and Eli Lilly for jacking up the price of insulin five thousand percent. Guess who's going to win that one."

"I love it," Berry said. "We join patients, doctors, nurses, and hospitals together. The inclusive 'we.' And there's a huge movement in voters now too."

"But," said Gath, "the payments to me from Medicare and Medicaid are ridiculously low. I can't feed my kids on them. And I've heard that there's no way that any of the big teaching hospitals can survive on Medicare payments either. Never."

"True!" said Fats happily. "And *that's our opportunity*! When push comes to shove, and the hospitals are hunkering down against us docs and nurses and patients, we bring them into a grand alliance with us, to join in on our one big demand: *Unless we docs and nurses and hospitals get paid at our current levels, which are way above Medicare, we will not go along.* The key is that alliance. If we stick together, we can't lose."

"But the public won't side with doctors going on strike," said Jude. "No way."

"And I won't either," said Gath. "I can't deny my patients. Go out on strike? We can't. It would be a national emergency—with us as the bad guys."

"Yop," said Fats. "So we gotta be *deft*. We don't just strike. We start by simply *threatening* a strike. Like the nurses did at Women's 2nd Best. Your union spent—what?—a whole year trying to get a deal. No deal got done, so you *threatened* to go out on a Monday morning a month away. And what happened?"

"They caved and settled on the Sunday night before," said Molly. "The mayor himself came in that night and made the deal. And Women's 2nd Best lost *24 million dollars*, just to *prepare* for the strike. Hiring nonunion workers to come in."

"Multiply that threat nationwide," said Fats. "Here's how it works. We start now, get a petition up, send it to every doc and nurse—and hospital—and patient-advocacy group and congressman." He unrolled a petition in the air. "*Two years from now, we plan to strike unless Medicare for All passes, with a guarantee of our current salaries—and payments to hospitals—intact. Will you sign up, with no commitment?* Doctors hate commitment—highest divorce rates, right? But at one year out, we do the same thing. More signatures, more notice in the media. And with six months to go? Lots of media attention. Three months? People getting nervous. It would be a disaster. One month? It goes viral. Cover of *Time* magazine. Front page of the *Times* itself. Headlines of 'A Real National Emergency.' Insurance starts to tremble. *We* do the work—and—"

A knock at the door.

"—if we handle his buildup right, we'll *never* have to actually go out on strike—because the cost, even *for one day*, for bosses, for all the BUDDIES clones nationwide and the other five rackets, is way too high."

Another knock.

Dulci Cacciatori poked her head in. "Pat P. Flambeau is here, with Krash. He wants to see Fats."

As always with authority, a gut clench, a chill. We all stared at one another. *Them? Both? Here? Had they somehow been listening in to all this? Taping it for evidence?*

"But," Dulci said, "I go, 'They're in checkout, a holy time, 'cept for emergencies, and are you one?' Pat P. goes, 'Holy time, holy smokes! Oh, well, then take your time. I'll just look around.'" She checked her watch. "There's no rush. He's havin' a ball—like he's a celebrity. Some people recognized him for his chickens—and poultry. He's a celebrity—never meets real folks. His security's uptight. Anyway, time's almost up?"

Fats nodded, stood up. "Okay, I know we didn't get into the nuts and bolts. Each of you has been a revolutionary, just by being in the House of God and here at the FMC. So I want *each of you* to come up with what your vision of resistance to BUDDIES, for all of us at the 4th Best, could be. The big message? All of us who are getting screwed by BUDDIES and INSURANCE and all the rest—we docs and nurses and Man's 4th and patients—have to ally and stick together. We start there next time." He paused. "One last thing. We got incredible talent in this room, in all different ways, from all us different docs and nurses including our very own Pancho Villa of the Mexican Medical Nation, and our beloved two"—he glanced at O'Toole, leaning against the wall in that same strange bicycle posture as Gilheeny and Quick— "make that *three* policemen."

"Two from the Dublin-in-exile constabulary," said Gilheeny. "Proud veterans of the grand Irish resistance, vide Easter 1916."

"One from Dublin's Mater Misericordiae, Jimmy Barnacle O'Toole. Jined today."

"Welcome, welcome," said Fats, turning toward the door.

"But," said Mo, "we medical students are coming out of school with about 400,000 dollars in debt. So a lot of us are choosing the high-paying, good-lifestyle specialties—Derm, Emergency, Anesthesia, some Surgery. Almost none of us go where we're most needed, like here on the front lines. How'm I going to pay back my loans?"

"How 'bout in return for free tuition—no loans needed—you do two years in a national medical service in an underserved place of your choice? Would you take—"

"Where do I sign!?" she shouted.

We all laughed.

"And, well, I hate to say this," Mo went on, for the first time sounding unsure. "I mean, this all seems pretty impossible. A lot of med students hate the current system, but we've given up. We don't even know what to *try* to get or how. It's too big."

"Honey," said Ro, touching her arm, "how could you believe otherwise? You haven't had our experience. What've we learned? As Fats said, 'Stick together.' What else? 'Don't settle. It's not that we only do what we *think* we can get. It's what we *dare* to do, together.' You can count on us walking with you, staying close, showing the way."

"Cool," said Mo, smiling, putting her hand on her mom's, squeezing it.

"Berry?" Fats was holding out his hands to her, palms up, offering.

She held his gaze, then nodded. "We all focus on how disease is contagious. But we don't focus on the contagion of health."

"Meaning?" Fats asked.

"Spirit. Within us, around us, and between us. Now."

We fell silent. Sobered. Enlivened. Pausing.

"So," Fats said, "we stick together *no matter what*. As Berry said, when things get tough, we don't take refuge in ourselves, but in our big, bad, fat 'n' ferocious . . . ?"

"*We!*"

"Two quick takeaways: one, we're gonna resist; two, we're all gonna come back and figure out the nuts and bolts, the 'how to.' Let's break, okay?" Nobody said anything. Fats cupped a hand to a plump ear. "I asked, 'Okay?' But I don't hear nuthin'!?"

We all said "Okay" in our different ways, and he coaxed us to say it louder and louder until even Naidoo and the Runt were yelling, "*Okay!!*"

"*Let's break!*" Fats shouted back. We left.

Berry looked at me, amazed. "Who the hell ever talks like this in medicine?"

And then we saw, in the middle of the crowd of patients waiting, Pat P. Flambeau, chest puffed out like a, well, chicken, strutting, glad-handing, beaming, and even, as we watched, bending to a kid in a wheelchair and listening intently and then taking out of his pocket what looked like a puffy stuffed toy chicken that emitted a loud "Cluck cluck *cluck*!" making the kid and others laugh and point. And then he was moving on to another, not a patient but one of the Runners he'd seen in the morning—was it just this morning?—the kid asking for his autograph on a FunRunners cap, Pat P. bending to hear the kid's name and taking a pen in his only hand and obliging. I was stunned by the smile on his face. He was really enjoying this.

Fats stopped, gestured to the raggedy multicolored crowd clustered around the big boss of the obscenely big BUDDIES. "Y'wanna see resistance how-to? This is it."

Flambeau's security guard, gun holstered and handy, was nervous, scanning, scanning. The rich feel that they are always at risk, sealed off in bubbles that kill off their empathy. Off to the side, awkward and avoiding, was the Krash.

"Hey, in't this great?" Flambeau yelled to us, a lollipop in his hand. "I love this! I hear you're hiring and accepting volunteers. Can y'fit me in?" Fats nodded. He extricated himself from the patients with a few final "Hiya, hiya, how are ya?"s and "Whut's yer name?"s and "How ya doin'?"s and "God bless"es and stood with us. "Oh boy—what spirit. Hell's bells, this spirit beats those damn screens any ole day o' the week. I love it."

"And they love you too, sir," said the Krash.

"Ooooh-kay. You're doin' a great job. This place is red-hot. SATPATs are back, OUTGOING dead. My dear mom in Bartlesville?" He shook his head sadly. "I lost her."

"Sorry to hear that, sir," said Krash, feigning sadness. "When did she pass?"

"Not dead. Gone. Eighty-seven and she's always in her 'I'-phone or laptop. I don't use 'em myself—Rowland does all my screens. I still do pen and paper, like with chickens. Saves a lotta time. My attention span is still tops. If I had an 'I'-phone, I'd never focus on anything impo'tant. Paper and pen were good enough for the chickens, so they're good enough for me. I wish I had time to visit with all o' you today, but I gotta talk with Fats and Krash." He gestured for them to follow him, but then stopped. "Hey—I heard you got these check-ins and checkouts every day? Maybe sometime I can sit in?"

All of us nodded assent. Was this guy . . . *for real*? "Boys," he said to Fats and Krash, "let's go."

They disappeared through the door that led down to the long, drippy 1816 tunnel that came out at the deep old bottom of the Pink.

Most of us went to see our last patients—left over from before checkout. I was done for the day, but I sensed that something was up with Fats and the other two. Berry left to pick up Spring—I stayed with Chuck.

We didn't have to wait long.

Fats came back, looking bad, those hundreds of tiny face muscles, usually so plumped up and supple, somehow sapped, drained down, tight, as if in pain. Pale.

"Man! Whut happened to you?"

"Need t'siddown." We went into the conference room. He dropped into a chair, like a massive beanbag. He said nothing. We waited. A lot more nothing.

"Want to go get something to eat?" I asked.

"Nope." Now I was *really* worried.

An enormous sigh. "Okay, so there we three were, walking side by side through this damp, spooky tunnel, two Securities protecting front and rear—it slopes down a lot, then levels out, and goes back up into the Pink. And Flambeau's walking between us, talking about how great the FMC's doing and how bad Man's Best is doing and then all of a sudden he stops, looks at me, lifts up that massive arm and hand slowly as if he's gonna level me, and then turns to his other side to look at Krash and slowly, slowwwly reaches around him and puts that hen-sized hand on his shoulder, tight, squeezing, squeezing, and looks him in the eye and says: 'Jared T. Krashinsky, I'm stickin' a fork in you, you turkey—you're done!'"

"What?" Chuck and I said in unison.

"Krash looks like he's been shot. He squeals, 'What? What are you talkin' about?' and Flambeau says, '*You're fired*. Security is already up in your office, to make sure you take only your personal belongings. You're *forked*. Get outta my LLC. Out. Now.' He nods to Security. 'Cyclops? Get 'im outta here.'

"'But why?' Krash asks. 'And where's my due process?'

"'Don't give me due process! Shitfire! You're all hat, no chickens! You're fired.'

"'But why?'

"'For doin' a shit job—money's down, prestige's down, maybe past 5th! Maybe outta the top 10! But the final straw is this morning. I get a call from a big-time Saudi. He says that at a party honoring a nephew, he hears something you did, to the nephew.'

"'I don't know any Saudi nephews. There must be some mistake.'

"'Does the name Mohammed Abdul ring a bell?'

"'No!'

"'No, because you never even asked him his name.'

"'I never met him!'

"'He counts that little to you, eh?' Krash stands there in shock. 'Well, he was on call one night when a Jewish patient, a Mr. Kripke, said to him, quote,

"I don't want to be treated by a damn Arab," and called you up to get him some other doc.'

"And Krash turns sheet white," Fats said.

"'And you decided,' Flambeau goes on, 'on your own in this important matter when you didn't call me for Chrissakes and ask for my help in making this—this crucial, delicate decision. Oh, no, not you, you big-shot putz! You just went ahead and decided—with extreme prejudice—for the Jew, and fucked it up "royally." Ergo, you're *forked*!'

"'But . . . but he signed out that night. He saw no other doctor. Problem solved.'

"'Not before you told Mohammed that he was off the case. It turns out that Mohammed is—wait for it—a blood relative of a royal Saudi. Of the Saudi-Kissy that I busted my butt to get! To save our ass! I got one and only one question for you.'

"Krash was so terrified," said Fats, "like he was wondering whether he would be turned over to the Saudi king or even to Kissinger himself to be personally executed by one of them and the only question that remained was whether he'd just be beheaded or tortured first. And then Flambeau asks him a question.

"'Why the hell,' he says, 'didn't you call me to ask for help in this decision?!'

"Krash shoots a glance at me.

"'Because,' he says to Flambeau, 'you always said that I had to be the decider.'

"'Idiot! I thought you were a mensch who didn't just follow a rule—like a computer—but that you could flex, like a human being, and decide when you can't decide and need help and call me! You put me and BUDDIES in the crosshairs of a royal kingdom—and we're barely out. But you're totally out. "President" Krashinksky, get the hell out of my institution!'

"'But . . . but if I had asked you, what would you have told me to do?'

"'Nothing.'

"'Nothing?'

"Flambeau looks at me and goes, 'As much nothing as possible. Law Number Thirteen of the House of God.'"

"He didn't!" I said to Fats.

"Did so. At that, Krash clutches his chest as if he's having a heart attack, gives me a look as if maybe I could still save him, but the two Securities grab him and drag him away on up the last slope as if he were a mannequin, up out of the tunnel into the Pink."

Chuck and I were speechless.

"There's more. Flambeau turns to me, shaking his head in pity.

"'The bad news,' he says, 'is that I hired him. I had my doubts. I mean, he wouldn't know a human trait if he found it in a Cracker Jack box, but I was persuaded by the board—not uninamiously, mind you—to hire him. The good news is that he convinced me to bring you on board. I shoulda hired *you* for that job.'"

"What?" I cried out.

"Settin' up on top of Man's 4th, bossed by the chicken man 'n' BUDDIES, *you*?"

"I know, I know," he said, chuckling, now back to his old overinflated Fat self.

"'So we got a vacancy,' he says. 'Guy like you should be runnin' this hospital. You too can have a version of my home in Bartlesville, Cluckingham Palace. Y'interested?'

"He sees that I'm in shock. Senses I'm about to say no. So he puts that big palm up between our faces like a stop sign. 'Don't say no yet. At least let's talk. I might just be able to give you what you want—even, say, help out with this bullshit discrimination trial goin' on against that poor Navajo gal—y'know I myself got Native 'Murcan roots, Oklahoma Choctaw.'

"'You can help with that?'

"'A statement I'd deny—vig-or-ous-ly—if it ever got out.'

"'It won't.'

"'I believe you, Fats. And that—that's why I'm offering you the job. Believability. A Krash you are not. And . . .' He smiled, Cheshire cat–like. 'And I could get some Big Pharma bucks for your boxcars and calcium—a great thing, that, for us old guys who can't remember where we put our keys, or our Ambien. I heard your phase three trial is perfect.'

"'Nobody knows that!'

"'Almost nobody. Don't fret. I'll keep it to myself.' An evil smile. 'Fats, make an appointment with my admin, Rowland. Ninety minutes. Let's do lunch. We can go out to any place you like—or I'll order in. Do it soon. We got a vacancy at the top of Man's Best. As CEO and former poultry provider, I hate an empty plate. God bless you, Fat Man, and God bless America.'"

We stared at him, amazed.

"You wouldn't do it, would you?" I asked. "No way, right?"

"Take the meeting?" Fats got a dreamy look in his eyes. "Sure."

"You?"

"Why not?"

"You know why—he's a thug, running a 26-billion-dollar BUDDIES *that has no reason to exist* but for squeezing money outta Man's 4th, and patients and doctors. He's as slippery as raw liver." Fats didn't seem to be listening, eyes elsewere, dreamy.

"Fats, listen!" He turned to me. "Why would you ever do it? *Seriously?*"

"Oh." He seemed to come to himself and consider this. "The best thing any of us can do, guys, is to work for change from the inside. Gotta be tough. But gotta be *deft.*"

Once again, he seemed pensive. "Roy, with everything running good here, maybe I can go back to Rosie and Chubby for, say, a week?" Suddenly his lip turned down. Tears came to his eyes. That mountain was shaking. "I miss them so much!"

"Good idea," I said. "Don't worry about us. We can handle all this for a while."

"Yeah, big guy," said Chuck, "as long as you don't get seduced."

His eyes got wide. "Me? Seduced?" He looked down at himself—a few more chins appearing—and gestured to his body. "Who in hell is gonna seduce this?"

26

A few weeks passed. Work and home had more or less come into balance. And in that inevitable miracle in New England, the bite of spring had started to loosen, giving the myth of summer credence. Not quite daffodil time, but crocus.

"Olive's happy today," Spring was saying, jumping into bed between us.

"Good for her," Berry said, yawning, yearning, I knew, for coffee and Internet. She grabbed her "I"-phone and went into the bathroom.

"Glad to hear that!" I said enthusiastically—so loudly that Cinnamon, like all dogs a lover of routine, raced over to me and barked thrice, his floppy ears flapping. "It's okay, Cinny. It's okay." I rubbed his ears, looked deep into his dark cataracted eyes. *I love this dog and he's getting old and if he dies how will I stand it?* "I remember you told me and Mom that Olive's been depressed. Lonely. No binkys."

"She's better now."

"Did you help her through it?"

"Da-ad. That's my *job*! Like Mom's job is to do it with me and you."

"Mom's helped me and you overcome our depressions?"

"Mom knows all about psychol-ing. I gave her a new name yesterday. Like in the circus? She's a 'trickcyclist.'"

I found myself chuckling all the way into the FMC. My good mood was catching—with the team and with some patients—not exactly an exaltation of larks, but, well, a kind of contagion of joy.

The check-in was the second session of our team project, for us to talk about our gender differences, in order to make better connections—building an open "we." Focusing on gender differences in the workplace.

We men and women faced one another across the table.

Molly read the women's first question to the men: "Do you ever feel, at work here or at other jobs, that other people are seeing you, or treating you, in a certain way because you're a man?"

We men fell silent, thinking. We looked at one another, puzzled. Finally, Fats broke the silence. "No, not really." Others joined in. "Nope." "Never felt that." "*Nunca.*"

A pause. Then a couple of us asked, in different ways, "Why? Do you?"

The women, like a series of explosive devices, detonated:

"All the time!"

"Every single day!"

"Don't you know?"

We were totally surprised and sat there stunned.

Seeing us flabbergasted, the women burst out laughing.

It was amazing to all of us. First, that we men realized the question did not *apply* to us. Second, that it was *a central fact* of each and every woman's experience at work—even at what we thought was a gender-neutral, open-minded place like the FMC.

We went back and forth, talking for the rest of the hour. By the end we felt more deeply aware of invisible differences and more connected in our "we." Berry asked if we'd like to keep going on the rest of the questions the next morning. Everyone said yes—except the Fat Man.

He sat there, stunned. In his expansive and creative worldview, he'd suddenly found a big fat hole. "Wow—*ow*! All these years, this . . . blindness to your experience? Blindness to my blindness? How'd I miss it? Guys, how did we all?"

"By getting isolated," said Berry. "We see truly only through each other's eyes." The women nodded. The men looked puzzled. "But time's up."

"Waitwait!" Fats said. "I can't wait till tomorrow. Can we keep goin' on it tonight?"

We could not. We went to see our patients.

My first patient was Nolan. I hadn't seen him in months—I figured he'd been sober, or else I would have heard from the cops or Horace. Both policemen were in the waiting room. Given how busy we'd gotten, they were helping out every day—even providing hands-on medical diagnosis and treatment. When I turned to lead Nolan back to my office, Gilheeny and Quick followed.

Nolan turned to them and, in a mean tone, said, "I don't want you to talk to my doc. This is private."

They stopped, startled. But not silenced.

"And are you," Quick said, "in your right mind to make this decision?" Nolan nodded. "Well, then, Quick abides." He crossed his arms over his thin chest, crossed his legs like a front tire aslant, and leaned against the oak-topped nursing station.

"However!" boomed Gilheeny. "We had wished to attend, to tell God's truth about what the hell's been goin' on that's drivin' Quick and his kin bonkers. And to make sure you tell Dr. Roy the *veritas* truth without any of yer bullshitology. And fourth, that we—policemen loyal to the end—will check out with Roy afterward to make sure he's been informed of the true soap opera of yer raggedy life." He stood up straight and, like a prophet, in-toned: "Luke Twenty-three. Calvary, lad, Calvary. Your choice. Your life."

"And," Quick said, "by Christ Jesus his cute self, a life that's extremely shitty."

I sat alone in the office with Nolan. He looked bad—worn, unshaven—with a scent of stale. Pissed off. I saw that he sensed my shock and my sadness for whatever he'd been going through. But he misread it as criticism.

"Okay," he said, "you're disappointed in me—join the crowd. I am too. I failed you as well as them—and myself. Things have turned bad."

"Are you still sober?"

He paused, struggled. "Let's just say mostly. No gun threats or car wrecks."

"The writing?"

"It's over." He poured out the story. Miss Heller had dumped him—telling him it was only for the sex. The publication of his story in the World's Best Literary thing had been put on hold, and the publisher of Nobel Prizers had rejected his novel about his time in Afghanistan. "He said to me, quote, 'It's old news now, old hat. War itself is old hat. We've been at it for too many dull years. It's gotten louche.'"

"'Louche'?" I said. "What the hell is 'louche'?"

He smiled. "I asked him that. He sneered and said, 'Not only louche, but boring.' And he never told me, and I didn't fuckin' look it up. He said the public wants to forget the wars, forget that soldiers are still there. That I could write a masterpiece and no one would buy it. That *War and Peace*, the greatest novel ever, would never get published today—no editor would even make it through that long, confusing first chapter—all those Russian names? 'Bottom line,' he said to me, 'I can't publish you.'"

"I'm really sorry. I know what it's like, and, Nolan, I . . . I am sorry. But y'can't listen to it. You just have to keep on—"

"Thanks for nothing." He got up to go. "Hey, I don't really mean that to *you*—I'm talkin' to myself. You're okay, and I know you tried hard, and, yeah, I got the part about your caring, but I'm past caring—or care. But hey, thanks for trying."

"Y'gotta stay sober or you're dead."

"I know. That's why I signed up for another tour in Afghanistan."

"What?"

"Part of the latest 'surge' that'll bring 'victory.' But hey—the money is double my last tour. The glorious Battle of Nawa Three. The Battle of the Bullshit."

"Oh." I sensed a sliver of opening up. "I'd be glad, right now, to talk about it."

He hesitated and then sat.

"I know. You're a good guy—but I'm not. If I'm anything good, it's when I'm totally focused by that sense of impending doom, leading my guys into the shit, making sure I bring 'em all back out. That's me at my best. War is hell, but contact with the enemy is a motherfucker! Even when you find yourself in the middle of a shit sandwich—especially then." He sensed my shock. "The two sides of being a war hero? One, people look up to you, as special. Two, savage joy."

"'Joy'?"

"Of killing your enemy. Being a warrior. Nuthin' like it. I mean, on earth. Best thing you can do with your clothes on." A thin smile. "Bein' the fuckin' *best*." He sagged, seemed to implode. Revived. "Hell, let's be honest. There's only one good thing about military training. You're taught not to leave the battle until all your men are taken care of or taken away dead. Comes in handy here at home. Last week I happened to be in Florida visiting a guy in my unit, and we're walking toward a bar and hear shots. And we see everybody running out of the bar, jumping through the plate glass, and like a reflex him and me start running *toward* the shooter, to kill him and to take care of the victims. That's my one and only skill set: when there's a massacre, I run toward it, not away. I know how to kill, how to rescue and protect. Outsiders like you can't know what it's like in here." He tapped his head. "I'm Father Courage." He considered this. Shuddered. A strange look flooded his eyes—sadness? Shame? He whispered, "Just one more fucked-up asshole enabling a sick empire."

He got up again, turned away to go. Stopped himself. Faced me.

That butterfly's wing. It can go one way or the other. Right here. Right now.

I felt such sorrow for him, trapped as he was in himself, damaged and trapped and wanting out of himself and into something else. I sent that sorrow out to him with all the compassion I could, holding his gaze.

He wavered, then looked away. "Take care of the policemen when I'm gone?"

I breathed out—I'd been holding my breath. "You think they're vulnerable?"

A thin smile. "Would they be policemen if they were not?" And left.

Chuck and I hurried up to Ward 34 to see Otto Vance, who was in dire straits on his deathbed.

Since he'd come back from his trip with Desirée to Louisiana, he had refused to eat. A visiting nurse put down feeding tubes, but he'd just vomit everything back up. By this time he had lost 50 pounds.

We had asked that the whole family Vance come in to witness a new treatment Chuck and I were going to try. They were gathered around the bed, scared and silent. Otto was a living skeleton, sunken eyed, gaunt cheeked, listless, like a photo from the Holocaust. He had said that he was going to die, and was in and out of stupor, barely strong enough to talk. All that he would allow was an IV for hydration. A nurse was attending him.

The day before, his wife had asked to talk to Chuck in private. Otto had told her what had happened to him in Louisiana, swearing her to secrecy. But now that he was dying, she had to tell Chuck, binding him to keep the secret. She said that in Louisiana he'd had a run-in with the local "voodoo priest."

Late one night the priest called him to a cemetery. She didn't know why he was called, but the two of them got into an argument. The priest waved a bottle of vile-smelling liquid in Otto's face and rubbed some pebbles into the skin of both arms. Then he told Otto that he'd "voodooed" him and that he'd die in the near future—and even doctors could not save him. The priest said that if Otto told anyone, he'd voodoo his wife and children. Otto had not eaten since.

Chuck and I talked about what we could do. Each of us had come across a few "spells" or "curses" or "evil spirits" in our doctoring—I with the Navajo, he in Tennessee. We'd seen how dire they could be, sometimes fatal. Together we fastened on a last-ditch effort that might just work. We'd admitted him to Man's 4th the night before.

Now, both of us wearing long, starched white doctor coats, Chuck and I walked straight spined into Otto's room. Chuck went to the side of the bed, I to the foot.

The family—about a dozen of them—trembling and frightened, moved away.

Desirée, ashen, limped heavily toward a wall, and stood in front of the crowd.

"Otto," I said, in a confident voice, "I know exactly what's wrong with you. Last night at midnight, a doctor friend of mine in Louisiana lured your voodoo priest to the cemetery. The doctor told the priest that he had uncovered the secret voodoo he'd put on you. The priest laughed at him—but then my friend almost choked him to death against a tree until the priest told him exactly what he'd done."

Otto's nubs of fingers slowly rose to his face. Other Vances stared, bug-eyed.

"The priest had waved a stinking potion under your nose and all around you, and scratched into the skin of your arms, scratched hard, some stuff that felt like little pebbles?"

Otto, a bit more alert, gave a nod.

"Well, that priest rubbed some lizard eggs into your skin, and they got into your stomach and hatched out some small lizards. And all but one of the lizards died, leaving *one big lizard*, which has been eating your food and the inner skin of your stomach. I'm now going to get that lizard out of your system and cure you. Chuck? Ready?"

Chuck had a syringe full of apomorphine, a powerful emetic. He lifted the syringe up, inspected it, squirted out a few drops from its tip.

Otto was now sitting up, wide-eyed, pressing himself back against the headboard to protect himself.

"Chuck? Go!"

Chuck pushed the needle into Otto's arm and injected the full dose.

Chuck and I left the room, telling the nurse to call us when Otto started vomiting.

It didn't take long.

When we went back in, Otto was retching, spasm after spasm, his head buried in a metal basin on the bed. When it looked as if he was stopping, I reached into my black bag and grabbed, quickly and secretly, a green lizard. At the next wave of retching, with Chuck distracting the family, I slid the lizard into the basin.

"Look, Otto!" I called out in a loud voice. "Look what came out of you. Otto, you are now cured! The voodoo curse is lifted!"

Eyes wide, Otto saw the green lizard, did a double take, and then jumped back to the head of the bed, slack-jawed. Dazed, he sank down into the pillows and fell into a deep sleep.

His pulse was 40, his breathing deep and slow. It was as if he were in a coma.

He would sleep for eleven hours, and when he awoke, he would be ravenous.

⌒

"See y'later," Fats said to Chuck and me just before noon at the nursing station. He was hurriedly trying to stuff his big upper body into the jacket of a dark pin-striped suit. Awkwardly. The pants were already on, thighs billowing out, big and tight.

"Need some help?" Chuck asked.

"Nah, I'm good. Trying to fit a fat guy into this suit is like unregulated health care: you get one part in and another part pops back out—you can't cover 'em all."

Chuck held one part in, while Fats and I struggled with another.

"Where are you going?" I asked.

"Today's my lunch with Flambeau. I can't believe I'm a little nervous."

"Really?" I pushed harder on a part. He nodded. "Why are you wearing a suit?"

"This?" I nodded. "My *mother* wore suits."

Chuck and I rolled our eyes. "And," I asked, "Pat P. is taking you out to the world's best restaurant?"

"Nah, I'm way too modest for that. I told him to order in from it." He asked shyly, "Y'sure you can't persuade Berry to keep going with us tonight? I mean, didja see how good it went? How deep we got? I'm on fire with this stuff. And tonight I'm free."

I gave him a look.

"Okay, okay, I'm just a hungry guy. I try to control it, but . . . but I can't?"

A plea? Answer it.

"Fats, some say that's your gift."

He stopped still. Chewed on this. Swallowed. "Yeah, maybe it is." But suddenly he seemed nervous about the meeting again. "Wish me luck."

As Chuck and I were walking through the Pink to the cafeteria, an alarm bell rang and a message blared out: "This is an emergency. A lone shooter in the BUDDIES Building, top floor. Security is in control. All those in the BUDDIES Building go into lockdown. Repeat. This is an—"

Chuck and I stopped, shocked. Then we found ourselves running through the scared crowds from the Pink to the BUDDIES elevators, and as we got there, the express elevator opened suddenly and something fell out of it onto the marble floor and it was a body awash in blood but it didn't fall all the way out. Its legs were still in it and the head was shot to hell so we couldn't tell who it was but it wasn't in a dark suit, thank God, and blood was pooling and spattered all over and a short-barreled assault rifle flashed in the harsh intermittent light as the elevator door kept trying to shut and banged against the mushed head and then shot back open again, shut and open, shut and open. Security arrived and shoved us away, and Chuck and I searched around until we found the service elevator and rode in silence as it crawled slowly up to the top floor and we got lost trying to find Flambeau's office and finally did and there were Pat P. and a crowd of doctors standing around something on the floor and we pushed our way through and it was a body on its back with a single neat bullet hole in its forehead and a widening plume of bright red blood covering the carpet and flowing out from where the occiput used to be but was now blown out in the exit wound and it was Fats.

This page intentionally left blank

27

Comfort must be given.

To all.

Even if there are not always two sides to a story.

Giving comfort, we are comforted.

"Yes," Berry says to me now. "We are."

I didn't realize that I'd been saying these things out loud.

"And if we're lucky," she goes on, "our suffering attracts compassion."

We're sitting on the back patio of Tierra Tranquila. Me on my treasured red metal folding chair, Berry beside me on a bench. At dawn today, this day of my close call with death, when the singing of the birds burst out with a certain joy at sunlight as if the language of the world had turned to singing, my eyes were drawn to a brand-new arrival in a family of bananas. The shoot had shot up overnight and was rolled into a tight cylinder. By the time we left for our walk up the mountain, it had begun to unfurl, the noon sun through the leaf coloring it a lime green, in contrast to the darker green of the family group.

Now, in the impatient dusk of the tropics, with less than an hour to go until that big eyelid shuts down over the day, and with the birds singing down the day to sleep, the new leaf has unrolled fully. It stands straight up, at the center of the group that arcs down in a circle all around it, the oldest leaves, the grandparents, rotting, almost going to ground. Gomer bananas going to ground.

Dusk on the equator is brief. You're sitting in bright afternoon and then, with a hint of dullness, it's dark, impenetrable even in a full moon. I feel a certain urgency to finish this story of death. Ever since my own fall this morning, and giving thanks for that butterfly's wing that had stopped me a half inch shy of that boulder. And being dead. The irony? In my seizure, I'd been dead to the world. Is that different from what the Fat Man knew, knows? But I had an aura of lettuce; his last sight was the barrel of a gun.

"Where'd you go, Roy?" Berry, beside me. "How's the pain?"

"Being alive helps live with it. Eye, face, head on fire. Rib cracked, knees battered and seeping blood, scraped hands—but *I'm still here!* Aren't I?"

"Unless this is heaven."

I think this over. Anything's possible now.

"How would I know?" I ask. "How would *we* know? I can't help thinking about Fats still being dead. Even after all these years. Dying at just this time of year. It's so fresh. I keep going back over it, over it . . ."

"How could you not? When I saw you flying past me, headfirst, down, toward all those rocks?" She shivers. In the heat, she actually shivers. "What do you feel?"

"Sorrow . . . gratitude . . ."

The night of his death, we all got together at our house. Cried, talked, raged, felt guilty, questioned, drank—well, not me—cried more until dawn. We were crushed. Humbo wept and wept. We took turns comforting him. And then, believe it or not—unable to sleep—we decided to go back to work. To help our patients through.

Soon almost all of them knew. We decided not to tell Spring. Cinnamon knew something was up—maybe because of the extra treats—and I explained it to him the best I could, a way of trying to explain it to myself, like Spring explained the world to Olive. Told him that it was the standard great American death by gunshot finally getting around to *our* lives. That sense we all had when, in the middle of a day, there would be "Breaking News" of a horrific shooting—"Twenty-three children and two teachers killed by a lone gunman who killed himself, et cetera." Over and over. Now it had come home to us. Inside a hospital, dedicated to saving life, not ending it.

If someone can be killed by an aggrieved, recently fired president of Man's

4th Best Hospital using a sniper rifle, inside a "secure" hospital office, *with its own secret-coded express elevator straight up to the penthouse?*

Well, then, none of us in this fucked-up gun country is safe.

The deaths grow. Humans get used to them. Burn out. Outrage dulls. Dumbs down. The price y'pay for freedom for guns. Idiocy. All for money.

Bitterness rises, takes over.

"Breathe," Berry says. "You're alive. You can breathe. Follow the breath."

The funeral was in the Orthodox Jewish tradition—by law it has to happen fast, within two days, or else. Hmmm. Or else *what?* Who knows? It was two days later in a small, dying synagogue in Brooklyn. Fats was an only child. His father was dead, leaving only his mother and a spinster aunt. Not many others came—almost none of our age.

All were in flat black. The Hebrew service was a mystery, except the mourner's chant, the ancient, gorgeous repetitions bringing fresh tears.

Gilheeny couldn't stop weeping, all great snorts and nose blowings. Quick had a death-mask face, dark unshaved shadow, inward-staring eyes. Rosie and Chubby flew in. Even Silicon Valley was said to be in shock. Berry stayed home with Spring.

The burial was in Queens. Familiar ground to me—my immigrant grandparents were buried there. Jews from each little town had formed their own social groups and unions, bought cemetery plots fenced with wrought iron. Mine was "the First Stanislauer Young Men's Benevolent Association." Crammed into steerage to find gold in New York, crammed into these plots in Queens—as we were now. But—hats off to them—they were with one another, bone to bone.

The sun was hot. Prayers were said. The Fat Man's mom, Fritzi, wailed and ripped her black sleeves as was the custom.

She was a small, round woman, obscured in black. I recalled a joke Fats had told us. A Jewish mother takes her young son to Coney Island. The son plays in the shallows. Suddenly, in the distance, a huge, dark wave rushes in, rears up, and—bam!—drops upon the son! Takes him away. Frantic, the mother prays to God: "Bring him back. I'll do *anything!*" A pause. And then, in the distance, another huge, dark wave rushes in, rears up, and—bam!— there he is, back again! The mother is ecstatic. He's fine! And then, looking up at the heavens and shaking a finger, she shouts: "He had a *hat!*"

Funny how our minds go funny at tragic times. What else can you do?

Pebbles danced upon the coffin lid. The giant coffin that had to be squeezed in among his tightly packed Ivano-Galicians. For our giant. But a giant we realized we knew little about, outside of work. No childhood friends came. No friends at all, but us.

We sat in the bar at the airport and cried some more, and Rosie told us a couple of stories that helped. He'd met her through his science—she'd been working in a lab at Stanford—and he'd wooed her not just with his brilliance and vision but with the fact that there was no deception in the wooing. He was as out there and frank as a child. On their disastrous first date, when he cooked dinner at his apartment—an elegant affair, candles, fine wine—his cat jumped up on the table—Fats had a cat?!—and its tail caught fire and they went running around trying to put it, and the cat, out. Fats swore off pets from that day on and made Rosie promise she would never get one. But one day when they were living together, Rosie wandered into an animal shelter and fell in love with a dog that was headed for euthanasia. She brought it home. It pooped in her pocketbook. There she was on the floor cleaning out her pocketbook with the dog sticking its nose into it, when Fats came home and just stood there in the doorway.

"I thought," she told us, "'This is the end of the relationship.' But then Fats looked at me and at the dog and smiled that . . . wonderful smile and said, 'Hey, we've got a dog!' And that turned out to be . . ." She wept. "Chubby."

We dodged the insane media coverage. Most of us managed to go back to work. Our waves of shock often turned to anger, with no softening in sight.

It was really *hard*.

We'd pass one another at the FMC, see in one another's eyes our own deadness and rage and occasional tears—and then we'd keep on keeping on, going to see our patients. At some point the tears began to dry up. Except at those moments when you find something of the dead's, or hear someone say something, or like one day when I found, in a crack under the Fat Man's stool at the nursing station, written on a discarded jumbo box of Devil Dogs, a note, with equations and biochemical symbols, about boxcars. A rush of tears, softening. Where was our center? The great weight that created our shared momentum? Sometimes with patients, moments of their suffering would bring back ours, and bring out our kindness.

Finally, after a week or so, Humbo—almost totally silent and withdrawn as he walked like a specter through the clinic with his patients—spoke up in check-in: "What we need to do with each other now is what Fats did with us—*levantarse*! He lift us up!"

Being with. Sticking together—the Fat Man's words—in our opened-up state, being with one another did start to give us, day by dark day, a flicker of light, even, eventually, a lifting up. We had cried into our "we," cried our grief and rage into it until—the human miracle—it softened us toward sorrow. We didn't have words back then for what happened, the *something else*. Now I do. I turn to Berry.

"Love, understanding, and sorrow," I say, "are all the same thing. Healing." She smiles at me, takes my hand. "Ouch!" My palm is raw.

"Sorry! Yes, the same. Taking refuge in our loving-kindness. A breath at a time."

So the Future of Medicine Clinic—Care, Compassion, and Cancer—went on. Flambeau appointed as interim president of Man's 4th a burly cardiologist of impeccable spirit and ethics, Dr. Jackson Kornfeld. Because of his love for the place, he agreed to serve. Both he and Flambeau kept OUTGOING down and the Runners up. We all felt valued. We kept putting one foot ahead of the other, walking with one another and walking with our patients at their crucial times of suffering—our doctor's job. What we signed up for, decades ago. None of us quit. We grew the place, adding doctors, PAs, nurses. The med students kept coming. That dank curtain of grief seemed to part, some. All the while we were in subdued resistance, preserving our little experiment in how medicine might just work humanely, together.

Until, after a few months, we were hit by two big waves.

First, the judge's verdict went against Jude. This meant that she, after a decade of training to be an orthopedic surgeon, would not be certified by Man's 4th to graduate, taking away any chance she had of making a living as a surgeon. We were crushed, enraged. Where was Paulie the Veal when I needed him? But Jude's priority was new life, a baby girl. Gath won an appeal to the board of medicine: she could continue to operate at the hospital he had joined, under his supervision.

Second, the *Register Star* report came out, with Gath's face on the front page and three *full double pages* inside. It told the truth. Under vicious pressure from the 4th Best board and BUDDIES, the paper stood firm. And so there it all was: the names of the surgeons who—like Schrödinger's cat—were able to "be operating in two different places at the same time, sometimes three," along with a list of the horrific outcomes. The headline that stuck, went viral?

"Man's Best Churns Patients for Cash: Double the Booking, Double the Money.'"

The 4th Best board claimed to have data, from a private investigation they paid for, by a stenotic and stern lawyer, on the effects of the double bookings on outcomes. It was seen only by the board chair and Flambeau.

Without comment, they locked it up, away, for good.

President Jackson Kornfeld asked to see it. They denied this. He resigned.

The new 4th Best president was Dr. Jack Rowk Junior. His inaugural speech was widely praised for an inspiring line: "My mission is to monetize money."

Flambeau announced Junior by saying, "He will be carrying the torch."

One morning, as Gath wrote notes in his office, an envelope was slipped under his door. He was fired. Ordered to leave the hospital by five. So much for his "Best Doctor of the Year" etched into the Pink. A staggering blow to us all. Gath wanted us to continue—we were the keepers of the Fat Man's dream, now booming, on all three floors. We did.

Maybe a year later, we were back on our feet, badly busy but staffed up, full of goodwill and sky-high PATSATs—but then Junior hit us hard with two *clicks*. The first brought back OUTGOING. The second threw out the Runners.

That did it. Most of us left. Mo and Ro, Molly and Angel—who'd delivered twins, sending the Runt celebrating on his racer and going over the handlebars but with only two broken wrists—and many of the younger docs stayed on.

Until one day BUDDIES decided that there would be no more Future of Medicine.

It was over. We each had been given a lot of money, the Fat Man's bequest from his fortuna plus shares of the roaring Boxcars for Boomers. Later, almost all of us went back to working in our own fields, a vision of resistance to injustice always with us, and our acting on it. Gilheeny and Quick left with memorable and startling good-byes.

"We've had enuf of bein' policemen in the USA," said the big red cop. "Too much rage and violence. The nightstick is no match for the guns, especially with yer new soft-nose military bullets."

"Jaysus weeps!" said Quick, tearing up. "And so, we two—without the wives—are goin' on a journey of the spirit. Forst to visit the seaweed sod on Arranmore Isle of the beehive stone huts, where our senselessy drunk kin recite scorchin' Gaelic poetry and sing sad songs that get yer tear ducts wobbling. And then, on to the Skelligs, where the first Christians, freshly good men of yer new man Jaysus, went and built, on crags like incisors in the maw of the sea, a church and dwellings—and a handball court. And why'd the monks go there?" He wrinkled up his paper white face to get the monks' words right. "'We come here to proclaim compassion, in order to save the world.'"

"But we'll be back, Dr. Roy, God willin', wherever you go. So good-bye for now."

Rosie Tsien and her Fat Man colleague and brother, Richard Tsien, and Oxford's Denis Noble last year shared the Nobel Prize in Medicine—showing how those cute atomic boxcars of calcium are the mechanism of memory, pointing to treatments of gomers and seniors. Sometimes now you see old folks wearing a pin in the shape of a boxcar that reminds them to take their boxcar pill by playing into their hearing aids that old-time tune:

"I've been workin' on the railroad, all the livelong day, ay ay ay . . .

I've been workin' on the railroad, just to pass the time awayy . . ."

As Berry put it lightly, "Even if you lose your mind, you don't have to lose your mantra." She went on. "Let's do our medicine skillfully, thoughtfully, kindly, and caringly—and also give a little dharma talk to our patients, from time to time."

The choice in medicine back then? The Fat Man's Dream or the Money.

The money won. The money wins. Not just in medicine, but in pretty much everything American now, and worldwide. The end of the Future of Medicine was due to screens and money, which is money and money.

In the past, way back before the screens, what was a good patient visit?

Your doctor greeted you, sat, and talked with you—chief complaint, history—then asked you to undress behind a curtain for the physical. During this, he or she wrote up what was learned so far. Then the physical. While you were dressing, he did what is now strange: he *paused*. He sat there and did nothing, as much nothing as possible—except he: *Considered. Mused. Sensed. Intuited. Put it all together. Came to a vision of what was wrong and how he might right it, and if not, how he could be with you in caring for you in your illness, no matter what.* He *integrated*. When you returned, he faced you and said, "Let's go over what I found and see what we can do about it."

Screens prevent us doing that. Machines never pause. Never have cause to pause.

Screens *iterate*. And *irritate*. Doctors *integrate*.

Now your visit to your doctor has become satire. You walk in—lucky if you get eye contact—and sit across the desk. Your doctor is trapped, hunched behind a computer screen, back or shoulder to you. The doc asks a question, you answer, the keyboard goes 'click-click-de-*click*!' faster and faster. On and on it goes, and you find yourself in the "Patient's Dilemma": Do I keep talking, or wait for a break in the action—usually the next question? Is he or she still listening or not? The new definition of "a good doctor"? One who can contort his or her body to touch-type while still making eye contact.

As you keep waiting, two questions may enter your mind:

What is she or he doing?

What you don't know is that your doctor is sitting there in front of that screen *seething*, because he is forced to sit in front of a screen *seething*, instead of what he wants to do: to talk and listen and be your doctor. He spends 60 percent of every workday—at least six hours—in front of that screen, more time than with patients. Family doctors spend an additional three hours at night at home, during 'pajama time,' digging out from under the pileup in the screen. This is the "Doctor's Dilemma."

Why is he or she doing this?

You might think she's doing this because it will be better for your health care. It may not. It may be worse. Worse for *your* care and—for sure—worse for the care of your doctor. It is better only for the money, the health-care industry. The machine was not primarily designed for care, but for billing. To make as much money as possible. We doctors are caught in this mess. We're not treating the patient; we're treating the screen.

And it's not that your doctor *wants* to turn his or her back on you.

It's the health-care industry that has turned its back on both you and your doctor.

And so now we docs *click* down the rabbit holes of these machines—screening us from the illogical, messy, authentic human—that never just pause. And people, always into their "I"-phones and "I"-pads and their other "I"-screens? Well, face it. People don't pause much anymore either, caught up in their "I."

Where's the hope?

Well, Man's 4th Best Hospital, crushed by the bankrupt BUDDIES, soon became Man's 4th *Beset* Hospital. Because of the ongoing seething at HEAL, the shooting of Fats, the *Register Star* revelation of data showing that double bookings harmed patients, and the slews of lawsuits, Man's 4th began to tumble down the rankings. Disappointed donors fled. It landed at Man's 19th Best. The House of God—fed by 799's human-friendly TORAH—floated along easily at 3rd Best.

The whistle-blower exposé brought attention to double bookings all over America. Congressional hearings were held. The practice mostly stopped. Too late for the Wambui Kamaus of the world, but still.

And sepsis? The big federal sepsis study was revealed to be fatally flawed in the American sample because the treatment was aimed for money, with doctors clicking, almost always, on "severe." The severe treatment for mild and medium killed people. The federal grant was canceled. Not to worry—a larger grant came from BIGPHARMAFDA, a trial of Xylolaxenda in non-profit Sweden, where the screens did data, not dollars.

And the most hopeful thing to come out of all of this?

News of the Fat Man's spectacularly senseless death spread like wildfire through the health-care community, jolting us. Literally every doctor and most health-care workers knew of him—mostly from the House of God. He had been a model doctor for many of us. His passing provoked a passion to "do something in his name." We of the House and Man's 4th let it be known that the "something" was some form of national health insurance.

It took quite a while, but just last year, Dr. Mocha "Mo" Ahern, a "Genius Grant" service-award-winning professor of medicine and founder of the Alliance for National Health Care—along with doctors, patients, nurses, some hospitals, and others—after many years and threatened strikes and, finally, the inevitable election of a two-thirds female Congress, got most of the Fat Man's and our dream to come true. And with payments to doctors, nurses, and hospitals on a par with for-profit insurance.

On national TV, she—seeming to us as fresh and young as back then—deleted that "sixty-five" and replaced it with "zero" and pressed "save." The Medicare, VA, and Indian screens, relieved of the burden of making money, became the national model standard. The for-profit private-insurance system, for those who wanted more coverage, did just fine.

BUDDIES sickened and died.

Man's Once Best, freed from the dead-whale weight that had crushed it, fired Jack Rowk Junior and shifted its mission from "monetizing money." No billing, so no Billing Building. No Coders 4 Cash. Man's rose rapidly in rank—leveling off last year again at 4th. Women's held at 2nd. HEAL crashed and burned and tried to sue everyone. Other kingpins of the six rackets of American health care got even more sick, deathly so.

The markets soared.

More hope? Shortly after we had left the FMC and were getting ready to sell our house and move, I heard the news. Remember our neighbor Henry Cabot-Lodge, who had often said to me, apropos of nothing: "Y'know, I really love pizza!"?

It turned out he really meant it, dined on it often, and always from Fabio and Antonella Pizza. One night, when his wife and kids were away at the mansion on Nantucket, he ordered out. He liked variety in his pies and was a huge fan of a new one: veal pizza. He also liked the new delivery girl—a high schooler working part-time named Magdalena, or Maggy. Maggy delivered the veal pizza, fought off his advances, and left.

The following morning Henry Cabot-Lodge was found dead, facedown in the pie, and on the floor beside him was a single slice, two bites taken out of it. Autopsy showed cyanide in the body and, strangely, *in only the one slice Henry had partially eaten.* Real strange. The how, the "whodunit," was never solved.

Paulie the Veal, ratted out by Lodge and still in jail, got word to me from his wife in Palermo that he would be out soon and wanted to buy my house and carriage house and would do the deal via a trusted emissary, in cash. His wife ended with: "Paulie heard about the tragic death of our beloved neighbor and sends you his congratulations."

The shooter? Even now, it's hard for me to mention him or write his name.

After all these years, after all this carnage, I'm sick and tired of all the shooters. Like so many of us, I'm so worn-out, so fed up.

Our daily horror has become mundane.

I plead sanity.

28

*S*eñor Roy?"

Miguel, our caretaker. Exactly my age, but looking 20 years younger. We live in one of the world's four "Blue Zones," rare places on Earth where the people routinely live to over 100, not as gomers, but active and healthy. Miguel and others walk up and down the mountain to Carmona routinely—2,000 feet. It's the diet, the farming, the deep family ties and social ties, and the outdoor life. A short, trim—and strong!—man with a square, tanned face and green eyes and always a sense of—what?—just being where he is. Berry and I have come to think of him as a person of spirit. He had been on the walk with us this morning when I'd fallen—I'd flown through the air past him and Berry both, and she told me that he had been beside himself, tremendously upset. I haven't seen him since. He's carrying something in his hand.

"Amigo!" I call out, with difficulty trying to get up.

"Espere!" He tells me to wait, and walks toward me. In his hand is a cane. He smiles and presents it to me, formally, like a ceremonial sword, and then steps back. He has fashioned it himself from a branch, carving the wood to a polished tan, but has left "spots" of underbark in brown so that, with the long "leg" and tapered "head and nose" of the hand rest at the top, it looks like a giraffe. He steps back, embarrassed at my enthusiasm. Gives me a thumbs-up. It is so touching.

He knows that Berry and I, every morning, take a walk together up the mountain overlooking the frisky Bay of Nicoya and the *Volcán Arenal* and, the other way, the plodding Pacific. Various walks—our ritual. He knows that now a cane will help. Spent the whole day carving it. I get up with the help of the cane—which I notice is at the perfect height for my hand—and walk to him and him to me. We hug. A saint. Shyly, he leaves.

A burst of birds singing. Singing as hard as just before dawn, knowing without evidence that the night is gathering, to pounce. Back and forth to one another, species to species, then joining the genus of birds. Back and forth frantically to locate and sing with their friends in other trees. Dogs take to barking; other dogs take it up, all down the valley toward the bay and up the mountain and over, one dog to another across the jungle and rock and water, a chain of dogs down the other side to the sea. Howlers join in, hidden in the fig trees, monkeys the size of babies, roaring like lions.

We sit together in silence, listening to this coda. A tardy cicada sings. We're so high up, there are no mosquitoes.

"What's on your mind?" I ask Berry.

"You'll be disappointed," she says.

"Being alive, I'm never going to be disappointed again."

"Well, lately, when I find myself *really* being in my mind, I try to shift it."

"To being out of your mind?"

She laughs. "Being mindful of what's happening *in* it, in this boring, scary tape of quote 'mine,' being aware of 'the Heavenly Messengers'—illness, old age, and death. Especially right now and, for obvious reasons, death."

"Why are they 'heavenly'?"

"Because when we find ourselves in one of them, like now, they wake us up. If we're mindful, they might just set us on the Eightfold Path toward ending suffering."

"Count me in. We need to meditate more, every day here, together."

"Nothing would make me happier, hon. I really mean that—you're so precious to me. Imagine if we both could live this opened up—without the epileptic seizures and scary falls? Even if only, sometime each day, in the brief time we have left together?"

"It would be all-time love, yeah."

More silence. A delicate calling out—a "trill"—of a lone bird.

"About 'mind'?" she goes on. "I keep thinking about what a Hindu yoga named Nisargadatta said: 'The mind creates the abyss; the heart crosses it.'"

"Beautiful. Luckily, my mind ain't working too well right now. Hey, heart!" I shout. "Get ready! Me 'n' my girl are gonna cross that damn abyss, together!"

"Cross your heart and hope to die?"

"Not that, no."

A lone bird calls out sharply, notes cut glass, all shards. Another answers.

"Y'know," I said, "I always thought that I'd lived a charmed life. But it's only now the charm's worn off that I've learned how to live. Thanks mostly to you. Suffering ain't optional—the First Noble Truth, right?" She nods. "Big suffering, little suffering—we all suffer. It's not a matter of the suffering. It's how we walk through it. If we try to walk through it alone, 'stand tall,' 'draw a line in the sand,' we'll suffer more and spread more suffering around. But if we walk through it *with* others, with *caring* others—and that's where we docs come in: *it's our job*, being with patients at the crucial times in their lives, yes, illness, old age, and death—we'll suffer less, spread less suffering around, and . . . and heal." I paused. "Heal both ways. Us and them."

"And awareness will arise," she said.

"And nobody dies. We'll be the exception."

"Good luck."

"Ahh, yes, all those decades I tried to be exceptional, to be 'the Best.'"

"Me too. I remember one day, growing up in Albany, I thought, 'You go to the best school and have the best teacher and live in the best city, the state capital, of the best state, the Empire State, of the best country, America, in the best continent, North America, on the best planet, Earth, in the best solar system and the best galaxy.'"

We laugh.

"Well, for the rest of the way with you, dear one . . ." I choke at the words, hers to me at our most loving moments. "I'll just try to live, with you, human-sized lives."

She smiles and takes my hand. We fall silent.

"But I'm still so bitter! Full of hatred for Krash—right here, right now. It never goes away. I mean, how do *you* handle it, your bitterness, your wish to kill?"

"Oh, so you want to start with the *easy* part?" She smiles—the smile helps. "Hatred's a poison. One of the Buddha's three human poisons, or defilements: greed, hatred, and ignorance. '*Karuna*' is the word for 'compassion.' If you hate someone, *try to bring compassion to your hatred.* Turn the unwholesome to the wholesome. And I try not to be locked up *alone* with my poisons. Even at my worst times, when they've taken over and I'm blinded, my faith shredded, I try to ask for help from others. When all I want to do is crawl back into my skin, curl up in myself, shades down—I try to remember that my solace comes from moving in the exact opposite direction, out of myself, asking for help. To resist together. With others. Without violence to ourselves or to others."

"Sounds good, but I'm so far from that, babe, it's ridiculous. Impossible."

"I know. Me too. But when I'm burning up in the fire of my hatred, I try to hold on to the bigger world?" She paused. "The Buddha said, 'In this world, hatred has never yet been dispelled by hatred; only love dispels hatred. This is the law, ancient and unchanging.'"

"If there's one thing I'm not, it's a Buddha. Let me have my hatred."

"And me mine too! Guess what. We're all merely human, yes. Living human-sized lives."

"I like that. Right now, it helps."

We fall silent. Sensing the day easing out on that ledge of sudden night.

I ask her, "How do you understand Fats now?"

She considers, for what seems a long time.

"He was lonely. Except for leading you all and, in his way, loving Rosie and Chubby, he was alone. Profoundly alone. He filled his life with his work—and was a great leader as long as he was *the* leader, and in resistance, to all those Hadassah arms."

We laugh.

"He could *see* the importance and depth of being in good connection, but couldn't quite get to living it, and leading it, into the mutual. And I think he realized that too. But he couldn't let go of that big self that had worked so well all his life, but which led to a constant comparison with others, coming out better than or worse than—but not *with*. Compare; don't identify. Trapped in competing. Hooked on 'more is better'?"

"But he hated all the shit about being 'the Best.'"

"He sure did. And he hated himself for getting caught up in it. That day when he said to you and Chuck, 'Who in hell's gonna seduce this'?"

"Yeah. It surprised us. His sense that maybe he wasn't enough? That he'd failed?"

"And—because for Fats there was always an 'and'—he was one of the most loving people, to all of you. I felt it too. But I sensed that maybe his love for Rosie was—I don't know—worrying him?" She smiles. "Hey—y'know what? *He was wonderful!*"

"And a wonder, yes!" I paused. "But are you saying that, deep down, he could never get out of himself, his 'self'?"

"This is going to sound very strange, Roy," she says mischievously, smiling, "but the 'self' is made up wholly of 'nonself' elements."

"*Whoa.* Very strange."

"Toldja. But again—he was wonderful, full of pure childish wonder. Inspiring!"

"Yeah. Let's hold that, that wonder, okay?"

She smiles and nods. I smile back, feeling, for the first time in a long while, a sense of joy. Smiles can give birth to joy, and joy to smiles, yeah.

"Y'know," I say, "I keep trying to see him fresh, his life, as if he were playing with imaginary flowers of medicine and science, and smiling at the ends of those fat fingers. He was a good man, profoundly good, his whole life looking for a place to do good in the world and—thinking he'd finally found a way with his clinic—coaxing us along to do good with him. And we did, for a while. Was he deeply, mutually, quote, 'related'? Or was he strangely, deeply alone? Maybe he was all work?" I sigh. "No. Bigger. At best he was free, a center of reality, everything being more real. We loved him, and he loved us even when we didn't love life during the House and the 4th, and he kept us alive with his crazy, funny caring, his belly laughs, and eyes sometimes twinkling, sometimes screwed up in laughter or calm with joy. As he sat there on his stool at the nursing station watching his creation—us—working so well in the world, he'd nod, smile and nod, and, rare for him, not say a word. When Potts died and I was with him alone, crying out and looking for hope, and he was crying with me, y'know what he did?"

"What?"

"'Linking pinkies.' As a kid in Brooklyn, in tough spots, he and a friend would link pinkies and just hold on for a while, looking into each other's eyes. We did it then. I still feel it, that big, fat pinkie around my thinner, smaller one, holding on. Two men actually looking into each other's teary eyes without looking away. And letting go. Smiling."

Berry seems so serious—it hits my heart and she reaches out and links pinkies and we just sob. Shoulders shaking, racking sobs. Everything.

We stop. Unlink. Hear birdsong again.

"And today I feel so comforted by my still *being* with you—wishing Spring were here too, and Cinny still alive—but I feel such gratitude for that butterfly's wing stopping me a half ouch—I mean, a half inch—short of that rock and—" I stop, suddenly feeling, yes, lifted up, and shout out to the birds and the bananas, jungle, mountain, *"So grateful!"* and back from the mouth of the mountain comes *So grateful so grateful so . . .* and the howlers in the fig trees go crazy and the birds stop—silent for a second—and start up louder and more raucous and singing their hearts out and on and on they go, singing, singing, *We're here we're here despite this lunatic all of us here singing our own team's song contrapuntally with them the others we're still here too! Lifted up!*

"An 'amazing'!" Berry cries out as Spring used to say as a child. "The singing reminds me how Navajo medicine men 'sing' their healing—oh, and how, last year in Italy at that retreat I taught at Lake Como, you and I walked past a man sitting in the sunshine on the porch of an eldercare home with a woman in a wheelchair who might have been his mother or even his dying wife, her body wasted, face gaunt—and he was singing to her, just singing."

"Beautiful."

"Beautiful. And just now I had the thought that you and I, well, we're so freed up that it's not like we're talking to each other as much as singing to each other, like birds."

"Yes."

Sudden, moonless dark. That big eyelid has come down over the day.

The birds start to calm, the near ones calling to the far ones, to make sure.

The jungle is alive with darkness. Snuffling and ruffling things, as if on signal, begin to move. Birds keep going for a while. Stars are out, without a moon. The Southern Cross, Orion.

"We're old," I say. "We sleep in pieces." She smiles. "And I love you more. Love you to death. Always learning more about you, your always being a step ahead of my understanding, blossoming into Buddhism rather than retiring to Florida to golf and quibble. Always out on our edges. Right now it feels like a new beginning—at our age, imagine?"

"Don't have to."

In the amber light coming strong and real through the screen walls of the living room to us out on the patio, I see her nod, her eyes shining.

"Yes, dear one," she says. "Old and aware, creating and resisting."

I feel, under my touch, my new giraffe cane, the hardwood smooth in my fingers. I stare into the giraffe's eye. "We should try, tomorrow morning, to do our walk."

"I hope so. How's the pain?"

"Too happy to really feel it."

"Hungry?"

"Y'know, I am hungry, yes."

"Daisy sent down dinner with Miguel, your favorites. *Plátanos maduros*, rice, beans, tortillas, chicken, her special salsa. Let me help you up."

She does. Arm in arm like old folks, we start toward the house.

A roaring sound—we stop—a four-wheel drive coming fast down the steep hill of our dirt road, too fast, skidding to a stop, and backing up and parking. Motor off. We hear two doors opening, slamming shut out of sync.

We stand on the patio, waiting.

"Dad? Mom?"

Choked with joy. Can't speak. Trembling.

Berry shouts, "Out here, hon."

She comes around the corner of the house out onto the long patio, comes fast, a slender young woman running and then grabbing me, bringing out an "Ouch!" and a "Sorry!" and then gently all three of us are hugging and crying with death-defying joy.

We pull away from one another and I notice a young man standing there on the edge of the patio, a handkerchief to his eyes—a young man wiping away a tear?

The tableau of three against one suddenly seems awkward. Spring gestures him over and introduces us and he looks nice, and his wiping away a tear at his age seems to me not only astonishing but enticing.

Here now is what we've been looking for in the world. This is hope.

Later, after Daisy's dinner, we talk until fatigue comes down on me hard like after being on call for ungodly stretches at the House or Man's 4th.

"Whoa! I can't stay awake anymore!"

"One thing, Dad? About the Fat Man?"

During dinner I had mentioned to Spring that, given what I'd gone through that day, I'd been thinking an awful lot about his obscene death. "Yes, dear?"

"Well, I sort of remember how bad you felt."

"And Olive felt too?"

"Da-*ad*!"

She laughs. Little bells still! Laughs never change.

Smiling, I look to Berry, she to me. Her eyes are wet, shining. Mine too. We look back to our child, this being who chanced into our lives on a butterfly's wing and brought love so big that right now it is nothing so much as the rare shared touch of the spirit.

LAWS OF MAN'S 4TH BEST HOSPITAL

I   Learn your trade, in the world.

II   Isolation is deadly; connection heals.

III   Connection comes first.

IV   Use the "we."

V   It's not just what we do; it's what we do next.

VI   It's not that we do what we think we can get; it's what we dare to do together.

VII   Without health-care workers, there's no health care.

VIII   Squeeze the money out of the machines.

IX   Put the human back in medicine.

X   Stick together, no matter what.

Samuel Shem, professor of medicine in Medical Humanities at NYU School of Medicine, is a novelist, playwright, and activist. His first novel, *The House of God*, was called "one of the two most important American medical novels of the twentieth century" by *The Lancet* and was chosen by *Publishers Weekly* as #2 on its list of the 10 Best Satires of All Time (between #1 *Don Quixote* and #3 *Catch-22*). His novel about psychiatric training, *Mount Misery*, was called "another classic—biting, humorous, superb" (*BookPage*). *The Spirit of the Place* won two American Best Literary Novel of the Year awards, and *At the Heart of the Universe* was described by Abraham Verghese as "poignant and tender, a novel about love, parenting, and the nature of home—a lovely transformative story." Shem and Janet Surrey's award-winning play, *Bill W. and Dr. Bob*, about the founding of Alcoholics Anonymous, ran off Broadway for a year. A graduate of Harvard and Harvard Medical School, Shem earned his PhD as a Rhodes Scholar at Oxford and was on the Harvard Medical School faculty for decades. Honored as a visiting artist at the American Academy in Rome, he is an in-demand speaker around the world, including more than sixty commencement speeches on "How to Stay Human in Medicine."

CONNECT ONLINE

samuelshem.wordpress.com

mans4thbesthospital.com